She put her ear to the door, hesitated just long enough to palm the baby-sized automatic, then plunged into the room. Chisholm was astride the window sill, framed against the starlight glow: his dark figure a silhouette on a screen of filtered grey.

"What are you doing?" Her shout was filled with panic.

"I'm leaving, sweetheart," came his voice, cheerful with the resignation of one who had been caught without a prayer and knew it. "Go back to bed, love. I'm letting you off the hook. I shouldn't have come here . . . It was a mistake. I'm going."

"No!" she screamed. "No!"

"Sorry, but it's for the best. I'm off. *Auf wiedersehen*." He started to move and the arm holding the gun came up. She fired . . .

CHAINS

A novel by
DOUGLAS SCOTT

TOR

A TOM DOHERTY ASSOCIATES BOOK

CHAINS

Copyright © 1984 by Douglas Scott

Reprinted by arrangement with Secker & Warburg

First Tor printing: December 1985

A TOR Book

Published by Tom Doherty Associates
49 West 24 Street
New York, N.Y. 10010

ISBN: 0-812-58840-1

Printed in the United States of America

0 9 8 7 6 5 4 3 2 1

Contents

One

The Prisoner

Chisholm surfaced from the whirling blackness to a dazzle of eye-burning light. He blinked painfully: the glare making his eyeballs smart as he tried to focus his vision and collect his fragmented wits.

His mind—like his lead-heavy eyes—hunted fitfully for a reassuring sign of reality somewhere in that assailing brightness. A full minute passed before he could keep his eyes wide enough open to identify the source of light. A single electric bulb was socketed high in the ceiling above him. It glared at him like a Cyclopean eye: unwinking, mesmeric, dulling his sluggish brain.

Chisholm tried to move. His limbs and body did not obey. His muscles received the feeble signals triggered by his slowly stirring mind but were incapable of immediate response. His flesh seemed to be made of jelly.

He tried again to move. This time the effort succeeded. Lancing pain tore at his right arm, racing from shoulder socket to wrist and back again in lightning currents. The base of his spine felt as if a steel spike had been driven into the bone and permanently lodged there. Chisholm cried out. His whole body jerked as the involuntary sound exploded from his lips. And with the contortion of his body came another sound: a metallic clinking, consequent to every spasmodic movement.

The pain brought remembrance of where he was. His wrists and ankles were fettered, with chains running to eye-bolts in the wall of the stone cell where he lay. The steel bands encircling his limbs had chafed the skin bloody and raw below the black serge of his trouser-legs and at his unprotected wrists. The pain at the base of his spine and in his racked shoulder-blades resulted from the unnatural sprawl of his body. How

1

long he had lain there in senseless oblivion he did not know.

He dragged himself into a position that fell far short of comfort but, nevertheless, lowered to a tolerable level the stabbing aches and racking stresses. Anger surged in his befuddled mind. Its intensity drowned at birth wayward bubbles of self-pity and despair that threatened to rise unsummoned.

Chisholm nursed the anger within him, let the emotion swell and fill him. It was the one positive feeling left to him. He clung to it now as if it were a life-raft in an ocean of doubts. It alone fortified him.

He jerked angrily at the chains, ignoring the sharp spears of pain roused by straining against the unyielding links. His hate simmered, concentrated darkly on the authors of his misery. He stared at the heavy metal door of his prison. The peep-panel was closed. He fixed his eyes on the small rectangular shutter; letting the venom flow from him as if it could pierce the steel like a ray and strike down his enemies beyond.

Why didn't they kill him? Why did they isolate him like this: caging him between four windowless walls with no human contact for hour upon hour, day upon day?

Chisholm began to tremble. The bout started – as it had so often started before – with a convulsive body shudder, then an uncontrollable shaking of his arms and legs. He knew it would pass. This much he had learned – although the learning had been traumatic and terror-filled. On the first half-dozen occasions, the shaking had seemed endless and accompanied by a mind-consuming horror. Now, he knew that the trembling would stop. He had to *think* himself calm. Will it. Ignore the shaking hands. He had to compel his mind from leaping about in a frenzy . . . Let the demon thoughts settle . . . Let them fall gently as scattered dust . . . Slowly . . . Like snowflakes . . . Down . . . Down . . .

The trembling stopped.

For the thousandth time, Chisholm considered the awful possibility that he really was mad. *They* said he was insane. Violently insane. But they were lying. His violence had been a spontaneous panic. It could be explained. And the hallucinations. They *were* hallucinations: manifestations of his tortured mind and not living memories of actual madness. They were dreams. And, however nightmarish, a dream is a dream is a dream: without substance.

Chisholm *knew* he was sane. He told himself over and over again that he was sane. They would never break him. Not with drugs. Not with chains. Not by aggravating the mind-tearing claustrophobia to which he was all too plainly susceptible.

It was his susceptibility to claustrophobia that had started the whole dreadful downward spiral into the misery he was now enduring. The claustrophobia – and the morphine that the U-boat commander had given him to ease the pains from the oil burns on his back – burns that had looked much worse than they actually were.

The horror had started on the U-boat. How long did they say he had been sealed up on that steel coffin – sixty-three days? It had seemed eons: a time without beginning or end. But there had been a beginning and it had ended, although Chisholm's recall of both was sketchy: lost in a continuous nightmare of fevered waking and frenzied dreaming where the boundaries between reality and unreality were without definition.

The combination of claustrophobia and drugs – coming as they had done on top of three stress-filled years of war at sea – had begun the disintegration of the man. Chisholm had recognised the process. He was a man falling apart at the seams. His tenaciously preserved hope of salvation was in *knowing* what was happening to him and never losing sight of the fact. Powerless to arrest the disintegration when the dark forces of unreason enveloped his mind, he had to fight his way back to rationality as soon as they relaxed their pressure: like a drowning man strikes for the surface when an upward glimpse detects a distant glimmer of light.

The U-boat commander had not been unkind. He had supervised the treatment of Chisholm's burns by a seaman medic and had even, for a time, given over the bunk in his tiny cabin to Chisholm. The arrangement had been short-lived as a result of Chisholm vacating the unfamiliar quarters in dementia; having awakened from drugged sleep in a state of total disorientation he had burst into the control-room like a stampeding buffalo. It had taken the surprised Germans some time to subdue the maniac in their midst as he had sought a way out from the bewildering confinement of the submarine.

Chisholm was moved to a hammock slung in the stern torpedo compartment: accommodation he shared with some engine-room mechanics who were less than enchanted with the arrangement. Their living conditions were primitive enough without a crazy foreigner in their midst.

It had not occurred to his captors that Chisholm's hold on reality had slipped only temporarily and was the result of an accumulation of shocks on a nervous system strained to breaking-point. Morphine-induced confusion had combined with claustrophobic panic to catalyse a violence of reaction of which Chisholm had no conscious awareness.

He was aware only of the confusion in his mind and a memory of slipping and slithering above an abyss of madness. Time and again, it seemed, the abyss had tried to suck him down into its dark depths. But he had fought the sublime temptation to surrender to it. He had clawed his way back from the void to be rewarded by periods of lucid rationality and a feeling of triumph. In such moments, he would gulp in the fresh air of his own reason, relieved beyond gratitude for the stimulus it provided. Every glimpse of mental daylight was a resuscitating assurance that he had not succumbed to the black forces of irreversible breakdown.

He had tried to communicate this knowledge to his captors. The seaman medic, whom he saw more than any other, had had a compassionate face – but the German sailor had been unable to understand a single word of English. Chisholm's desperate entreaties had elicited concern and pity – but not comprehension. Murmuring words that were intended to console and calm his patient, the medic would set about the task of sedating Chisholm: his manner sympathetic but firm, like a nanny administering medicine to a difficult child. The sight of the hypodermic needle had always been enough to panic Chisholm into resistance. And, each time, his resistance had been misunderstood. It never seemed to occur to the well-meaning submariner that Chisholm's fear was not of the needle itself but of the drugged nightmares its noxious fluid would induce. Twice, Chisholm had struggled so fiercely to keep the probing needle from his arm that help had to be summoned and he had had to be held while the drug was injected.

There was irony in the fact that Chisholm's struggles had been a despairing attempt to convince his captors that sedation was unnecessary. The result achieved was the opposite. The more he struggled, the more he convinced them that sedation was needed.

The attitude of the U-boat men was made plain without any resort to explanation. They had quite enough to contend with

4

on their deep-sea patrol without constantly looking over their shoulder to check on the antics of a captured British shipmaster. They had, most of them, seen men crack up in submarines before: excellent seamen with impressive records, men who had volunteered for the life. They seldom lasted the first week of training. Some had only to see the hatch close over their heads and they went green and pasty-faced with fear. A man either had the temperament or he didn't. Sympathy did not come into it in Chisholm's case. The U-boat crew were not unmoved by his distress. It was simply that they had other priorities.

Chisholm had only been fleetingly aware of the alarms and tensions of the U-boat's continued patrol after his capture. His own ship had been torpedoed just south of the Equator. The *Millerby* had been making a lone passage north, tracking close to the meridian of 30° West, and the U-boat had caught her at a location about midway between Recife and Ascension Island. It had come as no surprise, after the *Millerby* had gone down, when the submarine had surfaced and taken Chisholm aboard. It was common practice by U-boat commanders to make prisoners of ship captains.

But, if it had been no surprise to Chisholm to be singled out for captivity, the transfer from open boat to submarine had filled him with a bitter despair. His forced abandonment of his own crew to the mercy of the South Atlantic so soon after the abandonment of his ship added agony to agony. It was wrench enough to have lost his ship. To be further deprived of the responsibility he felt for the safety of his crew was like rubbing salt in an open wound. But he was given no choice other than to endure. Nor did it help to know that his deep and silently borne concern for his men was balanced by their very real concern for him. There was not one of them who did not believe that theirs was the preferable fate. Given the choice, each would gladly have accepted his chances in an open boat rather than accept the captivity to which their captain was doomed.

The U-boat had supplied the two boatloads of survivors with food, water and charts and then left them to their fate. Chisholm had been ushered below decks on the submarine with their cheers and shouts of good luck ringing across the water to him. And so had begun the long nightmare: the nightmare of being a man entirely alone, cut off by language from his captors and in many ways an embarrassing encumbrance to them.

Night, day and the passage of time were to have little meaning for Chisholm in the ensuing three weeks. The submarine had forged steadily south and then north again into the Indian Ocean in search of targets. She had torpedoed a second ship off Port Elizabeth and had later made a rendezvous with a tanker-submarine off Madagascar before returning to the Atlantic.

By then, Chisholm had grown weaker and weaker, removing any need for the Germans to immobilise him with drugs. So, they had eased up on this method of restraint. Although, he could hear the engine-room mechanics talking from time to time, the only man who spent any time with Chisholm was the sick-bay medic. He ministered to the British captain's needs, chatting away to him unintelligibly in German with a gruff good humour; spooning food into Chisholm's mouth when he became too weak to raise his head. Sometimes, the U-boat captain had come aft. It was his habit to ask Chisholm in stilted English how he was feeling. But Chisholm had become so used to spending days without uttering a word that the time he now required to frame a reply was interpreted as a desire to remain silent. The German officer would go off, shaking his head sadly and possibly regretting the decision to saddle himself with a supernumerary who used up precious food and air and would probably not survive the patrol.

When – returning at last from her long patrol – the U-boat had been attacked by British warships in the Bay of Biscay, Chisholm's anger at his compatriots on the surface had overridden his fears of permanent watery entombment. As the depth charges had exploded nearby, Chisholm had raged impotently, cursing the British Navy for their zeal and the possibility that they might rob him of his own personal victory over the U-boat.

In the event, the U-boat's eventual safe arrival in Brest brought no moment of triumph for Chisholm: no proud walk down the gangplank and final defiant gesture of farewell. Incapable of walking anywhere, he had been sedated yet again and had no conscious memory of leaving the U-boat, nor of his transfer to the grim fortress-like asylum to which he was taken.

He had awakened encaged, literally, in an iron-barred cot. Its high-barred sides extended up to the low ceiling, where they were firmly clasped into metal rails running the entire length of the ward. Twelve beds – all with similar restraints, were crowded into the narrow room and all of them were occupied.

Chisholm's first reaction was a flood of all-too-familiar panic: that heart-fluttering terror comparable to that shown by a bird trapped in a garden net. Chisholm fought it down by giving free flow to a rising tide of rage. The stinking bastards! How dare they do this to him? He spoke no words but they boiled up in him as a silent scream.

He had rattled at the bars of his imprisoning cot with the vehemence of one intent on wresting them free of the ceiling rails, but his strength was unequal to their security. Chisholm's fury drew the amused attention of a toothless sixty-year-old man in the next identically encaged bed. He, too, began to shake at the bars of his cot. He grinned insanely at Chisholm and punctuated his activities with elephantine bellows.

Chisholm desisted. He looked around the ward. Half the occupants were still asleep, but those who were awake had the same neglected dishevelment of appearance as Chisholm's immediate neighbour. But it was their eyes that took Chisholm's attention.

There were vacantly staring eyes, shifty secretive eyes, bulging fanatical eyes – and they had one thing in common: that strange luminescence that shines from the misty depths of disturbed minds, and is the mark of the psychotic. Through a range of expressions, from blank obliviousness to the world at large to ferret-like suspicion and cunning, there was no inmate of the ward who did not betray mental abnormality. In some, the abnormality was made more pronounced by physical defect: gross features and slavering, bulbous lips, protruding tongues, malformed shoulders and misshapen limbs.

As he looked around, Chisholm had gone cold with fear. He had no doubts about the kind of institution in which he had been incarcerated – and it was no prisoner-of-war camp. It was some kind of final resting place for the unstable derelicts of society – an asylum for the incurably insane.

He had spent two weeks in the ward. Two weeks of hellish memory. No doctor had visited him. A pattern had been established. At eight in the morning, the other inmates were herded from the room, shuffling out in a line, and they did not return until about seven in the evening, when they were locked up for the night. Chisholm had been kept in bed for two days, attended periodically by a couple of male nurses with the build of dancehall bouncers. On the third day, they had him on his feet and walking. On the fifth, he was allowed a period of exercise in a walled courtyard where a hundred or more shambling inmates perambulated. Some were lost in a world of their own but others ran hither and thither like children, emitting trumpeting noises or cackling demonically to themselves.

Chisholm had not pursued early attempts to engage the male nurses in conversation. They spoke to each other in French in a dialect and at a speed that defied Chisholm's understanding. They treated him as if he were a sack of potatoes that had to be bundled here or bundled there. Communication was a prod or a push, a "*venez*" or an "*allez*" accompanied by a gesticulation. Chisholm had retreated into his now habitual silence, while observing and memorising every detail of his surroundings. He had eaten the food set before him – it was unvaried and revolting – and had concentrated on regaining his physical strength.

He had made up his mind that at the earliest possible moment he would escape.

During the second week, he had been made to join the routine of the others. Eating with them in the drab common-room and exercising with them in the chilly yard. He was given the same grey denim clothes to wear. He was repelled by the demeanour and grotesque behaviour of the other inmates, by the stink of incontinence about them – and tried to keep himself to himself, avoiding the fights and screaming arguments that broke out every so often and had to be broken up by orderlies. Steering clear of some of the more persistent inmates, who grabbed him with steely fingers and babbled at him, had not been easy for Chisholm; but, somehow, he had managed.

Chisholm's first indication that he had not been removed without trace from the normal world came on his fifteenth day in the establishment he now knew to be named L'Asile des Perdus. He had been given a bath in tepid water, thrown a drab, off-white shift to cover his nakedness, and paraded before a doctor of pensionable age. The man poked and probed at Chisholm, spending some time examining the now-healed burn marks on his back. He asked no questions but made copious notes.

The questions were to come from another doctor, also a very old man, whom Chisholm took to be a psychiatrist. He had a gruff, matter-of-fact manner and a disconcerting habit of picking his nose while he spoke. His English was not fluent but comprehensible.

He had told Chisholm that the Germans occasionally sent prisoners and criminals to the institution for observation and assessment but he was the first English patient to have arrived. It was most unusual. What was Chisholm's occupation?

"I am a ship's captain," Chisholm had replied.

He could have created no more surprise than if he had declared he was Louis the Fourteenth or Pope Gregory the Great.

"But that is what it says on your record," the incredulous ancient replied. "Do you also know your name and the date of your birth and why you are here?"

Chisholm repeated his full name, his birth date, and said he did not know why he was there. He did believe, however, that as a prisoner of war he had certain rights and that his detention in this stinking slum was in flagrant contravention of the Geneva Convention. He would be grateful if the doctor would communicate these facts to the appropriate authority and arrange for his immediate transfer to a place where, at least, the terms of the Geneva Convention obtained.

If the doctor was impressed, he did not show it. Rather stiffly, he told Chisholm that he could not authorise his transfer anywhere unless he were satisfied that Chisholm did not present a danger to those with whom he came in contact. He had even lectured Chisholm on his good fortune on being committed to the care of an enlightened civilian establishment rather than a military one. The Germans were not noted for sympathetic treatment to psychotic criminals.

"I am not a criminal and I am not psychotic!" Chisholm had shouted in his face, knowing even as he did so that a calmer response would have sounded more convincing. By losing his temper, he was destroying his own case. But his wrath was righteous and could not be held in check.

The doctor had nodded sagely as if Chisholm's vehemence merely confirmed what he expected. He had read from a report on the desk in front of him, equating Chisholm's assertion with evidence that was clearly to the contrary.

". . . and he punched Coxwain Ritter on the face and body, pushing him so violently that he fell against the chart-table. Coxwain Ritter required five stiches in a head wound. Torpedo-man Hoffmann, having gone to Ritter's assistance, was attacked with the same ferocity. He was struck several blows in the face before being wrestled to the deck, whereupon the prisoner seized Hoffman round the neck and would have strangled him but for the intervention of the Executive Officer and myself . . ."

It was clearly a report of something that had happened on the U-boat, but Chisholm had no memory of it.

"Do you remember the incident?" the doctor asked Chisholm, who could only stare at the other man without confirming or denying the truth of the matter. Chisholm knew something *had* happened on the U-boat that had soured the attitudes of the submarine commander and some of the crew towards him, but the reasons had never been clear to him.

"Have you nothing to say?" the doctor had persisted.

"What do you expect me to say?" Chisholm had flared. "I don't even know what you're talking about."

When five days had elapsed without anything coming of his meetings with the doctors, he made his break. So well did he make use of all his patient observations that the ease with which he found himself outside the forbidding Asile des Perdus astonished him. It was then that he came face-to-face with a numbing reality. He had been so obsessed with the task of getting beyond the walls of his hated prison, that it was not until he had accomplished the feat that he realised he had given not a single thought to his next move.

Choosing a moment when a fracas among the inmates was distracting the orderlies, he had slipped down a labyrinth of passages and stairs to where he knew the kitchens were located. Although several pots were boiling away on the big iron stove, the kitchens were temporarily deserted and he had passed quickly through into a rear courtyard. A quick dash across the yard, through a series of stone sheds, and he was in the greenhouses flanking the large kitchen gardens. The twelve-foot wall surrounding the garden might have been an obstacle but for a compost recess whose sides he used as a stepladder.

It was not until Chisholm was free and crouched in the lane beyond the wall that he realised the enormity of the problem still facing him. He knew that he was somewhere in German-occupied France but, otherwise, had not the faintest idea of his whereabouts. He had no money, no food. He had the most rudimentary knowledge of the French language and none at all of German.

10

For the moment, the sheer joy of being at liberty had overridden all other considerations. It had been enough to settle for one primary aim – to put as much distance as possible between himself and L'Asile des Perdus.

Chisholm had stayed at large for forty-eight hours.

Even then, only because he was soaked to the skin and starving, had he shown himself to an elderly woman in a farmyard with the intention of asking for food. But the woman had taken one look at his filthy grey denim uniform and panicked. Her screams had brought a posse of workers from a nearby field. The men, arming themselves with spades and axe-handles, had made it plain by their attitude that they intended to beat Chisholm to a pulp and ask questions afterwards. They were in no doubt that they were dealing with the dangerous escapee from the asylum ten miles away, about whom there had been a warning on the radio.

Chisholm's attempts to explain that he meant no one any harm fell on deaf ears, and a vicious swing with an axe-handle was side-stepped more by good luck than agility. A hectic chase had ensued around the farm buildings with Chisholm seeming the inevitable loser until he snatched a sickle from a hook inside an open barn and showed that he would not hesitate to use it in self-defence.

The resulting impasse was only broken by the arrival of some German soldiers in a truck. Covered by their rifles, Chisholm had surrendered, preferring to throw himself on their mercy rather than that of the French farm-workers, who still seemed intent on his blood.

Chisholm had been detained in an army guardhouse for a night. In the morning, he had been hustled – hands handcuffed behind his back – into an enclosed truck. He had not been returned to L'Asile des Perdus. This time, his destination was a barrack-like building whose outline he only glimpsed as he was hurried across a cobbled yard. They had chained him in a cell. And it was in that same cell that they seemed determined to keep him in mind-breaking isolation for the rest of his life.

At regular intervals, he had been interrogated. Always a different interrogator and always the range and nature of the questions had baffled him. One day, he had been asked about his childhood relationship with his mother with the questioner going on and on about whether he had been breast or bottle-fed. On another occasion, the questions had been all about revolution and violence and whether or not he believed political change could be achieved without violence.

Sometimes, before the questioning started, they injected drugs into him. Then, as now, he would awaken with a foul taste in his mouth and he would have to make an effort to work out where he was and how he had got there. The chains that bound him were the only enduring reality. When he recognised them and felt their cruel grip on his wrists and ankles, he knew where he was and called up his anger. His anger was his strength.

Every so often, he rearranged his sitting position to ease his cramped legs but it seemed not to matter what position he adopted – his discomfort became as acute as ever. He longed for a change of clothing. His uniform trousers and jacket had been returned to him – they had probably burned the coarse grey asylum clothes in which he had been recaptured – but they were in a sorry state now. The gold braid on his sleeve was stained and turning a dirty green and the dark serge was filthy and soiled. He was aware that he must look grotesque: unrecognisable from the cleanshaven, fussy dresser who had paced the *Millerby*'s bridge. His long, uncut hair hung in ragged clumps to his shoulders and his straggle of whiskers and beard was matted and tangled.

He returned his attention to the door, staring again at the shuttered peep-hole and working now to summon the hate and anger that sustained him above all else. It anaesthetised him against his pain and his discomfort and such was his concentration that he was barely aware of the animal-like snarl that growled in his throat. He willed the door to open and reveal the human shape of an enemy against whom he could direct the liquid fury of his burning eyes. He could feel the strength of his hate lighting him like a torch within and was so conscious of its silent outpouring that it seemed to give him the power to shrivel to ashes anyone straying into its stream.

It was the sound of the heavy door opening, rather than Chisholm's actual sight of the man who stood there, that broke through his trancelike concentration and impressed upon him the fact that the door had opened and that someone *had* entered his cell.

The newcomer did not shrivel up and disappear. He stood, warily surveying Chisholm and making no attempt to come any closer to the chained man. His tone, when he spoke, was softly chiding. He spoke in English, with the twang of an accent that sounded more French than German.

"Why do you look so fierce, huh? I am not going to hurt you. I am your friend, eh? I have come to help you. I am not like the others. I've come to get you out of this dump. I really mean it. But you've got to trust me. So what do you say? Are we going to be friends?"

Chisholm stared at the man without a blink of trust, saying nothing.

After a long silence, his visitor tried again.

"Look, you've got to trust me. I really can get you out of here."

Still Chisholm said nothing.

"OK," said the man, "if that's the way you feel, I'll go. At least I tried . . ."

He turned on his heel and would have passed through the door, but Chisholm called out: "No . . . Wait!"

The man did just that. He waited.

"Who are you?" asked Chisholm.

A little smile appeared on the man's face. It could have been relief. It could have been triumph.

"Like I said, Captain . . . I'm your friend."

The visitor came several more times. He continued to show total sympathy for Chisholm, agreeing that it was barbaric to have him chained. He promised to make the strongest possible protest about it to someone he referred to as the Sturmbann-führer. Within the hour, two gaolers came and released Chisholm from his chains.

The visitor promised, too, to make representations on Chisholm's behalf to have him protected by the Geneva Convention. But one thing endeared him to Chisholm more than any other: he was the first human being he had encountered since his captivity in the U-boat to treat him as sane and rational. He scoffed at the generally accepted verdict on Chisholm that he was some kind of homicidal maniac. It was something he was prepared to stake his reputation on. And, he added, he was not an insignificant authority on the subject.

It was one of the few clues he offered to Chisholm about himself. Who he was and precisely what his position or relationship with the Germans was, he never made clear, warding off Chisholm's curiosity with hints that it was not in his best interests to know.

He never revealed his name but seemed to be amused that the Germans had nicknamed him Der Schulleiter – the Headmaster. This may have stemmed from his appearance, which was donnish: pale face, balding at the front and wispy, mouse-coloured hair rising in wings. A myopic stare gave the impression of absent-mindedness, but Chisholm guessed that this was an impression deliberately created.

If Chisholm never allowed himself wholly to trust his newfound champion, it had less to do with any obvious reasons for withholding that trust than with Chisholm's own state of mind. After all he had been through, there was in him now a reluctance to trust any other living person. In spite of Chisholm's caution, however, he would have been the first to admit that a change in his fortunes began from the day when the Headmaster first came into his life.

It culminated with the arrival in his cell one day of the mysterious visitor in a rare state of excitement. He could scarcely wait to announce his news. He had won a momentous victory. He had persuaded the Germans that Chisholm should be transferred to a hospital where he could expect the very best of treatment. It was staffed by both French and German personnel and was both comfortable and modern. Formerly, it had been a sanitorium for the very rich. Most important of all, however, Chisholm would be among his own kind. One section of the hospital housed a small number of Allied prisoners of war recovering from serious wounds and undergoing a period of convalescence before being transferred to POW camps in Germany.

"You will also have a very special friend there," the Headmaster confided conspiratorially, as if fearing that he might be overheard. "Her name is Nicole. She is a nurse. Now, forget that it was I who told you. Forget that my lips breathed her name. Remember only, when you hear the name, that she is a friend."

Two

Friends

There were no windows in the back of the truck. The only light penetrating the interior was that admitted by two narrow grilles in the heavy rear doors and a barred communication hatch to the driver's compartment. It was like a cell on wheels. Chisholm squirmed uneasily on the wooden bench-seat, unable to still the familiar stirrings of claustrophobic panic that had begun to gnaw away at him the moment the big heavy doors had been banged shut.

The two German soldiers stared at him with uneasy suspicion. They sat opposite him, their machine-pistols across their knees and with their hands across the trigger-guards. They were taking no chances with their shaggy-haired, wild-eyed charge.

The journey in the truck lasted less than two hours but, to Chisholm, it seemed an eternity. He endured it, fighting the almost unbearable impulse to throw himself at the truck doors and claw his way out into the freedom of fresh air and open space beyond. Some sixth sense told him that journey's end was near when the deep register of frequent gear changes made it clear that the truck was climbing a hill of many turns and considerable steepness.

His intuition was proved correct when, after a short distance on an easier and more even engine note, the truck came to a halt. Chisholm and the guards sat and waited until the heavy rear doors were opened from the outside and daylight streamed in. With the light came a tangy draught of air that Chisholm immediately recognised. He could smell the sea, not far off.

He shivered in the cold December air as he stepped from the truck. A veil of thin cloud covered a watery sun and he pulled his jacket close about him at the chilling whip of northerly breeze. He looked about him.

A broad expanse of lawn ended abruptly in a balustraded walk. Beyond and below was grey sea. Chisholm was given no time to admire the hilltop view. He was ushered in the opposite direction towards a long, low building with a paved terrace running along its entire length and fronting a line of french-windowed rooms facing the lawn and the sea.

Chisholm was escorted along the terrace – past what seemed to be the main entrance – so that he was able to glance through the sea-facing windows. Most of the rooms appeared to be spacious, single-bed apartments, spartan and clinical in furnishing; with gleaming wash-hand basins and sterile chrome fitments. Even the floors gleamed and Chisholm could almost catch the whiff of carbolic which, he guessed, permeated the atmosphere beyond the glass.

Some of the beds were occupied: by men with legs in traction, others with bandaged heads, some recumbent but without visible sign of injury. One of the long terrace rooms was a lounge, with chintz-covered couches and cushioned wicker chairs. Here, some bath-robed figures looked up from books and games of chess in idle curiosity as Chisholm passed by between his guards.

They skirted the end of the sprawling sanitorium, following a tarred drive that led to a series of outbuildings. One was plainly a laundry and another a boiler-house and power unit. The party of three marched on, beyond the outbuildings towards a cluster of green timber-built section huts that looked out of place amongst the orderly landscaped walks of the hospital grounds. The long huts – thrown up on what appeared to have been the only flat open space on the landward side of the hilltop parkland – was surrounded by a single barbed-wire fence with a gate and checkpoint at the only opening.

Chisholm was passed through and taken to an office in one of the sectional huts. Here, his guards handed over the papers relating to their charge and waited while an elderly corporal made out a receipt. The guards left and Chisholm stood under the watchful gaze of a white-clad orderly while the corporal laboriously typed out details on what seemed to be an endless number of forms. Finally, after shuttling back and forward between several filing cabinets and finding homes for all the documents, he barked out an instruction to the orderly. Chisholm was taken from the office and led to another of the

section huts. It had all the offices and accoutrements of a large hospital ward.

The orderly led him through two open six-bed sections. The occupants glowered at Chisholm in silence as he passed. Some wore British battledress tops over pyjama trousers, but there was no sign of welcome or friendship in their surly looks. Chisholm followed the orderly through narrow partitioned sections: a tiny kitchen to the right, a lobby-like dining area with lino-topped table and wooden benches. On through a toilets and showers section without doors of any kind. On past mysterious little rooms with closed doors that preserved their anonymity.

Finally, the orderly was opening one of those doors and Chisholm was ushered into a tiny room with just enough space to house four beds and afford the minimum of movement around them. Only one of the beds was occupied. A reddish-haired man of about twenty-four stared sourly up at Chisholm. He was almost hidden by the cage at the foot of his bed that protected his legs from the weight of blankets.

The man in the bed stared at Chisholm for a moment and then turned his head away: interest in the newcomer dissipated. The orderly threw Chisholm a towel, a pair of threadbare pyjamas and a thin wrap-around robe. Then Chisholm was taken back along the corridor and ordered to take a shower.

The water came through icy at first but warmed gradually. Chisholm luxuriated in the stream of warm water while the orderly sat on a bench nearby and smoked a cigarette. The white, odourless soap given to Chisholm was coarse and produced little lather as he worked it through his tangle of hair. He scrubbed at himself with a vigour that was almost frenzied, as if the cleansing would remove the indelible imprints on his mind made by his other prisons and the binding chains. The therapy was so sweet that the orderly finally had to call a halt to his ablutions.

The German spoke a little English but shook his head vehemently when Chisholm made signs that he would like to shave his straggly beard.

"Razor, nein! Verboten!" the man insisted.

Chisholm's disappointment was intense. He found himself almost pleading. But the orderly remained unmoved. Razors were verboten!

"I won't cut anybody's throat," Chisholm promised impatiently. He made snipping motions with his fingers. "How about scissors, then? Any damned thing that cuts. Look at me. I feel like Robinson bloody Crusoe!"

The man obviously understood only a little of what Chisholm was saying but was in no doubt at all about the urgency his prisoner attached to removing the unsightly hair. He was not totally unsympathetic.

"OK, I speak," he promised, nodding his head. "I speak."

He did not elaborate further: leaving Chisholm in ignorance of the authority to whom he would speak. So, Chisholm had to leave it at that. Wearing the pyjamas and the thin robe, he was escorted back to the cramped four-bed ward and left to make himself at home.

He sat on one of the empty beds and surveyed his new surroundings. They were a decided improvement on those of recent memory, although the other occupant of the room was doing his best to ignore him.

"I hope I'm not intruding," Chisholm said mildly. "If you don't like the arrangement, maybe you'd better speak to the management. If you're interested, my name is Chisholm."

The red-topped head turned and there was no friendliness in the anguished blue eyes that stared up at Chisholm.

"I don't give a goddamn who you are, Mister. I don't want to know."

Chisholm was taken aback by the bitterness in the other man's tone. Somewhere amongst his dismay and bewilderment, it registered with him that the other's accent was unmistakably North American.

"Sorry I spoke," he said flatly, stifling down a flare of angry resentment. Only the anguish in those blue eyes halted the rude retort that was not far from his lips. He shrugged casually. "Makes no difference to me."

But it did make a difference. He had buoyed himself up on the expectation of a friendly voice. He had looked forward to it like a lost traveller in the desert looks forward to his arrival at a waterhole: he does not expect the water to taste as sour as vinegar. The disappointment hurt.

Chisholm turned away and, kicking up his legs, lay back on the bed. He was filled with a grim sadness, a resigned kind of despair. He did not want to let the man in the other bed see the depth of his disappointment. And he shied away from the effort required to explain his overwhelming loneliness. He felt strangely incapable of making the patient conversation that might have penetrated the other man's bitterness and possibly eased his own. Simpler to retire behind his own shield – so easy to raise now – and remain there in unreachable retreat.

Scarcely aware that he was doing it, he began quietly to hum to himself. The tune was an old ballad, familiar to seafarers. He tum-ti-tummed softly, coming in with snatches of the words as they echoed on his memory: "*In the morning when I woke . . . Tum-ti-tum ti-tum ti-tum . . . No trousers, suit or waistcoat could I find . . .*"

He was unconscious of a slight stirring of movement in the other bed.

"*. . . And a policeman came and took my girl away . . .*"

"Stop it, for God's sake!"

Chisholm did not even hear the hoarsely muttered interruption.

"*. . . And the judge he guilty found her . . . For robbing a homeward bounder . . .*"

"For Christ's sake, will you stop it, goddamn you!"

The voice from the other bed was almost a shriek. It shattered the cocoon of Chisholm's private world. He broke off in surprise and, pushing himself up on an elbow, stared across at the thatch of red hair and a pair of burning blue eyes. Again, something in those eyes – there was torment, not just anger – stilled the temptation to strike back sharply.

"Sorry," Chisholm murmured. "I wasn't trying to annoy you . . . I didn't known I was doing it out loud. I . . . I sometimes talk to myself, too . . . I . . . I'm sorry."

He lay back and closed his eyes. And, once again, a feeling of incredible sadness washed over him. It had something to do with the pain that he had glimpsed in that anger-contorted face. The little-boy face. The American was only a kid. And he, Chisholm – at thirty – was older than Methusalah. A thousand years older than Methusalah!

Chisholm opened his eyes and, turning his head, stared across at the other bed. The young American was no longer staring in his direction. He had lain back and was gazing up at the ceiling. Chisholm groped around in his mind for words with which he could break the unrelenting silence.

"Look, chum, I know I may look like Ivan the Terrible but, until they give me the wherewithal to get a hair-cut and a shave,

19

you'll have to make allowances. I don't know what it is makes you so shirty with me, but it's pointless . . . We're in the same boat . . ."

"We're not in the same goddamned boat . . ." The young American's face was charged with emotion. "You've got both your goddamned feet!"

Chisholm jerked up into a sitting position. He stared at the cage over the American's legs. The awful purport of the other's words began to dawn on him.

"They told me about *you*. Don't tell me they didn't tell you all about me!" the American was saying. "That the guy you were getting for company was a cripple." The little boy face contorted. "I'm wise to their little games. Nothing they do is by accident. All the time, they're trying to get your guard down. I don't know what it is they put you up to – but it isn't going to work. The sooner you go back and tell them, the better."

Chisholm felt sick at the thought of the maiming injury concealed by the blanket-draped cage. And he was bewildered by the accusation that he was in some way in league with the unidentified "they" of whom the American spoke.

"You've got things all wrong," he said hoarsely. "Nobody put me up to anything. If you'll let me, I just want to be your friend . . ."

"Well, you're wasting your time, buddy. There's only one thing I want. And that's to be goddamned left alone!"

Chisholm smiled bitterly.

"Solitude is greatly overrated. Believe me, I *know*. What happened . . . to your legs?"

"I'm minus my left foot! That's what happened."

"I'm sorry."

"Not half so sorry as I am!"

Chisholm winced. Talking to this poor kid was like holding your face out to be slapped. No amount of sympathetic soft talk was going to get through to him. The boy was almost deranged by the horror of his disability. Almost as far out of his mind with it as Chisholm himself had been at the lowest moments of his lonely captivity. Chisholm recalled how he had shocked himself from depression by levelling contempt against himself. Now, he did not let his mind dwell on the possibility that he was acting with an arrogance of assumption that ran counter to most of his instincts. He had never truly subscribed to the belief that kindness demanded cruelty, so he had to hurdle a momentary hesitation.

"You're right," he said brutally. "You're so damned sorry for yourself that there isn't any room for anyone else to get in on the act. You're so far up to the neck in self-pity that you're drowning in the stuff. Well, OK, go ahead. Drown in it!"

Self-hate filled him as he delivered the savage words, blackening his countenance with a rage that the American interpreted as exclusively for his benefit. If the American's rebuffs had been slaps to Chisholm, the older man's counter-blast was like a flurry of crunching bone-smashing punches delivered with pulverising viciousness.

The American's little boy face crumpled like melting wax. Tears streamed from the anguished eyes, all ferocity gone. Trembling hands came up to cover the ravaged face and the younger man's body shook with unchecked sobs.

"Oh, God, I wish I was dead," he cried.

The passion of agony in the strangled words touched at Chisholm like red-hot rods.

He pushed himself off his bed and a single step took him to the other's side. He slipped an arm round the American's thin bony shoulders and cradled the red-thatched head against his chest. The young man sobbed against him like a broken-hearted child.

"I'm sorry . . . I'm sorry," Chisholm murmured. "That was too damned rough . . . I shouldn't have said what I did . . . God knows you're frightened and hurt and what happened to you is bloody cruel . . . But you've got a lot of life ahead of you yet . . . Don't wish you were dead . . . You didn't mean that. I know you didn't mean that . . ."

His words seemed pathetically inadequate but Chisholm poured them out, hoping that in the burning compassion of their utterance there was some balm. He willed the strength from his own body to drain into the frail wounded creature trembling against him.

Slowly, the sobbing subsided. The American's head lay cradled against Chisholm's chest and only occasionally now the thin shoulders heaved with an exhausted convulsive sigh. Chisholm eased him back on the pillow but kept a comforting, reassuring grip on the young man's wrist. The ravaged blue eyes cast a single upward glance at Chisholm but turned quickly away.

The American's first attempt to say something died away in

21

a choked sob.

"It's OK," Chisholm soothed. "Don't hurry it. You'll be fine in a minute."

But the younger man was fighting to recover his composure now and determined to achieve it.

"I'm sorry," he apologised. "I feel so goddamned ashamed . . . blubbing like a baby."

"There's no need to be sorry. And no need to be ashamed. Not after what you've been through. We all think we're granite, you know. But even rocks shed tears. Did you know that? They've got to give a little, too. We've all got to cry sometime. The pressure builds up in us like steam on a donkey engine. That's why Nature gave us a safety valve – to let off the excess. Crying's as natural as sitting on the john. We've got to let it all come out, or we'd burst."

Chisholm gave an encouraging smile.

"Have you got a name? Or do I just call you Red?"

"A lot of people call me Red. But that isn't my name."

"I get Chizz – but not often to my face. I let some people get away with it."

"I'm going to call you Chizz."

There was a tone of challenge in the statement. Chisholm grinned. The boy *did* have fighting spirit – and it was coming back fast.

"Fair enough, Red. I owe you that."

A shadow of a smile lit the younger man's face.

"When my brother wanted to annoy me, he used to call me Beanie. I'd get mad as hell."

"Why Beanie?"

"Because I loved baked beans. I could have lived on them." He studied Chisholm and, again, the shadow of a smile appeared. "You were right. You *do* look like Ivan the Terrible. You could sure use a haircut."

"Razors are verboten, according to the character who brought me over here from the office. But he promised to speak to somebody about it."

"Keitler probably."

"Who's Keitler?"

"He's the creep who runs this holiday camp. Watch him. He's a snake."

"You don't like him? Or this place?"

"Right both times. Rehabilitation Centre they call it. Maybe that's what it is for all the SS they have floating about here. It's more like the funny farm. Don't trust anybody here, Chizz — and I mean *anybody*!"

"A minute or two ago, you seemed to think that I had something to do with *them*?"

"I don't any longer. *They*'re subtle – but they're not that subtle. I thought you were another plant, put in here to wear me down."

"Why should anyone want to wear you down?"

"I don't know, for God's sake. I can't tell them anything. I wasn't even supposed to get involved in the fighting at Dieppe. I was only there as an observer and they know it."

"Dieppe?" said Chisholm, the surprise showing on his face. "You mean Dieppe in France? Do you mean our people have landed on this side of the channel?"

The American looked at Chisholm pop-eyed.

"You don't know about Dieppe? Where the hell have you been, Chizz – Outer Mongolia?"

Chisholm frowned.

"I think I would have preferred Outer Mongolia. Let's just say I've been in one form of cold storage or another for five . . . six months. I'm not sure just how long. I've been . . . what's the word? Incommunicado. I don't know if we've been winning the war – or losing it. How come there was fighting at Dieppe?"

"Dieppe was a goddamned disaster," the American said bitterly. "Not just for me – because it cost me my foot, and my freedom – but the whole goddamned thing! A raid in force, they called it, and I was just there for the ride. You never saw slaughter like it. The Canadian outfit I was with was wiped out. We never got off the goddamned beach – and a hell of a lot didn't even make it to the beach."

Sweat stood out on the younger man's forehead as he related to Chisholm some of the horror he had experienced at the calamitous Dieppe beachhead. Chisholm eventually steered the conversation away from that uneasy topic: wanting to hear of other events that had taken place during his absence from circulation. The more the American had to tell, the more Chisholm felt like Rip van Winkle.

As they talked, the tension that had marked their earlier exchanges vanished as if it had never existed. Chisholm learned that the other's name was Richard Thomson and that he held the rank of lieutenant in the US Army.

"My real friends call me Rick, not Red," he said. "I'd like for you to call me Rick, Chizz." For the first time, the boyish face creased into an unrestrained smile. "Will you listen to me!" he exclaimed. "A half hour ago, I hated the whole goddamned world. And you, too, because you walked in here on two feet and started singing like you owned the place and didn't have a single care. Now, I'm asking you to call me Rick and we're jawing away like we'd known each other all our lives!"

Chisholm grinned, an inner glow warming him at the transformation that had taken place in his newfound companion.

"Anything you say . . . Rick. It's matier than Richard — and a damned sight more dignified than Beanie. And don't think the jawing has stopped. I've got a thousand and one questions to ask you yet . . ." He paused. "You said a curious thing earlier on. You said *they* told you about me. What did you mean?"

Rick Thomson looked away from Chisholm, faintly embarrassed.

"I was shooting off my mouth. It was nothing. Scuttlebutt."

Chisholm wanted to know more.

"Keitler said I was going to get company. 'An interesting patient', he called you. He said I was not to be alarmed if you behaved strangely."

"Was that all?"

"The rest was just scuttlebutt. From the Canadians along the way . . . You must have passed them on your way in . . . I haven't exactly hit it off with them. They don't trust me and I don't trust them. It's my blame probably."

"What did they say?"

"They think I get preferential treatment. They don't seem to realise that Keitler deliberately stirs things up. That man makes trouble just for the hell of it. Anyway, Keitler or one of his stooges had been telling them that I was getting a nutcase in beside me . . . They were taunting me that I would have to keep one of my crutches on top of the bed instead of underneath it . . . That I would probably have to fight off this maniac in the middle of the night. Oh, you got quite an advance billing. . . Murder, rape, woman-beater . . . The Germans had to keep you in a straitjacket for most of the time. All bullshit, of course!"

"Yes, yes it is," Chisholm said quietly. But he had gone quite cold. The sensation at the pit of his stomach was fear. The question that burned on his mind was not how such a reputation had preceded him, but *why? Why?*

For some reason that Chisholm never discovered, the sectional block where he was confined in the grounds of the former sanitorium at St Cyr des Bains was called The Pavilion by its inmates. The nickname derived from the fact that some of the Canadian prisoners had been billeted in Brighton for some months prior to their wounding and capture at Dieppe, but what association there was between the Brighton landmark of the same name and the green timber building in the compound at St Cyr des Bains was obscure.

What Chisholm did find quickly was that the degree of freedom he was able to enjoy within The Pavilion's wooden walls was considerably more than at his previous places of detention. The inmates were even permitted to wander around an allotted area inside the wire perimeter, although most preferred the warmth of The Pavilion itself. None of them had been supplied with winter coats and it required a hardy constitution to exercise in the near-zero December temperatures.

There were six officers and six noncoms and other ranks in the two dormitory rooms through which Chisholm had passed on arrival. Most were ambulatory and almost fully recovered from their wounds, having been transferred to St Cyr des Bains from other hospitals. They had been told that they were all soon to be shipped to a new POW camp under construction in Poland.

Chisholm's first contact with any of the Canadians came early on his first day in The Pavilion. There was a sharp knock on the door of his and Rick's room. It was opened just wide enough to admit the bullet-like crewcut head of one of the Canadian noncoms, Corporal Malloy.

"Captain Lomax wants to meet the new guy," he announced.

"Is that a request or an order?" Rick asked with a sarcastic edge to his voice. "Lomax is Senior Officer," he added in an aside to Chisholm.

"The Captain just told me to deliver the message," Corporal Malloy said cheerfully. "I don't give a pig's ear one way or the other." He smiled in a mocking way. "You guys seem to be getting along just great."

25

Chisholm stood up.

"Where is this Captain Lomax?"

"In the bathhouse. He's waiting for you. I wouldn't keep him waiting too long if I were you."

Corporal Malloy's head disappeared and the door clicked shut. Chisholm frowned and looked down at Rick Thomson.

"I'll go and see what he wants. What's he like?"

"An iceberg. Doesn't show much on the surface, and what's underneath is all jagged and sharp. Watch him, Chizz, he's mean."

Lomax was sitting on the wooden bench in the bathhouse.

"Captain Lomax?" Chisholm proffered a hand. "My name's Chisholm."

Lomax ignored the outstretched hand. He stood up. He was taller than Chisholm by several inches.

"I'm the Senior Allied Officer here. You're Navy, I believe."

"Merchant Navy," Chisholm corrected him. "A civilian."

Lomax's lips parted in a thin smile. His eyes were icy.

"What you are doesn't really matter," he said. "I'm responsible for all the prisoners in this block. That will include you, whether I like it or not . . . Or whether you like it or not."

"You don't seem to like it a lot."

"I don't. I know where I am with men who understand military discipline. And they know exactly where they stand with me. But I'm not going to let the fact that you're Navy . . . that you're civilian . . . make any difference. There are certain rules around here and, while they are my responsibility, it's up to me to see that nobody steps out of line."

"Well, thank you for taking the trouble to put me in the picture, Captain," said Chisholm, his voice heavy with mock gratitude. "Once I know what the rules are, I'll try not to do anything that might embarrass you."

Lomax's stare never wavered.

"You sure as hell won't!" he said, and the threat in his tone was naked. "You try anything, Mister. Anything! And I personally will break you up in little pieces."

Chisholm was unaware that his fists had clenched white at his sides. He returned Lomax's stare with unblinking pugnacity.

"You're welcome to try, Captain. Just any time you feel like it."

It was Lomax who ended the staring match. It wasn't a

surrender. He turned his head away as if a great effort was required to control a temptation to violence.

"There's something you should know," he said evenly. "They warned us that you might be . . . awkward. We know you went for some defenceless Frenchwoman with a sickle. And we heard about the other guys you half-killed. OK, so maybe you're sick . . . I don't know. There were maybe even reasons why you did those things. But, here, you're not going to rock the boat. If there's going to be any rough stuff, I'm the guy who's gonna goddamned organise it!"

The anger that flared in Chisholm rose close to flashpoint. Lies, lies . . . All of it was lies. He wanted to ram the words back down Lomax's throat. But he kept his voice calm in spite of the fury churning inside him.

"Would it do any good to deny that garbage? Or do you believe everything the Nazis bloody well tell you?"

Lomax's expression did not change.

"Save your breath, Mister. We have our own way of finding things out around here. If you want to know, the Germans have gone out of their way to play down just how much of a nutcase you are. They just made it clear to me that if you make trouble, they'll make all of us carry the can. So, Mister, if you get the urge to throw your weight around, you come and see me. You lay one finger on any of my guys and, so help me, it'll be the last goddamn thing you ever do."

The temptation to bang Lomax's head against the wall and knock some of the obduracy from him was so strong in Chisholm that it was a physical effort to contain himself. He had to turn away and concentrate his eyes on his balled fists, clenching and unclenching the fingers to ease the tension from them. He compelled his anger to cool. Its hair-trigger quality astounded him; making him realise that the constant accusation of instability which he found so difficult to defend without outrage – was provoking in him some incipient form of paranoia. He said with a great weariness, "This is stupid. I'm not going to argue with you, Captain."

"Good," said Lomax, stony-faced as ever but unable to conceal the gleam of triumph that flashed in his eyes. "Now we know where we stand."

"No," corrected Chisholm. "I know where you stand. You think I'm crazy. Well, if it makes you happy, you go on thinking that. I haven't made my mind up about you yet. You may not be the stupidest son of a seacow that I've ever met in all my life – but I won't make any judgement without more evidence than my first impression."

He wheeled and walked away. He could feel Lomax's antagonistic stare following him.

"Wait!"

Chisholm stopped. He half-turned to look at Lomax. The slow movement of his body was cool, deliberate.

"Yes?"

"They've put you in with the Yank?"

"My good luck. They could have put me in with you."

The Canadian's face flickered with annoyance. As Chisholm continued to stare at him insolently, something new showed in the other man's scowl. It was a glimmer of uncertainty.

"He gets privileges. From the Germans . . . My guys don't like it. They're curious to know what he does to earn them."

"He does special work for them," said Chisholm, and was rewarded by Lomax's sudden look of alarm. It turned to one of lip-drawn fury as Chisholm added: "He tests out right-footed bedsocks for them."

"I suppose you think that's funny," Lomax snarled.

"Funny's not the word, Captain Lomax. Absurd. Like all the other notions you seem to have. Just what the hell is it that worries you about that kid in there? He's lost a foot and he's half out of his mind with the shock . . . And, instead of trying to help him, you insinuate God-knows-what because he's maybe getting an extra spoonful of sugar in his coffee. It's not funny, Captain Lomax – it's bloody tragic!"

This time, when Chisholm marched off, Lomax did not call him back. He stared silently after him with a scowl as black as thunder.

Rick Thomson scarcely looked round at Chisholm's return. In the tiny space at the end of the four beds, he was concentrating fiercely on six steps forward, turn, and six steps back – on his crutches. He was counting each step aloud and he ignored Chisholm until, with a grin of triumph, he announced: "Three hundred!"

It was not until Chisholm had congratulated him on his mobility that Rick realised that the cheering words were a trifle forced. They did not conceal a troubled air. Rick guessed the source of the depression and expressed his sympathetic understanding in one word: "Lomax?"

"Lomax," confirmed Chisholm. "He's convinced I'm a homicidal maniac – and I came within inches of proving him right. I could very cheerfully have kicked his teeth down his throat!"

"I know the feeling," sympathised Rick. He made a brave joke: "My trouble is that I kick with the leg I stand on."

The fact that Rick's spirits had revived – to the extent that he could now make light of the injury which, so recently, had been the source of suicidal despair – did much to dispel Chisholm's bewilderment and shock at his odd welcome to St Cyr des Bains. His own spirits perked up accordingly. For a time, the world beyond their four walls was forgotten as Chisholm – egged on by his audience of one – reminisced in happy vein about his misadventure-filled apprenticeship in the Merchant Navy.

A series of deliciously absurd escapades in Pernambuco had Rick rocking with laughter as Chisholm recounted his steps from one preposterous situation into another of even greater unlikelihood. The young American's blue eyes were bright with merriment as Chisholm launched into a Keystone Cops encounter with the local constabulary, but the story was never told. He saw the merriment fade from Rick's eyes as they fixed on a point beyond Chisholm's back. Chisholm turned and felt a startle of shock to discover the face of Wolfgang Keitler only inches from his own. The German had opened the door without a sound and advanced to the foot of Rick's bed without the pair being aware of his presence. Chisholm, who had been leaning against the cage on Rick's bed and half-perched on the rail at the end of the bed, sidled quickly to his feet; ignorant of the other's identity but resenting his stealthy intrusion and the way he had made Rick's face cloud with apprehension.

"I am Dr Keitler," the German announced with a smile of exaggerated warmth. "I am pleased to see that you two have got acquainted. You are to be congratulated, Captain Chisholm. You have achieved in hours what we have failed to do in months. You have made Lieutenant Thomson laugh."

Rick was still staring at Keitler with a mixture of fear and distrust but there was nothing sinister that Chisholm could see in the doctor's appearance. He was medium height, with a dumpiness of build: a rather mild-looking man. Lightish brown hair, that had been plastered down close to the scalp with water or brilliantine, added a touch of severity to the round face. The eyes burned with a bright intelligence. He beamed at Chisholm.

"I must say you look healthier than most of the patients they send here. I hope you will be comfortable with us. We take a personal interest in all our patients – and that is how we look on everyone in this block . . . as patients, not prisoners."

He regretted that there had to be some restrictions, but many were imposed in the best interests of the patients themselves. Razor blades, for instance, were not allowed. Psychologically disturbed patients – and Chisholm should realise that a man who had lost an arm could be as psychologically disturbed as a man with a brain injury – had to be kept apart from implements that could be used for self-destruction. Surely the Captain understood such things.

"Of course," agreed Chisholm, content to humour the doctor as this seemed to be the role expected of him and there seemed little point in contradicting him. Keitler's smile broadened. What a smiling man he was.

"Nurse!" he called out.

A slim, dark-haired girl in nurse's apron and cap appeared from the corridor at Keitler's summons. She was carrying a small leather bag and contrived to keep her eyes down looking at nobody.

"This is Nurse Baril," Keitler announced. "She is one of our French auxiliaries and I wish we had more like her. She suffers a lot of abuse from her own people down in the village because of the work she does. Is it not sad that some French are so blind and bigoted that they even shout traitor at someone engaged in her calling? She tends the sick but, because this is now a German hospital, her compatriots call it collaborating with the enemy."

The girl stole a shy look at Chisholm. Her scrutiny was cool, detached. She showed nothing in her expression of approval or otherwise of Keitler's introduction: as if she had heard it many times before.

"Nurse Baril will tidy you up," Keitler said to Chisholm. He beamed. "We like to keep our patients happy . . . Naturally, when I heard that your whiskers were making you feel wretched, I understood at once. I detest facial hair myself. It makes one feel unclean, eh?"

Keitler left and the girl unpacked a set of electric clippers and razor from the leather bag. She began work on Chisholm's overgrown locks with as little ado as a sheep shearer on piece work. She was efficient but none too tender and Chisholm winced once or twice as the clippers nipped the skin of his neck.

"Most barbers I know talk a lot," he said teasingly. "You don't have very much to say for yourself, Nurse Baril."

She did not reply but dug the clippers more fiercely than ever into the flesh of his neck in a fresh burst of industry.

"You're wasting your time with Nicole," Rick said with a mocking smile, as he watched the performance. "Nicole doesn't have much time for les Anglais – or les Americains, Chizz. She prefers stiff-necked Prussians."

The girl ignored the comment, apart from seeming to attack Chisholm's hair with greater fury than ever. It was Chisholm who started involuntarily at mention of her name. He jerked round so that she had to suspend operations.

"Nicole?" he echoed. "Your name is Nicole?"

"Oui." She shrugged impatiently. She wanted to get on with the hair-cutting, but Chisholm held up a hand.

"It's not true, is it, Nicole? About you preferring Germans?" His steady gaze seemed to fluster her.

"Please, Monsieur." Her eyes flashed warning signals against continuing with such questions. They begged him to desist. He did so, his own eyes flickering a tacit acknowledgement. When she continued the clipping, her left hand was resting on his shoulder. It was trembling.

Three

Way Out

Chisholm could not sleep. He lay on his back in the darkness, thoughts whirling. A low burn of excitement had gripped him since early evening.

A week at St Cyr des Bains had not reconciled him to the strange atmosphere that permeated The Pavilion. It was a place vibrant with baffling undercurrents and hostilities, where everything seemed to be out of proportion. It was like living in an enclosed hall of mirrors. Every image was distorted.

Rick Thomson was in no doubt that behind all the animosities in the prison ward – and fanning them furiously – was the smiling Dr Keitler. According to Rick, Keitler was behind the friction that flared frequently between the Canadian other-rank patients and their officers. And it was because of Keitler that both sets of Canadians seemed to despise the young American and treat Chisholm like a carrier of bubonic plague.

In spite of Rick, Chisholm was unconvinced that Keitler was somehow manipulating the prisoners and exploiting every petty difference. No, Rick – like everyone else in The Pavilion – tended to get things out of proportion. Keitler, with his phoney smile, was a creepy kind of individual but he was no bogeyman as far as Chisholm could see. As for the Canadians, they reminded Chisholm of the crew of an unhappy ship that had been dogged by bad luck and been too long away from home. They were what the Americans called "stir crazy": getting on their own nerves and everyone else's, seeing everything in the harsh exaggerated light of their own misfortunes and oblivious of all else. Their hostility to him had hurt and angered Chisholm, because he had done nothing to warrant it. Clearly, Lomax had declared him *persona non grata* and, in this respect, the Canadians had presented a more or less united front.

There had been signs that not all of them endorsed Lomax's hard line towards a fellow-prisoner but, if they spoke to Chisholm at all, it was guardedly, almost guiltily, with one eye skinned to make sure Lomax wasn't around.

Lying there in the dark, Chisholm was prepared to make allowances for the Canadians that they had not accorded him. They were, he told himself, the badly shocked survivors of an appalling massacre and had suffered terrible injuries. Their bodies might heal but the scars on their minds might stay with them for the rest of their lives. After what they'd been through they might distrust their own mothers, never mind a complete stranger who had been labelled insane and dangerous.

Chisholm had made no attempt to fight the slander that he was violent and unbalanced. He reckoned it would be a waste of breath. If the Canadians were prepared to judge a man on grapevine rumours without even listening to what the individual involved might have to say, then damn them. He certainly wasn't going to beg for a hearing. They could think what they damned well liked about him.

Chisholm peered across at Rick's bed in the gloom.

"Are you awake, Rick?"

"Yeah," came his voice. "I shoulda been an owl."

"You were wrong about Nurse Baril, Rick," said Chisholm.

"Oh yeah? I've noticed how you try to get her on her own whenever she's around. You're wasting your time, Chizz. She sleeps with German officers only. That's how she keeps her family in steaks when there isn't any meat in the shops. She's a whore, Chizz, and you don't have the kind of currency that interests her."

"She hates the Germans, Rick."

"Oh yeah?"

"Her father's a fisherman."

"I know. And he's thick with the Krauts, too. That's why they let him go to sea when most of the boats around here aren't allowed out of the harbour. And the Germans pay good prices for his fish. Ask Keitler. He's always on about Nurse Baril and her enlightened family. They sure know what side their bread's buttered on!"

Chisholm sighed.

"You've got it wrong, Rick. Nicole . . . Nurse Baril . . . and her old man . . . are on our side. They're going to help us get out of here."

Chisholm could hear the snorted exhalation of breath and the sudden movement as Rick pulled himself into a sitting position.

"Chizz, you're out of your goddamned mind!"

"Not too far out. I've escaped from one looney bin already, remember?"

"And how do you propose to get out of this booby hatch?"

"That's the least of our problems," Chisholm said. "The tricky bit is getting across the Channel to England." Again, there was a hiss of incredulity from the direction of the other bed.

"Jesus, Chizz, you mean it! You really goddamn mean it!" There was a short silence. Then: "How come you wait until the middle of the night to tell me?"

"Because you're not supposed to know . . . yet. Some people seem to think that you wouldn't be interested . . . in going over the wire, that is."

"Why, for God's sake?"

"They haven't seen you get around on those crutches of yours."

"I'd crawl all the way to the shore on my hands and knees if I thought I could get away." Rick's voice was shrill with outrage. "Christ, Chizz, you know it!"

"I know it," Chisholm affirmed quietly. "But I had to be absolutely sure. I wanted to hear you say it. That's why I'm telling you all this now."

"How much more is there to tell?"

There was a lot to tell. Rick listened in stunned silence. Chisholm told him how his first attempts to win the confidence of Nicole Baril had met with lies, evasion and threats to report him to Keitler. But the girl had not reported him. She was plainly terrified by Chisholm's approaches: her fear serving to confirm for him that she was under immense strain from the double game she was playing. Hers was a desperately difficult role to endure: being spat on in the street by her own people while, all the time, risking her life to rid her country of the conquerors whom she pretended to serve. Chisholm had made no headway with her until – without any intention of going through with it – he had threatened to call her bluff and go to Keitler himself. She had thrown herself on Chisholm's mercy rather than face a showdown. Her relief, when Chisholm finally managed to get it through to her that he had no intention of betraying her then or at any other time, had brought it home to him just how close to breaking-point the girl was.

She was quick to point out to him that the chances of escape to England without the help of the French Resistance were almost nil, particularly in the prohibited coastal area. If it had been as easy as Chisholm seemed to think, certain other inmates of The Pavilion would have been long gone. This was the first clue Chisholm was given that Nicole's dangerous double role was known to the Canadians and that some of them were in the escape queue ahead of him.

Nicole had not needed to name names for Chisholm to work out that the man in the Canadian camp at the centre of their escape plans was Lomax. He had to be the one who, according to Nicole, was becoming particularly difficult to deal with because he had got the idea in his head that the French Resistance were being deliberately unhelpful.

The suggestion that the Resistance were dragging their feet deeply offended Nicole because it was the opposite of the truth.

"We have a detailed plan to get six men out of here and on to a boat which can take them a few miles out to sea," she had told Chisholm. "But unless London can arrange a pick-up, our end of the operation is useless."

So far, London had been unable to provide the essential back-up.

"What's to stop the escape boat going right across the Channel to England?" Chisholm had wanted to know. He, himself, was prepared to take such a chance, even if it meant rowing all the way.

Nicole had pointed out that the boat was subject to regular checks by German patrols and always had to be back in harbour by a specific time, otherwise there would be a great hue and cry and it would be shot out of the water before it got half way to England. Then there would be repercussions ashore, with everyone connected to the boat being rounded up by the Gestapo. The entire Resistance group could be put out of action with the loss of the boat which, in any case, was vital to all their operations.

Rick Thomson listened to Chisholm's revelations with a mixture of astonishment and suspicion that bordered on disbelief. He could not credit that Nicole Baril was anything other than she pretended to be: a good-time girl whose favours were reserved for anything in a Nazi uniform.

"OK, so she fooled me," he conceded to Chisholm. "And maybe she didn't have to be hell of a clever to do that. But to fool Keitler is something else again. That cookie is trickier than a convention of lawyers. I just can't believe that the woman is born who could put anything over on him."

"You're obsessed with Keitler," Chisholm argued. "She probably only had to roll her eyes and waggle her backside at him. What makes you think that Keitler is any less susceptible to a piece of skirt than the rest of us?"

"She didn't fool *you*, Chizz. You saw through her in one minute flat . . . That day she came in here to cut your hair . . . I can't remember what it was you said to needle her but you said or did something that made her go white as a sheet. She tried to act like it was nothing but she stood there like she was fit to wet her pants . . . I just couldn't figure it out at the time."

Chisholm could almost feel the intensity of Rick's stare in the darkness. The American's words came to him with a faintly accusing ring.

"I don't get it, Chizz. If she's clever enough to fool Keitler— and everybody else around here—how come you twigged her the minute you clapped eyes on her? What makes you so goddamned smart?"

"I didn't twig her, Rick. I had a tip-off before I got here."

"A tip-off?" echoed Rick, his voice rising. "Who from for God's sake?"

"Who from doesn't matter, Rick. Somebody who tried to help me. Somebody I've got reason to feel grateful for. I was told to look out for a friend when I got here and that the friend had a name—Nicole. That's all there is to it."

"Is it?" asked Rick sharply. "How much more are you holding back?"

Chisholm sighed.

"Don't go sulky on me, Rick. It was for your own good that I didn't say anything to you about Nicole until now. I *had* to play things close to my chest. If I had been wrong about her, I didn't want you involved. That's all there was to it."

The silence from the other bed was now eloquent with regret. Chisholm knew that Rick was silently punishing himself for his petulant note of mistrust.

"I must have sounded bitchy," Rick said at last. "Sorry, Chizz. I didn't mean it. Blame it on this goddamned place!"

The voice took on a more hopeful note: "Do you really think we can make it out of here?"

"We're going to give it a try, Rick. We're going to give it a try!" A smile entered his voice as he added: "Even if it's the last thing we ever do."

"What about Lomax? Have you spoken to him?"

"No, Rick. I left that to Nicole. She was going to have a word with him before she finished her shift last night. I've been waiting for something to happen ever since. I reckoned he would go up in smoke. For all I know, he's having a nervous breakdown right at this minute, wondering about us and how the hell we got in on the act."

"He'll try to cut us out."

"You can bet your life on that, Rick. But something Nicole said makes me think Lomax may need us more than we need Lomax. It depends on the Resistance boys managing to beg, borrow or steal a boat that isn't going to be missed immediately – one that could be sailed to England. They vetoed the idea before when London said a pick-up couldn't be arranged. The French don't trust Lomax and his soldier boys not to get themselves lost if they tried the crossing on their own. They're liable to end up back in France – but I bloody well wouldn't, Rick! Sailoring's my job. I could get a boat to England!"

"A guy with only one foot isn't going to be much help to you, Chizz. Maybe I could paddle with a crutch?" Rick's voice was cheerful but Chisholm could detect an underlying note of anxiety. The reason was easily guessed. Rick feared that his handicap made him a candidate for being left behind. Chisholm chose his words deliberately.

"You can count on one thing, Rick. I won't be sailing anywhere without you. I've got your name down for the cook-steward's job. You won't need a crutch for that – just a chef's hat and a soup ladle."

The prisoners in The Pavilion were encouraged by their captors to exercise in the yard between 9.00 and 9.25 every morning. Then they had to assemble by their beds so that a squad of doctors and nurses might begin their morning round of inspection at precisely 9.30. As the medical team circulated, each prisoner was allotted his personal programme for the day and the senior nursing officer was given instructions on drugs, medicaments and treatment prescribed for the next twenty-four hours. The prisoner's personal programme would consist of timetabled periods for a variety of medical tests, supervised physiotherapy, X-ray examination, and rehabilitation assessment sessions.

The last were what Rick Thomson scathingly referred to as "Keitler's mindbending and Nazi-indoctrination classes", although Chisholm – from his own experience of them – was never able to make such a sinister interpretation of these man-to-man interviews. Keitler invariably handled these interviews himself. They were certainly interrogatory, but Chisholm found the questions personality oriented and harmless enough. Compared to the intensive grillings to which he had been subjected in his previous prison, Keitler's interviews were cosy little chats. He was always affable and did not seem to mind talking about his work on those occasions when Chisholm countered a question by asking about the object of it.

Keitler used these occasions to propagandise to some extent on the enlightened methods of German medicine and its practitioners, particularly himself. He liked to point out that medical and scientific knowledge took tremendous strides in wartime and that the prisoners at St Cyr des Bains received no less care and attention than the German wounded beyond the compound.

"The doctor learns much from his patient," he told Chisholm. "And that is how I see you, one and all – as patients. Not Germans or English or Americans. You are all individuals. I must diagnose and prescribe for you individually because the humanity of my profession demands it – but I learn much from the process. To me, every patient is like a unique laboratory culture to be painstakingly observed – and war throws up an abundance of fascinating specimens, as many in a month as the ordinary researching scientist might encounter in a lifetime."

"You make us sound like guinea-pigs," Chisholm had said.

Keitler had laughed, admitting that the observation was not without truth.

"We experiment," he confessed. "But we experiment in order to advance. Did you have a father in the last war, Captain Chisholm?"

"Yes . . . He was killed at Gallipoli. I was the son he never saw."

"Perhaps your father was lucky. Mine survived the war. But his life was pitiful . . . Shellshock, they called it." Keitler had

38

shaken his head sadly and, for a moment, had looked a very vulnerable human being. "It's ironic, is it not, that with the knowledge I've gained here, I might have made my father's life more tolerable and dignified than it was?"

He had smiled then, a hard smile.

"When I think of my father, Captain Chisholm, I have little reason for loving the British. But a doctor has to be quite objective, does he not? Tell me, has the death of your father warped your outlook in any way?"

And so, Keitler had steered the conversation back to the subject that, he maintained, held more than a passing interest for him – Chisholm's personality. The interviews - like everything else so thoroughly organised by the Germans for their prisoner patients – were treated by Chisholm as no more than diversions. He had only one thought on his mind: escape.

For this reason, he indulged in little verbal fencing with Keitler on the morning after he had confided in Rick Thomson about Nicole. Instead, his mind was occupied by the brief exchange of words he had had with Lomax during the 9.00 exercise period.

Lomax had shown no sign of likely co-operation in an escape plan.

His final words kept ringing in Chisholm's ears throughout most of his session with Keitler. The Canadian, haggard and gaunt-eyed as if his night had been sleepless, had warned him: "You stay away from Nurse Baril, Mr Sailor-Civilian! You're meddling in things that don't concern you! Just stay away from her and you won't get hurt!"

Chisholm's preoccupation did not escape Keitler.

"Am I boring you?" he asked. He had, for no apparent reason, been airing his views on the philosophical arguments of Oswald Spengler.

"I'm sorry," said Chisholm. "What you were saying was a bit over my head." He had never heard of Spengler.

"Come, come, Captain Chisholm, you're an intelligent man. Surely you see what Spengler was driving at when he defined the art of statesmanship. The statesman must have a clear idea of the course he is charting and a sure touch in handling every single occurrence and every single person he encounters. That is the Führer's genius. He has this clarity of purpose that enables him to turn impending disaster into decisive success. The secret of all victory lies in organisation of the non-obvious.

If you want to defeat an enemy, Captain, encourage him to concentrate on the obvious. Give him all the evidence he needs to confirm that what he sees in front of his nose is all there is to be seen. He will not look beyond the obvious for what is not obvious because what is obvious has substance. He will neglect what is not obvious because, without substance, it has no reason to exist and far less to be feared."

Chisholm tried hard not to look glassy-eyed. He looked at Keitler with an expression of apology.

"I'm afraid you're losing me. Maybe I'm just stupid . . ."

"Stupid, no," said Keitler and, contriving to sound superior, added, "lacking in guile, perhaps. Wouldn't it be true to say that you are a person who tends to take other people at their word? You are a fairly honest and straightforward person yourself and this is what you expect to find in others."

"Is this so terrible?" replied Chisholm defensively. After all Keitler's rambling on about Spengler, he had homed again on to Chisholm's personality. There seemed very little point to any of it. Keitler gleamed his most patronising smile.

"Let me put it this way, Captain Chisholm. When I tell you that, as a doctor, I am here to help you, I am quite sure that you believe me. You may think my methods are strange, you may not like my face or my manners or the uniform I wear – but you accept do you not, that the reason why I spend so much time on you and all my other patients here is because I am concerned for your welfare. You take me at my word, do you not?"

"Yes, I suppose so."

"And so you should," said Keitler. "You get better attention here than you would get in any British hospital. I insist on it being so. Why then does your American friend, Lieutenant Thomson, persist in the belief, that I want to harm rather than help him?"

"Isn't that something you should ask Lieutentant Thomson?" Chisholm's smile was bland.

"I have asked him," replied Keitler. "We moved him away from the others at his request and we have shown him numerous extra kindnesses. But the more we have spoiled him, the more suspicious and withdrawn he has become. I do not have to admit failure often in my rehabilitation programmes, Captain Chisholm, but with that young man I have to confess we have made very little headway." Keitler massaged his chin thoughtfully. "He seems to have taken to you, Captain

Chisholm. Perhaps you could convince him that we are genuinely trying to help him come to terms with his mutilation."

"Maybe you are trying too hard," Chisholm suggested diffidently. "He says he has no secrets that can be of any military value to you but that you have been using your little therapy sessions as a kind of third degree."

Keitler laughed.

"I am aware that the sum total of any military intelligence he possesses is without consequence or value and that he has this absurd notion about me. He is the victim of too much American propaganda, I'm afraid. To him, every nurse carrying a bedpan is a Gestapo agent in disguise and every doctor with a stethoscope in his pocket is an interrogator with a rubber truncheon to beat him. He sees everyone as an enemy who is determined to do him down. Did he tell you that we moved him because he thought the Canadian officers were trying to kill him? It was nonsense, of course, but he made himself so unpopular with them that it would only have been a matter of time before someone did try to do him an injury."

Chisholm said nothing. Keitler gave a weary sigh.

"Manic depression, acute persecution psychosis . . . These are just two of the unfortunate side effects one encounters when a man loses an arm or a leg or his genitals. In the past, we doctors concerned ourselves overmuch with the physical injury – although the body itself is surprisingly resilient – and too little with the mental implications, which are much more complex." Keitler beamed suddenly. "But we *are* learning, Captain Chisholm. We *are* learning."

Out of the blue then, Keitler asked Chisholm how he got along with the senior Canadian officer, Captain Lomax.

"I don't come into contact with him a great deal," Chisholm said truthfully.

"A quite remarkable man," commented Keitler. "A strong, forceful personality and, from all accounts, a first-class officer. By rights, of course, he should be dead. He would have been if he'd had the bad luck to have fallen into the hands of any other surgeon than Schumacher. Probably the best in Europe. He could have made a fortune in America in 1939 but he turned down the chance, to put on his country's uniform and live on a major's pay. He's a colonel now – and a stroke of luck for Captain Lomax and a lot of other Canadians that he was

41

stationed at Dieppe."

Keitler further volunteered the information that Lomax had a steel plate in his skull as a souvenir of Schumacher's life-saving operation on his brain.

"Like your friend, the American, he is his own worst enemy." Keitler added. "I have warned him time and again that he must not excite himself. It would take very little to cause a subdiural haematoma and undo all Schumacher's good work."

Chisholm wondered why Keitler was telling him all this. All doctors in his previous experience tended to be tighter than clams when it came to talking about other patients in their care. Chisholm took a deep breath and said: "Is there any reason why you are telling me this, Doctor?"

"It is something that all Captain Lomax's friends should know. For the Captain's own sake. Any undue excitement could kill him. I thought I should warn you."

Chisholm kept his eyes firmly on Keitler.

"And, of course, you warned everyone about me?" He had to make an effort to pronounce the libel: "That I was violent?"

Chisholm expected Keitler to show some sign of anger at his calculated provocation. But the German did not so much as blink.

"We have made no secret that you came here with some record of derangement," he said smoothly. "In the interest of all the patients. And your own. You see, Captain Chisholm, we believed that you would respond favourably to the kind of environment we provide here. And you have. Stress caused you to be violent – stress that was aggravated by isolation and restraint . . . Here, you are not isolated and you are not unduly restrained from moving around . . . With the result that the causes of stress are removed. I have not for one moment feared that there would be any recurrence of the behaviour abnormalities of the past. Indeed, you have been so composed and rational in all my little talks with you that it would be under false pretences to keep you here much longer. I am recommending your transfer to a seamen officers' camp just as soon as I can get down to the necessary paperwork. You can expect to be gone from here within the week."

Chisholm was taken aback but tried not to show the shock he felt. Here, at St Cyr des Bains with England not very far away, freedom was a very real possibility: an opportunity to be seized.

In Germany or Poland or wherever they took him, the chances of a successful break would become more remote with every mile travelled from the coast.

"Does the news displease you?" Keitler was asking him. "Perhaps you are too comfortable here?" he added with a laugh. He did not wait for a reply but stood up and offered Chisholm his hand.

"Good luck, Herr Captain. I shall not require to meet you again before you leave. I wish you a pleasant journey."

Chisholm was like a man with a fever. From the day of his arrival at St Cyr des Bains, he had felt completely in control of himself: thinking clearly, able to suppress sudden anxieties, concentrating positively on the single objective he was determined to achieve – his freedom. Now – with the shock of the news Keitler had delivered to him still raging in him – he felt like a swimmer caught by a fast ebb tide, whose strength he had underestimated. Fears and doubts beset him, compelling him to flail desperately against a current that threatened to overwhelm him. He could no longer wait for events to take their course and let himself ride with every favourable eddy as it presented itself, he had to generate the action.

There was a desperate recklessness in the urgency that gripped him. Previously, he had been circumspect in his meetings and conversations with Nicole Baril: choosing the moments carefully and without attracting attention. Now, he sought her out with the slimmest of pretexts in order to tell her that his removal from St Cyr des Bains was imminent and that if there was to be help for his escape bid it had to come within hours rather than days. The girl was alarmed by Chisholm's lack of caution in seeking her out. He had spotted her heading towards the dispensary and had followed her in despite the presence of the German pharmacist. There had been an awkward moment while the German had considered Chisholm's request for a laxative, but the man had not demurred and had retired to his tiny laboratory to mix a brew which, he promised, would work on a clogged bowel like dynamite.

Left alone with Nicole, the girl had almost frozen with fright when, low-voiced and scarcely pausing to draw breath, he had acquainted her with the urgency of the new situation. She would not have responded beyond a shaking of the head demanding his silence but for the desperate look on Chisholm's face. Realising that he was not to be put off, she acknowledged the need for haste. But he was to do nothing precipitate. He was to leave things to her. She promised that, by evening, she would be in touch with him or get a message to him via the Canadians.

The return of the pharmacist with a bottle of frothy brown liquid precluded further conversation. Chisholm left, clutching the concoction and thinking wryly that it must be about the last thing he needed. His insides were liquefying already as a result of the strange panic that had him in its grip.

Telling Rick Thomson of the unexpected development did nothing to ease his agitation. Indeed, it only served to make the American as jumpy and uncertain as himself. For Rick's immediate reaction, too, was a lowering fear that the talked-of escape was now in jeopardy. Neither man reckoned on the fidelity and speed with which Nicole Baril would honour her promise of swift action.

The night orderly had just made his 8 p.m. round – injections and temperatures – when Corporal Malloy appeared with a message for Chisholm. There was to be a conference in the shower-room in one hour's time, to which he was invited.

This time, Lomax did not come alone. With him was a lieutenant, whose name was Constantine, and a Sergeant Martineau. Lieutenant Constantine was a quietly spoken man who had been less aloof with Chisholm than some of the other officers. Once, he must have been a good-looking young man, but before he had sustained the face-burns that had left the skin blotchy and corrugated as if an attempt had been made to pare down his features with a carrot-grater. Martineau was a swarthy Quebecois who, apart from the stiff way he carried his left arm, showed little sign that part of his shoulder-blade and pectoral muscle were no longer there. Stripped, he looked as if a shark had taken a bite out of him behind the arm-pit.

"A deputation?" said Chisholm. "Should I feel honoured?"

Surprisingly, it was Martineau who spoke first for the trio.

"We need to talk with you. We don't need to pretend we like it."

"That's about the size of it," Lomax confirmed. He was staring hard at Chisholm, but his demeanour was calm. He was not simmering with violence, muscles twitching, as he had been that morning when he had warned Chisholm to stay away from Nicole Baril.

Constantine made the first positive contribution to the

44

conversation. his lipless face twisted into what might have been a smile.

"We need your co-operation, Captain . . . Chisholm, isn't it? It seems that you are as determined as we are to make a . . . home run. We have the promise of outside help . . . But it seems that there won't be any unless we take you along. This means that we have had to overcome certain reservations . . . You understand?"

"I have reservations of my own," said Chisholm. "That doesn't mean we can't work something out. But if there's something about me that bothers you, I want to know what it is." He stared at Lomax. "If you want to get something off your chest, now's the time."

"In a nutshell, we're not sure that we can trust you," said Lomax icily. "There's too much about you that smells. The same goes for your friend, the Yank. Him we do not trust at all!"

Constantine cut short the angry reply that was on Chisholm's lips.

"With respect, sir, we're not going to get anywhere with this kind of talk. We've never known for sure that the Yank was telling tales to the Germans. Maybe it wasn't him at all. We can't even be sure that the French girl is what she says she is. We don't really know any more about her than we know about Captain Chisholm here. We've got to start taking chances. We've got to start taking a hell of a lot on trust or none of us is ever going to get out of this goddamned place!"

"I agree," said Chisholm.

"The Lieutenant's right," said Martineau. "We could sit round on our fannies talking 'til we all got grey beards. We gotta do something—even if we have to fight our way out."

Lomax favoured Martineau with a look that seemed to express some doubt about the Sergeant's intellect. He said: "Sure, we'll storm the main gate with wet sponges." He shook his head. "No, Sergeant, an excess of stupidity isn't going to get us to England any better than an excess of caution. It looks though that I'm the odd one out on my own escape committee . . . So, OK, we all swim together or we all sink together."

He looked suddenly weary. Turning away from the others, he put both hands to his head.

"Are you all right, sir?" asked Constantine, getting up from his comfortable perch on the metal splashguard of one of the

45

showers.

"My head aches like hell," Lomax said. "You're going to have to manage without me. I think I'll go and lie down for a spell."

Spurning Constantine's offer to help him, he staggered off, saying he would be all right. "You've got some details to work out," he told the Lieutenant. "I'll go along with whatever you decide. It's all up to the girl anyway."

With Lomax gone, there was no more beating around the bush. Chisholm listened while Constantine gave an account of a meeting he and Lomax had had with Nicole Baril earlier in the evening.

The substance of it was that the Resistance were ready to activate their plan to spring a maximum of six prisoners. The earliest opportunity would occur in forty-eight hours' time, the evening of Friday. The next earliest would be the following Friday. It was up to the prisoners themselves to decide the six escapees, with one exception. Essential to the second stage of the escape was that one of the party was the sea captain because, without an experienced seaman to take charge, the sea journey to England would almost certainly end in disaster.

"So you see, you're the key man," Constantine told Chisholm. "We go with you, now, or we sit around here for God knows how long, waiting for London to send a pick-up boat. We could all be in Poland by the time the guys across the Channel get round to doing that."

Chisholm had expected that the escape party would have to break out of their compound and make their way to the village to rendezvous with the Resistance. It was a matter to which he had given a lot of thought, so he was surprised when Constantine told him that nothing quite so desperate was required. They just had to be ready to leave at the appointed hour. The wire would be cut for them, they would have to walk a few hundred yards to transport that would be waiting, and they would go out the way they had come in – by the road. The Resistance had it all worked out. And they were running all the risks. That was why they didn't want to foul things up by trusting a boat to a bunch of farm boys from Saskatchewan, which they seemed to think the Canadians were.

It was not until Chisholm and the two Canadians touched on the actual composition of the escape party that a conflict of opinions arose. Both Constantine and Martineau had assumed that Chisholm and five Canadians would make up the six. They were astonished when Chisholm disabused them of the idea. Rick Thomson had to be one of the six or they were going to have to find another navigator. They argued but, when they saw that Chisholm was not going to give an inch, they reluctantly conceded a place for Rick, complaining bitterly that Chisholm had them over a barrel and asserting that Captain Lomax would more than likely veto the arrangement.

But morning brought no veto from Captain Lomax. Chisholm was performing his usual solitary perambulation in the yard during the nine o' clock exercise period when Constantine detached himself from the Canadian huddle and walked beside him.

"We drew lots to see who would drop out," he told Chisholm. "Captain Lomax won't be coming with us. He drew the short straw." He added meaningfully: "You ain't the most popular guy around here right now. If I were you, I'd steer well clear of the Captain today."

For Chisholm, it seemed like a day without end. Now that he had been pronounced fit by Keitler for removal to a prison camp, he found that his name had been removed from the usual daily programme of activities. He did not have to surrender a pin-prick of blood at the lab unit at ten, nor return at eleven with a labelled bottle containing his urine. There was no physiotherapy under the supervision of a big-bosomed fraulein followed by a ritual of being weighed in kilogrammes and the information recorded on the growing file that kept track of every movement of his temperature, bowels, blood pressure and pulse-rate. There was no chummy chat with Keitler about egocentricity, kleptomania, father fixations, sex starvation, Freud, or the works of Spengler. Every minute dragged.

In the afternoon, with Rick off somewhere doing special exercises to strengthen his quadraceps, Chisholm lay on his bed and tried to sleep. From the morrow onwards, there was no saying how long he might have to go without that commodity. But sleep would not come. He was contemplating this capricious fact when Nicole Baril flitted silently into the room. She could not stay long. She had come to let him know that all was in readiness for the following night and she gave him a brief rundown on what he and the others had to do. In particular, they were to put on every bit of warm clothing that they could but she would have a final check with them. She was due to

47

start night duty from next day and would be in and out of The Pavilion from 6 p.m. onwards. With the promise to see him then, she left.

Chisholm never saw her again.

Four

The Break

It was not Nurse Baril who, shortly after six, came to the room shared by Chisholm and Rick Thomson. It was a girl whom Chisholm had never seen before.

"Nurse Baril will not be coming on duty tonight," she told them. "I have come in her place. It is all right," she assured them as their expressions both showed alarm, "you can trust me. I know everything."

The Resistance group, it transpired, had insisted that Nicole have an alibi for the night of the escape: to allay the suspicions of one of the German officers. The man had been taking an undue interest in Nicole's activities: largely, it seemed, because she had rejected his attentions. To divert his suspicions and provide Nicole with a cast-iron alibi, she had switched her duty rota and would be dancing the night away at Deauville with the German while the escape operation took place at St Cyr des Bains.

"Nicole is in and out of here so much, you understand?" said her replacement. "It would be too easy for the Germans to put two and two together and realise that she must be the contact you have with the outside."

"What about you?" asked Chisholm. "Won't they suspect you?"

The girl shrugged.

"There is always risk. But we know what we are doing."

Her name was Violette. Like Nicole, she was concerned that the escapers should have warm clothing for the adventure that lay ahead. No overcoats had been issued and the prisoners were in for a miserable time from the elements if they had to face them in their uniforms and flimsy hospital garb.

Chisholm and Rick had long ago decided that the blankets

49

from their beds would be leaving with them but had run into difficulties tailoring a cloak for Rick and his crutches.

"We need string or bandages for ties," Chisholm told Violette. "We'll improvise something. But it would help if we had a knife, or scissors. Something to make arm-holes, Or even a hole to get the head through. We could make poncho capes."

Violette approved. She told Chisholm to slip along to the little office used by the nurses in about twenty minutes. She would try to find something that would help his makeshift tailoring efforts, but she would have to get the German orderly out of the way first.

As he passed through the Canadian sections to keep his assignation with Violette, Chisholm could feel a tingle of excitement permeating his entire body. As the hour drew near for the break for freedom, the calm that he had tried to maintain throughout the day became more and more fragile. He felt strangely light-headed, longing to channel his pent-up nervous energy into decisive physical action. He was like a highly tuned greyhound, eager to be free of the trap and running.

None of the Canadians spoke to him as he passed through. He could sense their tension, too. Constantine's disfigured face wrinkled into what may have been a smile. It may just as easily have been a nervous contortion of facial muscle or a tacit signal of recognition. Chisholm gained a small consolation from the realisation that all of the Canadians were as twitchy as he felt.

The white-coated German orderly emerged from the nurses' tiny box-like office as he approached. The man was carrying an enamel mug and looked at Chisholm questioningly. Chisholm beamed a broad disarming smile and gestured with his hands that he intended to go into the small office. The German watched as Chisholm knocked and entered.

The nurse called Violette was seated at a cabinet with a fold-down leaf that served as a desk. She said nothing but signalled with her eyes. Chisholm followed the direction of her eyes. A pair of long surgical scissors rested on the desk flap.

The girl could see through the little square spy window that the German orderly was still lingering beyond the door. She rose brightly and lifted a cotton shift from a shelf where a variety of fresh-laundered handtowels and other such items were neatly stacked. The girl dropped the cotton garment on top of the scissors briefly and then scooped it up again to hand to Chisholm. The scissors had disappeared and Chisholm smiled acknowledgement as he felt solid metal through the folded cotton bedwear he now held in his hands.

Violette chatted away officiously to him in French as she bundled him out through the door of the small office, as if she were busy and anxious to be rid of him. She even chided the still-hovering orderly: asking him if he had nothing better to do than stand staring when there was work to be done. Then she pranced back into the tiny office with the air of one who is harassed on all sides.

Chisholm pushed past the bewildered German with another broad smile and a shrug of the shoulders. He did not look back as he made his way past the beds of the Canadian OR prisoners. He was halfway through the officers' section when Lomax barred his progress.

"I can't talk now," Chisholm muttered and would have squeezed past but Lomax caught his sleeve. The tug was just enough to slacken Chisholm's hold on his bundle. The scissors slipped from the fold of cotton shift and clattered to the floor.

A live hand-grenade tumbling to the floor could not have caused more consternation. Although Chisholm swooped like a hawk to retrieve the scissors and conceal them again in the cotton gown, it was not before most of the Canadian officers had moved or craned forward to get a glimpse of whatever it was Chisholm had dropped. Their reactions to seeing the scissors were almost uniform. Eyes popped with surprise and then heads turned to glance over shoulders to see if any of the German staff were about and had caught sight of the offending article.

There were audible sighs of relief that there was not a German in the vicinity. Chisholm found that some of the Canadians were regarding him with a respect that bordered on awe. Every man knew that cutting implements of any kind were *verboten* in The Pavilion.

Lomax had gone red in the face: a confusion of surprise and embarrassment that he might unwittingly have triggered an incident which could have had search squads and security guards trampling all over the place. But he did not apologise.

"Sweet suffering Jesus!" he blasphemed in a low-voiced growl. "Where in hell did you get your hands on them?"

"I borrowed them," said Chisholm.

"You should have let us know. In here, we pool what we steal."

"I just this minute got the bloody things."

"The new girl?"

"She helped."

"I don't like last-minute changes. Nurse Baril should have warned us instead of just chickening out."

"The way I heard it, she was following orders. There's nothing we can do about it. It's too late."

The Canadian's expression – which seemed to be perpetually angry – broke into softer lines. He seemed suddenly old-looking and ineffably weary.

"Yeah," he murmured, "it's too late."

On an impulse, Chisholm said: "Look, I'm sorry you're not going tonight."

Lomax stared at him with a tired kind of hate.

"Are you, you bastard?" he asked, his eyes boring at Chisholm like drills. "*Are you?*"

Rick was precariously balanced on one leg on top of his bed when Chisholm returned. He was peering at a tiny grille set into the ceiling. He kept placing the flat of his hand over the grille and then removing it. He grinned down at Chisholm.

"I don't get it," he said.

"You looking for bats in the attic?" Chisholm asked with a frown. "What are you doing up there? You lose your balance and you're liable to break the one good leg you've got, to say nothing of your neck."

The American climbed down.

"My curiosity was aroused by a scientific phenomenon." He shook his head. "I still haven't worked out the answer."

"Well, I've got us a pair of scissors," replied Chisholm, "and I have need of your services. Be a pal, Rick, and keep a watch while I do a quick conversion job on our blankets. What's your preference – a Mexicana-style poncho or a knee-length woolly vest to go under your jacket and tuck down inside your trousers?"

Chisholm unfolded the cotton hospital shift and laid the long narrow surgical scissors on the bed. Rick seized them.

"Just what I needed to finish my experiment," he said.

"Some other time, Rick." Chisholm relieved him of the scissors. "Now, be a good boy and get on those crutches of yours and outside that door. If anybody comes, start whistling the Marseillaise."

"You're a goddamned bully, Chizz," Rick said good-naturedly. "Aren't you even interested in my experiment?"

Chisholm propped a crutch under the American's arm and urged him towards the door.

"Later, Rick. The Master Race will be doing their rounds in another hour. We don't have much time. Please."

"OK, OK, but think about it, Chizz. You ask yourself why this place has little ventilators all over the ceiling . . . According to the laws of convection, you should be able to feel hot air going out or cold air coming in — but there's nothing up there. Nothing!"

"You think about it, Rick. I've got work to do."

He closed the door on the still protesting American and turned immediately to the job in hand. Taking the first blanket, he made a diagonal fold and spread it over the bed. Then, judging the middle, he began to cut into the fold, following a semi-circular direction. The hole he made in this way was not quite big enough to admit his head. He refolded the blanket and began again, making a wider cut.

"Somebody's coming this way." The warning was whispered by Rick from the doorway, but Chisholm had completed his work and there was no evidence of it to be seen except for the incriminating scissors.

"Put them under my pillow," hissed Rick. "Quick!"

Chisholm was just withdrawing his hand when the German orderly strode into the room. He looked from Chisholm to Rick and back again. Then he nodded at Chisholm.

"You! Come!" he ordered.

With a bewildered shrug of his shoulders at Rick, Chisholm followed the orderly into the corridor. They reached the Canadian officers' section as a procession of two arrived from the other direction: the nurse called Violette, preceded by the substantial figure of the prisoner compound's nursing superintendent.

The latter was a husky, hard-faced woman not noted for her sense of humour or feminine grace. Her name was Dietrich and, inevitably, the English-speaking inmates had nick-named her "Marlene": a liberty that the filmstar of the same name would scarcely have considered flattering.

Marlene regulated the activities of the hospital staff with the same unsmiling authority that she brought to bear on the lives of the patients. The doctors walked in awe of her and, it was rumoured, the tough SS convalescents across in the main sanitorium hid when she approached.

Now, she halted Chisholm and his escort in their tracks with a monosyllabic bark. She fixed Chisholm on the end of her rapier-like stare.

"Herr Cheetz-hoom, Vye do you vahnt to speak with Herr-Doktor Keitler? Heh? Vot trouble you make now? Heh?"

Chisholm stared back at her, slack-jawed: partly stunned by her heavily accented parade-ground bark and partly by mystification at what she was saying.

"Ach!" she exclaimed and shouldered past him with all the elegance of a Tiger tank. She had no more to say to Chisholm and bore down on one of the Canadian officers who had had the temerity to choose that moment to light a cigarette. She was lecturing this unfortunate on his manners when the orderly threw a nervous look at Chisholm and said: "Come!"

Chisholm had no choice but to follow hard on the heels of the orderly, who seemed intent on distancing himself as quickly as possible from the fearsome supervisor. The man did not slacken his pace until he was halfway across the muddy ground that separated The Pavilion from the administrative unit.

"What's this all about?" Chisholm asked, catching up with him. "I didn't ask to see Dr Keitler. I didn't ask to see anyone."

The orderly would not or could not understand. He had been given orders and he was going to carry them out.

Outside Keitler's office, Chisholm was ordered to take a seat under the glowering eye of a black-uniformed sergeant at a desk near the door. The orderly departed. Chisholm waited impatiently.

He was still waiting an hour later. By then, more than a feverish impatience filled him. He was all but consumed by a host of anxieties. He had visions of still being seated in the draughty outer office while the appointed hour came and went when he should have been creeping through the cut wire beyond The Pavilion. Several times he asked the black-uniformed sergeant how long he was to be kept waiting. He was peremptorily told to keep silent on each occasion.

Ninety minutes passed before the outside door opened and Keitler strode in. He was in uniform and was already discarding his greatcoat as he entered his office and cheerfully called to Chisholm to come right in. Chisholm faced him uncertainly as he took up position with his back to the stove, warming his hands behind him. Keitler was smiling and there was a faint whiff of brandy from his breath. His uniform was quite resplendent although Chisholm could not tell from the insignia what rank the German held. It was a field rather than a dress uniform, he guessed. Grey was the field colour. Chisholm wondered why an officer should wear what looked like a lance-corporal's chevron on the right sleeve, noting too that Keitler had a plain black patch on the right collar. Did that mean he was a doctor or was that indicated by the green piping on the epaulettes?

"There seems to have been a mistake, Doctor," Chisholm said, when it was clear that Keitler was in no hurry to speak. "I made no request to see you."

Keitler's smile widened.

"No, it was I who sent for you," he said. "I shall miss our little talks. I have a small gift for you . . . The spirit of Christmas, eh? And a small going-away present."

He smiled again, enjoying Chisholm's surprise.

"It is nothing, Captain Chisholm. Just a tin of cigarettes that our soldiers captured . . . I was lucky enough to get some. The spoils of war, you could say . . ." He crossed to his desk, opened a drawer, and took a flat, oblong tin. He handed it to Chisholm. "See, they are English – a naval brand. Most appropriate, don't you think?"

Chisholm took the fifty tin of Senior Service and stared at Keitler in bewilderment.

"I . . . I don't know what to say. Thank you."

The German made a gesture with his hands, deprecating the need for thanks.

"Please, please, it is nothing . . ." He frowned briefly. "I know that some of our people treated you roughly . . . Before you came here. I regret it. I deplore any kind of brutality. A small gift does not make amends but, perhaps, it will help you to think not unkindly of me. Eh?"

Keitler strode to the door, opened it, and called to the sergeant in the outer office. "Take Captain Chisholm back to his quarters, Sergeant," he ordered in German. "And take a lamp. It's a dreadful night. You could drown in that mud out there."

Dazedly clutching the tin of cigarettes, Chisholm was escorted back to The Pavilion. There was relief in him that the unexpected episode with Keitler had turned out to be so bizarre and inconsequential. Almost an anti-climax after all his fearful imaginings. It had been unreal. Had it all been just a drunken whim of Keitler's – he had seemed sober enough – or was it just plain eccentricity? Chisholm was baffled. He scarcely felt the cold rain on his cheeks as he slithered along behind the Sergeant's flashlight. Nor did he pause to contemplate its significance – either as aid or hindrance – for the adventures the night still held.

Inside The Pavilion, the yellow light streaming from the nurses' office was like a beacon amidst the blue-tinged glow of the wards' night lighting. Neither the new male orderly now on duty nor the nurse called Violette made a move to accompany Chisholm to his room. He made his way through the first Canadian section, feeling his progress watched by eyes from every bed: the stares curious, enquiring, like that of schoolboys in a dormitory watching the return after lights out of some enterprising rascal from a forbidden assignation.

As he tiptoed through the officers' ward, Chisholm sensed more than curiosity in the silent stares. There was something about the quickened tempo in the sound of sharp nasal breathing from Lomax's bed that suggested currents of hostility. The tension in the ward was almost tangible, as if at a given signal the inmates would leap from their beds and confront Chisholm. He had no doubt that every man was not only wide awake but tuned to a high pitch of alertness and breathlessly expectant. Then he realised the reason: the summons from Keitler and the impression created by that big cow of an Overnurse that he, Chisholm, was the instigator of it.

Chisholm stopped at the foot of Lomax's bed.

"You can relax, Captain Lomax," he said in a loud whisper. "All of you can," he added to the ward at large. "Nothing's happened to upset the applecart."

"What the hell did you want with Keitler?" hissed Lomax.

"I didn't want Keitler, Captain. It was him who sent for me. He's been hitting the brandy or sniffing ether, or something. He thinks he's Santa Claus. Look, he gave me a going-away present – a fifty tin of fags."

The strangled expostulation that erupted from Lomax's throat conveyed both outrage and disbelief.

"I'm going to cancel tonight's party," he declared flatly in the next breath.

"You're not bloody well stopping me!" Chisholm replied with vehemence. "You can suit yourself about your own people but you're not telling me what to do."

He did not wait for further argument. He stomped angrily away, heedless of the crash made by the side-door as it swung shut after him.

Chisholm stopped in the corridor outside his and Rick's room and leaned against the wall. He was still fizzing with anger. There was no way he was going to accept postponement of the escape. It was tonight or never! Nobody—particularly Lomax—was going to take this last chance of freedom from him! It was not a matter of reasoning and calculating risk any more. It had to be *now* and damn the consequences. His promise to Rick that they would get out or die in the attempt had contained an element of bravado. Not any more. It was a sign of how truly desperate he had become when he acknowledged to himself that if the choice was now between death in the next few hours or being locked up for another month, the first option was the more preferable.

He held out his hands in front of him and watched their trembling. They did not shake from fear. Anger had reduced him to this. Anger at Lomax and rage against anything likely to present an obstacle at this eleventh hour between himself and the freedom that seemed only minutes away.

Chisholm willed the trembling of his hands to stop. He had to be cool and detached—strong for himself and strong for Rick, who was going to need his support. God, he would have to watch his temper. He had wanted to hit Lomax back there: lash out at him in sheer frustration. To cancel the escape now would have been sour grapes on Lomax's part. He had missed out, so he was making sure nobody else was going through the wire. The trouble was that Lomax was obviously as desperate to escape as he was. Chisholm could almost appreciate the Canadian's bloody-mindedness in the circumstances. If their positions had been reversed, Chisholm knew he would have been homicidal. It was almost possible to forgive the Canadian.

The thought helped to calm Chisholm. He stared at his outstretched hands with the triumph of one who has proved the mastery of mind over matter. The hands were now rock steady. He was in control.

He pushed open the door of his room. It was a surprise to find it in darkness. Rick had not switched on the blue glow of the night light when the main lighting in the block had been doused by a central switch as usual at nine-thirty.

Chisholm groped for and found the night-light switch. The tiny blue bulb set in one wall came to life. The sapphire blush thrown out had no greater illuminative power than a candle. The ghostly luminence left corners of shadow in pools unreached by its frosty pallor, but it took Chisholm only an instant to discern that the room was empty. Rick Thomson was not there.

The discovery was so unexpected that Chisholm stood staring at the American's empty bed for fully a minute. He had not paid that much attention as he had passed through the toilets area moments before but he was fairly sure that no one had been occupying any of the doorless cubicles. He would have noticed.

On an impulse, Chisholm ran a hand under the top blanket of his bed. The makeshift poncho was underneath, as he had left it. Rick's, too, was undisturbed. Chisholm lifted the pillow on Rick's bed. The long-bladed surgical scissors were not there. He wondered where Rick might have hidden them, and searched around. They were nowhere to be found.

The area under the four beds in the room was deep shadow, screened from the glow of blue light. On his hands and knees, feeling below the beds, Chisholm encountered nothing but cold lino. He scrambled to his feet from below Rick's bed, cold fear tickling at his spine, as he pulled after him two items that he had not expected to find there – Rick's crutches.

He was baffled. Where could Rick have gone without them? Had he been probing at the ceiling again and fallen? Had he crawled somewhere badly injured, hoping to find help, and passed out?

Chisholm peered at the bed and the floor beside it, looking for some clue to the mystery; eyes straining in the feeble demi-light from the blue eye on the wall. He bent to the floor to investigate a shadowy speck. It was like touching paint that had almost dried. He examined his fingers. It was not paint. It was blood.

He found more stains, not quite dry. Then a dry and clearly identifiable smudge, as if a foot or other object had scuffed across and spread the telltale sign.

Heart beating wildly, Chisholm tracked to the corridor and along it: following the trail of blood. It did not indicate excessive bleeding: more the regular fugitive drip from a nosebleed that a hand across the nostrils is not wholly holding in check.

In the corridor, as throughout the interior of the block, the only light came from the little blue-glow bulbs set at regular intervals along the walls. Chisholm, crouched low to touch and feel the shadowy trail he followed, found that the signs petered out in the shower bay. He cast around with his eyes, probing every shadowed place. He found Rick in the end shower stall. The young American was slumped against one wall in deep shadow.

Chisholm pulled him out, not at first seeing the ringed haft buried in his chest. It was the single blade of the scissors not employed in the stabbing, whose movement against his own body he could feel, that alerted Chisholm to the other blade dagger-like in Rick's side. He cried out at their discovery. He stared at the American with an anguish that was like a rock on his soul as he realised that Rick Thomson had made the ultimate escape from the pains and sorrows of this world. He was dead.

"Suicide," said Constantine.

"Or murder," said Lomax, staring fiercely at Chisholm. "You saw the state he was in when I said I was going to call everything off. What happened, Sailorman? Did you have one of your crazy spells and take it out on this poor bastard? Look at you, for Christ's sake! You're covered in his blood!"

Chisholm, crouching beside Rick's body, was bathed in the beam of the pencil flashlight held in Lomax's hand. He was still too stunned by the knowledge that Rick was dead to treat Lomax's accusation as anything other than absurd. He made a helpless gesture with his hands, as if to acknowledge the futility in denying that the blood on them and smearing his jacket was Rick's.

"I found him in the shower . . . I lifted him out . . ."

"It could be the truth, sir. I think the Yank took his own life . . . For the sake of all of us." It was Constantine who had spoken.

"What are you talking about?" rasped Lomax.

"When I spoke to him earlier, he wanted to back out from the escape. He was mighty upset . . . He thought he was just going to be a hindrance – him being on one leg, that is. And it bothered him that you were having to stand down to make a place for him. He felt guilty about it."

Chisholm stared questioningly at Constantine.

"But that's crazy. Rick was desperate to go. He would never have killed himself!"

"He tried before," replied Constantine. "When they first brought him here. He was always wishing himself dead. Ask anybody. We all heard him at it. Now the poor devil's gone and done it."

Lomax turned the flashlight away from Chisholm and shone it on the dead American's face. The eyes were still wide open and staring. Chisholm could not bear to look. Never in his life had he felt burdened down with such a sense of loss as he now felt. He got to his feet and turned away with a sorrowing shudder.

"So what the hell do we do?" murmured Lomax.

It was Constantine, the calmest of the three, who said, "We leave the Yank where he is and we go through with the plan. We owe it to him now. And it means that you can go with us, sir."

Lomax made a surprising show of reluctance.

"There's going to be hell to pay here tomorrow. Maybe it's my job to stay with the others and face the music. It's my duty as SCO."

"We went over that before, sir," said Constantine. "When we first picked the escape team. There was no question of you not going. You were quite happy to let Lieutenant Macdonald take over from you as SCO."

Lomax allowed himself to be convinced not only that the escape should go ahead but that he should be one of the six who made the break. Chisholm retreated into a brooding silence, numbed by the shock of events and strangely disinterested in his own fate or the success of the escape. He wanted his freedom, but freedom that demanded a down-payment as obscenely exorbitant as Rick Thomson's life had come nowhere in his reckoning. It no longer seemed to matter to him what happened. Life or death, imprisonment or freedom: none of them seemed important now that Rick would not be there to share with him the success or failure of the enterprise they had planned together.

Chisholm could not believe that Rick had taken his own life, noble as Constantine made the deed sound. Rick had become too devoted in these last few days to living and the prospect of winning freedom. But if he had not taken his own life, who had? Lomax? To regain the sixth place on the escape team? No, surely not. There was something twisted and ruthlessly brutish in Lomax's make-up but it was fanciful to think that even he would stoop to murder for such an end.

The only solution that made any sense to Chisholm was the belief that Rick, in the pursuit of that crazy experiment he had talked about, had somehow impaled himself on the scissors and had crawled or staggered as far as the shower-room before collapsing and dying. It would never have happened, of course, if Chisholm had been present to prevent it – and, in his mind, he savagely cursed Keitler and his idiotic whim of giving him a tin of cigarettes for the whole needless tragedy.

Chisholm was so locked in the withdrawn bitterness that held him in the hour after his discovery of Rick, that he was later to find it difficult to recall all that happened. He did what he had to do with a numb indifference, saying little or nothing to the Canadians: allowing Lomax to organise and command. The why and how of Rick's death were not discussed further. He was dead and that was that. Theories and explanations would have to wait for another day, another place. All that mattered now was the successful execution of the escape plan which the French patriots outside were at last putting into action and which, for so long, the Canadians had carefully prepared.

Security in The Pavilion was light by German standards: only the night-nurse and one orderly after 10 p.m. At 10.30, the French nurse reported to Sergeant Martineau in the OR ward that the first part of the plan had succeeded. The German orderly was already deep in a drugged sleep. Later, the Germans would reconstruct how the orderly had left the freshly brewed pot of coffee unattended near Martineau's bed while the orderly had investigated a diversionary "emergency" in the officers' ward. They would also find a stolen supply of the drug – with which Martineau had doctored the coffee – under the Sergeant's mattress.

Having given Martineau the all-clear, the nurse then retired to her office to drink her own coffee from the doctored pot: ensuring that she took no further part in the night's proceedings and, hopefully, as a result, diverting German suspicion of complicity away from herself.

61

There was time for the Canadian escapers to make their farewells with the men who were being left behind. These were limited to quick exchanges of good luck wishes except in the case of the lieutenant whose name was Macdonald. Lomax spent valuable minutes acquainting the young man with the responsibility that would evolve to him in his new role of Senior Canadian Officer. Lomax regretted relinquishing the burden inasmuch that the Germans might take some kind of reprisals for the escape on those who were left behind, but he expressed the hope that Macdonald would understand that he, Lomax, had a first duty to escape and avenge Dieppe by fighting Germans.

Chisholm realised how crude had been his own plans for "breaking out" of The Pavilion when he saw how thoroughly the Canadians had prepared their departure. Although they could have left unhindered by the front door, this option had been ruled out because the door was in full view of the guard-hut some hundred metres opposite. So, a rear exit had been preferred.

This was achieved via one of the lock-fast rooms close to the one occupied by Chisholm and Rick Thomson. The Canadians had secretly manufactured their own key for the unused room and had already done an impressive piece of work on its one and only window. Instead of having to force it, Sergeant Martineau removed two screws with an ingeniously homemade screwdriver and the entire frame, glass and all, was lifted out. The six escapers climbed out. Fifty metres away was the compound wire, unlit, with a grove of tall-standing sycamores beyond.

They made the short dash to the wire one at a time. Constantine was first to go. He located the part of the high fence which, as Nurse Baril had promised, had been expertly cut from the outside. The two noncoms, Martineau and Malloy, followed Constantine. Chisholm was next. Then Raoul Gilbert, a lieutenant in the Regiment de la Chaudiere. Lomax was last to leave. They gathered under the sycamores, where there was some protection from the battering rain and high gusty wind.

With Lomax leading, the six crept to the edge of the trees, following a route that was parallel to the fence through which they had just escaped. They emerged from the trees opposite a cluster of buildings. Two tallish brick chimneys rising like pencils identified the laundry and the boiler-house. A high-backed open truck stood in the yard behind the boiler-house. The whole area was in darkness and looked deserted. Not far from the truck was a shadowy mini-mountain of coke, heaped in the open.

Before crossing from the trees, Lomax went round each man in turn with whispered instructions. He repeated that there was to be no talking from that point on: none at all. Absolute silence was imperative until he indicated otherwise. They moved quickly across the open space.

Malloy, using a rear wheel as a foot-hold, swiftly scaled the high side of the truck. He straddled the top and remained there, assisting the others, as they pulled themselves up over the top and into the truck. There was a soft landing inside. The floor of the truck was carpeted by piles of sacks – from which their contents of coke had recently been emptied.

Once all the escapers were inside, they began silently to stack the sacks towards the cab end of the truck: making spaces to accommodate themselves in a sitting position and keeping sufficient of the dirty and rain-sodden sacks to pull over their heads for concealment. Then they waited.

Their waiting seemed eternal but it was less than thirty minutes before they heard a door opening. They could not see the shaft of light from the doorway that made the rain look like silver rods. They heard only voices, German and French. Goodnights were spoken. Three men climbed into the cab of the truck: the French driver, his mate, and one German guard. It was all as Nurse Baril had said it would be.

The truck started up. It reversed in a half circle. Then it moved forward, lumbering slowly past the boiler-house complex, and following a turn-and-turn-again route along the interlocking grid of roadways at the rear of the sanitorium.

As they passed along the side of the main sanitorium, the wind carried the strains of symphonic music briefly and faintly to them. A radio somewhere, playing Wagner.

There was a stop and a protracted exchange of conversation in German. The topics were social, slightly ribald, unmarked by military punctiliousness or a zeal of security. They were at the main gate.

There was a second stop, very short – an outer checkpoint – then the big truck was negotiating the steep twisting road that Chisholm remembered from the day of his arrival at St Cyr des Bains. He sat, hating the suffocating cover of wet sacks and yet frightened to shed their protection. Alternately, he shivered with cold and sweated with fear. There was no elation in him at the knowledge that, at last, he was escaping. He could not rid his mind of Rick Thomson's staring eyes and the sprawl of the body with the long shears blade thrust between the ribs.

Five

A Smell of Treason

The truck halted. The six escapers heard the cab doors being opened and then slammed shut. There was the sound of voices and unhurried footsteps. The sounds receded, finally punctuated by the closing of a distant door. The silence was broken only by the wild soughing of the wind and the batter of rain against the sides of the truck.

Still, no man spoke. The escapers remained hunched and silent amid the soggy sanctuary of the sacks. They did not hear the sea-booted approach of the solitary figure who emerged from shadow and padded stealthily towards the stationary truck. Their first indication of his presence was the sharp double rap on the tail of the truck and his whispered call.

The six moved quickly: discarding the wet sacking and clambering from the shelter of the truck's high sides. Chisholm dropped on to wet cobbles and slipped on one knee before finding his balance. Rain slanted into his face as he took in his surroundings. He could make out the dim outline of a row of buildings on one side. The barest chink of light showed from the nearest. As his eyes grew accustomed to the dark, Chisholm identified the blacked-out building as an inn or bistro. Then he could make out shop fronts adjacent to the inn.

The darkness on the side of the street opposite the inn was total. But, from this void came the angry slap of water against concrete and, beyond that, the constant swish and tumble of waves against a far breakwater.

The man in the seaboots paused briefly beside Chisholm.

"Le Vieux Bassin," he said by way of explanation, seeing Chisholm peering at the dark of the harbour. "Come! We must hurry. A foot patrol passes along here every half hour."

The truck was parked on the broad cobbled thoroughfare

that was St Cyr des Bains' main street and market area: flanked on one side by the Old Harbour and on the other by the picturesque sprawl of shops, houses and pensions that, in bygone summers, had made the village a magnet for tourists spilling south from Le Havre and Honfleur. Chisholm and his companions got little impression of the village's charm on that bleak midwinter night. They were hustled by their guide along the deserted quayside to where a straight-stemmed sailing yawl strained against her moorings.

Chisholm's first impression of the yawl, with its tall pencil of mast writing gyrating patterns against the lowering black overhead, was of immense solidity. There was a stoutness of timber and plumpness of line to suggest that the vessel had been designed to weather angry seas rather than win beauty contests. She was Chisholm's senior by many years: a survivor from an age when sail had not yet surrendered the crown to steam. She heaved restlessly at her moorings, but with an easy lumbering grace that was almost contemptuous of the wind-whipped harbour waters.

There was no time to admire the sea veteran's weathered solidity or savour the tarry fragrance that emanated from her oaken timbers. The six escapers were helped by their guide to make the short descent on to a slippery deck that rose and fell as they dropped to it via a first precarious foothold on black-painted gunwale. A second stranger had opened a corner of the main hatch and it was to this that the escapers were shepherded. One by one they clambered down a short rope ladder into the inky blackness of the hold. Here, the atmosphere was ripe with the salty stench of fish. The timbered floor was like a skating rink.

Chisholm was the last man to climb into the black void. He had to steel himself against the flood of panic that filled his being: the familiar dread of enclosed space. His panic intensified as a voice from above adjured the occupants of the hold to endure their discomfort in silence. It would only be for a few hours.

Heedless of what was happening around him, Chisholm braced himself against the heaving of the yawl and willed his mind to positive thought. Freedom was now only short hours away: in minutes that could be counted off. He could count the seconds off . . . And it would be daylight before he had got to twenty thousand. There was light at the end of the tunnel this time. Not like on the submarine or that dungeon where they had chained him. There, night and day had been meaningless and the future had held no hope of relief. Now, it was different. The prize of freedom was almost within grasp. A little patience now and it would be his. He forced the fear in him to subside and slowly it gave way before his will.

With mastery of himself came the awareness that he was not alone. He realised almost with surprise that, around him, others were suffering forms of discomfort nearly as acute as his own. Two of the Canadians had already succumbed to the constant motion of the yawl and the stale fishy odours of the hold and were retching miserably in the darkness. A third cursed angrily as one of the unfortunates staggered into him and showered him with vomit.

Lomax struck a match and, by its light, allotted places to each man and ordered them to sit. The cursing man – it was Constantine – retired to one corner of the hold, still cursing. Chisholm sank to his haunches in another. The two sick men were left the freedom of the centre of the empty hold to indulge their nausea. After lighting three matches and holding them until they flickered out, Lomax, who had parked himself down with his back against the forward bulkhead, repeated the need for silence. He rebuked the complaining Constantine sharply and warned the retching men to choke to death quietly or he would render them permanently quiet with his own two hands. He exhorted all to try to get some sleep.

The encouragement to sleep seemed, in the circumstances, to be ludicrous to Chisholm but – wet and uncomfortable as he was – the total darkness, the rocking motion of the yawl, and the acute concentration of his consciousness inward and away from external things, all combined to induce a drowsiness. He found himself dosing fitfully.

He had no idea of how much of the night had passed when he became alertly awake. The darkness was as inpenetrable as before but a variety of new sounds assailed the ear. The hollow echo of feet passing to and fro on the deck overhead. The thud of ropes and the creak of a windlass. The distant coming to life of a diesel engine and the guttural shouts of men calling to one another as orders were relayed and acknowledged.

Now, the movement of the yawl was different. The storm sounds of the night had gone. There was a positive and gentle rhythm in the yawl's easy rocking. Chisholm could sense the vessel's new freedom as she glided from the quayside, released from her moorings. Now, she was turning. Now, she was moving forward and the throb of diesel engine seemed to deepen as the propeller began to bite water.

Although he could see nothing, instinct and a hazy notion of the geography of St Cyr des Bains gave Chisholm a mind's eye picture of the scene above decks. He could feel the sudden surge of water against the starboard side of the yawl as she emerged from the cut of the old harbour into the riverway. There was a tug of current and then the drift round of the bow as the yawl began to ride with the stream towards the sea. The engine beat steadied and, now, the forward surge was pronounced. There was no cross motion now. The lift was fore and aft as the bow lifted and dipped into the chop of the estuary.

Suddenly, the engine note died and the vessel was drifting lazily. Another sound manifested itself, coming closer and closer: the heavy aeroplane roaring of a high-powered motor. The sound closed and then faltered to an idling tenor.

Chisholm's blood ran cold at the sound of a megaphoned voice. A Germanic voice. There was a bump as the second vessel rubbed briefly against the solid flank of the yawl. Heavy boots sounded on the deck above. More voices. German and French. The exchanges went on for fully five minutes. More footfalls. Then the aeroplane roar of the other boat screamed to a new pitch.

The noise seemed to fill the darkened hold where Chisholm and his five companions crouched with nerves stretched. The noise drifted slowly away and receded to a distant whine. In the meantime, the yawl's diesel resumed its deeper note as the gear of the propeller shaft engaged and the yawl pitched more deeply into a heightening swell. Chisholm felt a warm surge of relief. Unless his scenario was wrong, the yawl had got clearance from the estuary patrol craft and was now heading for the open sea.

They emerged stiff and cold into a grey December morning. A fresh breeze from west by north was bowling squalls of sleet and rain from the wide spaces of the Atlantic. The escapers huddled in the lee of the low after deck-house, gratefully clutching the mugs of hot, bitter coffee their French hosts had prepared for them.

The diesel engine was now silent and the yawl, *Therese*, was tacking north-east under sail and making about seven knots. Chisholm felt a thrill of sheer pleasure as he looked up at the groaning spread of stretched canvas. Had it crossed his mind that the yawl would win no beauty contests? She was majestic now, with the tall mast aquiver with the weight of the main lug and the triangular staysail ballooning elegantly forward. At the stern, the wind filled the gaff-mounted spanker as it leaned out to starboard.

The man he took to be the skipper of the yawl sought Chisholm out.

"You are the sea captain, Monsieur?"

Chisholm acknowledged the fact.

"I do not envy you your passage to England, Capitaine. You will need all the Saints to watch over you." The skipper gave an expressive shrug. "The craft we have for you is small and has suffered neglect – but the Germans have taken everything, you understand?"

"I understand," Chisholm said gravely. "But desperate men can't choose, eh? You are Nicole's father?"

"You do not need to know who I am, Capitaine. You are not yet beyond the reach of the Germans – and what you do not know can cause us no harm. You understand? If by any chance you are recaptured, your story must be that you stole the boat from a shed on the riverside near the old fish-houses. Not from the harbour. You slipped down the river by night. You have never seen or heard of the *Therese*. Understand?"

"Yes, I've got that. I understand."

"The others must be told, too."

"They will be. We stole the boat from a shed. Near the old fish-houses. On the riverside. Exact enough to be convincing – and vague enough, too."

The skipper smiled.

"It is near enough the truth. That is where the boat was found some days ago. You do not need to know who did the stealing. Come, you had better see it. In an hour, we must start fishing and, by then, you must be on your way to England."

He led Chisholm forward. The boat was lashed to the deck under a tarpaulin.

Chisholm's heart sank when the tarpaulin was removed. The blue-painted ten-foot dinghy had indeed been neglected. The paint was flaking in places and it dismayed Chisholm to think how dried up the timbers might be. His concern did not escape the *Therese*'s skipper. He produced half a dozen two-litre cans.

"You and your crew will need hse," he said apologetically.

Chisholm nodded. Privately, he wondered how the Canadians would relish baling water out of their tiny craft all the way to England. In fact, the five Canadians stood pale and dumb-founded when introduced to the dinghy on which their salvation depended. Even Lomax was shaken.

"Will it float?" he asked uncertainly.

He was soon to get his answer. The *Therese* came about, lowered her sails, and manoeuvred slowly on the auxiliary to make a lee for the boat-lowering operation. Everything on the *Therese* was done by what Chisholm called "the armstrong system", that is, muscle rather than mechanical power. With fore and aft painters secured, the dinghy was hoisted over the side on a short-armed derrick, operated manually. Chisholm went with it. He stepped and rigged the mast, dropped the rudder into place, lashed the tiller in the midships position, and then accepted the two oars and sail that were handed down to him from the deck of the *Therese*. Already, more than a foot of water was sloshing about over the bilge-boards of the dinghy.

"What are you waiting for?" he roared up at the Canadians. "Are you coming with me to England or are you waiting for a cross-Channel ferry? The service isn't as good as it used to be."

Constantine was first over the side. The others continued to stare goggle-eyed at Chisholm and the boat, which seemed to be filling with water.

"Come on, damn you!" Chisholm bellowed. "And bring those tin cans. I need hands to bale before this bloody thing sinks."

After four hours constant baling, the battle to keep the water in the dinghy at a tolerable level appeared to have been won. But Chisholm's unseamanlike crew were on the verge of exhaustion. At times, it had seemed that all their frantic efforts were to have been in vain. Water had been coming in through the seams faster than the baling Canadians had been able to remove it. With the water rising almost to the level of the thwarts and the weight of the occupants reducing the freeboard nearly to zero, the boat had been in imminent danger of swamping. It had wallowed perilously, making no way as the sail flapped ineffectively. Chisholm had lowered the sail and, allowing the small craft to drift, had seized one of the baling tins and shown by example the effort and method that was required to keep the sea at bay. Sergeant Martineau – perhaps anxious to show the officers that, where men's work was involved, he would not be found wanting – proved Chisholm's most apt pupil. He bent his back with a will and achieved a rhythm and an efficiency that Chisholm himself would not have cared to have challenged. The others followed suit and before too long, Chisholm was able to relinquish his baler and think of hoisting the sail again. It was the most basic of sails – a standing lug: which meant a minimum of crew work. The yard and sail did not have to be moved every time Chisholm changed tack: remaining to windward of the mast on one tack and to leeward on the other. Thankfully, too, there was no swinging boom on the sail foot to clip his unwary crew members between the shoulder blades and knock them over the side. The Canadians tended to move about the boat without any apparent thought for its equilibrium.

Chisholm educated them as they went along. He was a fair, if harsh-tongued, tutor. They learned quickly that instant obedience earned a terse "Well done" or similar encouragement, and so great seemed the accolade that they took care not to repeat mistakes made by others.

Before they had left the *Therese*, her skipper had shown Chisholm a chart and pinpointed the yawl's position for him. He had also given him his sole navigation aid – a cheap wrist compass not unlike the kind that Chisholm had seen on sale at Woolworth's toy counter before the war. He would have grudged paying sixpence for it.

"The wind will be my best compass," Chisholm had told the Frenchman. "*If* you can give me a reasonably accurate weather forecast for the next thirty-six hours."

The statement had brought a smile to the weather-beaten face of the skipper. If Chisholm was prepared to rely on the word of a German, he would gladly pass on the forecast issued at only six that morning by the Kriegsmarine HQ at Brest. It had been relayed to the skipper by the German naval officer in charge of the patrol boat that had stopped the *Therese* in the estuary.

The Kriegsmarine meteorologists had warned that the squally weather in the Channel would continue for at least another twenty-four hours, with westerly winds reaching fresh to gale force. They would veer slowly and, as they did so, the frequent showers could be expected to be of sleet and snow rather than rain.

The information, although not making things easy, simplified the navigational problem facing Chisholm. He would have to make some sea to westward and then use the direction from which the wind was coming as a guide to his true course. By tacking to make a mean course that kept the weather on the port bow, he would make the northerly progress that sooner or later would bring him up somewhere in the vicinity of the Isle of Wight. Much would depend on his ability to read the weather, but he trusted his instinct to do so more than he trusted the toy compass. The latter might be all right for a boy scout on dry land but, in a tossing dinghy. would be as useful as a roulette wheel.

By four in the afternoon, the light began to go. By then, the dinghy's seams had tightened sufficiently to allow the baling to be done by two of the Canadians while the other three rested. Chisholm remained at the tiller, tending the sheet with one hand and the steering with the other. He made short tacks at first, accustoming himself to the feel of the dinghy and becoming more adept at bringing her about. Then he settled to a routine of thirty minutes to port and thirty to starboard. He sat statuesque on the stern sheet, head hunched into his shoulders and jaw thrust forward so that his face was set and immobile against the driving spray and slanting rain. Only when he brought the dinghy about did he move position, shifting over to sit always on the weather side of the tiller-shaft.

None of the Canadians volunteered to take over the handling of the tiny boat, nor did he invite them to do so. As darkness fell, the task became one of feel and instinct; like reading braille with the toes. But it was the wind and sea that Chisholm had to read through his seat-of-the-pants contact with the timber of his maritime steed and his finger-tip reining of rudder and sail. Thick flurries of snow iced his hair and eyebrows and caked his front. Icy trickles of water invaded his clothing at neck and sleeves and insinuated themselves to the dry parts of his body.

In spite of his companions – the Canadians huddled as low as they could in the boat to escape the bitter lash of wind and spray – Chisholm was like a man alone. He was scarcely aware of their presence, so rapt was his concentration and the demands the battle made on his flesh and powers of endurance. In order to ignore the unrelenting cold and appalling bodily discomfort, he became again the man in chains: reaching to the uttermost reserves of his will and forcing his mind to overcome stark physical reality so that his consciousness operated at a level unreached by pain.

For hour after hour after hour throughout the long night, the ordeal went on. From time to time, one or other of the five Canadians – awed by the obstinate quality of the single-mindedness with which he stuck to his task – expressed concern that he gave himself no respite. He acknowledged their solicitude with a minimum of words, brushing their fears for him aside with an aloof kind of impatience. His authority was not disputed and there was relief, albeit unspoken, when he made it plain that getting to England was more important than his physical well-being.

Dawn found them alone on a friendless sea. There were now breaks in the low, scurrying clouds and the frosty sharpness of the wind confirmed for Chisholm the suspicion that it had veered almost to due north. There was no concealment of the teeth-chattering misery that afflicted his landsmen companions. Nor was he able to hide his own. Much as he tried to pretend otherwise, spasms of shivering made his whole body tremble. His face felt raw, as if it had been sand-papered, and it needed only an involuntary twitch of a cheek muscle to make it feel that bloody cracks were opening in the skin.

By noon, in spite of his exhortations to bale and keep warm, the Canadians had all but abandoned their attempts to eject the water still permeating through the dinghy's seams. They wanted only to huddle, their wet clothes pulled about them with collars about the ears, seeking escape from the never-ceasing wind. And, as they ignored Chisholm, so his own will to cajole and upbraid them diminished. Exhaustion and his own suffering from the predatory cold sapped him to a point almost beyond caring. The longing to lie down and cover his head became so intense that his mind wandered from his now almost automaton-like handling of the dinghy, only for it to be jerked back as the tiny craft was caught by the lee and the sail flapped wildly.

It now required an effort to see. He found himself blinking his eyes in order to keep them wide enough open to peer painfully aloft or take in the endless rise and fall of weaving horizon. The converted trawler seemed to rise from the sea without him ever being aware that it was in the vicinity. One moment, there was nothing to be seen and, in the next, there was the rusted grey hull less than a cable's length away. Chisholm gazed at it in astonishment and then felt on overwhelming desire to burst into tears. A tattered white ensign cracked like a whip at her gaff.

A duffel-coated figure on the bridge had a megaphone in hand. Chisholm heard himself hailed in the broad twang of the Buchan coast. No voice had sounded sweeter to his ears. Just as the trawler *Daydream* from Peterhead had been converted to trawl for mines with paravanes and sweeps, so – it seemed – had her skipper been converted to naval officer with two and a half rings on his sleeve. But grey paint on his ship and gold braid on his sleeve had not changed his accent.

An excess of words was not used in establishing identities and deciding on a course of action. Somehow, Chisholm got the sail down – more hindered than helped by his shivering crew – and made fast a line from the trawler with hands that were purple and numb. The dinghy was hauled alongside the trawler as, with a touch of engine and a hardover helm, the larger vessel made a lee for the smaller.

Strong hands pulled the Canadians aboard and a blue-sweatered sailor joined Chisholm in the dinghy. He saw Chisholm safely up the ladder, then handed the dinghy's sails, mast and oars on to the deck of the trawler. Two swift blows of an axe brought water gushing through the boat's bottom. The small craft was sinking rapidly as the seaman deftly released the forward painter before nimbly skipping across the thwarts to let go the stern painter. He swung on to the ladder as the swamping craft drifted away from the trawler's side.

Chisholm gazed expressionlessly at the drifting dinghy from the trawler's deck. As it escaped from the navy ship's lee, seas broke over the sinking craft and soon hid it from sight. It seemed an unjust reward for a job well done.

At first, freedom was better even than Chisholm had hoped it would be. The kindness of the minesweeper skipper and his crew was overwhelming: towels and blankets and thick woolly sweaters and rum to beat the cold. Especially rum. Then bacon and eggs – as much as they could eat.

At the hospital in Portsmouth, it was much the same. Doctors, nurses, other patients regarded the six escapers with an awe that bordered on hero-worship. Not enough could be done for them. Even the lieutenant from the office of the Naval Intelligence Officer – who had come to interrogate them about their escape and fulfil the bureaucratic necessities of identification – had been considerate and unstinting in his admiration of the feat they had accomplished. As far as he knew, no others had made a direct cross-Channel escape since just after Dunkirk. Since the Germans had made the Channel and Atlantic coasts of France an armed camp, the long trek south and over the Pyrenees was the escape route likelier to be favoured with success. He congratulated them on pulling off something that, in official circles, was considered impossible.

It took less than a week for the taste of freedom to turn sour in Chisholm's mouth. He was totally unprepared for the change of climate when it came.

Christmas Day in the hospital had been something to remember. How the staff had conjured up the dinner menu in wartime Britain, Chisholm did not know: a five-course spread with turkey and all the trimmings as the centrepiece. The wards had been awash with an astonishing variety of wines, beers and spirits. The parties and the carol singsongs had gone on all day, with normal hospital discipline relaxed to the point of ceasing to exist. Even Lomax had got a little drunk and been infected by the general goodwill. He had gone out of his way to shake Chisholm's hand and wish him a merry Christmas. Then he had smiled ruefully.

"I owe you one," he had said. "We'd never have made it to England without you. It don't change the way I feel about you. I still don't like you. But I wouldn't be standing here today if it weren't for you – and a debt is a debt. Any time I can do you a favour and you want to call in the shot, just you get in touch."

Chisholm, his own goodwill buoyed up with brandy, found Lomax's ambivalence faintly amusing. He did not take offence at being pronounced disliked and he foresaw no occasion arising when he would be seeking favours from Lomax.

"After tomorrow, we'll probably never meet again," he had said. "Not this side of hell."

Lomax had grinned lop-sidedly and, for the first time since Chisholm had known him, made a joke: "If I get there first, I'll keep a place warm for you."

Some of the glow of Christmas stayed with Chisholm into Boxing Day morning. He shaved and dressed in a mood of glorious wellbeing. The grey civilian suit that had been found for him was an excellent fit. He luxuriated in the feel of a spotless white shirt and a collar that had not been starched too much. He lingered over the task of running a grey-and-blue striped tie into the collar and knotting it round his neck so that it sat perfectly.

They were all leaving: the five Canadians and Chisholm. All were fit enough for the journey to London, where they were to face some routine interviews about their experience. All, too, had been equipped with documents from the Portsmouth hospital which had to be handed over to the Medical Officer at the Transit Centre where they would be housed.

A crowd of nurses gave them a rousing send off as they boarded the grey naval bus that was to take them to the station. A British army sergeant and a private had arrived from London to act as the small party's guides and escort. A compartment for all eight men had been reserved on the London train. Chisholm spent most of the journey to Victoria looking out the window while the Canadians talked about pubs and clubs in London and speculated on the possibility of visiting them soon. The chatter of their talk seemed a distant buzz to Chisholm. It held no interest for him. The green Hampshire countryside, touched white where the sun had not reached the morning frost, was a sight that sent his soul soaring in a joyously private way. This was the reality of freedom: to see this soft green land flashing before his eyes in a continuous and changing vista. He kept wiping away condensation from the window so that he would not miss a glimpse of a friendly spire or red-walled farmhouse, nor spy the plough-horse snorting breath-clouds in the winter air. This was what he had waited so long to see. This, truly, was coming home.

Two roomy saloon cars, painted a drab stone colour, were waiting for them at Victoria Station. In a rear corner seat of one, Chisholm's interest was again on the passing scene beyond the window and not on the desultory conversation within the car. His eyes greedily took in the strangely reassuring sight of Londoners hurrying about their everyday business. Every second passer-by was in uniform: a lot of casually strolling Americans, some Polish officers with their quaint square-cornered caps, French sailors with red pom-poms on their hats, airmen in blue, a Sikh naval officer in a neat sky-coloured turban. There were workers in cloth caps, gas mask satchels slung from their shoulders. Chisholm guessed that the satchels contained Thermos flasks and sandwiches and copies of the *Daily Mirror*. There were gents in bowler hats and carrying rolled umbrellas, typists and office secretaries in bum-freezer coats and coloured kerchiefs on their heads.

The scars of bombing were everywhere. At Hyde Park corner, Chisholm's driver pulled in to let two fire engines go screaming past with bells ringing. They raced along Knightsbridge, the noise of the clanging bells receding in the distance. Sand-bag barriers and windows covered in sticky tape gave a wartime cosmetic to the opulent face of Park Lane. The car crawled behind a bus at Marble Arch and into Oxford Street. It accelerated free into Baker Street and travelled its length before turning towards Marylebone Station.

Chisholm climbed stiffly out of the car and looked up at the building that was their destination, the Great Central Hotel. Now conscripted for military service, the hotel had shed its peacetime grandeur to become the London Transit Camp. Chisholm and the five Canadians were herded to a reception room on the second floor, furnished in the manner of a temporary employment exchange set up in the annexe of a village hall.

Across a trestle table, the six men supplied to a small team of uniformed clerks the personal details of name, service number, date of birth and other particulars. Then they waited to be taken individually for interview in rooms along the corridor.

Chisholm was still waiting two hours later, his impatience only kept at bay by a mug of tea which one of the soldier-clerks had kindly brought him. Four hours were to pass before his name was called and he was invited to step along the corridor.

He was shown into a small, austere room containing only six items of furniture. There was a plain, brown-varnished table in the middle of the room. It had two equally nondescript chairs at one side and a third at the other. A card-table sat a little to the side of the larger table. A fourth chair was propped against it. Chisholm had scarcely time to be unimpressed by the spartan surroundings when a civilian entered the room followed by an army captain and a sergeant.

The Sergeant went immediately to the card table, laid some papers on it, pulled out the chair and seated himself. The civilian and the Captain sat down at one side of the larger table and indicated to Chisholm that he should take the chair facing them.

"Sorry to keep you waiting," said the civilian, "but we're rather fussy in this department. A lot of formalities – but we've found it doesn't pay to rush them."

He opened a folder in front of him and peered at the documents it contained through his heavy-lensed spectacles. When he looked up to stare at Chisholm, the thick glass seemed to magnify his eyes to about twice their normal size.

"You're a bit of a mystery man, Captain Chisholm," he said. "We've heard a great deal about you, a lot of it contradictory. We don't know quite what to make of it. However . . ." he rubbed his hands together in anticipatory fashion and favoured Chisholm with an oily smile ". . . I'm sure that you will keep nothing back from us . . . You will be very frank."

Chisholm's frown was one of innocent puzzlement.

"I'll tell you whatever you want to know. So, there's no need to beat about the bush. I quite understand that you've got to satisfy yourselves that I am who I say I am, so fair enough. Fire away."

"Very well, Captain." The eyes behind the thick glasses narrowed to almond shapes. "I shall not beat about the bush. Tell me, are you a homosexual?"

"A what!" Chisholm shot out of his chair and stared angrily at his questioner.

"You heard me, Captain. Are you a homosexual?"

"No, I bloody well am not!"

"You deny it?"

"Of course I bloody well deny it! What kind of question is it to ask, anyway? What has it got to do with proving who I am?"

"I'm not interested in who you are, Captain Chisholm. I *know* who you are. I want to find out *what* you are." The eyes staring from behind the glasses were fish-like, as devoid of emotion as the questioner's carefully modulated voice.

A deep anger flared in Chisholm.

"I don't know who *you* are, Mister. And I don't know what you are. But you just keep asking me questions like that and I'll take you apart to find out."

The threat seemed to cause the other man mild pain.

"Please don't raise your voice, Captain Chisholm. And please don't threaten me with violence. This is not a routine examination to establish your identity. This is an official inquiry on behalf of His Majesty's Government – albeit a preliminary one – into activities that might be deemed to be

78

injurious to the State. Until I satisfy myself on that score, I am going to have to ask you questions, searching questions; questions that you may not like. It will save all of us a good deal of time and pain if you just sit down and answer them truthfully." He waited a moment and then added: "I *can* have you restrained while I interrogate you. Would you prefer it that way?"

Chisholm subsided into his seat. His anger had given way to bewilderment.

"I don't know what the hell you're going on about."

"Puzzles, Captain Chisholm. Riddles. Strange irregularities. That's what I'm on about. Unexplained happenings. A beastly odour is assailing my nostrils, Captain Chisholm. I want to identify it, to find its source. I have the whiff of treachery in my nose, Captain – a smell of treason."

Six

Suspect

The crunch came after six hours of questioning. That was when the bespectacled interrogator – his name, Chisholm discovered, was Benson – had finally lost patience with Chisholm. Fat lower lip trembling and spittle flying from below his overprominent front teeth, he had leaned across the table and shouted in Chisholm's face: "You're a liar! A fucking liar!"

It was too much for Chisholm. Head aching, nerves stretched at the injustice of it all and made to feel unclean by this man's vile questioning, he had seen red. Seizing Benson by the lapels and breathing hate into the unlovely face so close to his own, he yanked his interrogator bodily across the table and – without letting go – propelled him across the room in a swift turning movement and bundled him with a crash into the opposite wall. Benson's thick eyeglasses went flying and the breath exploded from his body as Chisholm – still holding him by the lapels – bounced him against the wall a second time and a third time for good measure. Then he let go. The interrogator slid to the floor, his back against the wall. His eyes were popping and he seemed to have great difficulty breathing.

The army Captain and the Sergeant, stunned by the speed in which it had all happened, moved belatedly to restrain Chisholm. When, however, they saw that Chisholm threatened no more violence, they did not put a hand on him.

The Captain retrieved the fallen spectacles – they were unbroken – and bent to tend Benson. He seemed only to be winded and was beginning to recover. The Captain straightened himself and shook his head sadly as he glanced at Chisholm.

"There'll be bloody hell to pay now," he said.

"He asked for it," snapped Chisholm. He was breathing

heavily, like a quarter-miler who had just put in a sprint finish. "I'm not a bloody criminal. Who the hell does he think he is . . . the head of the Gestapo?"

"He was only doing his job."

"Was he, by God! I'm surprised he still has so many teeth. I thought somebody would have kicked them down his throat long before now!"

The Captain turned to the Sergeant.

"You'd better get hold of Cartwright or Jenkins. Tooled up, just in case." He threw an apprehensive glance in Chisholm's direction. "I don't think our friend will give us any further trouble."

Benson was stirring. He moaned softly. The Captain tossed an afterthought to the departing Sergeant: "Oh, and Sergeant Wilkins, you'd better see if there's a doctor in the house. Mr Benson doesn't look too well."

When the Sergeant returned, he had a stern-looking military policeman with him. The redcap favoured Chisholm with a warning glower that invited him to mix things with him if he dared. He patted the service revolver at his side and his grim little smile spoke volumes.

Benson was, by then, on his feet and arguing low-voiced with the army Captain about the wrath that was going to descend on Chisholm as a result of the dastardly assault. His department had ways and means of putting upstart bastards like him in their place and he, personally, was going to see to it that the bloody madman got all that was coming at him. Aware of Chisholm's eyes on them, the Captain edged Benson out of the room. He closed the door, but the sound of their raised voices carried quite clearly to Chisholm from outside.

"You were a witness," he heard Benson tell the Captain.

"Yes, I was," came the Captain's voice, "and I think you went too damned far. You grilled that poor blighter in there for close on six hours and had him so that he didn't know whether he was coming or going. A blind man could see he's completely baffled by it all. He just doesn't know what's hit him."

"I know what bloody well hit me!" came Benson's outraged reply. "He did!"

"Only because you kept provoking him. With all respect, sir, you went over the score. That's not the way we do things in MI Nine and, do I need to remind you, sir, that this is still our show?"

"It stopped being your show, Captain Kirkwood, when your boss called in my department. I am not one of your bloody wartime amateurs, Captain. I was in this game when you were in kindergarten. I know how to handle scum like Chisholm and you don't break his kind by being nice to them."

"You're assuming that he's guilty . . ."

"That's how I work, Kirkwood. That's how I always get results. When you're a little older and wiser, you will learn that I am never called in to investigate innocent men. They only send for me when the rat is in the trap. I'm not a rat-catcher, Captain . . . I'm the one who knows all there is to know about rodents. I'm the one who makes them spill their guts."

"Well, it hasn't worked this time, has it? That poor bugger in there hasn't got a clue what it is you're trying to get out of him."

"We'll see. I'm going to apply for a detention order."

"Then you'd better have a word with my CO first. We have a directive from the PM's office not to hold anyone for more than forty-eight hours unless we have the strongest possible grounds for suspicion."

"And that's exactly what we have, Kirkwood – the strongest possible grounds. You smelt a rat and tipped off the Colonel. He agreed or he wouldn't have sent for the fire brigade. That puts it out of your hands now, old boy, and out of your Colonel's, too. I'm going back to the office now to report to one of the senior partners and I'll only need to whisper that the firm are possibly involved and there will be detention orders flying all over the place."

"For the Canadians as well?"

"On the face of it, no. We might ask that they all be kept in one place for a day or two but not necessarily under lock and key. No, I'm interested in the odd man out – the one man who wasn't shot up at Dieppe; the one man whose stock answer to pertinent questions is 'I don't know' or, worse, that he can't remember; the one man who denies he is in any way violent and yet reacts like King Kong when you needle him . . ."

Chisholm missed what else Benson said because the redcap chose that moment to open the door and tell the two men in the corridor that their conversation could be quite clearly overheard inside the room.

"That you they was on about?" the MP asked Chisholm, with an air almost of disinterest. "Proper rascal you are by the sound of it."

Chisholm made no reply.

The room had no window. There was no inside handle on the door. The only ventilation came from two mesh-covered panels just below ceiling level. There was one light, but no switch to operate it. The bulb shone from the centre of the ceiling and was protected by a stout glass holder with metal rims.

The bed, against one wall, had a pillow and four blankets. In a corner was a porcelain toilet bowl, no higher than a bidet. It had a button-operated flush and no seat. The floor was covered by a khaki-coloured lino. The walls were cream and looked freshly painted. In one wall, a broad mirror had been inset.

The cell – because no word more accurately described the room – held a depressing familiarity for Chisholm. It was only slightly fresher and more comfortable than the succession of cells in which he had been confined during the previous six months. But, in many ways, this new cell was the worst of all – because this was not a French or a German cell and his captors were not the henchmen of a totally alien regime. This cell was on British soil and he was the prisoner of men enjoying the same birthright and common heritage as himself.

If, in the bad moments before, he had questioned his sanity, it was during the first hours of his imprisonment on British soil that Chisholm came closest to convincing himself of his own madness. Too much that had happened to him defied his attempts to rationalise away. Why had the U-boat captain kept him drugged if he was as sane as he liked to believe? Why had he been locked up in a French lunatic asylum? Why had French peasants reacted to him as if he were a monster? Why had the Germans kept him in chains? Why had the Canadian prisoners been so hostile to him? Why, now, was he being treated by his own people as if he were a criminal? Why was it that the loathsome Benson had kept on at him so relentlessly: trying to make him admit that (a) he was some kind of sexual pervert and (b) he had committed treasonable acts because of it?

Time and again, Chisholm had challenged Benson to come right out and tell him what crime it was he had committed. But Benson had prevaricated, insisting that Chisholm should confine himself to answering his question. More than once, he had said in his infuriatingly patronising way: "We both know what you've been up to, Captain Chisholm, don't we? But I want you to tell my *why*!"

Bewilderment, more than obstinacy, had delayed the inevitable explosion of Chisholm's rage. Benson's temper had been the first to go. His snapping resort to the use of gutter insult had instantaneously triggered a reaction that had been predictable in all but its ferocity.

Now, Chisholm was back in a locked cell – and cut off again, it seemed, from any friendly agency. Until the door had slammed shut, he had kept alive the hope that – at any moment – someone would discover that he was the victim of a monumental mistake and that he would be released with profuse apologies ringing in his ears. He had clung to that hope throughout the humiliation of being hustled in handcuffs out of the London Transit Camp building and into a waiting car. He had clung to it as the car had sped through London's blacked-out streets.

From landmarks he knew, Chisholm had recognised a westerly route through Ealing and Uxbridge, but a series of country lanes had disoriented him. He guessed that the general direction of the car's meandering was north-west into Buckinghamshire and that High Wycombe could not be far away when it had stopped at a lodged gateway and security passes were shown to an armed guard. There was a short drive through country parkland into the gravelled forecourt of a country mansion.

He was hustled down a series of dimly lit passages into a cellar complex. In an austere anteroom, he had been strip-searched by two military policemen. They had then allowed him to redress partially. His shoes, tie and belt had been withheld. Still clutching his trousers to keep them from falling around his ankles, he had been unceremoniously pushed into the windowless cell. When the door had clicked shut, his belief – that this treatment of him was a mistake of a quickly remediable nature – died.

In the first hours, he paced the room like a caged animal, torn in turn by numb despair and bitter consuming rage. As before – when it had seemed that God and man alike had abandoned him – the positive emotion displaced the negative, and he sustained himself solely on a profound anger. So long as it burned, he would never bow to the unacceptable. So long as it smouldered, he would endure.

He was hollow-eyed from lack of sleep when the door of his cell opened. He was left a tray containing breakfast: two slices of toast, two rashers of bacon and a mug of tea. There was no cutlery, so he made the toast and bacon into a sandwich and ate ravenously. His hunger surprised him. He made the tea last, sipping it slowly.

At ten in the morning, they came for him. He was taken to a room on the first floor. It was furnished partly as a lounge, partly like an office, and contained a sofa, several armchairs, two desks and three metal filing cabinets. Benson scowled at him from behind one of the desks.

Chisholm was told to sit in an armchair, facing his interrogator of the day before. The MP escort was dismissed.

"We'll be right outside the door, sir," one of them said.

"I'll buzz if I need you," said Benson. He allowed his right hand to hover near a bell-push on his desk, drawing Chisholm's attention to it. The warning was not lost on Chisholm but he gave no indication that this was so. He had anticipated a second meeting with Benson and he had made his mind up on how he would conduct himself.

Benson pushed a packet of cigarettes across the desk.

"Have a cigarette," he invited.

Chisholm would have given his right arm for a smoke but he shook his head in refusal. He said nothing. Benson's hard little smile was smug.

"Please yourself. I was only trying to be friendly."

Chisholm stared at him but still said nothing. Benson shrugged.

"Nothing has changed since yesterday," he said. "You are going to have to tell me all I want to know, Captain Chisholm. You are not going to be difficult, are you?"

Chisholm made no reply.

Benson tried again. Chisholm met his slightly mocking approach with a stony silence.

The interrogator shrugged. He got up from behind the desk and walked over to a window that looked out on a broad lawn. Rooks were sending up a raucous din from high sycamores beyond the lawn.

"I admit I lost patience with you yesterday," Benson said. "I won't make that mistake today. I have an order for your indefinite detention. Sit there like a Trappist monk if you like. We have all the time in the world."

Chisholm stared at him with contempt, saying nothing.

As the morning wore on, he continued to meet all Benson's

approaches with the same contemptuous silence. There were questions, little homilies, more questions. Chisholm met them all with silence.

"You killed the American, didn't you?"

Silence.

"Was it a lovers' quarrel?"

Silence.

"Was it because of the American's death that you went through with the escape? Were you afraid of what the Germans would do to you when they found out that you had knifed your little playmate?"

Silence.

"This doctor – Keitler – you were very friendly with him. But you double-crossed him, too, didn't you? Instead of tipping him off about the escape plan, you decided to skedaddle with the Canadians yourself. Why? Did you have a fit of conscience about the game you were playing? Is that why the American had to be bumped off? You wanted to go and he wanted to stay? Did he threaten to blow the whistle? Was that why you killed him?"

Silence.

Benson tried a different tack.

"This attitude won't help you, you know. It's tantamount to an admission of guilt. The only chance you have is to tell me everything. You have a good record. If there are mitigating circumstances, these will be taken into account. Better men than you have broken under pressure and done things they were ashamed of. Your only hope is in being frank. Tell me everything. We know what you were up to – but you've got to fill in the gaps, help us to understand why."

Chisholm stared hard at Benson.

"There is only one thing I have to say to you," he said slowly. "And that is that you are the most evil-minded bastard I have ever met!"

Saying it made Chisholm feel better. He continued to stare hard at Benson, the loathing for the man showing in his eyes. Benson, in spite of his superior air and self-confidence, flinched with uncertainty before the naked hatred in the look.

He continued to ask questions, but the slightly mocking confidence that had been there before was no longer in evidence. He started demanding answers and seemed impatient to get them. Chisholm sensed a minor victory in the anxiety that edged the other man's voice. It became more marked as Chisholm resorted to a silence that he did not intend to break again unless the whole tenor of interrogation underwent a radical change.

The morning interrogation ended without any wavering in Chisholm's refusal to co-operate. Benson tried again in the afternoon to break his silence. He failed.

The following day, the pattern was repeated. The afternoon session ended unexpectedly. A note was handed in to Benson. He read it, a deep frown growing on his face. He abruptly terminated the interview and Chisholm was returned to his cell. There was no further attempt at interrogation that day.

Next morning, Chisholm was again taken to the room on the first floor. Sitting behind the desk that Benson had previously occupied was a naval officer in his mid-forties. He wore the braid of Commander, RN, and his face was set in a grave, rather worried, expression. He stared at Chisholm with alert, searching, blue eyes. He did not beat about the bush.

"I want to ask you one question," he said brusquely. "And I want you to answer it."

The blue eyes stared at Chisholm.

"I've spoken to people who know you, Captain Chisholm. They all tell me the same thing: that you are a first-class mariner and have always been a credit to the service to which you belong. My question is this . . . During the time you were in German hands, did you willingly or unwillingly perform any service that could be construed as aiding and abetting the enemy?"

"No. Never!"

"Can you tell me then, why the Germans should think that you were worthy of special favours?"

"Favours!" snorted Chisholm, his anger rising. "Favours! Like being chained hand and foot to a wall! By locking me up in an asylum with a lot of gibbering lunatics! Is that what you call favours?"

"They treated you badly?"

"They didn't beat me up or pull out my fingernails. They didn't torture me in that sense. But what they did was torture just the same . . . How would you like being chained up like a rabid dog, Commander? How would you like to spend day after day, week after week, in solitary confinement – with the only thing to break the monotony of it being dragged out into the daylight to be asked idiotic questions by morons? What would you call 'being badly treated', Commander, in the light of the treatment that has been handed out to me in the last three days?"

The words had poured from Chisholm in a torrent, leaving him almost breathless. Chest heaving, his fierce eyes challenged the Commander.

Surprise had registered on the naval officer's gravely set face. Now the merest suggestion of a smile wrinkled his lips.

"I was told that you were not too loquacious, Captain. I seem to have been misinformed. Have you been harshly treated here?"

"Not by Gestapo standards, no. Your technique and theirs seem to be not dissimilar. All that I would like to know is what I've done to deserve it."

"You have been told why we had to detain you?"

"No, I bloody well haven't. I've been told nothing. I've been asked a lot of stupid questions and been subjected to more vile innuendo than my stomach can take – but nobody has told me anything."

"I see," said the Commander.

"You see, do you?" exploded Chisholm. "Well, that's fine and dandy. That makes one of us. Well, I don't see a damned thing! I want to know what the hell this is all about!"

The other man deliberated before replying.

"Captain Chisholm, can you understand that, where national security is concerned, secrecy is a way of life? It surrounds the activities of both the government and military departments to whom you were referred as an escaped prisoner of war, or – if you prefer it – a person who landed in this country by unorthodox means. Do you accept that?"

"Yes."

"Would you also accept that where an unorthodox entry occurs, the authorities must – without divulging too much of the reasons for their interest – investigate any irregularity or inconsistency that comes to light as a result?"

"Yes."

"Well, that happens to have happened in your case."

Chisholm digested this crumb of information thoughtfully.

"Are you trying to tell me, Commander, that you want to find out whatever it is you think I know, without telling me what *you* know?"

"In a nutshell, yes."

"Well, it won't work. I've done nothing I need to apologise for – and you'd better believe it . . . Because you're going to get nothing out of me, not a damned word, unless somebody comes across square with me and tells me what the hell this is all about!"

"We are not obliged to tell you anything, Captain Chisholm."

"Nor are you obliged to deal in damned lies! But that's what seems to be the stock in trade around here – lies! Well, let me put the record straight for you. I am not, as one of your charming colleagues put it, 'a fucking liar'! I am not a liar, full stop! And I am not a homosexual, or any other kind of sex pervert! You'd better believe, too – because it is the truth – that I do not go round killing people. I am not a murderer . . . yet. I won't guarantee to stay that way if your buck-toothed chum keeps chipping away at me to make me confess to things I've never done . . ."

"Are you finished?"

"No, I haven't. I want to get it through to somebody – and you'll have to do – that I've had as much as I can take. I don't know what it is you want out of me but you're not going to get it until somebody starts believing me. When that happens and when you start treating me accordingly, I'll be happy to tell you anything I know. Until then, you're going to get nothing from me! Not a damned thing!"

The Commander's watchful eyes had remained trained on Chisholm's face for every instant of his passionate discourse. When Chisholm finally halted, the Commander sank back in his chair, reflective, in no hurry to break the silence that ensued. The only sound penetrating the room was the distant racket from the rook colony beyond the lawn. An age seemed to pass before the naval officer leaned forward towards the desk again with the air of one who has made an important decision.

"I'll make a deal with you, Captain Chisholm," he said deliberately. "If you *are* a man who tells lies, you have mastered the art. You make your points with some conviction. But I want to make no judgements at this stage. I simply want you to trust me as you, yourself, want to be trusted. I promise you that I shall be as frank and truthful with you as I possibly can. I promise, too, that I shall not pre-judge your position. I shall listen carefully to all that you care to tell me. In return, I want you to give me your own detailed account of everything that has happened to you from the day you lost your ship."

Chisholm's instinct was to trust this man. Before he could make any reply, however, the Commander had an afterthought.

"I want to meet you half-way, Captain. To prove my good faith. Are there any questions you want to ask me . . . Anything that might put your mind more at ease? If I can give you the answers, I shall."

Chisholm thought for a moment.

"There's so much I just don't understand," he said. He shook his head in perplexity. "For instance, you talked of irregularities. What did you mean? What kind of irregularities?"

"Your status in captivity is one, Captain. And not yours alone. Neither you nor the five men who escaped with you were officially listed as prisoners of war. You show surprise . . . It was also a surprise to us. Your five companions were presumed to have lost their lives at Dieppe and you were presumed to have been lost with your ship. As a rule, the Germans have not been slow to register the names of captured men with the Red Cross in Switzerland – but they didn't do so with any of you. We should like to know why."

Chisholm shook his head.

"I . . . I just have no idea."

"On its own, it isn't perhaps all that important. Delays do occur, particularly if a man is hospitalised. The prisoner may not be registered until he is actually installed in an official camp."

"But you must have known I was a prisoner. My crew must have told what happened. They saw me taken aboard the U-boat . . ."

Chisholm's tongue dried in his mouth and his voice faltered to a halt as he saw the look on the other man's face. He was already guessing a horrible truth as he managed to whisper: "My crew . . ."

The Commander's face said it all.

"We know that at least one boat got away after the *Millerby* was torpedoed . . . It was found drifting in the South Atlantic six weeks after your ship was sunk. No one in the boat was alive . . ."

"There were no survivors?"

"Only you, Captain Chisholm."

A skewer driven into his body could have caused Chisholm no greater pain than the Commander's softly spoken words. He bowed his head, stricken with grief and a sense of failure. He covered his face with his hands, remembering. All those men! *His* men. "We're the lucky ones," they'd told him to cheer him up when the U-boat had taken him from them. The lucky ones! God, how they must have suffered in that desolate ocean; thirst, madness, some seeking drowning as their bodies shrivelled and their minds snapped.

"With me, they would have had a chance." Chisholm breathed the words, scarcely aware that he had spoken aloud. "When they needed me I wasn't there."

"I know what you must feel," the Commander said softly. "You mustn't blame yourself."

"Blame myself?" echoed Chisholm, staring at the Commander. "I could have saved them. I know it."

"I know how you feel."

"Do you? Do you? They're dead and I'm alive. Can you understand what that means? Do you know what it's like to lose a ship?"

"Yes, I do," came the answer.

Their eyes met and, for a moment, there was a communion of a shared and very special agony. The Commander did not reveal the circumstances of the experience that, Chisholm knew, had been as traumatic as his own. When, however, they resumed talking, a subtle change had taken place in their attitudes. Much of the anger and resentment that had seethed in Chisholm was at rest and he talked without any obligation of reserve. Similarly, a layer of dispassionate formality fell away from his interrogator. Where, before, there had been a stiffness, there was a certain sympathy. It was as if they had both found a wavelength of communication from which all others were excluded.

Chisholm held nothing back. He told it all, from the beginning: furnishing the Commander with a detail of remembered experience that went far beyond anything he had confided to another living soul. His proneness to claustrophobia had always been a secret shame to him, yet he spoke about it now with a candour that astonished him. He not only revealed every recalled incident of his long ordeal but relived the mental torment that surrounded the blanks: those episodes buried in black mists below consciousness and memory and which had caused him to agonise over his own sanity.

He recalled the Dickensian horror of the conditions in L'Asile des Perdus, his escape from it, and the consequent chained imprisonment by black-uniformed gaolers whom he took to be Gestapo. He recalled, too, the awakening of new hope in him from the moment that the man he remembered as The Schoolmaster had walked into his cell; and the sheer joy he had experienced in this first contact with anyone who not only believed he was sane but had sufficient authority to improve his lot.

Occasionally, as Chisholm told of the more reasonable conditions he had found at St Cyr des Bains, the Commander chipped in with a question. He answered without reserve. Yes, it was true that he hadn't got on well with the Canadians and Captain Lomax in particular. And, yes, it had surprised him. He couldn't give a reason for this. They didn't like the American and they seemed determined to dislike anyone who had anything to do with Rick Thomson. But there was more to it that that. Lomax had seemed to hate Chisholm on sight. It was an almost obsessive hatred that annoyed Chisholm because it was so unreasonable and undeserved.

"He had a reason," said the Commander. "Or, at least, there is an explanation. I'll tell you about it. But, first, tell me about the nurse, Nicole Baril. Did she make it known to you that she was in the Resistance?"

Chisholm hesitated. His conscience still pricked him about the rather cruel way he had enlisted Nicole's co-operation. He recounted the circumstances to the Commander.

"You were tipped off by this man you called The Schoolmaster and you threatened to expose her to the Germans?" The Commander's voice had a shocked tone and a frown darkened his face.

"She kept denying that she could help. She threatened to report me to the Germans. I just called her bluff. I would never have turned her in."

"Somebody did," said the Commander.

"What do you mean?"

"She hasn't been seen since the night of your escape. We have reasons to believe she'll never be seen again – alive."

Chisholm was shocked. He recalled the note being delivered to Benson on the previous day and the abrupt termination of his interrogation. Had that been connected with what the Commander had now revealed?

"You think the Germans arrested her?"

"We're certain of it. But don't ask me how we found out."

"Nicole didn't turn up on the night of the escape. She sent another girl in her place. Did you know that?"

"Yes, we know about that. And it puzzles us very much, Captain Chisholm. Because she is one of several unexplained mysteries in this whole business. We know nothing about her. Nothing at all."

Chisholm could feel a strange dryness in his mouth.

"She couldn't have been a phoney . . . Is that what you're suggesting? She could have shopped us any time. We would never have got away . . ."

"I'm not suggesting anything. All I am saying is that Nicole Baril was well known to us. We knew of no other female in the group."

"Do you think . . ?" Chisholm could hardly bring himself to put into words the question that was burning on his mind. "Do you think . . . Was it because of us . . . Was it because of the escape . . ? That the Germans got on to Nicole?"

The Commander stared sadly at Chisholm.

"Not just Nicole, Captain. They got everybody. The whole group."

Chisholm shrank back against his chair.

"No, no . . . Not because of us." He wanted to shout the denial but his voice was just a whisper.

"Do you think it was a coincidence? Do you believe in coincidences, Captain Chisholm?"

"I don't know what to believe," he cried, trying but failing not to sound shrill.

"Then you will understand our dilemma. Whom do we believe? Do we accept your version of events? Or do we accept the depositions of the five men with whom you escaped from France? Their stories are substantially the same. Yours is quite different."

"They would never have got away without me."

"They all admit that freely, Captain Chisholm. No one was more emphatic on that point than their senior officer, Captain Lomax. He was quite extravagant in his praise for your seamanship and the part you played in getting them to England. He was less complimentary about you in the very full report he made about this mysterious rehabilitation centre at St Cyr des Bains."

"That doesn't surprise me," said Chisholm bitterly. "The only real friend I had in the place was Rick Thomson. They treated him like a leper, too. They trusted no one outside their own little clique. And it was on Lomax's say-so, I'm sure. I told you I was poison as far as he was concerned . . . From the word go."

"And you don't know why?"

"No."

"Did you know that the Canadians had access to the dossiers the Germans had on you and Lieutenant Thomson, the American?"

"No."

"Lieutenant Gilbert read them. He was having a session with one of the doctors and the doctor was called out of the room. The papers were lying on the desk in front of Gilbert and he read them. His German is very good . . ."

"I know that," said Chisholm. "Everybody knew it. He was called on a lot as an interpreter. But no one ever mentioned dossiers to me. The Germans had files and charts on everybody . . . but they were very careful with them. They locked them away like the crown jewels. They never left them lying around."

"Except this once. Apparently it was the day you arrived at St Cyr des Bains."

"And?"

"Lieutenant Gilbert said the reports were couched in rather high-flown medical terms – the kind psychologists use. Yours had quite a lot to say about your mental problems . . . That you were given to inexplicable bouts of violence, which you couldn't remember about afterwards . . . That you gave a lot of trouble until it was realised that the key to your behaviour was repressed guilt arising from a predilection for sexual gratification with small boys . . ."

Chisholm let the Commander go no further. He was on his feet, his face white with outrage.

"For Christ's sake! It's lies – all of it!"

"There was more. About how you had been responsive to a humane understanding of your problems and how much you appreciated that the German approach to them was enlightened compared with attitudes in your own country, where society was dominated by moralistic norms inherited from the Jews."

Chisholm could scarcely believe his ears.

"Next, you'll be saying I applied to join the Nazi Party. It's beyond belief. Surely no one in his right mind actually swallowed that . . . that crap."

"Captain Lomax did," said the Commander. "You said that he hated you on sight. Hate is probably too mild a word. Especially with his family history."

Chisholm regarded the other quizzically.

"What family history?"

"Lomax had a brother. When he was eight and the brother was seven, they were abducted by a sex pervert and kept prisoner in some out-of-the-way backwoods cabin. The man abused the boys but Lomax escaped while he was occupied with his young brother. A search party found him in the woods, half-starved and half out of his mind. Then they found the cabin and the young brother. He was dead, terribly cut up. They never found the man responsible."

Horror and revulsion were etched on Chisholm's face. He felt a shudder of pity go through him for Lomax. No wonder the Canadian had reacted to him with unadulterated odium. Innocence or guilt had been irrelevant. It would have needed only a whisper that Chisholm was a homosexual to have aroused in Lomax a detestation that bordered on the murderous.

"I feel sick," Chisholm said. He had to sit, head bowed and still, until the swimming nausea passed. His head was reeling with unanswered questions avalanching on his mind. He raised his head and stared at the Commander in bewilderment.

"You have helped me to understand one thing: why Lomax hated my guts . . . But that still leaves a hell of a lot that needs to be explained . . . I don't know who that dossier was about, but it wasn't about me. It makes no sense. Why should anyone go to the trouble of concocting filth like that? Why? Why?"

"We have asked ourselves the same question," said the Commander. "It only makes sense if what the documents said was true."

Chisholm went cold at the Commander's matter-of-fact statement and its almost unassailable logic. That the Germans would go to a good deal of trouble to concoct a false assessment of a prisoner's mental health seemed highly unlikely. What purpose could it serve? Having done so, why – unless it was intended – should they leave it lying around to be read by the one Canadian officer linguistically capable of understanding it? If the aim had been to make the Canadians dislike Chisholm, it had been successful. But why should they go to such elaborate lengths? Chisholm was surely of no great importance and the end result seemed monumentally petty. The effort to perpetrate such a mischief seemed to far outweigh any possible gain.

Chisholm continued in the face of the Commander's logic to deny the libellous content of the dossier Gilbert had seen. He was equally adamant in declaring as false the dossier on Lieutenant Rick Thomson.

This apparently branded the American as a latent homosexual and, worse, a potential traitor: a young man so alienated to America's participation in the war and so sympathetic to the German cause that he deserved every privilege that his captors could bestow on him.

The Commander heard out Chisholm's stout defence of Rick.

"I promised to keep an open mind," he said, "But consider these points, Captain Chisholm. Because of the very real doubts the Canadians had about you and the American, they did not want you muscling in on their escape plans. But you muscled in on them in spite of that. You forced the hand of Nicole Baril and you were instrumental in persuading her group to adopt a sea escape plan in which you had an essential part . . . No – " he held up a hand " – let me finish. You made sure that, without you, no escape could take place. You also insisted on the American going along and more or less blackmailed the Canadians into acceptance. Isn't this so?"

"Only up to a point," protested Chisholm. "It was the Resistance people who insisted that getting across the channel was a non-starter without an experienced seaman. I may have taken advantage of that – but it was their idea, not mine. And if the Canadians were so damned sure that Rick and I were traitors, why did they go along with it? Why didn't they just tell me to go to hell?"

"Because they were desperate to get out of that place, Captain. Would it surprise you to know that not one of them actually believed they would ever make it to England? But they were all agreed that to try and fail was preferable to making no attempt at all. They were also agreed on something else . . .

That, if they were betrayed, neither you nor the American were going to survive . . ."

"I don't understand," said Chisholm.

"You were under sentence of death, Captain Chisholm. If anything had gone wrong with your escape, you were going to die . . . Regardless of the consequences."

Horrific as the implications were to Chisholm, his mind was racing ahead of the one that was immediate to himself. He was remembering Rick Thomson and how he had died. Anger gleamed like a battle-light in his eyes.

"They killed Rick. The bastards killed Rick! They had to take a chance on me because they needed me. But they didn't need, Rick. So, they killed him. I thought it was an accident . . . I blamed myself, because I wasn't there . . ."

The Commander had eased himself upright in his chair and he was watching Chisholm intensely.

"You think the Canadians killed the American?"

"I didn't think it possible they would go to that length. I couldn't believe they would go as far as murder. But after what you've just said, I can see that I am the one who was too damned trusting. They were ready to kill both of us . . . But they needed me. The bastards needed me."

"None of them has expressed any regret over Lieutenant Thomson's death," said the Commander, his eyes still on Chisholm's face. "But they all swear emphatically that they had nothing to do with it. They seem to think that whoever murdered him did them all a good turn – that his untimely demise was probably the critical factor in your escape succeeding. Indeed, they are reluctant to condemn the man who – they all believe – did kill Thomson."

"And who is that?"

"You, Captain Chisholm. You."

Seven

Operation Thumbscrew

The men seated round the long table could hear from less than quarter of a mile away the constant drone of traffic rising from Trafalgar Square. The top of Nelson's Column could be glimpsed through the window behind the presiding officer's chair.

There were eighteen men at the table. The majority were in uniform. Those who were not seemed to favour dark suits that might all have been cut from the same bolt of cloth. The order convening the meeting had come from the highest possible strata of command: the office of the War Cabinet. It brought together at one table – and that made the event a rarity – a wide diversity of highly secret (and highly secretive) agencies who pursued their nefarious activities in spite of, rather than in conjunction with, each other. Their work was allied but conducted within jealously guarded lines of demarcation.

Almost every branch of governmental and military security was represented, and three Allied nations. The British contingent was the largest, with representatives from MI5, MI6, MI9(b), OES and Naval Intelligence. There were several Americans present, all in uniform. They, too, represented organisations whose operations were cloaked under cryptic connotations of letters: MIS-X, CPM and MID. The solitary Canadian presence was embodied in the person of a fierce looking provost-major whose waxed moustaches were as sharp at the points as darts. He had spent the journey from Pirbright to the city composing harangues with which to assert the Canadian viewpoint.

Chisholm – if he had been privy to the discussions – would have been impressed by the range and sweep of authority exerted by the represented bodies. He would have been flattered by the frequency with which his name came up at the table but shocked, perhaps, at the seeming indifference to the prolongation or otherwise of his already chequered life. More important things were at stake and whether Chisholm lived or died was irrelevant.

In the view of the OES representative, the escape of Chisholm and five men who had been wounded at Dieppe had been a catastrophe of the first order. Or, at least, it had been the catalyst of disaster: occurring at the wrong place, at the wrong time, and producing a sequence of costly misfortunes that far outweighed the value he placed on the survival of five Canadian soldiers and a sea captain.

He found the ready support of Chisholm's first interrogator. Benson – nicknamed "Tiger" by colleagues in one of the murkier divisions of the SIS where he had worked – rose to agree with the OES man. He suggested darkly that the sea captain, in particular, had probably been a closet Nazi all his life and that his collaboration with the enemy was not so much at question as the extent of it. If the man could not be broken, made to confess all and brought to trial, then the solution might be to set him at liberty and arrange that a suitably fatal accident would overtake him at an early date.

This drew frowns of shocked disapproval from some, also some embarrassed smiles that quickly disappeared when it was realised that Benson was not only in deadly earnest but advocating a "solution" that would not be creating a precedent.

A grey-haired former academic with a senior position in MI6 drily congratulated Benson on displaying the subtlety for which he was rightly renowned. With a disarming smile, he questioned the need to have assembled such a vast array of brains and glittering talent around one table when the entire matter could have been expeditiously settled by Benson, a hired car, and a compliant coroner.

Benson went red in the face and reminded his mocker that, in war, certain departments were given *carte blanche* under the emergency powers with the object of eliminating enemies of the State. The whole design of such powers was to allow departments such as his own to act decisively in those instances where the normal machinery of justice and retribution were ineffective.

It was the presiding officer who finally steered the discussion away from what promised to be a lengthy debate on any one organisation's prerogative to apply the ultimate sanction in cases where they were not the only interested parties.

Benson, however, made one final attempt to baulk the presiding officer and justify his own position. It was as clear as a pikestaff to him, he opined, that the sea captain and the American, Thomson, had bartered for their own freedom with a promise to betray the entire French Resistance ring at St Cyr des Bains to the Germans. It was likely, too, that the sea captain – a man he knew from his own experience to be extremely violent – had killed his American friend: perhaps as the result of a quarrel, or because he thought that the American, with his disability, would be a liability on the escape to England. The fact that the Germans had allowed five wounded Canadians to escape with Chisholm had been window-dressing to deceive the French Resistance group and give them a false sense of security. The Germans, in any case, had probably decided that the escapers would never reach England in the flimsy craft available. They had probably left the boat lying around where it would be stolen by the French, because they had requisitioned everything else that was seaworthy. They must have been well aware of the boat's near dilapidated state.

That was Benson's case against Chisholm. The sea captain was a traitor and a killer and, if he were shot out of hand, it would be no more than he deserved.

The presiding officer tolerantly allowed Benson to have his say. Then he indicated that he was going to have his and that he wanted no more uninvited interruptions.

"I would remind you all of the purpose of this meeting," he said. "That is: to assess *all* the implications of what I shall call the St Cyr des Bains affair. It affects all of you in different ways."

He outlined them. MI5 had to consider a possible attempted intrusion into Britain of disaffected elements. MI6 and OES had to consider the damage done to their cross-Channel operations: how it had been inflicted by the Germans and how it would affect future operations. MI9 and, in particular, its Department "b" had to consider not only the efficacy of their screening procedures – which he was not criticising – but, in the light of this case, what actions might be required of them on the strength of evidence that was largely circumstantial and downright confusing.

The presiding officer glanced down the table towards the Canadian provost officer from Pirbright.

"The Canadian forces in this country have rightly demanded participation in a matter that concerns them. That is why George Brockway is here today. He may be a stranger to most of you, but he is an old friend of mine. You may dismiss as apocryphal the legend that the Mountie always gets his man. I can tell you that it's no legend as far as George Brockway is concerned, it's true. As an investigative officer with RCNWMP Intelligence Branch, he has tracked down more villains and spies than the rest of us put together. Glad to have you here, George."

The fierce-faced officer with the waxed moustaches nodded his acknowledgement. The presiding officer's attention was then transferred along the table to where four American officers sat in a group.

"There is an American involvement, too," he said. "Already, some British officers have seen fit to form conclusions on the behaviour of an American officer, one Lieutenant Thomson, who was severely wounded at Dieppe and taken prisoner. These conclusions have not been endorsed by anyone at his former base who knew the man and, indeed, they were vigorously denied by the sea captain, Chisholm – as you will see from the various interrogation reports in your possession."

The presiding officer stared expectantly at the most senior of the American officers.

"We have not heard a word from your side of the house, Major Hibberd. But, unless my reading of your faces was wrong, you have not been in full agreement with all that has been said here this morning?"

The American smiled.

"We have been conscious, sir, that what we have before us is a paper mountain of surmise and speculation. We have very few facts. Until we are confronted with good, solid, concrete facts, we believe it would be idle to pronouce one way or another on just what the hell happened on the other side of the Channel. We'd like to see these guys who got away and maybe come to a few conclusions of our own. For a start, we don't buy the story that our guy was a Nazi stooge. He was hand-picked for the Dieppe show – as an observer – but he never filed his report. For all we know, he could have formed some impressions that didn't make him too popular with the other guys in the hospital prison . . . But that's speculation, too. All we know for sure is that the poor guy is dead. We're not ready to guess who was responsible or why he got wiped out—but we owe it to him to get at the truth." Major Hibberd smiled. "That, we reckon, is about as far away from us at this minute as the mountains of Tibet!"

"Thank you, Major," said the presiding officer. "If it is any comfort to you, I share your reluctance to impugn a dead officer. It's too easy to pass judgement on someone who can never contradict you. My instinct is to walk very warily when there are as many complications and side issues as this affair provides. It positively bristles with unknown factors. One of the most baffling is the German hospital establishment at St Cyr des Bains, with its strange Commandant, on whom we have so many contradictory reports. Why were prisoners hospitalised in this place? Or, rather, why were they sent there for so-called convalescence?"

The presiding officer glanced along the table to a man in Royal Navy uniform and cocked an enquiring eyebrow in his direction.

"Commander Vaughan."

"Yes, sir?"

"None of the circulated material mentions that your people were interested in the German complex at St Cyr des Bains *before* the six men escaped from it. Can you tell us why?"

Commander Vaughan, whom Chisholm would have instantly recognised as his sympathetic inquisitor, regarded the presiding officer gravely.

"We weren't sure just why the Germans took over the old sanitorium. There were rumours on the ground about the place . . . That they were perfecting a new secret weapon there was one. Another had it that it was a crucial communications centre for the Atlantic wall defences, while outwardly a hospital. But they ringed it with steel. They don't usually go to such trouble for a hospital. That's why the French girl, Nicole Baril, was infiltrated . . . Her special objective was to find out just what was going on there."

"And was she able to send back any clues?"

"No, sir. We were going to pull her out when she, herself, was satisfied that she had got the whole picture. She was to say when."

"Her job wasn't to organise an escape line?"

"No, sir. Her group did provide an exit route for people we wanted out of France, but not for runners . . . prisoners of war. The St Cyr route was reserved exclusively for our own trained personnel returning from operations."

"So this escape was an embarrassment to you?"

"We knew that someone was wanting out – by a pickup from the French yawl. But we tried to discourage the idea. We didn't want unprogrammed stunts of this sort getting in the way of operations with a much higher priority."

"I see," said the presiding officer. "Did you know that there were any prisoners of war at St Cyr des Bains?"

"Not in that neighbourhood, no. Not until the six men turned up on this side of the Channel. We got the surprise of our lives."

"And you believe the escape compromised the French network?"

"We can't be absolutely sure. What we do know is that within twenty-four hours of the six men getting out, the entire St Cyr des Bains network was blown. The French girl, Baril, disappeared – and we have a confirmed report that a young woman was executed by firing squad four days later at Gestapo headquarters in Caen. We are almost certain it was Nicole Baril."

"And the others have been arrested?"

"We are in no doubt about that, sir. They have just vanished without trace."

"What about their radio operator? I take it that he was the one who somehow got this information to you?"

"No, sir. Our information came from other sources. The Germans are now operating our radio at St Cyr des Bains."

"You are sure of that?"

"Quite sure, sir. They are maintaining the pre-arranged schedules but it's a stranger operating the key. The signature is all wrong and he's omitting the required codeword that would signify that the signals are genuine. We have, of course, given no indication that we know what has happened. We are playing the Germans along."

"What conclusions have you reached about the affair, Commander Vaughan?"

"Only one. That the truth – as Major Hibberd said – is as far away from us as the mountains of Tibet."

"You have the advantage of having interrogated the six escapers and assessing whether or not they have been telling the truth. Yet, you express no opinions in your report, which is most comprehensive by the way. How do you account for the disparities that your own investigations have revealed? Everyone can't have been telling the truth. Someone has been lying to you."

"Not necessarily, sir. Perhaps they have all been telling the truth as they see it. Or as they have been conditioned to see it."

"I don't follow you," said the presiding officer.

"The key, sir, is the German commander at St Cyr des Bains – a doctor. But what kind of doctor? A doctor of what? Misinformation? All the escapers give a quite different picture of him, varying from harmless eccentric to evil monster. There is no doubt he tried to politicise them . . . In a way that antagonised some but merely amused others. He certainly ran his establishment and its prisoner compound like no other I've ever heard of . . ."

"What are you suggesting, Commander?"

"That we have a much bigger threat here than any of the single constituent issues might lead us to believe. We've got a riddle here that has to be solved with all the means at our disposal."

"And how do you propose we crack it?"

"It would need a special team. Or a team of specialists, if you like. A team that would get all the co-operation it requires from the various services. There are enough resources represented around this table to supply the team – and ensure that red tape is cut to a minimum. Parish boundaries might have to be crossed and recrossed – and without screams of protest every time it happened."

There was a polite cough from the American end of the table.

"May I ask a question?" The speaker was Major Hibberd. "Is the Commander suggesting that we stage a military operation . . . Like a commando raid on St Cyr des Bains?"

Commander Vaughan smiled.

"Only if in the final analysis it was necessary. I hadn't at this stage envisaged anything quite so spectacular."

"But your target is this bogyman at St Cyr?"

"Possibly. He is the one who makes me nervous – a bogyman, as you say. But there's more to it than that. It is just possible that he bungled when those six men made it across the Channel. Maybe they weren't supposed to make it and tell us what they know."

"They haven't given you all that much to go on so far," put in the presiding officer.

"On the contrary," Vaughan replied. "They've given us quite a lot. And unless I'm mistaken, there's a lot more to come."

"More interrogation?"

"If need be. But simply asking questions may not be enough. I feel we've got to make things happen. Take a lateral approach. We're not getting the right answers because we've been asking the wrong questions. It's like searching for buried treasure. You know it's there – but we're digging at the wrong end of the island. We might even be on the wrong island."

"There may be nothing there at all," said the presiding officer.

"Oh, there's something there all right, sir," said Vaughan. "I had another session with Chisholm last night, over a bottle of Scotch. I find he's responsive to kindness. Bully him and he fights back like hell. That's beside the point . . . He told me something about Keitler that set off enough alarm bells to convince me that we've stirred up a very murky pond indeed."

"I trust you will illuminate us in your own good time, Commander."

"Oh, yes, sir. I'm sorry. I seem to be hogging the show. The point is that I got the information from Chisholm almost by accident, the lateral approach, if you like. I was trying to build a picture of Keitler from the conversations he had with Chisholm. I was prompting him by suggesting that he was responsive to Keitler and more or less tolerated him in much the same way as he got on with me. Because Keitler was invariably respectful towards him and never unkind to him. Chisholm agreed. He said he tended to treat others as they treated him. Then he said that most people wanted to trust doctors, because they were a caring profession. Keitler, although he had his share of odd little habits, seemed a basically humane man and merited some respect. One does not automatically withhold respect for a doctor, because he wears a uniform – German or otherwise." Vaughan slapped the palm of his hand on the table in front of him. "That remark, gentlemen, brought me up with a jerk. There I was trying to build a picture of Keitler from his conversations, as I had done when I'd spoken to the Canadian escapers, and all I had was a mass of contradictions. It had not occurred to me that I might quickly have learned more about Keitler if I had asked what he was wearing."

"I thought all doctors wore white coats," observed the presiding officer. "What would that tell you?"

"But that's the point precisely," said Vaughan, with the gleam in his eye of a conjuror about to pluck a rabbit from a hat. "Keitler was no exception. He *always* wore a white coat when he was around the prisoners. The Canadians never saw him without it. Chisholm was the only man to have seen the uniform under it. That was on the night of the escape. I asked Chisholm to describe that uniform to me in detail."

"And?" prompted the presiding officer.

"Keitler may be a doctor, sir . . . But he also appears to be a high-ranking officer in the German Security Service – either the SD or the Sipo. Chisholm recalled it as odd that a Colonel in the German Army should have a lance-corporal's stripe on one sleeve . . ."

Commander Vaughan paused, aware that he had the rapt attention of every man in the room. He continued: "The chevron worn by the SD is not a lance-corporal's stripe or even a good-conduct stripe, sir. It is worn only by the elite of the SS with a special entitlement. The stripe signifies service to the Nazi Party from the days before it took power. Worn by a man of Keitler's rank, it signifies that Keitler is, if not one of Hitler's intimate comrades, at least very close to the original hierarchy. In the Security Service, that would mean Himmler."

There was a buzz of exchanged comment round the table at Vaughan's revelation. It was left to the presiding officer to ask the question that others were already whispering to each other around the table.

"And what significance do you read into that, Commander Vaughan?"

"I want to know," said Vaughan softly, "I want to know why one of Himmler's chums is running an SS convalescent home in a prohibited zone of France. It could be interpreted at its face value – a nice little sinecure for a good party man. But, in the light of recent events, that possible explanation is wholly unacceptable to me. I suspect something a damned sight more sinister, gentlemen. Something big enough to have cost the life of one American officer in enemy hands. Something important enough to have cost us a well-organised and efficient network inside the enemy camp and to have seen a brave young woman die in front of a firing squad. By now, all her comrades are probably dead, too. Why? Bad luck? Coincidence? The fortunes of war? What is it that all those deaths conceal from us? Until we know . . . Until we know for sure, I for one am going to find it difficult to sleep at nights."

A hush preceded the renewal of discussion at the table. There was a twenty-minute recess for lunch, no more, then the talking started again. The winter dusk of late afternoon had descended before the gathering finally broke up. By then, the seeds of "Operation Thumbscrew" had been sown. The codename for the operation had been decided speedily and without debate – but the choice was not inappropriate. Much pain was to be caused before the last secret was extracted.

Vaughan eyed the two men comfortably sprawled in separate corners of the settee opposite him. He was sitting back in the depths of a spacious armchair that was covered in the same mahogany-coloured hide as the settee. A low oak table occupied the intervening space and, on it, rested cut-crystal glasses, a near-empty bottle of Scotch and a soda siphon.

The three men were the only occupants of the oak-panelled lounge – one of three such lounges named after famous men of empire – in Vaughan's club in St James's. The Clive Room was the least used, even when the club was busy, and it was for this reason that Vaughan and his guests had retired there. Now, at two in the morning, the need for privacy that had governed their choice no longer applied. The premises were deserted but for them and a night steward, who, looked in occasionally to stoke the big open fire and to enquire if they had need of his service.

Vaughan's companions were the American, Major Hibberd, and Brockway, the Canadian provost officer. The three had been assigned the task of defining the objectives of "Operation Thumbscrew", drawing up a plan of action and – subject to approval from higher up – implementing that plan.

By two in the morning, the three men had progressed beyond a harmonious understanding of each other's interpretation of their common brief. It had not been plain sailing. There had been awkward moments initially. They had come together as strangers and some preliminary fencing had been required, with rights to be asserted, suspicions to be overcome. A leisurely dinner at Vaughan's club had worked wonders. And a long exchange of views afterwards had brought about a mutuality of respect, even liking, between the three.

Vaughan was pleased at the outcome. He had feared head-on personality clashes as the inevitable consequence of the ordained fusion of three such distinctly dissimilar characters. But each man had been quick to recognise admirable strengths in his companions and each had sensed instinctively that a positive alliance of those strengths was not only desirable but would synthesize into a single force of formidable potency.

They agreed that their differing nationalities and existing loyalties would have to be secondary to the demands of fulfilling their task dispassionately as a unit. Hibberd summed up their accord.

"We left our caps in the cloakroom, gentlemen," he said. "If we're going to work as a team, that's where they've got to stay . . . Along with any preconceptions we've got, any axes we may want to grind, any claims we might be tempted to stake . . . The way I see it, we've been appointed to be the three wise men of this little show. So, I guess we've got to play it like three wise men: all saying our little piece, all listening real good when the other guy says his, and then all giving one hundred per cent support to whatever decision we come up with."

"We speak with one voice," said Brockway, beaming his approval.

"And we act with one mind," said Vaughan.

"I'll drink to that," said Hibberd.

Brockway raised his glass.

"To our unholy trinity," he proposed: a suggestion that led to their faintly blasphemous choice of cover designations for secret communications passing between them. Vaughan became "GA" – although he thought that the "A" for Almighty was too extravagant. Hibberd became "JC" and hoped he wouldn't be crucified for it, adding that, if ever asked about it, he would say the initials stood for Julius Caesar, or Joseph Carbolic because he was the Joe Soap of the outfit. Brockway was delighted to accept "HG" because he was "neither holy nor ghostly but it sometimes paid a policeman to be both".

They amicably divided their spheres of activity three ways, according to the expertise and resources at their command.

Vaughan seemed the best person to devise and initiate intelligence-gathering in Occupied France. He would liaise with MI6 and OES, having an intimate association with both organisations.

Brockway would head the UK investigative effort, which would be concentrated initially on the six escapers from St Cyr des Bains. Somewhere amid the contradictions and confusion of the escapers' stories were vital clues to treachery and misdeed on an incalculable scale. Brockway would find them by fair means or foul. His was the policeman's role and, if need be, he would conduct it with back-up from Scotland Yard's Special Branch, MI5, and possibly some of Hibberd's specialists.

Hibbert was to be responsible for the team's co-ordination of effort and communications. In his central role, he would provide back-up research and intelligence, locate and direct specialist personnel, and act as general trouble-shooter in emergency situations.

Vaughan reiterated the belief that they could not allow themselves the luxury of waiting for things to happen.

"We've got to stir the pot," he said. "We can't just wait and hope that we'll make a breakthrough by doing the orthodox things." He told the others what he had in mind. "There's our communication channel to the Baril Resistance group. We're at one end and Jerry's at the other. For the moment, Jerry doesn't know that we know that the network has been broken up – but he knows that sooner or later we may find out. I think we should initiate a little mischief there before Jerry realises we're on to his game."

"How do we do that without giving the game away ourselves?" asked Hibberd.

"We've got to take a chance on that," said Vaughan. "It's going to take time to get one of our own people into St Cyr des Bains again and find out what's going on there. So, first, why don't we ask Jerry himself to answer some of our questions?"

"They'll stall – or sling back false information," said Brockway.

"Of course they will!" Vaughan leaned forward in his chair, eyes alight. "But don't you see? No matter how they respond, they'll be telling us *something*! They will try to mislead us. But that's a game two can play – and we've got to get in first by misleading them."

He outlined his plan. The German-controlled radio at St Cyr des Bains had so far made no mention of assisting six Allied prisoners to escape across the Channel. Possibly they were waiting for London to broach the subject first by signalling their successful arrival. The time was perhaps past when London should have replied but their silence could be accounted for if the escape had not worked out according to plan.

Vaughan's idea was to signal that only two survivors had been picked up on the English side of the Channel and were now in hospital. Also, these survivors had told an incredible tale about escaping from the sanitorium at St Cyr. Neither man had been on any notified list of prisoners in German hands, although they claimed to have been nearly six months in captivity. Could this be investigated and the fact confirmed that more prisoners were still being held at the sanitorium? There was another disturbing factor. One of the St Cyr survivors had accused the other of murdering an American officer on the night of the escape. Could any information be obtained on this?

Although Brockway feared that the Germans controlling the Resistance radio would reply in a wholly negative fashion, he and Hibberd helped Vaughan to compose the text of a message for coding and transmission to France. It was 4 a.m. when the trio's conference in the Clive Room was finally adjourned.

Four days passed, during which the three men were kept busy translating the idea of "Operation Thumbscrew" into a working reality. On the fifth day, a Royal Corps of Signals operator in a listening base in the south of England picked up the callsign and counterfeit signature on the key operating from St Cyr des Bains. It came right on schedule. The message was decoded and sent by Despatch Rider to Vaughan in his new operations room near Trafalgar Square.

The Commander found that his hands were trembling as he opened the big yellow envelope marked "Most Secret". The message inside read:

FROM BOULANGER TO CHEVALIER
YOUR RECENT ARRIVALS WERE TWO OF SIX RELAYED THROUGH THIS OFFICE. OUR CONTACT AT THEIR FORMER PLACE OF RESIDENCE CONFIRMS SMALL NUMBER OF FRIENDS REMAINING. ALL IN GOOD HEART AND WELL TREATED BY HOSTS. RESIDENCE RESERVED

FOR SERIOUS DISABLED. THIS MAY ACCOUNT DELAYS IN NOTIFICATION.

CONFIRM UNEXPECTED PASSING OF UNCLE SAM'S BOY. RESULT OF ACCIDENT INVOLVING DRUNK SAILOR WITH LONG RECORD AS TROUBLEMAKER. UNTRUSTWORTHY FELLOW TOO FRIENDLY WITH WRONG PEOPLE.

REQUEST YOU SUPPLY NAMES OF YOUR TWO ARRIVALS. THEIR FRIENDS AT FORMER RESIDENCE MOST ANXIOUS AND KEEP ASKING FOR NEWS.

Eight

Memento of a Dead Lover

Early January brought a light covering of snow and a relaxation in the severity of Chisholm's confinement. Walking in the parkland grounds of the Special Detention Centre, he delighted in the serenity of the surroundings. Out here, amid the time-weathered oaks and the gaunt, leafless sycamores, he had an ephemeral taste of freedom. He scuffed the snow with the toes of his shoes, reliving the boyhood pleasures of long-gone winters and dwelling in a private serenity that was undisturbed by an ever-present personal shadow: the uniformed escort who plodded twenty paces in his rear, rifle on shoulder.

For a week now, they had allowed Chisholm to exercise in the grounds; walking where he pleased, with the one stipulation that he must not approach within fifty yards of the high boundary fence. So, he circled the sprawling mansion-house, keeping the fence at regulation distance. From talk he had overheard, he had a rough idea of the Centre's location, mentally pinpointing it between Beaconsfield and Amersham.

He had lost count of the number of times he had been interrogated, sometimes with a stenographer present, sometimes without. The Navy Commander, Vaughan, had been the most empathetic of his questioners: constantly encouraging his confidence by introducing the conviviality of a bottle of whisky, or whistling up pots of tea and plates of sandwiches, which they consumed before a roaring fire when the mind-dredging sessions of talk stretched to the midnight hour and beyond. The social trappings put a civilised veneer on the otherwise barbarous inequity of Chisholm's arbitrary detention.

But it was in a fatalistic frame of mind that he was summoned into the presence of Commander Vaughan during the second week of 1943. Chisholm had not seen Vaughan for several days and he drew no comfort from the naval officer's grim expression. He looked graver than ever–which was saying quite a lot–and his eyes were dark and ringed with fatigue. He signalled to Chisholm to take a seat, but it was a vague offhand nod of the head. He made no other sign to acknowledge Chisholm's existence: saying nothing, just sitting there absorbed in the gloom of his own thoughts. Chisholm, sensitive to the possibility that Vaughan's unhappiness centred on him, ventured to ask: "Bad news?"

Vaughan roused himself.

"No, no . . . I'm sorry." The denial was not quite true. He had heard only that morning that a good friend had been killed in the Med. The Germans had thrown 190 aircraft against shipping off the North African coast, sinking four ships and damaging the cruiser *Ajax*. Vaughan was privately grieving for his lost friend and conscious that he had died fighting the kind of war that Vaughan himself would have preferred: on the high seas, face to face with the enemy. But Fate, or the Admiralty, had decreed otherwise. In Vaughan's war, the face of the enemy was never seen. The battles were waged from holes in the ground hundreds of miles apart, like chess by remote control. And, like chess, Vaughan's war needed pawns.

He smiled at Chisholm.

"I've got good news for you. It has been decided that there's no need to keep you locked up here any longer."

As his words registered, Chisholm's face brightened like the slow breaking of an Indian Ocean dawn.

"You . . . You're letting me go?"

"Not completely. We'll want to keep in touch. And there are conditions. Documents to sign . . . This is a secret establishment–and I have to warn you that if you so much as whisper a word about its existence, you'll be whisked off to the Tower faster than you can blink. All of us who come here are under the same rules, so it's not just a question of gagging you personally. Having said that, the gag applies in a number of things. There will be an embargo on your communicating by word of mouth or any other means the details of your experiences in German hands. All that comes under the heading of highly sensitive material and is subject to a strict security blanket. You can tell your friends, if you have to, that you escaped from France–but that's as far as you're permitted to go. Absolutely no details.

Do you understand?"

Chisholm nodded. "Careless talk costs lives. Ask any merchant seaman. We know more than most about the cost side."

"Yes . . . Yes, I daresay you do," Vaughan murmured. He leaned back in his chair, the air of preoccupation returning.

"Does this mean that I'm off the hook?" Chisholm asked. "That you believe everything I've been saying since you penned me up in here?"

"I believe you have told me the truth." Vaughan hesitated momentarily. "But you are not off any hook. I said that we would want to keep in touch with you." He changed the subject abruptly. "What will you do with yourself? You're going to have time on your hands."

"There's only one thing I want to do. And that's get back to sea where I belong."

Vaughan frowned.

"I'm afraid that's out of the question for the time being. Look, you'll have a lot of leave due. Why don't you treat this . . . this remission, for want of a better word . . . as a holiday?"

"What would you suggest?" Chisholm could not keep the bitterness from his voice: "A fortnight at Blackpool? The beach shouldn't be too crowded at this time of year."

Vaughan ignored the sarcasm.

"It would suit us if you didn't move too far from London. Is there some place where you could stay?"

"My sister usually puts me up when I'm on leave. She lives in London."

"Yes, I know." Vaughan smiled. "She's very highly thought of by the SSTO. We checked her out."

"Of course!" said Chisholm, with heavy sarcasm. "I just hope you didn't let your friend, Benson, loose on her. He'd have wanted to drum her out of the Wrens."

"There was nothing like that, I can assure you. All our inquiries have been made with the utmost discretion. As it happens, your sister has a high security clearance. Her integrity has never been in question."

"Does she know I didn't go down with the *Millerby*? Heaven knows she had enough heartache to put up with when her husband didn't make it back from Dunkirk without her thinking I was a goner, too."

"She knows you are alive . . . That you were picked up by the

114

U-boat. Beyond that, she knows nothing. You'll be able to give her a happy surprise by turning up in person. But no details, remember! Not even to her. You got out of France but you're not allowed to talk about it to anyone."

Chisholm suddenly felt more cheerful.

"That'll make two of us then. She's the one who's always had to be tight as a clam about what Wren officers do in Whitehall to justify two blue stripes on their sleeves. Not that I ever gave her credit for more than brewing tea for some desk-bound admiral."

Vaughan's answering smile was polite rather than amused. He pursed his lips thoughtfully.

"Let's forget your sister for a moment, shall we?" he said. "There's something else . . ." He hesitated. "I . . . We . . . It has been suggested that you might care to perform a small last service for a friend . . ."

Vaughan seemed strangely reluctant to come out with what was on his mind. He clearly found it embarrassing. Then he plunged straight in: "Your friend, Lieutenant Thomson, had a girlfriend in Brighton. Did you know?"

"No." Chisholm puzzled. "There was a girl in the States he talked about . . . But I don't think it was a deep involvement . . . He never mentioned anyone in Brighton."

"Well, there was a girl there," said Vaughan, still uncomfortable. "All I know about her is what I've been told. The point is that he bought a gift for her before he embarked for Dieppe. It's been sitting in the safe of the regimental paymaster at Newhaven since last August. Apparently, he left instructions that if he didn't make the return trip, the package was to be sent on to her."

"And has it been?"

"No," said Vaughan. "That's where you come in. Nothing was done about the package because although Lieutenant Thomson was posted as missing, he was never officially listed as dead. There are procedures . . . red tape. Now, the American Army are ready to release the gift to its intended owner. And they want you to deliver it."

"Me?" Chisholm was quite stunned. "Why me?"

"It wasn't my idea," said Vaughan. "I don't know what I would do if I were in your position. But I said I would ask you. It's a gesture by the Americans. In their own words, they don't buy the story that Lieutenant Thomson was a Nazi stooge.

They know that all along you've maintained Thomson's innocence of any complicity with the Germans – as you've maintained your own innocence. The Americans appreciate that you and you alone have stuck up for their man. Anyway, it's entirely your decision. Nobody's going to force you to do it."

"It's a compliment to me, I suppose. The girl must have been special to Rick . . . But he never mentioned her."

"She must have been special enough. The little gee-gaw he bought for her is a brooch – platinum with an inlay of diamonds. Must have set him back fifty or sixty quid."

Chisholm made a face.

"That's quite a lot of money. He must have been in love."

"Or star-struck," said Vaughan. "The girl's a singer and quite a celebrity down in Sussex. Quite a force's favourite. Entertains at all the base concerts. The darling of Southern Command."

Vaughan reached into a drawer and pulled out a framed photograph. He pushed it across the desk to Chisholm.

"That's the young lady. It was with other personal effects that Thomson left at the Newhaven billet. It used to sit beside his bed."

Chisholm studied the photo. It was the kind of glossy reproduction that theatrical people have taken for publicity purposes. It showed a sultry raven-haired beauty in a low-cut sequined evening dress. Scrawled across an area of bosom in blue ink was the inscription: "All my love – Anina".

Chisholm gave a soft whistle. "She's quite something, isn't she?"

"You'll go and see her then?"

"Somebody should – if it's what Rick wanted. It might as well be me."

Vaughan breathed a sigh of relief.

"Thanks. I wasn't sure what your reaction would be. The Yanks are strangely sentimental people . . . And they're pretty sore at the Canadians over this business – because of the accusations that have been flying around. They thought very highly of your friend, Thomson, and I suppose this is their way of letting you know that they're in your corner."

"It's nice to know who your friends are," said Chisholm, with some feeling.

"Yes," agreed Vaughan, but avoided looking directly at Chisholm. He had been wishing that Hibberd himself had been the one to tell Chisholm about the girl. He had located the photo in Thomson's locker in Newhaven. Or Brockway should have told Chisholm. He was the one who'd got so excited about the damned girl; and this whole thing was, after all, Brockway's idea.

Chisholm's sister wept all over him when he arrived out of the blue on the doorstep of her flat in Westminster. He was the brother back from the dead. She had not built up false hopes when she had heard of the *Millerby*'s loss. Not like the first time, when her husband, David, had been posted missing in France. Then, she had buoyed herself up with the conviction he was alive. His death had been all the harder to accept when, after two months of unwarranted optimism, the telegram had come from the War Office confirming the worst.

An official of the shipping company had called on her personally to tell her that the *Millerby* had gone down. She had accepted then that it was unlikely she would ever see her brother again, and had put on a brave face as she had gone about her WRNS duties at the headquarters of HM Sea Transport. There, she was Second Officer York – a year or two older than most of the Wrens around her – highly efficient, unflappable, so mature and sensible. Only a few knew she was a war widow. She wore two blue rings on her sleeve, not her heart.

Millie York had scarcely been able to take it in when, after quietly grieving for her brother for six months, a two-and-a-half ringer from Staff had taken her aside and told her that the *Millerby*'s master had not gone down with his ship. He had been picked up by the U-boat. And, now, when she was still trying to get used to the idea that young Heck – as he had always been to her – was alive and probably behind barbed wire somewhere in Germany, he had turned up on her doorstep.

His gaunt appearance shocked her. He had lost weight. And there was a troubled weariness about his eyes that had never been there before. For the first hours of their reunion, she only had to look at him and it was enough to start a fresh fountain-burst of tears.

"Oh, I'm sorry. I just can't help it, Heck," she apologised. "I'm just so happy to see you."

"Nobody calls me Heck," he protested, with feigned exasperation. "The man of the house in our family has always

117

been Chizz to his nearest and dearest. That's the way it's been for generations and I demand my hereditary rights as a matter of respect."

"Chizz!" Millie repeated indignantly. "It's like a name out of a kiddies' comic. I've always hated it. I always felt it cheapened Dad – and it cheapens you."

"It's better than Heck. Mother must have been out of her mind, calling me Hector."

"You know she thought it was heroic."

Chisholm's face went suddenly bleak.

"That's why I've never liked the name," he said flatly. "There's nothing heroic about me."

His expression, the tone of his voice, made her look at him sharply.

"Is there something you want to tell your big sister, love? Is something wrong?"

"No . . . Nothing's wrong."

"Was it bad . . . ? Over there, I mean? Did they treat you badly?"

"No, no," he lied. "Anyway, it's all over now. I'm home, and that's what matters. Everything's fine . . . fine."

But everything wasn't fine. He stared down at his wrists, where the chains had been. There were no marks there now but the flesh seemed to burn. It was as if the chains were still there. He was free now, free – but the chains still held him.

Chisholm found an empty first-class carriage and settled himself in a window seat. He had had seven days of freedom but he had found that, more and more, he was avoiding the company of others and wanting to be on his own. The desire was like a gnawing impatience in him now, as the train sat in the station waiting the minute of departure. Chisholm fretted at the delay: anxious for the train to leave before some stranger invaded the compartment and started yapping at him about the weather, the war, or the state of the railways.

To his relief, the train started to move. He relaxed immediately. He gave himself over to thinking about the bizarre errand that was taking him to Brighton. He wondered just how much the girl knew of Rick's fate.

She must know that Rick had been reported missing. Or did she? Rick would not have been able to warn her beforehand that he was about to embark on a raid into Europe. In all probability, Rick had gone off without a hint of what was in store for him. They had probably parted with an arrangement to meet again the following weekend: made a date that only Rick knew might never be kept.

It was possible that, in her ignorance, the girl thought to this day that Rick had stood her up: simply ditched her. It happened all the time: wartime romances were transitory. The chances were that, whatever feelings the girl may have had for Rick the previous August, she felt less than loving towards him now. She had not been notified of his failure to return from Dieppe. She was not Rick's next of kin. Just a girl that he knew.

Chisholm had liked the Major Hibberd who had called on him and passed over the package for the girl. The Major had apologised for what he described as "an exercise in North American sentimentality". It would be nice for the girl to have the keepsake, he had said, and hoped Chisholm would forgive him for his cowardice in not facing her. By getting Chisholm to deliver the brooch, he was chickening out of a task for which he had no relish. He had hoped Chisholm would understand: facing an enemy machine-gun post was one thing – all in the line of duty, as it were – but facing a broken-hearted girl was something else again. Just the thought of it turned him to a jelly.

"You and Rick seemed to have been real good buddies," he had said. "Commander Vaughan has told us how you really went to bat for the guy. That meant a hell of a lot to us. We knew him as a loner, a quiet sort of guy. None of us really knew him that well. He wasn't easy to get close to. But he never struck us as a quitter – or a Nazi-lover, like those Canadians made out. He was as American as apple pie, Old Glory and Plymouth Rock."

In view of this. Hibberd had hoped that Chisholm would not look on the request to visit the girl as an imposition. The US Army wanted to fulfil the last wish Rick had made before he had gone off to battle and, in doing so, they wanted Chisholm to look on their invitation as a kind of honour. That was how it was intended.

Chisholm saw his errand more as an obligation than an honour. He owed it to Rick. Vaughan, Hibberd, the Americans had really nothing to do with it. His debt was to Rick. The memory of his discovery of Rick, impaled on those surgical scissors, filled Chisholm's dream-haunted nights. Reproaching him. Accusing him. Perplexing him with its bizarre abiding mystery.

Over Brighton, a watery sun rode the sky: a pale opaque disc floating in a filmy vapour of cloud. Chisholm pulled the collar of his trench-coat up around his neck and strode out along Queen's Road. A chill breeze blowing up from the sea ruffled his hair and iced the tip of his nose. He had time to kill. He escaped the wind momentarily by cutting along past the Public Library, following a haphazard course that finally brought him out near the Palace Pier. There was no shelter from the wind in Marine Parade, not that he sought any. He walked briskly, head high, taking an almost masochistic pleasure from the whip of salt air on his face.

He walked until the morning was gone. Hungry, he selected an unpretentious café for lunch. There were still some hours to go before there was any likelihood of seeing Anina Calvi. Hibberd had been unable to provide the girl's current address – she had moved digs several times in the past few months – but had suggested catching her at the venue of one of her shows. This, Chisholm intended. Anina Calvi was scheduled to appear that evening at the Beaumaris Hotel.

Lunch was a disappointment. The menu offered a main course choice of sausage, mash and beans or sausage, mash and peas. As he toyed with two sausages containing a breadcrumb mixture and next to no meat, he found that Anna Calvi's face was smiling down at him from the wall opposite his table. When he had finished his meal, he took a closer look at the poster. It displayed a blow-up of the photo Vaughan had shown him.

The poster advertised: "Grand Garrison Concert & Late Dance". It was to be held that evening in the Ballroom of the Beaumaris Hotel. Anina Calvi, described as "Sweetheart of the Forces", was top of the bill. Admission was five shillings, with members of the Armed Services admitted at half price.

Chisholm decided that it was time he reconnoitred the Beaumaris Hotel. He liked its atmosphere from the moment he walked through the imposing pillared entrance.

A pretty blonde receptionist was disposed to chat with him. Yes, there were plenty of rooms available. No, of course it didn't matter that he had no luggage. Would he be requiring dinner? It was being served early to allow guests to attend a concert and dance in the ballroom. A barber's shop, sir? There used to be one in the hotel but, unfortunately, it had to close. The war, sir. You know how it is. They could send out for anything the gentleman needed.

Chisholm's room was on the first floor. He telephoned Millie in London.

"You're spending the night in Brighton?" she echoed his words. "What on earth are you doing there?"

"Just visiting a friend of a friend."

"Is the friend of a friend young, female and not bad to look at?"

"All of those things," he replied with a laugh, "but it's not what you're thinking. I'm not sowing any wild oats. I've just decided to spoil myself for the night. I've got this courtesy call to make, but it shouldn't take long. I'm going to have a few drinks and a slap-up dinner, with no expense spared. This place doesn't seem to have discovered yet that there's a war going on. Either that or the chef knows his way about the black market. They have sirloin steak on the menu tonight and, thanks to the rather cute blonde on reception, mine's already ordered."

"And I'll be having an omelette made with powdered egg," wailed Millie with mock jealousy. His seeming high spirits cheered her. It had alarmed her that, since his return, he seemed to have lost the knack of enjoying himself. He had become strangely withdrawn – and it worried her.

"You have yourself a ball, young Heck," she exhorted, before finally hanging up.

He made a brief expedition to shop for toiletries and then returned to the Beaumaris to enjoy a leisurely bath. A notice on the bathroom wall requested guests to restrict their baths to a depth of five inches in the interests of national economy. He ignored it and three-quarter filled the tub. He reckoned the national economy owed him a bath or two for the days he had been deprived of that luxury.

The spacious reception lounge of the Beaumaris had a deserted look when he went downstairs at 4.30. The absence of people pleased him. Armed with an evening paper, he found himself a comfortable corner and ordered tea. It arrived in an ornate silver pot, with matching jugs and bone china crockery, served by a demure waitress in black uniform dress and white frilly apron.

Chisholm was pouring himself a second cup from the silver

pot when he became aware of a bustle of activity near the reception desk. A group of army officers had arrived and were collecting room keys. There was something vaguely familiar about the tallest of the officers, who had detached himself from the others and was idly surveying the lounge. When his eyes met Chisholm's, recognition was instantaneous and mutual. A moment later, Lomax was crossing the lounge towards Chisholm.

"Well, well, well, this is a surprise!" The Canadian's face was a study as he towered over Chisholm. He displayed the questioning bewilderment of the upright citizen who has chanced upon the town drunk at a gospel meeting. The Canadian's surprise was matched by Chisholm's. He recovered enough to force a tight little smile and remark on the smallness of the world.

"Can I offer you a cup of tea, Captain Lomax?"

The Canadian thanked him but declined. He also pointed to the new crown on one epaulette. "It's Major now. I've been promoted. May I ask what brings you to this neck of the woods?"

"I have a call to make in the neighbourhood. I'm staying here overnight."

"In the Beaumaris?"

"Yes," said Chisholm.

"Are you, by God?" Lomax grinned. "You couldn't have known, then? That this is Canadian territory? There are twenty of us living here. We've got the whole of the north wing to ourselves."

The coincidence startled Chisholm. More than that, it disturbed him. Somewhere in the back of his mind, an alarm bell was sounding a warning. He was remembering past Canadian associations with Brighton . . . How they had even nicknamed their quarters in St Cyr des Bains "The Pavilion" after the pretentious Regency edifice in Brighton. However fortuitous this encounter with Lomax might be, Chisholm realised that it was an encounter he had wanted to happen. Ever since that first interview with Vaughan in the Detention Centre, he had wanted to face Lomax – knowing what he knew now about the man – and forcing the Canadian to re-examine his antipathy towards him.

"I've been hoping we would meet again," he told Lomax. "But I had no idea you were here."

"You've changed your tune. Last time we talked, you said you didn't think we'd meet again this side of hell."

"And you said you owed me one—a favour, Major Lomax."

"I meant it."

"Did you? Did you really? Well, now I'd like to collect it." Chisholm's eyes challenged Lomax. "You've caused me more misery than you'll ever know. Because of you and your chums, I've had to suffer the kind of degradation that no man should ever be made to suffer. I should hate you, Major Lomax. But I don't hate you. Because I can begin to understand why you never wanted to do me any favours before."

"Just what is this favour that you want?" Lomax's tone was tinged with suspicion. He seemed suddenly uncomfortable at the relentless, soul-piercing scrutiny of Chisholm's eyes. Chisholm had risen to his feet, not in an aggressive way but exhibiting a calm and control that the other found strangely unnerving. Chisholm said: "I want you to listen to what I have to say, Major Lomax. That's the only favour I want. But I want you to listen good. Because what I am going to tell you is the truth, the whole truth and nothing but the truth."

Chisholm articulated the words slowly and with a calmness that edged every syllable with steel. Lomax spread his hands in a placatory fashion.

"OK, OK . . . I owe you that. Let's sit down, eh? You got something on your chest—so, go ahead and spill it."

And spill it, Chisholm did. He fired the words like bullets, fast and true and with the accuracy of a marksman who is shooting for his life and knows it. His object was total conviction.

Without frills or embroidery—and all the more eloquent because of that—he put it to Lomax that the Canadian's judgement of him had been wrong from the day of their first meeting at St Cyr des Bains. Further, that judgement had been poisoned deliberately by malicious falsehoods that had been manufactured by someone who knew—as Chisholm now knew—the full story of the vile outrage that had befallen Lomax and his brother in childhood in Canada.

Lomax had wanted to interrupt at this stage but Chisholm insisted on being heard out because what he still had to say was of importance. He wanted Lomax to know that he fully understood the aversion he must harbour for any man he suspected to be twisted enough and sick enough in the mind to

123

abuse children. He, Chisholm, shared Lomax's total abhorrence for all such monsters. But what Lomax had to believe was that Chisholm was not and never had been a pervert of this kind. With solemnity and all the conviction he could muster, Chisholm swore that he had never in his life indulged, or even been tempted to indulge, in sexual acts with a member of his own sex. His appetites were healthy and had been strictly confined to relationships with consenting women. And that, so help him, was the truth, the whole truth and nothing but the truth.

When he had finished, Lomax made no immediate reply. He was shaken by Chisholm's sincerity, by its passion. Chisholm mistook the reason for the Canadian's silence.

"Do you believe me, damn you?" he demanded, naked agony in the low-voiced appeal.

There was torment of a different kind in Lomax's stricken look. It arose from the shocking certainty that Chisholm spoke the truth. And this truth was exploding against his mind with its significance. Lomax was realising for the very first time the monumental nature of the wrong he had caused Chisholm.

"God forgive me," he said softly, but his eyes were asking Chisholm for his forgiveness. He shook his head in a bewildered way. "The truth is I *wanted* to believe you were the kind of bastard they said you were. I *needed* to hate you—even when it didn't make sense to me. Do you think it never crossed my mind that you were wrong for the part? That you couldn't be what they said you were?"

"Yet, you never gave me the benefit of the doubt."

"No," whispered Lomax, his voice almost inaudible, "because I needed someone like you to hate. I always have . . . Ever since . . ." He left the rest unsaid. Again, he shook his head as if to clear a fog of bewilderment. "What I can't understand is why. Gilbert wasn't lying. He saw the German report they had on you. It was there in black and white. If it wasn't true, why? *Why?*"

"Do you think I haven't asked myself the same question a hundred times?" Chisholm's voice had the same tortured quality as Lomax's, but was pitched a few decibels louder. It caused the group near the desk to turn and stare in their direction, but neither man was aware of the curiosity their intense conversation was provoking.

"Gilbert was *meant* to read that report on me," Chisholm was saying. "And he was *meant* to go running back to you with it. I can see *how* it was done . . . now. But not *why*. What was the *reason?*"

"It was that goddamned place!" said Lomax softly. He seemed to be staring into distance, his mind going back. "It was that goddamned place! And that smiling bastard who ran it! Your Yank friend got one thing right: Keitler was evil."

"Maybe a damned sight more evil than I've ever given him credit for," Chisholm agreed, and frowned as his own memory took him back to St Cyr des Bains. "Maybe Rick was right about Keitler all along and I was wrong. I could never understand why Rick loathed that man quite so much as he did."

"And maybe I was wrong about the Yank, too," Lomax murmured thoughtfully. "I was wrong about you . . . I'm beginning to think I've been wrong about a hell of a lot of things. I've not only been blind, I've been goddamned stupid!" His voice rose as he made the final assertion and he stood up suddenly, like one who has just made a surprising self-discovery. Chisholm blinked up at him, a little startled by the unexpected speed of the other's movement. Lomax had shed his air of contemplative perplexity. He had an air of purpose.

"We're going to talk again in the very near future, Captain Chisholm, but right now you'll have to give me a raincheck. There are a couple of things I've got to straighten out and I'm going to come straight back to you. What room are you in?"

"One-one-five."

"I'll remember that. I'll get to you there or leave a message at the desk." He stretched out a hand, which a still startled Chisholm stood up to grip with his own. "I could spend the rest of my life apologising to you," Lomax went on, "but apologies don't mean a damned thing. I'm going to try to make amends. Then, if you feel like forgiving me for being a goddamned fool, you can."

Before Chisholm could even think of a reply, Lomax gave a final shake to his hand and turned and strode off. Chisholm saw the tall Canadian have a word with the blonde at reception and then hurry towards the lift. He glanced at the light panel indicating its movements. Then he turned away impatiently and made for the main staircase. He disappeared upstairs, taking the steps two at a time.

* * *

Chisholm recognised Anina Calvi the moment she stepped into the dining-room of the Beaumaris. The glossy photograph of her scarcely did justice to her looks. She was more strikingly attractive in the flesh: the raven-black hair an arched frame for the perfect oval of her face, the eyes dark and animated. She held herself erect but she moved across the room with a fluent grace that was feline in its languor.

She wore a white evening-dress and black matinée coat with brocade trimmings. The dress sheathed an enticing body. A red-faced waiter danced attendance upon her, hurriedly moving chairs here and there so that her progress between the closely set tables was unimpeded. Then he held a chair for her at the table of her choice. She ignored the fussing presence until, all too plainly, she dismissed him with a single imperious flash of her wide, dark eyes.

The same dark eyes now surveyed the room and the handful of early diners. They briefly met Chisholm's gaze and passed on immediately. Chisholm had intended waiting until after the concert before seeking Anina Calvi out and introducing himself. Seeing her alone, he changed his mind. He crossed to her table.

"Miss Anina Calvi?" he enquired.

He found himself scrutinised by the wide, dark eyes. There was no hint of friendliness in the scrutiny. It was clinical.

"I am Anina Calvi. Who are you?" The question was impatiently direct.

"My name is Chisholm. Look, I hope you don't mind me butting in on you like this, but I've come down specially from London to see you . . . I am a friend of a friend and I have a gift from him that he wanted you to have."

The eyes treated Chisholm to a sceptical look.

"A gift?"

"A piece of jewellery, I believe. Miss Calvi, what I have to tell you won't take a moment, but it might be easier said sitting down . . . May I? Or would you care to join me at my table?"

"That's an original line, Mr . . . Chisholm. The answer is no, you may not sit down, and no, I do not want to join you at your table. Why don't you just push off?"

Chisholm flushed.

"You don't seem to understand, Miss Calvi. I . . . I have some bad news for you. I thought it would be better if . . ."

"Mr Chisholm," she interrupted, "if you've come to tell me

that Mafeking has been relieved, I've got news for *you*. I've already heard. Now will you do as I said and just push off? I'm expecting a friend at any minute."

"I'm sorry," mumbled Chisholm. Her abrasive manner was the last thing he had expected and he was embarrassed. He was making a complete fool of himself. He fumbled in his pocket for the package containing the brooch and placed it on the table.

"All I want to do, Miss Calvi, is give you this. Rick Thomson wanted you to have it."

"Rick who?" Her look was one of disinterest rather than puzzlement.

"Lieutenant Richard Thomson, United States Army," said Chisholm.

"Never heard of him."

Chisholm winced as if he had been struck. Did this girl have so many boyfriends that she had simply lost track of Rick and had forgotten him already? Or was it possible that Rick had never actually met her? Red-faced, he said: "Lieutenant Thomson was wounded and captured at Dieppe last August. I am sorry to have to tell you that he died in captivity."

The information provoked no emotion in Anina Calvi. For all the reaction it produced, he could have been talking about the weather.

"Am I supposed to be heartbroken?" she asked.

"You obviously don't give a damn!" snapped Chisholm. He was no longer embarrassed. He was angry.

The girl picked up the package, shrugged her shoulders, and let it fall on the table again.

"Why did this Rick want me to have this?"

"I had assumed because you meant a great deal to him. He wanted you to have it if anything happened to him."

She arched her jet-black eyebrows.

"You're not a soldier . . . Are you? Where do you come into this?"

"I'm in the Merchant Navy. I lost my ship . . . Rick and I became friends in France."

She looked at him with curiosity.

"*You* were a prisoner? I don't understand. How did you get here?"

"That's a long story. Let's just say I was lucky: I got out. End of story. The point is, Miss Calvi, that I was Rick Thomson's friend and I was given to understand that you were a close friend, too – when he was stationed at Newhaven last summer. He kept your picture next to his bedside."

Anina Calvi sighed. She picked the package up again and, opening the shiny black handbag at her elbow, dropped the package inside. She snapped the bag shut.

"I'll put it with my other souvenirs," she said, and flashed her teeth in a that's-that kind of smile. "I have lots of admirers, Mr Chisholm. Half the soldiers in Sussex carry my photo around in their wallets. On every other ship from Dover to Plymouth, you'll find my face on locker doors and pinned on mess-room walls. I meet thousands of servicemen, Mr Chisholm, and I dish out photos by the hundred. I'm sorry I can't remember your friend Rick."

"Not quite so sorry as I am," said Chisholm. Her insensitivity sickened him. She didn't know Rick from Adam, but it hadn't stopped her pocketing the brooch like a dockside whore salting away an unexpected bonus. Chisholm was vaguely aware of the arrival at the table of a third person. A stiff-backed, middle-aged man in British military uniform was hovering just behind Chisholm's elbow. He had the insignia of lieutenant-colonel.

"Evening, sweetie," he announced himself. "Sorry I couldn't make it for six on the dot."

Chisholm turned to stare at a scrubbed, bland face sporting a silver moustache.

"Just going, were you, chum?" the face asked Chisholm, with meaning. Chisholm did not reply. He turned back to Anina Calvi.

"I would like to say it has been a pleasure meeting you, Miss Calvi . . . But that wouldn't be strictly true. It has been more an education." Chisholm made the tiniest inclination of his head and, turning on his heel, made his way back to his own table. The loud voice of the Colonel followed him.

"Cheeky devil! That damned civilian wasn't annoying you, darling, was he?"

Nine

The Next Man To Die

The sirloin steak was excellently cooked but Chisholm did not enjoy his dinner. His encounter with Anina Calvi had depressed him. The girl had earned a very low rating in his estimation. She had the kind of looks to stir any man but her physical attributes were cancelled out by a monstrous vanity and capricious nature that made her anything but endearing. She rated minus marks, too, for her choice of dinner escort. The man she had been with was old enough to be her father – and that alone was enough to sour Chisholm. He found it galling to think that any girl who had won Rick's admiration was of a type who pandered after sugar-daddy figures. It suggested a mercenary streak a yard wide.

Poor Rick! What could he have possibly seen in the girl? Had he been – as Vaughan had hinted – simply starstruck? A stage-door Romeo who had got no closer to the glamorous creature he idolised than a gallery seat in some theatre? It was the puzzle of what possible spell Anina Calvi could have woven on Rick that persuaded Chisholm to attend the concert in the ballroom.

He did not expect to be impressed by Anina Calvi on stage. But, albeit reluctantly, he was. Her performance was a revelation. The difference between the personality of the girl in the dining-room and that projected from a spotlit stage to a predominantly male audience was startling. Chisholm marvelled at the girl's sheer professionalism. He had heard better singing voices, but it was the way she allied the whole of her being to her husky contralto that brought a spellbinding quality to her stage artistry. Every movement of her body and limbs, every tilt of her head, every spark from those wide dark eyes contributed to the captivating intimacy she created with her audience. She was, to the servicemen packing the auditorium, no crooning replica of the girl next door – the girl next door was far, far away and forgotten – but the exotic goddess of their fantasies: a goddess shedding unreachability to betray tempestuous desires to be possessed and enslaved.

Her performance was a *tour de force*, so much so that Chisholm emerged at the end of it unable to equate the enchantress he had seen with the cold, insensitive creature whose reaction to a soldier's death had been indifference.

"Captain Chisholm!"

The sound of his name being called startled Chisholm as he made his way through the press of humanity spilling from the ballroom. He turned and, in the sea of faces, saw the upraised khaki arm waved in signal and, beneath it, the purple-red beacon that was Lieutenant Constantine's scarred countenance. The Canadian elbowed his way through the throng to Chisholm's side. He pumped Chisholm's hand, greeting him like a long-lost friend.

Eyes still beaming, he said: "The Major said you were in the hotel. I was hoping I'd run into you." He lowered his gaze and shuffled in an embarrassed kind of way. "We heard they gave you a rough time on account of us . . . I'm sorry." The eyes brightened again. "I'd like to buy you a drink. I'm not going to take no for an answer."

They found a bar corner to themselves in the cocktail lounge of the Beaumaris. Chisholm noticed how people stood back from Constantine, making space for him as if they couldn't bear too close proximity to that burned face. There would be a quick stare, an involuntary grimace and an edged retreat. Then they would keep their distance, self-consciously avoiding to look him directly in the face.

"It's all right," said Constantine, as if tuned in to Chisholm's thoughts. "I'm getting used to it now." He grinned. "I reckon I wouldn't win any beauty competitions."

Constantine had always been the friendliest of the Canadians and Chisholm felt a pang of sympathy for him now. Disfigured as he was, he had every right to feel bitter and sorry for himself – but there was no trace of self-pity in the Canadian.

"I thought you and the others would all be back in Canada now," Chisholm said.

"You forget that we're all volunteers in this man's army and that we came over here to do a job. The job's not finished."

"From what I've heard about Dieppe, I would have thought

130

that you'd all done your bit."

"We got our baptism, that's all. You don't throw that kind of experience away. You use it. Besides–" Constantine tapped a finger on his crimson cheek "–I've got a score to settle now."

"Are all of you in Brighton?" Chisholm asked.

Constantine shook his head.

"Only three of us–old Ironhead, Gilbert and myself. Martineau and Malloy were sent back to what was left of their outfits. They're trying to piece the Division together again and their mob has been re-training at Aldershot." Constantine's scarred face bunched into a frown. "I don't suppose you heard about Malloy?"

Chisholm's blank response was answer enough. Constantine enlightened him.

"The poor devil went completely bananas. They'll be shipping *him* back home–in a straitjacket!"

"Malloy? But . . ." Chisholm's surprise was tinged with horror and, more, an element of fellow-feeling for the unfortunate corporal. Still vivid in his own mind was his knowledge of what it was like to be branded insane. The odd thing was, too, that Malloy had never struck him as being unstable. He remembered the Corporal as a surly individual, with a mocking impudent way about him, but far from being a candidate for the madhouse. Indeed, he had been possibly the fittest and strongest of the six escapers, with no outward sign of whatever wounds had landed him at St Cyr des Bains.

"What happened to him?" Chisholm asked Constantine.

"He just flipped his lid. It was on the tank range at Aldershot. The minute the guns started to go bang, he just went crazy. It took six men to get him under control."

Chisholm gave a sad shake to his head.

"I can't say I ever liked him much. Civility was never his strong point. But he had all his wits about him . . ."

"He cracked before," said Constantine. "It must have always been on the cards that he would crack again."

Constantine stared at Chisholm in surprise when it became plain to him that the sea captain knew nothing of Malloy's history. The Corporal, it transpired, had been one of Keitler's prize patients.

"Didn't you know that Malloy was one of Keitler's miracles?" the Canadian asked. "He was always boasting what he did for Malloy."

It was news to Chisholm. He confessed he did not even know why Malloy had been hospitalised in the first place. So, Constantine told him.

Malloy had been found huddled on the beach at Dieppe in a state of total shock. He had been so traumatised that his power of speech had gone. He had been little more than a shuffling idiot when, finally, he had been taken to St Cyr des Bains and put in Keitler's care. Keitler had subjected him to some kind of electric shock therapy and, one day, Malloy's speech had returned as dramatically as it had gone. He had retained no memory of Dieppe, however, other than recalling that the landing-craft taking him ashore had been sunk and he had been thrown into the water.

"Poor devil!" Chisholm echoed the comment that Constantine had used some moments before. "I had no idea. There was no way of telling just by looking at him. He seemed so fit compared with everyone else."

"You looked in pretty good shape to us, too," Constantine reminded him. "If I remember right, you needed a shave – but you were all in one piece. Lomax was convinced you were a German plant. You know he ordered us to give you a wide berth?"

Chisholm nodded grimly.

"Captain . . . I mean, Major Lomax . . . had his reasons. How about you? Did you think I was a German plant?"

Constantine's lipless mouth twisted into a grinning shape. He gave a soft laugh.

"If I had thought you were a German plant, I would have killed you," he said. He was not joking. If Chisholm harboured any doubts, they scattered before the steady gaze in the Canadian's ice-blue eyes. Constantine had meant exactly what he said.

"I'm glad I got the benefit of the doubt," Chisholm murmured. Again, the Canadian gave a soft laugh.

"I like to keep an open mind. If drastic action is called for, I have to be absolutely sure. I was never quite sure what to make of you. You weren't skulky enough to be spying for Keitler. You're all on the surface, too open. I don't think you could be devious if you tried."

Chisholm made a face.

"I suppose that's a compliment?"

"Not necessarily. You can be honest to a fault. People can

use you without you ever realising that you're being used. The thought did occur to me that Keitler was using you."

"I seem to recall him telling me just what you've told me . . . Something about being too open for my own good."

"He would know. Now, there's a man who really was devious. Clever, too. But vain. Too vain. Look at the way he boasted about Malloy."

"Not to me," said Chisholm. "The first I heard about Malloy was from you a few minutes ago."

"Then you were lucky. Keitler never stopped boasting to us about the miracle he performed on Malloy . . . How he made him whole again and restored his power of speech. Well, it wasn't so much of a miracle after all, was it? The first time the poor guy hears the guns go bang, he goes completely out of his skull."

The crowd in the cocktail bar of the Beaumaris thinned as the strains of music drifted along from the ballroom; signifying that the chairs had been cleared away from the floor area and the dance was beginning. Constantine, with a wry remark to Chisholm about girls running a mile from the sight of his face, made it plain that dancing was a pleasure he intended to forego. He seemed pleased that Chisholm showed no inclination to forsake the bar for the dance-floor. They remained where they were, talking.

Like Lomax, Constantine seemed to have it on his conscience that what he had told the interrogators at the London Transit Camp had resulted in Chisholm being given a bad time. The rumour had circulated that Chisholm had been whisked off to Brixton Prison.

"I'm sorry if we landed you in the mire," Constantine tried to apologise, "but they put us on the spot. I couldn't get out of telling them exactly how things were in that pig-pen at St Cyr. These guys were real thorough. They wanted to know everything, but everything – from the colour of Keitler's eyes to the mess they dished up for breakfast on Sunday mornings. And they wanted to know all about you, Captain. They always got back to you."

"They were doing their job", said Chisholm, manfully resisting a more bitter comment. Constantine was less restrained.

"It's the way the bastards go about it. They keep twisting your words, trying to trip you up. I kept losing my temper with one guy." He gave a snort of disgust. "You get yourself fried for King and country and then these bastards grill you until you feel like a goddamned thief!" His own choice of words stopped him short. He grinned suddenly in his grotesque way. "Hey – fried and grilled! What am I saying? That makes me a real pork chop!"

His amusement forced a smile from Chisholm in response. The smile died, half-formed, as his eye caught the glamorous gowned figure of Anina Calvi framed for a moment in the doorway. She paused only momentarily and then moved toward the bar. She came straight towards Chisholm.

"Mr Chisholm, I didn't know you were a friend of Lieutenant Constantine's." She trilled the words out pleasantly. She was all smiles, no trace of the bitchiness he had glimpsed earlier in the evening. Chisholm found himself strangely tongue-tied. He flung a desperate help-me look at Constantine.

The Canadian was grinning more widely than ever.

"Hey, I didn't know you two were old friends!"

"Not quite old friends," Chisholm corrected him. "Miss Calvi and I met for the first time this evening."

"And I made a very bad impression," the girl put in, with a flashing smile that was for Chisholm alone. "I was all tensed up for the concert and I had that boring ass, Teddy Green, as a dinner date. I'm afraid I was unforgivably rude to Mr Chisholm."

Chisholm made no attempt to contradict her. He was not yet ready to forgive. But the force of that smile was disarming. He found himself asking her with studied politeness if he could get her a drink, as the bar was about to close.

She said she would love a drink and asked for a glass of Algerian red wine by name. The choice surprised him, as did his discovery that the bar stocked the wine. She was clearly no stranger to the Beaumaris. As he ordered up two more whiskies and soda for Constantine and himself, the Canadian led Anina Calvi to a vacant table.

Whatever Constantine's misgivings about the effect of his scarred face on the opposite sex, he seemed totally at ease in Anina Calvi's company. She, in turn, showed no sign of being repelled by the flaming ugliness of his features. The pair were deep in animated conversation when Chisholm arrived with the drinks. Anina Calvi broke off to welcome Chisholm with another dazzling smile.

134

"You did not tell me you were a hero," she said to Chisholm, her wide eyes faintly reproachful. "Paul here has been telling me that he owes his life to you."

"Then he has been talking out of school, and exaggerating," said Chisholm, placing the glasses on the table. "Don't believe a word he says."

"Oh, you men!" Anina pretended exasperation. "You're so tight-lipped about everything. First, Paul tells me that you saved his life. Then, he says he's not allowed to tell me where or how. Now, you're trying to make out that it was nothing at all. Are you going to get a medal, too? Paul says he can't even remember what it was he did to deserve his. Isn't that right, Paul?"

Constantine was laughing.

"It's the truth. They probably mixed me up with somebody else."

"Dieppe?" asked Chisholm.

The Canadian shrugged modestly.

"Yeah. I reckon they must have drawn the names out of a hat. My lot were more or less wiped out so there sure as hell weren't any witnesses. The citation could refer to a hundred other guys besides me. They just pulled my name out for a Military Cross. Posthumous at that. They didn't expect me back to collect the gong."

"Congratulations anyway," said Chisholm.

"Aw, bullshit," said Constantine, embarrassed. His embarrassment increased when he realised that his spontaneous comment was less than appropriate in mixed company. He apologised profusely to Anina Calvi, who was amused and in no way upset.

Constantine surprised Chisholm then by leaving him alone with Anina Calvi. He insisted that he should go and find both Lomax and Gilbert. He talked of making a real party of it and hinted that the Canadians' mess, in another part of the hotel, could be a lively place. It was not governed by silly English licensing laws. He seemed, all of a sudden, just a little bit drunk. The realisation struck Chisholm that his own state of unworried well-being – a complete absence of care about past or future events – was due almost entirely to having stowed away more liquor in one evening than in the previous twelve months.

He was, nonetheless, a little dismayed by Constantine's

sudden departure. After that first off-putting encounter with Anina Calvi, he had no relish to be left alone with her. Indeed, the temptation was strong to make some excuse and extract himself from the situation in which he found himself.

A number of things conspired against any such drastic action. The girl's performance on stage had had a strangely erosive effect on the antipathy he felt towards her. Her own eagerness to erase the bad impression she had created continued the process. It was completed by the congenialising effect of several whiskies. He was mellowed by their lingering glow. There was no harm in being civil.

But even his intention, to retain a certain aloofness while being civil, was slowly but surely dissipating as time wore on and Constantine did not return. Mentally, Chisholm started making excuses to himself for the Anina Calvi he had glimpsed at dinner. He really should not have thrust himself on her uninvited, the way he had. And could he really blame her for not remembering Rick if, as seemed likely, he was just another face in a crowd for whom she had autographed photos? It occurred to him that if he were to blame anyone for what had happened, he should reserve his anger for Vaughan or Hibberd, who were responsible for involving him, not this girl.

The more Chisholm talked with Anina Calvi, the greater became the ease with which he forgot his reasons for wanting to dislike her. More so, when it became abundantly clear that her attitude towards Rick's gift had undergone a complete change during the course of the evening.

Sipping her red wine, her wide dark eyes heavy with unhappiness, she said that she could not possibly keep the gift. It was not the worthless trinket she had, at first, taken it to be; but a beautifully fashioned brooch with real diamonds and set in platinum. More a lover's gift than a token from an unknown admirer. She had no right to such a precious gift. She was unworthy of it.

Tears sparkled in her eyes as she spoke of the dilemma in which the totally unexpected gift had placed her.

"Tell me what I must do," she pleaded softly with Chisholm. He was nonplussed.

"He wanted you to have the brooch. Is that not reason enough for keeping it?"

His answer did not satisfy her. She shook her head vehemently.

136

"No—don't you understand? He was a stranger. One I'm sorry now I didn't know. But I didn't know him. You saw . . . at dinner . . . I couldn't even remember his name. I'd feel guilty about it for the rest of my life if I just took his brooch . . . Knowing that, in a way, he loved me, wanted me even . . . And I didn't know he existed . . . I returned the feelings he had . . . with nothing. Don't you see I want to do something in return now . . . Something for him . . . Something that will give his gift meaning for me?"

Chisholm could not argue with the solution which, she became convinced, was the one she should accept. She was due to sing in the near future at a big function to raise money for war orphans. Her decision was that she would donate the brooch to a special auction of gifts being organised by a film star to swell the funds.

If Chisholm had voluntarily erected any barriers between himself and Anina Calvi, they melted away in the happy afterglow of her decision about the brooch. Having come to terms with her troubled conscience, she radiated an infectious joy. And if, earlier, Chisholm had found her wide expressive eyes easily resistible, that ceased to be the case when he and he alone became the object of all their warmth and vitality. She did not equivocate about her change of mood and heart. She blamed herself for their bad beginning and it made her unhappy. Now, she wanted no bad feeling between them. It mattered to her that they become friends. Shyly, she admitted that part of the reason she had reacted in rather prickly fashion to Chisholm at dinner was because she found him a rather attractive man and he had caught her off-guard. It was purely a defensive mechanism and a terrible failing, especially if she felt she had been caught at a disadvantage. The more attractive the man, the worse was the impression she usually managed to give.

Chisholm was flattered that anyone so vitally feminine and sexually enchanting should tell him to his face that he was attractive but he basked in the attention she lavished on his every utterance. She contrived to make him feel that the universe did not extend beyond the surrounding tables and that he was the sun at its centre.

The lounge emptied and the barman closed the bar without Chisholm being more than vaguely aware of it. Nor did it bother him that Constantine seemed to have been gone a long time. Desires that had been subdued within him for far too long were beginning to leap in his mind like volcanic sparks. The circumstances of his meeting with Anina Calvi, the reasons for the pair of them chatting away like old friends in an empty hotel lounge, the chances of them ever meeting again, all began to lose significance to one fact that grew like a mountain and overshadowed all else. He was a man who needed a woman. The need was like a physical pain, and his awareness of it was a torture that intensified with every intimate glance of her eyes and each delicate tremble of her thrusting breasts.

Their conversation did not stray across forbidden frontiers. It was confined to exploratory probes: searching, seeking and often finding areas of exciting compatibility. They exchanged fragmentary details of the paths their lives had taken to this crossing of the ways.

Chisholm delighted her with vivid cameos from his nomadic journeyings. They were not only rich in colour but, in their telling, revealed the nature of the man. Like all good story-tellers, he carried self-depreciation to an art: never casting himself as the hero but, more usually, as the innocent who survived to smile at his own follies.

Anina Calvi, in turn, revealed a colourful enough background of her own. She was Argentinian by birth, with Italian, Spanish, English and Welsh blood in her veins. The blood mixture was rich enough – blue in places, with three separate aristocratic lines merging in as many generations. She had been born to wealth and made no pretence of not enjoying the advantages it brought her.

The family estancia on the banks of the Tigre near Buenos Aires boasted thirty-six rooms and a dozen servants. In spite of an Italian grandfather, the family was essentially British by tradition and identification and her parents were prominent members of the British Community

In 1939, her brother had shipped immediately to Britain to join the Royal Navy. He had been killed at Narvik.

Anina had left home in 1941, to study music in Madrid. At the time, she had hoped to become a concert cellist. In her own words, however, the virtuosi of that instrument had nothing to fear from her as a rival. She had dismayed her family by quitting her studies and working in night-clubs as a singer. After a disastrous love affair, she had made her way to London where she found work as a translator: doing jobs for the Spanish

Embassy and a publisher friend of her father's. She also found she was in demand as a singer, without ever seeking to make a career of it. It had all started at a party where an impromptu performance had taken a trick and led to a flood of invitations to work professionally.

"You were terrific tonight," Chisholm told her. "Do you realise that I went to that concert tonight determined to be unimpressed. But you bowled me over – me and every other man in the place. I would have given you a hundred to one at seven o'clock tonight that if anybody would be on their feet clapping and shouting for more, it wouldn't be me – but I was. I came, I saw, and was conquered."

The admission pleased her.

"So, you were impressed?"

"Impressed is the wrong word. Bewitched is nearer the truth. When you sang 'All of Me', I wondered what on earth I ever saw in the Al Bowly record. You gave it something that really got me. I forgot that there were a couple of hundred other blokes in that hall . . . You could have been singing it just for me."

Her eyes twinkled.

"But I was," she said.

"Now, you're teasing me."

"Does it hurt?"

"In a deliciously pleasant way."

"Do you realise we are the only two people left in here?"

He glanced around the empty cocktail lounge. From some way off came the steady thump of a bass drum.

"Everybody must be tripping the light fantastic," he said. "Do you want to move?"

"No. We're just getting to know each other and I'm happy. Two's company. Do you think that Paul has forgotten all about us?"

"I don't really care. Not when we're just getting to know each other."

"Now, you're teasing me."

"Does it hurt?"

"Unbearably."

He was hunched across the table looking directly at her. She leaned towards him, returning his stare steadily with eyes that smiled, until their faces almost touched. Then she kissed him softly on the lips. It was a brief contact. Her face retreated from his again, the eyes still mischievously alight.

"Now you know something else about me," she murmured. "I'm not shy."

Chisholm's longing for her was like a bomb ticking inside him, ready to explode. The kiss and the look in her eyes had the effect of a blow-torch applied to a very short fuse. But the bomb did not go off. Constantine chose that precise moment to return. If the Canadian noticed the rapt intimacy he was interrupting, he elected to pretend otherwise. He purported to be much more concerned about the party he had been wanting to organise and the fact that his failure to do so would cause Chisholm and Anina immense disappointment.

"Look, folks, I'm sorry," he apologised, "but we're just going to have to forget it. I can't find Raoul or the Major anywhere and our Mess is like a morgue. They closed the bar early on account of the dance. There's stuff left there to make coffee or tea and I could rustle up some digestive biscuits . . . But who the hell wants to celebrate on goddamned tea and biscuits!"

Chisholm had no more enthusiasm for tea and biscuits than, at that moment, he had for Constantine's company. He had other things on his mind and Constantine did not figure in them at all. He almost grinned his relief when the Canadian said rather sheepishly: "Would you two mind it a whole lot if I just said goodnight and faded out of the picture? I've been on my feet since five in the morning and I'm so goddamned tired that I'm liable to pass out on you if I don't get the weight off my legs. I really am bushed."

He got no arguments to detain him.

"That's what I call a diplomat," Chisholm observed after Constantine had said his goodnights and departed, leaving the twin doors swinging gently on their hinges in his wake. Chisholm and Anina had risen to say their farewells to the Canadian and they were now standing in the middle of the empty lounge. Chisholm turned the girl to face him and said: "Now, what was that you were saying about not being shy?"

She looked up at him, eyes glinting with amusement. He needed no further encouragement. Pulling her into his arms, he kissed her with a passion born of long hunger. Their tongues met and twined. Their thighs touched to explode sparking currents of quivering sensation.

When they broke apart, they were breathless. He could still feel the tremble of her body against his. He was dizzy with

140

desire for her; scarcely daring to move or attempt to speak in case the heady wonder of it was a dream of acute fragility. He thought it must be when she suddenly drew back from him and turned away, reaching for a little matinée bag that lay discarded at their table. His sense of loss was momentary for, as quickly as she had withdrawn from his embrace, she was back in his arms: arching her body shamelessly into his and seeking his mouth eagerly with hers.

Without relaxation of the intensity of her kiss, her right hand sought out his left: prising it gently away from the curving hollow where her slim waist merged with the firm fleshy bulge of her hips. She pressed something into his open hand but it was not until she relented in the tongue-searching ardour of her kiss that he realised what the object was.

"Give me fifteen minutes. I'll be waiting for you."

She murmured the words and shivered out of his embrace with a wriggle of her shapely shoulders. Then she was gone. He watched the slowly dying movements of the panelled doors through which she had passed. Their back and forward motion became weaker and eventually stopped.

Chisholm opened his hand and looked down at the hotel-room key and attached number disc that lay in his palm. In the distance, the dance-band's bass drum was still throbbing out its resonant beat. Its unchanging rhythm was lethargic and dull compared with the thunder in his ears of his own heartbeat.

She was sitting combing her hair, her back to him, when he let himself into the room only five doors away from his own. Unloosed, her raven-dark hair fell in a tumble almost to her waist. She brushed it with slow sensuous strokes, a smile playing on her lips as their eyes met in the mirror.

"You're not frightened of me, are you?" she teased. "You look scared."

"I'm scared I'll wake up. You are real, aren't you? Or am I dreaming this?"

She put the brush on the dressing-table and, rising, she turned to face him.

"Why don't you touch me and find out?"

The full-length négligé she wore was unfastened, hanging loosely and giving her glimpsed nakedness a tantalising quality. Bare half-moons of breast showed: their twin halves hid coyly behind curtains of lace. Her belly was firm and flat above the dark triangle of hair where her long straight legs flowed with curving symmetry into the willowy sweep of her body.

"You're the most beautiful creature I've ever seen," he blurted out.

She gave an elegant little shake of the shoulders and the négligé fluttered to her ankles. She stepped out of it and, with the grace of a ballerina taking a curtain call, she extended one arm high and executed a flourish with the other: completing the movement with a combination of bow and curtsy.

"*Voilà!*" she called softly. "You said you liked 'All of Me'. Now, you see all of me." She gave a throaty chuckle. "I warned you that I was not shy. Are you?"

"No," he managed to say. The word came out as a croak.

She came towards him then and he allowed her to assist his undress as his own hands fumbled with stubborn buttons. She gentled his haste, contriving at the same time to let her cool fingers linger on his flesh and send exquisite tremors shivering through his body.

Her lack of shyness out of bed was matched by her lack of inhibition in it. There was nothing virginal about her love-making. She seemed to have infinite insights into the art of rousing the fiercest bodily pleasures and prolonging their ecstasy through near unendurable peaks. She used her body and his with the abandon and willing joy of a houri dedicated to the provision of every refinement of sexual gratification.

Chisholm's first thrusting union with her was over-hasty and clumsy: a consequence perhaps of many months of long, rather than voluntary, celibacy. But she concealed any disappointment she might have felt. Instead, she was extravagant in her encouragement and cried out with writhing pleasure at the ferocity of his penetration and the stamina he showed. He began to believe it when her eager mouth and hands stimulated him to fresh endeavours that drew from her squeals of shuddering passion.

Their bouts of coupling were punctuated by intervals of happy somnolence and conversational exploration. She teased him into telling why he had survived for more than thirty years without being lured into marriage. He laughed but told her the truth. His life had simply never allowed him to let him get to know any girl long enough. Perhaps, if he had been on regular runs between the same ports, it might have been different. But most of his life had been on tramp ships: travelling anywhere that cargoes were available and seldom visiting the same place twice.

She saddened him by speculating that he and she were like ships that passed in the night. Having found her, he did not want to want to believe that it was all going to end with the morning light. But she did not encourage him to contemplate a relationship that would survive the dawn. She ended talk of it — and his dismay at the prospect — by snuggling close to him and rousing his physical desire to new heights: excluding all care and thought of what the morning might bring.

The frenzy over, she lay back with a groan of animal pleasure.

"Oh, my sweet Chizz," she sighed, "you are a tiger. Was it as good for you as it was for me?"

"You know it was," he murmured sleepily. "I didn't know it could be like this . . . One long thrill . . . like a roller-coaster that goes on and on . . . All the way to heaven."

She laughed softly.

"A roller-coaster! A shilling a ride?"

"I didn't mean it like that, you minx. It was a compliment. When I was younger, a trip on a roller-coaster was the biggest thrill in the world. Now, I know better but even when I first went to sea I was mad about them. Every place we went, I would walk for miles just to try a new one."

"You preferred them to girls?"

"I was an innocent. I still am."

"Liar!" She laughed.

Chisholm smiled to himself in the dark. He still had roller-coasters on his mind and was thinking of his first visit as a young apprentice to Anina's native city of Buenos Aires.

"Did you ever go to Retiro Park?"

"Where?"

"Retiro Park."

"One park is pretty much like the next one. I've never heard of that one."

"But you must have, Anina. Retiro Park in Buenos Aires."

"Don't know it," she said, lazily indifferent. "There are dozens of parks in Buenos Aires. Just like London."

Her reaction puzzled Chisholm. He had not meant just any kind of park, like Hyde Park or Regent's Park. He had been talking about Retiro Park with it super-colossal roller-coaster: arguably the biggest funfair in the Southern Hemisphere, if not the world. He would have pursued the subject further but it was forgotten as a soft hand insinuated itself between his legs and began to stroke the flesh of his thigh. His flagging senses prickled to life. He caught his breath sharply. The rapidity of his arousal surprised him, as the appetite of the girl beside him amazed him. He slid a hand of his own across her body and over a smooth hillock of breast. A proud nipple hardened under his touch and she sighed. Chisholm suspended further astonishment at his own powers of durability and surrendered himself to the immediate joys of possessing and being possessed.

It was still dark when he awoke with a start. Anina was deep in sleep, one arm draped languidly across his stomach. Somewhere in the depths of the hotel, there were noises of activity: a door banging shut, the clank of a bucket on a stone floor.

Chisholm peered at the luminous dial of his watch on the bedside table. It was 6.30. He got up without disturbing the sleeping girl and groped round the room for his clothes. Dressed, he bent over the bed and brushed the sleeping girl's cheek with his lips. She stirred slightly and settled once more into steady rhythmic breathing.

"See you at breakfast," Chisholm whispered softly. He tiptoed from the room and stole along the corridor to his own room. Fumbling with the key, he could not get it to turn in the lock. Then, with surprise, he discovered the reason. The door was not locked. He smiled ruefully. So much for the haste he had been in to get into Anina Calvi's bed! He must have been in too much of a hurry to put down the catch on the lock the night before.

He switched on the light and took a few steps into the room. He stopped abruptly in mid-stride, giving a soft cry of shock that leapt involuntarily from his throat.

Slumped in the blue cane armchair near the window was the khaki-uniformed body of Major Lomax. His head hung to one side, the eyes wide open and staring grotesquely.

Chisholm did not need to touch him to know that he was looking at a corpse.

Ten

A Man Called Thorn

Lieutenant Calvin T. Thorn looked at his watch for the fortieth time since 5 a.m. and decided he was crazy. Upstairs, there was a warm bed lying empty and he, voluntarily, had spent the night in the lobby lounge of the Beaumaris Hotel.

He could easily have pulled rank on Sergeant Weaver and let him do the night shift but, unaccountably restless at midnight, he had told Weaver to get some sleep while he stuck around in the lobby for a spell. He had remained there all night. The night was really his time; when he came alive.

As a young cop in New York – long before he joined the plain clothes detail as a detective – he had acquired a taste for being one of the night people. There was something about working the city in the hours before dawn that the day people could never appreciate. Something that tickled the old adrenalin button and gave the night hawk a feeling of superiority. It came perhaps from a sense of looking after the world while the great mass of humanity slept.

Brighton, however – and the lobby of the Beaumaris – was not quite in New York's league for stimulating the senses. New York had exciting vibrations that never stopped. The city dosed fitfully, rather than slept. When midnight struck, Brighton went into deep coma.

Thorn fingered the stubble on his chin and asked himself for the umpteenth time what he could conceivably have imagined would happen in the Beaumaris Hotel that was worth the loss of a night's sleep. Clearly, he had an excessive devotion to duty. Nothing was going to happen. Nothing ever did on surveillance work. Not unless you sloped off for a cup of coffee or took five minutes off to visit the john.

He supposed that that was the real reason he had never gone

to bed: the fear that if he turned his back for one minute, all hell would break loose.

It needled Thorn now that, of all the assignments that had come his way as a Military Intelligence Department officer, this one had excited him more than any other. His briefing had been intensive and Major Hibberd had led him to believe that it was to be a whole lot more than an ordinary surveillance job. There would be ceaseless watching and waiting, yes, but his role was to be more than passive observer. Hibberd had expected something to happen – he couldn't say what – and, when it did, he hoped Thorn would recognise it as a signal to act. It was a matter for Thorn's judgement to choose the moment when his intervention was necessary.

"We don't want somebody getting killed and we don't want the civil police butting in," Hibberd had said. "You've got to be ready to jump in and control things before they get out of hand."

It both excited Thorn and alarmed him that this part of his brief was so vague. He was being trusted to dispense with his cover and use his initiative – but not until the precise moment when, in his own judgement, there occurred a development that warranted it. This gave Thorn the opportunity to do the wrong thing, no matter what he did. If he acted prematurely, he could screw the whole thing up. If he didn't act or left it too late, Hibberd would have his head on a plate.

Still, it made a change from most of the assignments that had come Thorn's way in wartime Britain. These had been anti-climactic, to say the least: investigations of smoke that had turned out to reveal not only no fire but no trace of smoke.

Already, Thorn had developed a strong, almost affectionate affinity for the man whose footsteps he had faithfully dogged for more than a week. It was enhanced by the fact that his quarry seemed not to have the slightest suspicion of being watched. Knowing Chisholm's history helped, too.

"He's a nice but rather naive guy and I hate having to use him as bait," Hibberd had told Thorn, briefing him for the Brighton diversion, "but this is a long shot and we need to try for every long shot we've got."

"You're sure he's clean?" Thorn had asked.

"We're banking on it. The Krauts have tied a patsy label round his neck. They fingered him for us – and they sure as hell are not going to finger their own man. That means that some of the company this guy Chisholm used to keep may not be just as clean as they seem to be."

"One of the Canadians? One of the guys who got out of France with him?"

"I know it's crazy, but that's the way it looks. That's what's so baffling about this goddamned mess. The Krauts want us to think Chisholm sold out to them. Why? The answer must be that they're trying to protect the guy they really turned – one of the Canadians. One of five heroes who have all been given a clean bill of health."

"Couldn't they be re-interrogated?"

"They have been. And we came up with the same answers. No, Lieutenant, if there's a traitor in this little woodpile, we're going to have to flush him out."

"What if there isn't a traitor? What if they really are all clean?"

"Then the Krauts will be laughing all over their faces and we'll have egg all over ours. Maybe this is all one great big waste of time. But we've got to be sure one way or the other. It depends on how you handle it. You're the one who's got to find out!"

"Where does the Calvi girl fit in?" Thorn had wanted to know.

"Ah, now there's an interesting little parcel of goods that needs careful handling," Hibberd had said, and had filled in the known facts on Anina Calvi as supplied by Brockway. The girl had come under Brockway's scrutiny in the summer of 1942 because of a relatively minor security breach by a Canadian officer: no more than an indiscreet remark about Canadian army morale that had somehow reached German ears and been quoted in a propaganda broadcast. Brockway had been alarmed by the fact that Anina Calvi had been a frequent dinner companion of the officer concerned and that she seemed to be acquainted with a very large number of officers in Southern Command. If she was passing information to the Germans, she had access to military indiscretion on a dangerously grand scale.

The girl's foreign-sounding name might alone have started Brockway's moustache-tips quivering like sensitive antennae. Little escaped his suspicion. He had gone into her background thoroughly, his senses going on red alert when he discovered that Anina Calvi did translation work for the Spanish Embassy and, feasibly, had the means of transmitting information to Germany via her diplomat friends.

But, in spite of her foreign name, alien birth, and associations with a Fascist government, Anina Calvi had come out whiter than the driven snow from the security check Brockway had ordered. Her family in Argentina were openly pro-British and had proved their support in countless ways. The Foreign Office had been outraged by Brockway's inquiries and senior officials there had been prepared to stake their careers by taking up cudgels on behalf of the Calvi clan, whose loyalty to the British cause was – in their view – beyond dispute. As for the girl herself, she had worked tirelessly as an entertainer and done a magnificent job for the armed forces. There was not a shred of evidence that she was motivated by anything other than the strongest devotion to Britain, as – it was pointed out – her brother had been. And he had given his life to Britain. Brockway had also discovered that Anina Calvi had friends in high places who were not above using their influence to make life awkward for "prying busybodies", as a senior civil servant described him. Brockway was warned several times about getting his fingers burnt if he persisted in his "stupid vendetta against a defenceless young woman of flawless character". Finally, he was ordered to drop the case.

Brockway had done as he was told. But he had never closed the file on Anina Calvi. Indeed, after the débâcle of Dieppe, with its catastrophic loss of Canadian lives, the file on the Argentinian-born singer was one of several "open" files to which he returned again and again: convinced that someone had passed advanced details of the operation to the Germans.

When a photograph of Anina Calvi had been found among the American Rick Thomson's personal effects and it emerged that the girl had previously been acquainted with some of the Canadian escapers from St Cyr des Bains, Brockway had been unable to resist the temptation to exploit matters in his own way. It was not his fashion to sit and wait for events to prove him right or wrong. Sometimes they needed a judicious nudge.

The clock above the reception desk was at 6.37 when he decided he had had enough. Weaver could take over the lobby watch while he snatched a couple of hours' sleep. Thorn moved stiffly towards the lift with the weariness of someone twice his thirty-one years. He pushed the call button and waited. There was the quick hum of powered mechanism and metallic disengagement of locking gear as the cab began its slow descent from the floor above. When the doors opened, Thorn found himself staring with some shock at the body of Major Lomax.

A shout brought the night porter scurrying from his glass sanctuary. Together, they carried Lomax out into the lobby. Thorn's mind was in a turmoil. There was no visible sign of injury on Lomax. How had he died? His skin was ice-cold to the touch and the pallor of this face had a grey-green tinge as if the process of atrophy had already begun. Had he been lying dead in the elevator for half the night? No, impossible. The night porter had used the elevator several times and, most recently, less than a half-hour before. Did that mean that someone had, even more recently, dumped the body in the lift? It was wrong, perhaps, to have moved the body but impractical to have left it where it was – so, Thorn had no qualms on that score. He had, in any case, made a cursory scrutiny that was still expert enough to have impressed all the details indelibly on his mind. The left shoe, for instance. It had slipped, half off the dead man's foot: suggesting that he might have been dragged to the elevator.

It was the night porter who revealed to Thorn that one of the Canadian officers billeted in the north wing was a doctor. Only two evenings ago, he had helped with an elderly woman who had collapsed on the lobby. Thorn sent the porter to fetch the doctor and used the time to make a quick examination of Lomax's pockets: not knowing what he hoped he might find that would make him any wiser on how the Canadian had died or how he had got in the elevator.

The doctor arrived in pyjamas with an army warm pulled over the top. He probed and peered at the dead man's eyes before closing the lids. He was non-committal about any conclusions he may have reached at the end of his swift examination: fending off Thorn's questions and clearly resenting the curiosity of an American officer who had no right to be so inquisitive.

"I'll take over here," he told Thorn. "There's really nothing to keep you now."

Thorn was tempted to show him his special service ID and let the doctor know that his curiosity was official, but he decided against it. He shrugged good-naturedly.

"I didn't mean to be nosy, Doc. You find a dead guy in an elevator, you wonder things. I thought the poor guy had been murdered."

The doctor's stiff little smile was deprecatory.

"I think we shall find that the Major died a natural death. Or, more correctly, from the after-effects of wounds he suffered on active service. He really should have been invalided out of the service but that's easier said than done with guys as tough as Major Lomax." The doctor shook his head sadly. "He knew better than anyone that the end could come quickly . . . Not as soon as this . . . But the risk was always there."

He excused himself brusquely and went off to arrange for an ambulance to remove Lomax's body. Thorn stared for a final moment at the blanket-draped corpse. Was this the kind of outcome that the bright boys in charge of "Operation Thumbscrew" had reckoned on? Or was it just an unfortunate coincidence that one of the principal figures in their complicated scenario should drop down dead? Thorn had the suspicion that the possibility of Lomax's death was something that had not crossed the minds of Hibberd or Brockway and news of it was going to come as an unpleasant shock. As for the coincidence factor, Thorn did not go a bundle on coincidences. Neither big ones nor little ones. Somewhere, there was a connection between the mysteries of St Cyr des Bains and the sudden death of a Canadian major in a Brighton hotel – and Calvin T. Thorn was determined to find it. Whether or not Major Hibberd and company were likely to agree with his timing or not, Thorn came to the decision that it was time he stopped hiding behind pillars. That wasn't how he had won four commendations as a young detective on Homicide. It was time he dealt himself into the action.

Until he had found Lomax dead in his room, coincidence was not a subject to which Chisholm had given lengthy thought. He knew that coincidences did occur from time to time and could be mind-boggling in the intricacy of myriad factors governing their occurrence. Lightning *could* strike in the same place twice. Perhaps even *three* times.

The time to sit up and take notice was when lightning visited the same victim not twice or thrice but with a regularity that far out-scored the likelihoods of chance. Where a pattern developed, coincidence went out the window. And where there was a pattern, *there had to be an explanation*.

The discovery of Lomax's body had visited Chisholm with

the kind of shock not inconsistent with the stark realisation that lightning had struck in his vicinity once too often for the phenomenon to be the indiscriminate workings of chance. He could not bring himself to believe that Lomax had simply walked into his room and dropped down dead in so inconsiderate a manner that the circumstances could not have been better designed to direct further suspicion and calumny like an avalanche on Chisholm's head.

But, if it was not chance, if it was no accident, who or what was responsible? Why was he being singled out so implacably that he could sense but not see the web of evil that held him like a fly? The agencies at work were unseen but they were human agencies. Dead men do not walk into untenanted hotel rooms. *Someone* had carried Lomax into his room and *someone* had had to borrow or steal a key – perhaps a chambermaid's – to get entry. But *who*? And *why*?

Chisholm sat for long enough staring at Lomax's body; trying not to panic and yet paralysed by indecision. He knew that he should telephone reception and report his discovery. He knew a doctor should be summoned, and possibly the police, too. But he could not bring himself to do what he knew to be the correct and law-abiding things he should do – because he knew only too well to what he would be exposing himself by doing the right things. There would be the questions: questions he was unable to answer and questions he would not want to answer. Could he involve Anina? Not voluntarily. The nightmare possibility of more interrogation and an inability to offer convincing explanations terrified him.

What could he say about his knowledge of Lomax's head injury and the man's vulnerability to sudden death? Someone else had known about that vulnerability but it wouldn't be someone else they accused of manslaughter. His one merciful stroke of luck was that he had returned to his room and found the body himself. What if one of the hotel staff had beaten him to it? He shuddered to think of the implications.

Chisholm forced himself to consider the problem calmly. If, as he was certain, someone had deliberately planted the Canadian officer in his room in a calculated attempt to burden him with a mountain of awkward explanations, why shouldn't he frustrate his unknown enemy's calculations by removing the corpse to a less incriminating location?

His mind made up, Chisholm checked a second time to

151

ascertain that the Canadian showed no outward sign of physical injury. There was none that he could see. It was likely then that Lomax *had* died from some form of over-excitement, just as Keitler had warned Chisholm might happen. Well, no one was going to accuse Hector Chisholm of provoking the fatal rise in Lomax's blood pressure. He had been otherwise engaged: working up unprecedented extremes in his own blood heat that were now all but forgotten.

Making sure that the corridor was empty, Chisholm manhandled Lomax's dead weight along to the lift-shaft. He depressed the call button and underwent agonies of anxiety at the age the cab took to make the short ascent from the lobby. The doors jerked open with what seemed a fearful noise and he bundled the body inside. A shoe came half off Lomax's foot in the process but Chisholm was beyond caring about such a detail. His one care was to get back to his room as quickly as possible without being seen. He had almost reached his door when the lift doors shuddered together automatically.

Inside his room, he eased the door shut silently and leaned against it, as breathless as if he had run up several flights of stairs. His hands were shaking and, standing back from the door, he flexed the fingers: staring at them, wrinkling his nose. His hands seemed to give off the odour of death. The whiff of decay teased at his nostrils, nauseating him. He felt unclean, contaminated by dead flesh.

He went into the narrow bathroom recess, stripping off his clothes as he went. The water he ran into the bath was only tepid but he did not care. He soaped himself furiously, immersed himself briefly to rinse away the lather, and then began the soaping process all over again.

When he had shaved and dressed, he sat on the edge of his bed wondering what his next move should be. The panicky bewilderment that had filled him earlier now gave way to a slow burning of deep-seated anger. There was no doubt in him now that, in his innocent stupidity, he had somehow aided his own entrapment in a web of deception. So much wool had been pulled over his eyes that the wonder of it was that he had been able to move a step without tripping headlong? Where had it begun? At St Cyr des Bains? Or even before that – in the chained misery of a windowless cell. Was that where the first evil seeds were sown? There was the bizarre questioning by jackbooted Nazi officers. . . .

Were you ever breast-fed as a child?
Did you love or hate your mother?
Have you ever had incestuous thoughts about your sister?
Do you believe in the survival of the fittest?
What qualities do you look for in a friend?
If you were alone in your cabin on your ship, would you stand to
attention if your national anthem was played on the radio?

Chisholm recalled the questions like fragments of a nightmare but retained only a hazy idea of how he had answered
them. What obscene purpose had the questioning served! No
inquisitor at the gates of hell could have been more thorough in
probing the caverns of the soul. They had drugged his mind
into a malleable state and then turned it inside out. But why,
why, why?

A sudden thought rose as he reached back into his own
nightmares: a thought so uncharitable that he wanted to reject
it as speedily as it had occurred to him. But he could not reject
it. It lodged in his consciousness and stuck as painfully as fish-
bone in his gullet.

What if his friend, the man they called *Der Schulleiter*, was not
the friend he had seemed! *What if he was one of them*?

There, it was out! He asked the question aloud. *What if he was
one of them*? Simply letting the words form filled him with a
sorrow akin to that of Caesar's when he had seen the knife of
Brutus raised against him. Could it be true? Had he even been
betrayed by the one person he had trusted as friend and ally? By
the man who had pulled him back from the black pit of despair,
who had saved him from himself by returning his instinctive
enmity with patience and kindness? Chisholm recalled his
emotions at his reluctant discovery that The Schoolmaster
genuinely wanted to help him. Tears of gratitude had brimmed
in his eyes. Because he had believed the man to be his saviour,
his deliverer.

But into what way-stations of hell had he delivered him?

All his gifts had been illusory. St Cyr des Bains had seemed
like paradise – but only a fool, as Chisholm had been a fool,
would have thought so. Even the freedom to which he had
eventually been delivered had been a false freedom, because the
poison that had contaminated him in France had clung to him
and could not be washed away .

To what else had the Schoolmaster delivered him?

To the smiling enigma that was Keitler; to the ready-stoked

hostility of the Canadians who should have been his friends; to the genuine friendship of Rick Thomson and the desolation and haunting mystery of his death.

Rick's had been the first unaccountable death to touch Chisholm. The second had been Nicole Baril's. And then more – the French patriots who had helped him. He had dismissed as mischance and fanciful any direct relation between himself and the way death seemed to follow in his wake. But now, cataloguing in his mind the trail of misfortune that led from a windowless cell in France to a hotel room in Brighton, he knew with a gnawing certainty that all the events were related: like links in a single chain. And the chain imprisoned him.

Nothing that had happened had been fortuitous. That was what Lomax's death spelled out to him. There was a pattern.

Was that what Lomax had sensed the evening before? Was that why he had to die? Not by chance. Not by coincidence. But to conceal the emerging pattern. To hide and preserve the shadowy outline of a sinister and baffling design.

The sudden knock on his room door startled Chisholm. Guardedly, almost guiltily, he opened the door a few inches. An American army officer stood in the corridor. Lieutenant Calvin T. Thorn had given up lurking behind pillars.

"Hi there, Captain Chisholm. I'd like to speak with you. Mind if I come in?"

Reluctantly, Chisholm opened the door. He was puzzled and his steady stare at the American was quizzical. Thorn answered the stare with a smile that was broad and friendly.

"The name's Thorn – Cal Thorn. You don't know me but I know you."

"What do you want?"

"We had a bit of excitement in the lobby, Captain. An acquaintance of yours showed up there dead. A Major Lomax."

Chisholm seemed to bite his lip. It was a nervous reaction rather than surprise.

"Oh," he said, "Major Lomax? I'm sorry."

"You don't look too surprised. Just how sorry are you, Captain?"

Anger rose in Chisholm. Thorn saw it and it reassured him. It was not the reaction of a guilty man. He saw Chisholm's fists clench and it seemed for a fraction of a second that his answer was to be a punch on the jaw. But Chisholm's answer was violent only in the emphasis he put on the words he hurled at Thorn in a slow deliberate snarl.

"I don't know who you are, chum, but I'll tell you how sorry I am . . . And that's more sorry than you're ever likely to know."

Thorn looked at him sharply.

"Would you like to explain that?" Seeing resentment flare in Chisholm's eyes, he added in a gentler, disarming tone: "I have the authority to ask, Captain. I know that you and Major Lomax didn't exactly hit it off."

Chisholm caught his breath. He said, cautiously:

"This visit – it's official then?"

"Yes, Captain Chisholm. It's official. You said you were more sorry about Major Lomax's death than I'll ever know. What did you mean?"

Chisholm shrugged wearily.

"Just what I said. Major Lomax's death is the last thing I wanted . . . We . . . Like you said, we didn't hit it off . . . Until last night . . . Last night, we cleared up some misunderstandings there were between us. He apologised for getting the wrong impression about me . . ."

"And?"

"And he was going to do something about it. He seemed quite charged up with it but I don't know what he had in mind."

"What exactly did he say?"

"That he had some checking up to do. Then we were going to have another talk."

"Now, he's dead," Thorn said soberly.

"Murdered!" Chisholm blurted out.

It was Thorn's turn to catch his breath.

"Now why should you say that?"

"Because somebody wanted him dead. He knew *something*!"

"What makes you think he was murdered?"

"He had a plate in his head – a war wound. His brain was damaged. He knew that if he ever got himself too worked up emotionally, it could kill him. He took pills to keep his blood pressure down . . ."

"Are you suggesting that somebody deliberately got him worked up, knowing he could drop down dead? Who?"

"Somebody who didn't want him to talk to me again."

There was an air of desperate defiance about Chisholm that disturbed Thorn.

"You're pretty worked up yourself, Captain. What's eating you?"

"Being pushed around!" Chisholm flung back at him angrily. "That's what's eating me. People have been pushing me around for so damned long that I've had just about as much as I can take! Well, it's not going to happen any more! I'm going to do the pushing now—and God help anybody who stands in the way!"

His fiercely challenging glare clearly included Thorn in the threat but, far from discomfiting Thorn, it warmed his heart. He wanted to cheer. If only Hibberd and Brockway could see Chisholm now with his blood up. The puppet was really straining at his strings: threatening to snap them free and strangle somebody with them. Thorn grinned at Chisholm.

"Goddam it, Captain, I think you'll do. I think you'll do."

Chisholm blinked in surprise.

"You're going to need help," Thorn went on. "That is, if you're set on busting a few heads. What do you say we do this together?"

Chisholm stared at him without comprehension.

"Together?"

"Yes, Captain. You and me." He continued to grin maddeningly.

"I just don't understand."

"There's a hell of a lot you don't understand," said Thorn, "but I'm taking it on my own head to level with you. Maybe if somebody had levelled with you before, Lomax might still be alive. I don't know. What I do know is that I'm not taking any chances on you going the same way. You, whether you know it or not, are the key to this whole goddamned mess, and you're precious. I'm going to look after you because, believe me, you need looking after."

He was still not making sense to Chisholm. Thorn sighed.

"Don't you understand what I'm saying, Captain? Somebody has been playing you for a patsy and I want to nail the bastard every bit as much as you do—but we do it together. We need each other. And if I'm going to use you, it'll be with your eyes open. You'll know what you're getting into."

"Just who or what are you?" Chisholm asked, bewildered.

Thorn pulled a card from his breast pocket.

"I'm an officer with the US Military Intelligence Department. And there's a good chance my boss will have me fried in oil for talking to you, let alone telling you this. But he can like it or lump it. He told me to play it by ear and that's just what I'm doing."

"You're sticking your neck out for *me*?" There was a tinge of suspicion in Chisholm's tone.

"All the way out," said Thorn quietly.

"Why?"

"A feeling, that's all. And maybe because I've gotten to know you a whole lot better than you'll ever guess. But you clinched it yourself. I didn't know how I was going to play it when I came into this room . . . Needle you a bit, maybe . . . And see if you lay down and let me stamp all over you . . . But you came out swinging. You *want* the bastards who shut up Lomax. You want them as badly as I do."

"And you think I can help?"

"That's still up to you. But it'll be because you want to. No setting you up without you knowing the risks. I said I needed you and I meant it. You're the key. But you're going to need me a whole lot more. Because when it comes to fighting dirty, you're a babe in arms. That work's for pros – and I'm one."

A flicker of comprehension lit Chisholm's eyes.

"Do you know a Major Hibberd?"

"He's my boss."

"You know why I came to Brighton?"

Thorn nodded.

"I've been on your tail since the first day you were let loose in London. There's not a hell of a lot I don't know about you, Captain."

Chisholm was shaken, but said nothing. Thorn smiled then, in a way that softened the faint reproach in his next words.

"I can even tell when you've been doing things you shouldn't," he said. "Like lugging dead bodies around and dumping them in elevators."

Chisholm coloured.

"What makes you think that?"

"I told you I was a pro, Captain. I learned all about stiffs when I was a New York cop. It wasn't all that difficult to work out."

Still, Chisholm said nothing. Thorn moved around the room. He pointed to the bed.

"Your bed hasn't been slept in." He waved a warning hand at Chisholm. "Don't tell me where you spent the night. I can guess—and I'm envious. That's something I should have figured a whole lot sooner than I did." He stared thoughtfully up at the ceiling, as if making a calculation. "Let me get this right now. Whoever put Lomax in the elevator, did it between six-fifteen and about quarter of seven. My guess is that you got back here sometime after six and found the Major stiffer than a frozen turkey. It must have been quite a shock?"

Chisholm did not reply. Thorn moved towards the window, sniffing the air.

"You should have opened a window and let that cold January wind blow in," he said. "This place still has that dead man stink about it. Did you find him on the floor? Or was it in that chair? Yeah, the chair. He was cramped up pretty badly."

"Does it matter?" Chisholm asked wearily.

"No," said Thorn. "I know and I reckon you know that if he died by getting so riled up that his heart gave up on him, nobody's going to pin a murder rap on you. There's no way it could be made to stick. Mind you, I reckon maybe English law has something to say about moving a body . . ."

"It would have to be proved," said Chisholm defensively, not sure just where the conversation was going. Thorn laughed.

"You're right there," he agreed. "Look, Captain, I'm not trying to pin anything on you. Moving that body was the best thing you could have done. Somebody dealt you a hand from a stacked deck. You rearranged the cards, and that's good strategy. They're not going to be too happy when they find out that you're still in the game. That means that they might try again. Tell me, why do you think that Lomax was planted in your room? Why did somebody go to all the trouble and all the risk of planting him on you?"

"To make things look bad for me. God knows that I've had a hard enough time getting people to believe what I say when I'm telling the gospel truth."

"Yeah," murmured Thorn, "I know what they put you through." He shrugged. "The trouble with people in my game is that they sometimes find it easier to accept a big lie than a small truth. And the trouble with this mess is that the big lie is a good one. So goddamned big that we can't even guess what it is." He shook his head in frustration. "What the hell was their motive?"

"In lumbering me with a dead body?" Chisholm had no doubt about the motive. "Somebody wanted me stuck with a manslaughter charge?"

Thorn looked at him sharply.

"A manslaughter charge? What's that?"

"You would probably call it second or third degree murder," said Chisholm.

"But how would they have made it stick?"

"Whoever did it must have known that Lomax and I had never seen eye to eye. He thought I was a bloody sex pervert, for Christ's sake! We were always at each other's throats. They must have known, too, that a heated argument could probably kill him . . . And that if anybody could make him go off the deep end, it was me. So how was I going to explain him lying dead in my room? Or that I didn't wish him dead? Murder, they might draw the line at – but manslaughter, culpable homicide . . . The way my luck's been running, I wouldn't give tuppence for my chances."

Thorn nodded thoughtfully.

"What if somebody else was supposed to have found the body in your room? That might have made things worse for you. If there was a hint that you had concealed the death for several hours . . . What I am trying to figure out is: who was the number one target . . . You or Lomax? Or were they aiming to get rid of two birds with one stone?"

"There's something you're maybe not taking into account," said Chisholm, lowering his eyes a little shame-facedly. "It's not something I'd want to shout from the roof-tops. But I've got an alibi for most of the night . . . Just along the corridor in room one-three-seven."

Thorn blinked up at Chisholm, a frown forming on his face.

"The singer? Along the corridor? But . . ."

"You don't believe me?"

"Yeah, but . . . I checked. Her room's on the fourth floor." Seeing the look on Chisholm's face, he added. "You don't have to take my word for it."

Thorn crossed and lifted up the house telephone.

"Hall porter," came the voice. "Can I help you?"

"Sure," drawled Thorn. "My friend's got a room on the first floor but I can't remember the number. I think it's one-three-seven. Would you check for me, please?"

"Just a moment, sir." There was a delay, then: "Room one-three-seven, sir. That's Colonel Green's room."

"That's him," said Thorn, and passed the telephone quickly to Chisholm. "Would you just repeat that for me?"

Chisholm heard the reply.

"Very well, sir. Room one-three-seven is occupied by Colonel E. H. Green. Will that be all, sir?"

Chisholm dropped the receiver back on the cradle without replying. He stared at Thorn, disbelieving.

"What where you saying about an alibi?" asked Thorn.

Eleven

Picture of a Frame

The room was the same in which "Operation Thumbscrew" had been born. This time, however, there was no eighteen-strong gathering dispersed around the long table. Only four men were present. Vaughan, Hibberd and Brockway sat uncomfortably in adjacent seats at one side of the table, studiously looking anywhere but at the sturdy, bull-like figure wearing Brigadier's tabs who – choosing not to sit in case it was taken as a signal of informality – was holding the floor and addressing them in clipped and strangely high-pitched tones. The squeaky voice was totally at odds with the Brigadier's heavy build and it grated on his three listeners. Their faces betrayed the kind of auricular distress normally associated with reaction to an out-of-tune fiddle, played badly; but it was as much the substance of the homily as its grating delivery that pained Vaughan and his companions.

In his days as a university don, the Brigadier had been noted for the sadistic pleasure he seemed to draw from the verbal assassination of his intellectual inferiors. He was accomplished in the art and it may have been for this reason that he had risen swiftly to an exalted position in the administrative hierarchy of Britain's intelligence services. The Brigadier seemed to be an automatic choice as spokesman for High Authority on those occasions when it was not only necessary to make known the express wishes of the decision-makers but also to voice the displeasure of that august body.

For fifteen minutes now he had been flagellating the unfortunate Vaughan's self-esteem with invective which he handled like a scourge: flicking at him with acerbic postulation that was weighted to cut and then drawing back from the next blow by imparting a carefully measured meiosis that tore at the open wound with the barb in its tip.

Vaughan, as both the advocate and architect of "Operation Thumbscrew" had been singled out for official opprobrium because of a drastic change of mind on the wisdom of the enterprise. It was now being described by those who saw any merit in it as "probably ill-conceived". This was ecstatic praise compared with the views of a more numerous body who saw no merit in it whatsoever and who were, in their more charitable moods, prepared to damn the project as "asinine" and its authors as "feeble-minded".

It did not matter that "Operation Thumbscrew" had evolved as a corporate decision. The representatives of the various departments had no sooner assented to its creation than they were scurrying back to their headquarters voicing second thoughts and spreading the gravest misgivings about what they referred to as "Vaughan's three-ring circus". Thus, promised co-operation had been withheld and inter-departmental harmony had been replaced with bloody-minded prevarication on the one hand and outright hostility on the other. Rivals of Vaughan, who were jealous of the *carte blanche* he had been given to conscript key personnel, took the opportunity to denigrate the operation and whisper accusations of empire-building.

The nudges and whispers had reached such a pitch that High Authority had been forced to review the situation. Dismayed by the lack of hard evidence that St Cyr des Bains was the centre of a sinister German undertaking likely to influence the course of the war, they had endorsed the mounting criticisms of "Thumbscrew" and had entrusted their hatchet-man, the Brigadier, with the task of performing a wing-clipping operation on Vaughan. It was a task the Brigadier relished. He had done his homework well and set about demolishing the idea of "Thumbscrew" by enumerating its foundational weaknesses and passing scathing comment on its relevance in the face of more easily defined priorities. He likened it to the harnessing of sophisticated pile-driving machinery to crack open a peanut: a task made all the more futile by the failure of all concerned to locate the peanut and the very real possibility that it did not even exist. Without once telling Vaughan to his face that he was an incompetent fool, the Brigadier managed to cast such doubt on Vaughan's ability to think or act rationally that no direct accusation was necessary.

After fifteen minutes demolition work on the concept of "Operation Thumbscrew", and Vaughan's ego, the Brigadier got down to particulars.

"Ten days ago," he squeaked at Vaughan, "you despatched an agent and a radio operator to France for the express purpose of investigating the enemy establishment at St Cyr des Bains. It must now be apparent, even to someone of limited intellect, that this particular exercise has failed. Is this not so, Vaughan?"

"I am not ready to say it is a failure, sir. Not yet."

The Brigadier stared at Vaughan as if he were witless.

"Oh, it has been a success?"

"I didn't say that, sir," said Vaughan.

"No, because these men are almost certainly dead. You send two men to their deaths but you are not, at this stage, prepared to say whether their mission was a success or a failure?"

Vaughan coloured.

"We cannot be sure they're dead, sir. We had to drop them fifty kilometres from the coast and they had orders to avoid even our known friends. They may have had difficulty entering the prohibited area . . ."

"Were they not ordered to radio the fact that they were safely down in France and were operational?"

"Yes, sir. Within forty-eight hours."

"But you have heard nothing in ten days?"

"I'm afraid not, sir."

The Brigadier stared at Vaughan with contempt.

"You amaze me, Commander. You amaze me. I expected something better of a man of your experience. Are you unwilling to acknowledge the loss of two highly trained operatives because you are a complete and bloody fool? Or is it because you do not want to admit that it was you who sent them on a fool's errand and that you are the person directly responsible for their deaths."

Vaughan's fists were clenching and unclenching below the table.

"If anything has happened to these men, the responsibility is mine, sir. I'm not trying to deny it."

"Then face the facts, Commander!" The Brigadier's declaration was shrill, a piped command. "Face the facts! You are not going to hear from these men again. There is no point deluding yourself on that score any more than in clinging to the delusion that this whole crack-brained operation is anything more than a scandalous waste of resources and personnel.''

"We need time . . .'' Vaughan started to protest but the Brigadier cut him short.

"You've had all the time you're going to get, Commander,'' he snapped. "And my time isn't so plentiful that I can let it be taken up endlessly with grandiose follies such as this operation of yours.''

Vaughan did not reply. He sat, lips drawn, repressing waves of dismay and intense anger. The Brigadier turned and walked across to a hat-stand by the door and retrieved a bulky brief case from the hook on which he had hung it. He opened the brief-case and, extracting a small piece of paper, returned to flourish it in Vaughan's face.

"I am sure that you have a plausible explanation for this particular idiocy.'' he drawled sarcastically in his reedy voice. He placed the piece of paper on the table and let Vaughan, Brockway and Hibberd examine it in turn. It was a receipt from Garrard's, the Regent Street jewellers, for an expensive brooch. In spite of the demands on his time, which he had mentioned, the Brigadier had a great deal to say about the receipt. Not least, he demanded to know the name of the genius who had authorised the purchase of the brooch.

"I signed the chit,'' said Vaughan, hating the Brigadier for the way he made him feel like a schoolboy being forced to confess to masturbating in the lavatory.

"It was all my idea,'' chipped in Brockway, his moustache bristling. "I talked the Commander into it. He wasn't all that keen.''

"It was a joint decision,'' said Hibberd, who had never encountered anyone quite like the Brigadier before and was appalled by the man. He qualified his share of the responsibility by adding: "It seemed a good idea at the time.''

"A good idea!'' the Brigadier echoed incredulously. "A good idea! You involve a perfectly innocent girl and this mentally unstable seaman chap in what I can only describe as a purposeless stunt and you call it a good idea! I call it a madness! The most charitable interpretation I can put on it is that it was a stupid aberration on the part of you all.'' He rounded on Brockway. "And you, sir. Were you not warned before that your harassment of the young lady in question amounted to persecution?''

Brockway returned the Brigadier's stare belligerently.

"She was the subject of a security check, that's all! There was no harassment of the girl. She didn't even know about it."

The Brigadier received the statement without giving any indication that he believed it for an instant. He changed the direction of his attack.

"A pity, of course, about this Canadian officer's death," he observed. "I am sure that you three gentlemen will, naturally, be anxious to absolve yourselves of any responsibility for that?"

Vaughan half-rose, his hands on the arms of his chair.

"We all regret Major Lomax's death, sir," he protested sharply. "But it's too early to be sure of its significance, or to say it was avoidable or unavoidable. Any conclusions we might reach in advance of the post-mortem findings would be premature."

While Vaughan spoke, the Brigadier kept nodding his head as if in agreement. But his eyes mocked Vaughan.

"Naturally, naturally," he said. "You are quite happy to postpone any judgement on the matter and wait in the hope that the post-mortem will vindicate you. You know that there is no evidence of foul play. Therefore, no blame can possibly be attached to yourselves."

"We have by no means ruled out foul play," Brockway said icily. "Indeed, there may be a much greater significance in Major Lomax's death than you seem to think, sir. It is also imperative that no currency is given to the idea that his death is anything other than a natural consequence of the wounds he suffered at Dieppe. I have personally instructed that our interest is to be kept unobtrusive. If there's a chance of our suspicions proving founded, we don't want the facts advertised. In the meantime, we've got to give our men on the spot time to complete their inquiries. Until they do, it's far too soon to jump to conclusions. Good heavens, sir, it was only yesterday the man died."

The Brigadier's face twitched with annoyance all the time Brockway was speaking. But he allowed him to finish.

"Only yesterday," he parroted Brockway's words. "Only yesterday? Twenty-four hours is a long time in our business. I cannot believe that you have been any less active than I during the last twenty-four hours in acquainting yourself of the facts surrounding your unfortunate compatriot's death."

"We have two men in Brighton who are keeping us

informed," snapped Brockway.

The Brigadier smirked.

"Then you will know—as I have taken the trouble to find out—that the doctor in Brighton who signed the death certificate gave the likely cause of death as a brain haemorrhage. Are you suggesting, my dear chap, that this brain haemorrhage was induced by someone who wanted Lomax out of the way?"

"There is every possibility that his death *was* provoked," Brockway replied evenly.

"There is another possibility that is much more likely," the Brigadier piped shrilly. "and that is that the absurd devotion you three gentlemen have for theatricalities is what killed Lomax! You deliberately created a situation—one that may make sense to you but makes none to me—and its one incontradictable consequence is that the Canadian Army has been robbed of the services of a brave and highly esteemed officer. You, gentlemen, may consider this outcome to be rather bad luck. I represent a view that considers it unforgivable!"

He placed such emphasis on the last word that the three officers facing him were dared to contradict him at their peril. His chest heaved with the emotion of righteousness proclaimed. In a calm voice, he went on: "There is only one more thing I have to say, gentlemen. Your folly is to go no further. 'Operation Thumbscrew' is cancelled. It is over. That is the order that I have been empowered to hand down to you. It is final and it is irrevocable."

Vaughan and Hibberd remained rooted to their chairs, stunned. Brockway got angrily to his feet with such outrage that his chair fell over behind him.

"You're telling us to close the book?" The Canadian's voice rang with disbelief.

"I am telling you to wind things down, dismantle the operation. No more, no less. All special personnel will be returned immediately to their parent units and no more initiatives will be taken in pursuit of 'Thumbscrew' objectives outwith the normal activities of your respective departments. Is that understood? I am sure that there is a mountain of much more important matters demanding your attention than this molehill that has distracted you for far too long."

The Brigadier collected his cap and brief-case and with a curt "Good-day, gentlemen," marched from the room. As the door closed behind him, Brockway hit the table with his fist and gave voice to a single-word obscenity.

"That," declared Hibberd in a shocked voice, "is the most disgusting specimen of homo sapiens that I've seen walking upright. Was he real? Or did I imagine it?"

"He thinks he's real," said Vaughan morosely. "And unique! The rest of humanity was put on the earth for him to piss on from a great height." He pounded a fist angrily on the table. "We needed longer!" he declaimed bitterly. "We're after shark and they think we're fishing for bloody minnows!"

Chisholm's raincoat still lay draped across the chair where he had tossed it the night before on his return from Brighton. The sight of it greeted his sister, Millie, when she arrived home from night duty at eight in the morning. She shook her head with a despair that was softened by affection. Her brother still had the untidy habits of the small boy she remembered from long ago. She sighed. It was time young Heck had a wife to look after him.

She picked up the coat and went to hang it in the hall passage. As she swept through the living-room doorway, the coat swung against the panelled door and there was a sound like a muffled pistol shot. She reached into Chisholm's coat pocket to find out what it was that had rapped on the door. Her fingers closed round a small glass jar. She inspected it. It was coloured dark brown and had a black screw top. It rattled when she shook it.

Curious now, she unscrewed the top and emptied some white pills into her hand. She stared at them with a little flutter of alarm. The fear rose that her brother was ill and had been doping himself on the quiet, so that she wouldn't worry. But that wasn't like Heck. He was the kind who would rather die than let an aspirin past his lips. She put the jar on the sideboard and made a mental note to question her brother about the pills later.

Chisholm, who had slept like a dead man for ten hours, wakened at the sound of Millie moving about in the next room. He got up and they had breakfast together. He spent most of it fending off questions about what he had done in Brighton. They were on their second cup of tea before Millie remembered about the pills.

The dark brown jar, which she placed on the table in front of him, mystified Chisholm. He, too, spilled some of the white tablets into his hand and examined them.

"They're not mine," he declared. "You say you found them in my coat?"

"Yes. I went to hang up your coat in the hall and banged it against the door in the passing. I wasn't meaning to pry . . . I just wondered what on earth you had in your pocket."

"They're not my pills."

"Well how did they get into your pocket?"

"Search me. I haven't the faintest idea."

"Didn't you feel them? A thing like that knocking against your leg."

"I never had my coat on yesterday. I carried it over my arm."

Millie looked at him reproachfully.

"Then it's a wonder you didn't catch your death of cold. It's still the middle of winter, you know. You should look after yourself."

Chisholm grinned.

"You sound more like our dear departed mother every day."

"I mean it," she said severely. "You don't look after yourself properly." Returning to the subject of the pills, she said: "Somebody must have mistaken your coat for theirs on the train. Or in Brighton. Were there any Navy officers there? Those dark trench-coats all look the same."

"Yes . . ." he agreed in a vague sort of manner. He was casting his mind back to Brighton. Perhaps that *was* where the pills had been put in his pocket. An accident? Deliberately? No, surely not. What on earth were they?

Chisholm did not share his fleeting suspicions with Millie. He had no intention of troubling her with what had happened in Brighton.

She was tired from her night duty and needed little persuasion from Chisholm to be packed off to bed. He chased her with the promise to clear away the breakfast things and wash up the dishes.

As he rinsed cups and saucers in the tiny kitchenette, his mind returned to the events of Brighton. So much had happened that a sensation of trauma still befuddled his mind: Anina, Lomax and then Thorn.

What a surprise packet Cal Thorn had turned out to be. So like Rick in some ways and yet totally unlike him. Maybe it was only the accent that was similar. Thorn was that much older, wiser in the ways of the world, rock like in the easy confidence he exuded. Not a man who would be easily perturbed or fooled.

If he had chosen to do so, the American could have made life extremely awkward for Chisholm. Instead, he had stuck his neck out for him with almost anarchic disregard for the consequences. One of the things Chisholm had instinctively sensed and liked about Thorn was his contempt of anything that smacked of mindless conformity to convention. Thorn, Chisholm guessed, was one of those lucky mavericks who always did things in his own unorthodox way and invariably got away with it.

Chisholm knew that, at first, he had had no choice but to trust Thorn. But, after two hours of verbal fencing with the man, that had ceased to matter. Chisholm had sensed that it was Thorn's strong humanity that had made him declare himself as he had, rather than any profound belief that Chisholm could be of real practical help. It had nothing to do with prudence or wisdom or self-interest – but a great deal with Thorn's very own measure of right and wrong. Like a hunter tormented by the sight of his own decoy-beast squealing and threshing against its tethers, Thorn had set Chisholm free and resolved to catch his tiger some other way.

His intervention had come at a critical moment in Chisholm's troubled life. At a moment when he had felt himself alone and encircled by forces of incalculable malevolence. Almost in the instant when Chisholm had found the resolution to stop being their prey and to defend himself tooth and nail, Thorn had appeared and declared himself friend and ally in the fight. The knowledge that he was no longer *alone* had sent Chisholm's morale rocketing sky-high.

It had stayed high despite immediate setbacks to the hopes of both men that they could get quick answers to a number of puzzling questions. At the top of Chisholm's list was the painfully embarrassing question of why Anina had invited him to a room that had been reserved for her haughty dinner companion of the evening before. Why there instead of her own room on the fourth floor?

Of equal moment was close investigation of the two Canadian officers who, like Chisholm and Lomax, had links with St Cyr des Bains. If there was a renegade amongst the six escapers, then either Constantine or Gilbert had to be the man playing a deadly double game. With Lomax dead, Martineau in Aldershot, and Malloy in hospital, the choice of suspects had shrunk to two.

But neither Anina nor the two Canadians were anywhere to be found in the Beaumaris by the time Thorn and Chisholm had finished exchanging theories on who might have planted Lomax's corpse in Chisholm's room. Chisholm had been reluctant to admit even to himself that Anina Calvi might have played a part in ensuring he spent most of the night away from his room. Thorn, less starry-eyed, had pointed to the possibility with scant regard for Chisholm's blushes.

"So maybe she made a sucker of you," Thorn had observed. "That don't make you unique. Dames have been making saps outa guys like you and me ever since Eve discovered that most of her assets were under a fig leaf."

Chisholm was enough of a realist to concede that the speed with which Anina had fallen into his arms might not have been entirely due to his irresistible charm. She might well have had an ulterior motive. Indeed, the more he thought about it, the more he had to admit that he had been such a pushover that he would have turned cart-wheels for her if she had but crooked her little finger and suggested it. So eager and flattered had he been, that he had fallen at her behest like an overripe plum into the picker's hand. He could acknowledge that fact, but its acceptance did nothing to erase an overwhelming sense of sorrow.

The sorrow stayed with him when, on Thorn's suggestion, he had returned to the room along the corridor where he had left Anina asleep; not to confront his lover of a night with unpleasant truths and force a showdown but to gauge as subtly as he could her reaction to his reappearance. If she were part of a conspiracy to compromise him with a corpse, then his reappearance as if nothing untoward had happened would come as a shock.

But the room—ostensibly the reserved accommodation of Colonel E. H. Green—had been empty, the door swinging open. Chisholm had gone inside, filled with a growing sense of anti-climax: having braced himself for the role that Thorn had encouraged him to play. The big double bed had been carefully remade, with no hint that it had ever been occupied.

Chisholm, without further consultation with Thorn, had gone hurrying downstairs to the reception desk. The girl in attendance had met his enquiry about Miss Anina Calvi's room number with a polite smile of regret. Miss Calvi had checked out of the hotel only twenty minutes or so ago.

Returning to his room, Chisholm had found Thorn fast asleep in the chair that a couple of hours before had been occupied by Lomax's body. The night had made up on him. Chisholm's news that the bird had flown brought the American to angry wakefulness. The anger was directed at himself for failing to anticipate Anina's flight and at Weaver for not tipping him off from the lobby. In fact, the Canadian Sergeant had tried unsuccessfully to locate Thorn. The last place he had expected Thorn to be was in Chisholm's room.

Thorn's dismay increased when he learned from Weaver that both Gilbert and Constantine had also left the hotel, although it was still not 8.30 in the morning. Apparently, the two lieutenants had departed before eight with a group of a dozen or more Canadian officers. Weaver had seen no point in following them because he could not have done so discreetly and, in any case, because he knew exactly where they could be found. They had gone to a training lecture at Fareham, near Portsmouth, and would be occupied there for the whole day before returning to the Beaumaris in the evening.

One way or another, it had been a frustrating start for the newly founded "pro-am" partnership of Thorn and Chisholm, as Thorn had described it. Thorn had been a little embarrassed that, having solicited Chisholm's active co-operation as a willing accomplice rather than unsuspecting pawn, his strategy had become bogged down within the space of a few minutes. He need not have worried on Chisholm's account. Having made his declaration of war and identified Thorn's enemies as his own, Chisholm had a personal commitment to action that was not going to be deterred by setbacks nor appeased by a secondary role. Having been released like an imprisoned genie from a bottle, there was no way Chisholm was now going to be persuaded back inside and the cork replaced. Thorn's problem with Chisholm was going to be restraining the force that he had, with the best of motives, unleashed. Perhaps sensing this, Thorn had evolved a way of harnessing Chisholm's determination to become fully involved.

If Chisholm wanted to play detective, that was OK with Thorn – but it had to be done within the role that events had so far cast him. For instance, there was no harm in him asking around the Beaumaris about Lomax. The Canadian Major had arranged to meet him that day. His concern would be seen as natural. Thorn had not been optimistic that Chisholm would learn very much about Lomax, however, and advised him not to push too hard with any enquiries he made. It would be better, he had suggested, if Chisholm were to concentrate on trying to find out where Anina Calvi had gone in such a hurry. With a sly smile, Thorn had said: "You've got the best reason in the world for wanting to find her. You're in love with her. Goddamit, you maybe even want to marry her." Seeing Chisholm's expression, he had added: "You won't have to pretend too hard, will you? You still can't quite believe she's maybe mixed up in this."

Thorn, himself, elected to do some checking on the mysterious Colonel E. H. Green. He, too, fitted into the jigsaw and Thorn wanted to find out where.

Playing detective on that eventful morning in Brighton had gone some way to way to satisfying Chisholm's need to be involved, but the novelty had been beginning to wear thin by afternoon when a great deal of legwork found him back where he had started – at the Beaumaris – with nothing to show for his efforts. It was then he had his first stroke of luck. He was standing near the reception desk when a taxi-driver presented himself there and asked if the gentleman who had been enquiring at the station rank about his girl friend was still at the hotel. Overhearing, Chisholm had immediately identified himself as the gentleman.

The taxi-driver remembered taking Anina to the station from the Beaumaris all too vividly. She was not the kind of fare that was easily forgotten.

"Had a row with you, guvnor?" the taxi-driver asked sympathetically. "She wasn't in too sweet a temper. Near bit my head off, she did, and I was only chatting to her friendly like."

In addition to this insight into Anina's state of mind, the only information the taxi-driver had was that the young lady had taken the 8.40 train to London. Chisholm had pressed a couple of pound notes into the man's hand and thanked him profusely for his help. He had been intensely relieved that at least he would have something to report to Thorn.

But Thorn had not shown up at the Beaumaris at three as they had arranged. Instead, at about fifteen minutes after the hour, he had telephoned. If Chisholm had expected a pat on the head for his efforts, it was not forthcoming. Thorn had not seemed over-impressed by Chisholm's discovery that Anina Calvi was in London.

"Where in London?" he had asked impatiently, and had let Chisholm know that the sooner he got himself up to London and started distributing largesse around the taxi-drivers at Victoria the sooner he was likely to come up with some really solid information.

"You keep looking for that lady love of yours," he advised. "I'll be in touch. Just give me a phone number where I can reach you."

Chisholm had given him Millie's flat number and taken the first train for Victoria. There, he had spent several hours talking to taxi-drivers who might have been on the rank in the morning – but he drew a blank. Not one remembered picking up Anina Calvi.

Going over his Brighton adventures in the light of a new day, Chisholm wondered where and how a small brown jar of pills had found its way into his coat pocket. He had to admit defeat there, too. But he resolved to mention the jar of pills to Thorn.

He spent the morning at Victoria asking questions, hoping that the drivers who had been there the previous morning would again be on the stance. A number were but none remembered getting Anina as a fare. He returned to the flat and waited, hoping that Thorn would ring. It was late afternoon when he finally did. The American sounded tired and irritated.

"Is something wrong?" Chisholm asked.

"Plenty," said Thorn. "Look, it's complicated. I'll tell you about it when I see you. Can you meet me around six?"

They agreed to rendezvous at a pub on the south side of the Strand. Chisholm was there early and sipping a half pint of beer at the crowded bar when he saw Thorn come in. The American took one look at the elbowing throng and shook his head to Chisholm's offer of a drink.

"Let's blow," he said. "This joint is like Madison Square Gardens on fight night."

They walked towards Charing Cross. The blacked-out Strand was milling with off-duty servicemen and office-workers heading for home. Negotiating a way past sandbagged entries and avoiding collisions with other pedestrians demanded a care that made conversation impossible. Thorn led the way down a pitch-dark sidestreet with such impatient haste that Chisholm nearly lost him. He didn't slow down until he reached the

Embankment and found a spot that was reasonably sheltered from the wind. He leaned against a parapet looking down on the dark water of the Thames. He looked down at the river in brooding fashion, saying nothing.

"It was warmer in the pub," Chisholm pointed out good-naturedly. "Something's worrying you."

"You're goddamned right something's worrying me," Thorn replied with feeling. He made a gesture of apology for his angry tone. "I'm still trying to take it in. Somebody has pulled the plug at headquarters and cancelled the whole goddamned show. Hibberd and his buddies, who were running things, have all had their backsides kicked. I'll be lucky if I don't wind up doing beach patrols on some slab of rock in the Aleutians."

Chisholm, whose knowledge of the "show" Thorn talked about went no further than the fragments he had gleaned from the American, was more puzzled than alarmed by the other's dismay. Brighton, and not the wider ramifications, was uppermost on his mind.

"How does this affect what happened at Brighton?" he asked.

"It means that the hounds have been called off. If there was a mess at Brighton—and you and I know there was a goddamned mess—it's all going to be swept under the carpet and forgotten."

"But Lomax was murdered! And somebody put his body in my bloody room. You can't just pretend it never happened!"

Thorn grinned ruefully in the dark at Chisholm's words.

"But that's exactly what I did, old buddy. You moved the evidence because it pointed straight at you. OK, so I helped you conceal a crime, but it's a crime that looks even less like a crime now—because it suited us to pretend it never happened." He gave a short, humourless laugh. "Do you know how many people know you had a stiff in your hotel room, my friend? Three."

"Three?" queried Chisholm.

"Yeah, three," said Thorn. "You, me, and the guy who put him there."

"You haven't told Major Hibberd?"

"Nope. And a whole lot more besides. Not that I've been deliberately holding out. I just haven't had the chance. As far as Hibberd knows, I'm still stalking you like I was the last of the Mohicans."

"But Hibberd knows about Lomax?"

"He knows the guy is dead and that there's something fishy about the way he died. But all that he and the rest of them at headquarters know is what I told my contact man at Brighton to pass on to them. And that is that we're looking into things in our own softly-softly way and keeping everything quiet and peaceful like they wanted. The last things the guys in London wanted was a squad of Brighton bobbies tramping all over the Beaumaris . . . And the last thing anybody wants is to panic the guy we're after. Our best chance of finding out exactly what he's up to is by letting him think he's got clean away with it."

"But he *will* get clean away with it if, like you say, the whole thing's going to be swept under the carpet!" It was Chisholm's turn to be angry. "You can't bloody well back out now!"

Thorn bridled at the suggestion.

"Who said anything about backing out?" he snapped back, and immediately regretted the whip of his tongue. More good-humouredly, he added: "I never was much of a one for taking orders. Even when I was a cop. 'That son of a bitch, Thorn', my old captain used to say, 'he'll have us all back walking a beat for not doing what he's told'. That's the way I was, see. I had my own ways of getting round the guys at City Hall."

"So, what do we do now?"

"Well, I sure know what I'm going to do. I'm going to sleep on it. Maybe it'll all look better in the morning. And maybe it won't. Major Hibberd wants to see me nine o'clock sharp – probably to tell me that the big boys have put the kybosh on everything and that I've been drafted to the infantry."

"What makes you think they have . . . Put the kybosh on everything?"

"Because I called the shop just before I rang you. My orders were spelled out loud and clear. All bets are off. All personnel report at oh-nine-hundred. The big show has been cancelled. Pay off all the extras. There ain't gonna be a cast of thousands in this here movie."

"Cast of thousands?" Chisholm couldn't think what Thorn was talking about. The American smiled.

"An exaggeration, maybe. But you started something, Captain Hector Chisholm, when you got out of that French fun-palace. They even had a Commando battalion standing by to go and take the lid off that joint. Now, it's off."

Chisholm was staggered.

"But it's just a hospital—a convalescent home with barbed wire."

"Sure it is," drawled Thorn, "So, don't you go blabbing about what I just said about Commando battalions. You could get us both hung."

Thorn's billet in London was a requisitioned hotel near the British Museum. It was his intention to return there after his meeting with Chisholm. Instead, he allowed Chisholm to persuade him to return to Millie's flat for a pot-luck meal and a couple of drinks. They caught Millie on the point of leaving for night duty. She insisted on opening a hoarded tin of ham for their meal and fussed round them like a mother hen until it was time for her to go. It did not escape Chisholm that his sister and Cal Thorn got on as if they had known each other all their lives. Thorn's fatigue and irritability vanished and he seemed inordinately pleased with life when, after they had eaten, he and Chisholm relaxed with glasses of whisky before Millie's spluttering gas fire.

It was then that Chisholm remembered the jar of pills. Like Chisholm, Thorn was at a loss as to how they could have found their way into Chisholm's pocket. He could read no special significance into the fact nor connect them with events at Brighton. Thorn did notice, however, that the jar had once borne a label—probably a pharmacist's—and that some of the paper still adhered to the glass.

"No harm in finding out what kind of pills they are. I'll get them analysed," Thorn offered—and, with no objection from Chisholm, pocketed the jar. He was not optimistic that the pills would prove to be of the slightest relevance but, in his policeman's way, he was not prepared to discount the tiniest scrap of unexplained detail.

Indeed, he did not return directly to his billet when he bade Chisholm goodnight and left the flat in Westminster. He was lucky enough to find a taxi near Parliament Square and, on an impulse, told the driver to take him to Scotland Yard. He had been a not infrequent visitor at the Metropolitan Police headquarters since his arrival in Britain and had made a number of friends there.

The best of these, a Superintendent Weller, was not in his office but his deputy—who had met Thorn only once—greeted the American like an old friend. Thorn tipped some pills into the palm of his hand and held them out for inspection. Could he have them analysed, as an obligement?

"Let's go and find out," suggested Weller's deputy. Thorn followed him through a maze of corridors to the forensic laboratories. A helpful lab technician emptied a few pills from the jar into an envelope, which he docketed with Thorn's name, service department and telephone number. He promised Thorn that he would have the result of the analysis some time the following day.

"I think I could guess what they are right now," he said to Thorn, "but it'll be tomorrow before I could say for sure."

"What do you think they are?" Thorn prompted.

The pharmacist tipped one of the pills into his hand from the unsealed envelope.

"Overdose material," he said confidently. "We see a lot of them." He tasted the pill with the tip of his tongue. "Yep, it's a barbiturate. Pheno-barbitone I would say. Or sodium barbitone."

The off-the-cuff verdict had no special meaning for Thorn that night. He filed it at the back of his mind. It was still there next morning as he sat in the office he shared with Major Hibberd, idly sifting through a number of intelligence and other reports that had come in overnight. It was only 8.30 and he did not expect to see Hibberd for another half hour.

Among a number of yellow envelopes, a white one stood out. Printed on the back in a single line were the words: "Dept. of Pathology, Eastern Road, Brighton, Sussex." Thorn turned it over. The front had been rubber-stamped in two places: once with an RAMC unit frank and once with a Canadian Army divisional HQ stamp. An economy label partly obscured the latter and bore Major Hibberd's name and departmental address.

Thorn tore it open and extracted four sheets of carbon-typed flimsy. They contained the autopsy report on Major Henry Valentine Lomax, deceased. As Thorn glanced over the sheets, one word leapt up at him from the third page: the word "barbiturate."

In Lomax's stomach had been found traces of the barbiturate, sodium barbitone, amounting to the equivalent of three 40 mg tablets. Even as the fact registered with Thorn, it did so with a question-mark in parenthesis alongside. Three tablets was a long way from being an overdose, never mind a fatal overdose.

He read on. Below an underlined heading, *Cause of Death*, the word "barbiturate" occurred again. The pathologist's conclusion, stripped of its medical double-dutch, was that Major Lomax had died from a brain haemorrhage as a direct result of ingestion into his system of approximately 120 milligrams of the barbiturate, sodium barbitone.

The details were all impersonally cloaked in clinical terms that baffled Thorn but the gist was quite clear. A relatively mild amount of sodium barbitone had reacted on Lomax's damaged brain with as equally a lethal effect as a bullet fired from a .45 revolver.

Under *General Remarks*, the pathologist had recorded – without wishing to anticipate or prejudice the findings of a Coroner's Inquiry – that the medical facts gave rise to questions that he was not competent to answer but should not be overlooked.

It would be a cause for some concern if a barbiturate drug had been prescribed for the deceased by a medical practitioner who was familiar with the deceased's history of head injury. Death would have been the inevitable result to the deceased from a barbiturate intake of as low a dosage as 80 milligrammes. This being the case, it was hard to believe that the deceased had not been warned of the likely fatal consequences of resort to even the smallest amounts of hypnosedative drugs.

These facts, he hoped, would be borne in mind by those whose function it was to establish whether the drug was self-administered with intent or by accident, or prescribed or offered in ignorance. Anyone who had undergone surgery in the area of the occipital lobe – as the deceased had done – ran the gravest risk at all times from a number of drugs and, in drawing this to the attention of those privy to this report, lives might be saved in future if the implications were noted by all who were in a position to avert the occurrence of similar tragedies.

The pathologist was clearly disturbed by the possibility that Lomax's death had resulted from some ignorance, oversight or incompetence on the part of the medical profession. But it was no careless sin of omission that stared Thorn in the face. It was murder.

That was why an unlabelled jar of sodium barbitone tablets had been planted in Chisholm's coat pocket. Not only had murder been committed but it had been set up *to look like murder*.

With difficulty, the sea captain might just have been able to explain away the presence of a body in his room. He would have had a hell of a job explaining away a body *and* a jar of death-dealing pills. Clearly, the murderer had not bargained on Chisholm finding Lomax in the first place, nor subsequently the pills. A more likely scenario was that a porter or chamber-maid should have found the body, and the police called in. They would have searched the room as a matter of course. And Chisholm's belongings. But Chisholm had spoiled things by returning to his room too soon, before the trap had been sprung.

As Thorn thought about the crime and how it had been carried out, he sensed in the deed a degree of haste and perhaps an element of clever improvisation between one move and the next. The perpetrators were clever all right, but far from infallible. They had made mistakes.

Thorn realised, almost with a start, that he was now thinking of murderers in the plural. It was not the work of one person, but at least two. Working as a team. And one of them was Anina Calvi.

Twelve

Sing Like a Swan

Chisholm sat nervously silent in the passenger seat of the jeep as it bucked and pitched along the narrow by-road. Huge ruts scarred the surface of the unmade track. Frozen ridges of mud had been cemented rock-hard by three consecutive nights of February frost.

"How far to the cottage?"

"Under a mile. We're nearly there."

A shadowy figure stood ahead, arms waving.

Thorn, at the wheel of the jeep, swerved the vehicle off the track and brought it to a halt in a tree-flanked lay-by alongside a fifteen-hundredweight army truck already parked there. He switched off the engine.

A second figure loomed up out of the gloom. It was Brockway.

"Everything OK, sir?" Thorn asked, as he swung his long legs out of the jeep.

"Quiet as the grave," answered Brockway. He turned briefly away to call softly to the great-coated soldier who had diverted the jeep. "Keep a look-out further along, Corporal. If anything or anyone comes up this lane, I want 'em stopped before they get this far."

The soldier touched the narrow visor of his red-topped cap in acknowledgement.

"Yes, sir. Leave it to me sir."

He disappeared into the night, taking the direction from which the jeep had approached. The sound of his heavy boots, crunching on to frozen mud, faded slowly. Brockway rejoined Thorn.

"I've got another man watching the cottage. The girl's been inside all evening. In bed now, I reckon. Her blackout isn't as good as it should be but there hasn't been a glimmer of light since just after eleven."

Chisholm had stayed inside the jeep and Brockway nodded in his direction.

"How's our man?" he asked Thorn.

"A little bit nervy, but he'll be OK," said Thorn. "He knows what's expected of him."

"No second thoughts?"

"No. He has scores to settle. He wants to see it through."

"I hope to God it works," said Brockway.

"We'll find out soon enough," answered Thorn. "We ain't gonna get no medals if it goes wrong." He moved round the jeep and tapped lightly on the windscreen. "It's time, Chizz."

Chisholm got out of the jeep and joined the others, blowing on his hands. He wore no overcoat and was shivering in the frosty night. He shielded his eyes as Thorn bathed him in the light of a pocket flashlight.

"Will he do?" the American asked Brockway. Chisholm looked and felt like a tramp. His grey suit was crumpled and mud-stained. His chin was dark with three days' stubble.

"Christ!" exclaimed Brockway. "You look like you been sleeping in the woods. She'll get a shock when she sees you."

"That's the general idea," said Chisholm. "How long do we stand around here? I'm bloody frozen."

"You can get going whenever you like. You know what you've got to do?"

"Yes. We've been over it a hundred times."

"Good," said Brockway. He cleared his throat in a fussy, nervous kind of way. "We're grateful for what you're doing, Captain Chisholm. We appreciate it, truly." More brusquely, he added: "We'll stay well out of sight, but we won't be far away."

They walked along the lane, screened from view by the briar hedge that skirted one side. Another of Brockway's redcaps loomed from the shadows to meet them at a turn in the lane.

"All quiet, sir," he reported.

Brockway turned to Chisholm.

"The cottage is just around the bend. It stands about fifty yards or so back from the road, all on its own. There's not another for miles. We won't go any further."

"Right," said Chisholm, "I'll be on my way."

"Good luck, Chizz," whispered Thorn. He accompanied

Chisholm to the bend and then watched as he clambered over a low stone wall and crossed a flat expanse of rimy lawn towards the dark shape of cottage beyond.

Chisholm took a deep breath and started hammering with a fist on the front door. With only brief pauses, he kept it up for fully a minute. Then he waited, listening. He could hear movements inside.

"Anina," he called out. "Anina! Let me in!"

There was the sound of a heavy bolt being drawn back on the other side of the door. The door opened a few inches.

"Who is it?" came the voice of Anina Calvi from the dark wedge of space.

"It's me, Anina. Chizz Chisholm. Let me in, please. Hurry! I'm frozen stiff."

A chain was removed and the door opened. He pushed past her into the unlit interior. She closed the door, replaced the chain, and guided him into an L-shaped kitchen-cum-living-room. He had stumbled into the middle of it before she found the light-switch and flooded it with light. As he stood there, a hand half-raised against the sudden dazzle of light, she let out a cry at the sight of his dishevelled state and unshaven face. Now that the moment had come to face her, his mouth had gone strangely dry and a panicky dread filled him. He avoided her eyes by making a pretence of rubbing his hands together for warmth. He was shivering. He really was cold. But his shaking misery was as much due to the jangled state of his nerves as his low body heat.

"Hector, what has happened to you?" The questions came in a tumbling rush. "How did you get here? How did you find out about this place? Who told you I was here?"

He played desperately for time. His wits were scattered to the four winds. He let the questions bounce off him, unanswered, as he struggled to pull himself together.

"I need a drink, Anina," he blurted out. "Something to stop my damned teeth from chattering. Please! Anything!"

The little shrug she gave, no more than a heave of the shoulders and toss of the hands, bristled with impatience and irritation. Her anxious face was pale with shock. But she desisted from talk and brushed past him towards a mahogany sideboard. From the cabinet section she extracted a bottle and poured a generous measure from it into a glass. He gulped it down gratefully.

"I need your help, Anina," he said.

She stared at him apprehensively, her dark eyebrows arched still in an impatient frown.

"Look at the state of you." The scolding tone of her words covered unspoken anxieties. "How did you find your way here? How did you know I would be here?"

"I took a chance on you being here," he replied. "And finding out about this place wasn't difficult. The theatrical agency in Brighton who book your concerts . . . I phoned them . . . They gave me your address, eventually."

"They had no right to."

"I spun them a story . . . Said you were wanted for an American tour with Bob Hope and I had to contact you right away . . . They were falling over themselves to help after that . . ." He was watching her face, the way her lips were pursed. "You don't look too pleased to see me, Anina."

The frown deepened perceptibly. She pulled her long housecoat more closely around her body.

"Why should I be pleased?" she burst out. "You frightened the life out of me. I was fast asleep. Do you expect me to dance with joy at being wakened in the middle of the night?"

"I'm sorry I frightened you, Anina. This place takes a bit of finding in the dark."

"Look at your clothes! Have you any idea what you look like?"

"I'm sorry for the way I look, Anina."

"You said you needed help . . ."

He turned away from her, letting his shoulders droop. He didn't want her to see his face in case he fumbled the big lie that was coming.

"I'm in big trouble . . . The police are looking for me . . . They were taking me back to Brighton . . . I jumped off a train . . . This side of Haywards Heath . . . Nearly killed myself . . . But I gave them the slip . . ."

He turned. She was staring at him, pop-eyed.

"The police!" She got the words out in a tortured whisper of disbelief. "Why? What in God's name have you done?"

He found he could look her in the eye now. Lying wasn't quite as difficult as he had feared. After the first half dozen, it got easier.

"That night at the Beaumaris, Anina . . . A Canadian army

officer was found dead . . . At first, it looked like an accident . . . Now, they're saying it was murder—and that I did it."

"Oh, no!"

Her hands had gone up to her face. If the horror she expressed was feigned, she was making it look good.

"You shouldn't have come here, Hector. Can't you see what an impossible position you're putting me in? I don't want any trouble. I don't want to be involved."

He let disappointment show on his face.

"You're throwing me out?"

"I want you to leave of your own accord. Now! Before anyone finds you here. I'll give you food, money, anything! But you've got to go!"

"We could go together . . . We could make it to Ireland . . ."

"No! No! You're out of your mind!"

She was well and truly agitated now. The eyes that had beguiled him were dark with hate. His showed only sorrow. Sorrow at all that he read in her face.

"That night we had . . . It meant nothing to you, Anina? I was just another ship that passed in the night?"

His calm regret seemed to infuriate her more. But it was the fury of forced retreat. She became defensive.

"How could you expect it to mean anything to me? You were a stranger. You still are! I was amusing myself . . . I felt sorry for you."

She knew how to hurt, damn her! Chisholm winced at the angry taunt in her voice, but he endured her scorn. He had been shrinking from hurting her. Now, she was making it easier for him.

"You've got interesting friends, Anina. If you won't help me get out of the country, maybe they will." He prodded the suggestion into the dialogue from nowhere, taking her by surprise and pricking the rising balloon of her rancour. He held his breath as she stared at him, puzzled.

"Friends?" she said.

"Yes, Anina. You don't need to pretend with me any more. Your Little Miss Innocent is wasted on me. I *know* you're working for the Germans."

"You're insane!"

Fury again masked her face, but it had not altogether covered the quick start of fear his softly spoken assertion had provoked. He smiled.

"There's no need to worry, Anina. I get on excellently with the Germans. If I hadn't been so damned matey with them when I was a prisoner, I wouldn't be in the jam I'm in right now. But you did your little bit, too, didn't you? In Brighton. You tried to set me up good."

"I don't know what you're talking about," she snapped back at him. "And I'm not listening to any more. I'm going to telephone the police."

He shrugged carelessly.

"Go ahead. They've got a lot more to hang you for than they've got on me. Damnit, I *know* I didn't kill that Canadian in Brighton – which is more than I can say for you. The only crime I've committed was like I said . . . I was too pally with the Jerries . . . And somebody seems hellbent on making me pay for it . . ."

She had taken tentative steps towards the wall telephone hanging near the door but made no move to pick it up. She glanced at him over her shoulder, uncertainty flickering in her eyes.

"Go ahead," he urged her. "Phone the damned police!"

She turned away from the telephone. Her anger was bottled for the moment: under control. She was puzzled, watchful, wary of him.

"Hector . . . I don't really want to turn you in," she said, but her change of heart made her sound less than wholly convincing. She shook her head as if in great confusion. ". . . All this fanciful nonsense, where do you get it?"

He sighed wearily.

"Anina, let's stop the kidding, eh? Don't you want to get out? Can't you see that it's only a matter of time before they get you? They've been watching you, too, you know. They had security people all over the Beaumaris that night. I thought it was me they were after . . . But I'm not all that important to them. It was you they were after. You and your Canadian chum." She had gone chalky white. He was drawing blood with every thrust. Still, she would not admit defeat.

"Nothing you're saying makes any sense," she persisted, "I just don't know what you're talking about. Those accusations . . . They're absurd . . . Fantasies."

He greeted this with shaking head and a pitying look.

"Anina, Anina," he sighed. "Save your act for somebody else. You're a phoney and I know you're a phoney. You gave yourself away to me."

She stared at him with stark fear. Her lips trembled with a reply but the words died in her throat. Chisholm turned the screw.

"Who are you, Anina? You can tell me about it now. Is the real Anina Calvi dead? I know there was a real Anina Calvi – but you're not her. You're not the real thing. You weren't born and brought up in Buenos Aires any more than I was."

This time a sound did emerge from her trembling lips: a strangled whisper of denial.

"No, no . . . You're wrong . . . I am Anina Calvi."

He shook his head, his eyes never leaving hers, disbelieving.

"No, Señorita – or should it be Fraulein? I don't think you've ever been in Argentina in your life. Certainly not BA. You'd never heard of Retiro Park. That was careless, Anina. Very careless. Like a Londoner saying he'd never heard of Buckingham Palace or Billingsgate Fish Market. I bet you've never even picked a *collectivo* off a tree."

"I have!" she cried desperately, her naked panic feverish. "I have!"

He laughed at her.

"Anina." There was gentle reproach in the way he spoke her name. "Anina, a *collectivo* doesn't grow on a tree like an apple. It's a taxi-bus. BA's swarming with the damned things."

Her face crumpled. She had lost and they both knew it. As the realisation sank in, it seemed to calm her.

"What are you going to do?" she asked quietly.

He took a step towards her and reached out a hand, letting it rest lightly on her shoulder. She seemed to wince at the touch, but she did not shake the hand away. He spoke soft-voiced.

"I said I wanted to get to Ireland . . . I still do. Come with me."

She looked up at him, eyes darting, trying to read more from his face than he allowed to show.

"I underestimated you," she said. "You're not quite as stupid as you look."

He laughed softly.

"And I love you, too!"

She seemed not to hear the rejoinder. No flicker of amusement came back from her eyes. Their scrutiny was intense, unwavering.

"Is this a trap?" She darted the question at him.

"A trap?"

"Answer me!"

"No, of course it isn't a trap," he said. But for the first time, he was conscious of his words sounding lame. Her direct counter-attack had caught him wrong-footed and unprepared.

"I don't trust you," she said flatly, sensing the uncertainty in him. He felt himself forced further on to the defensive. But he did not give ground.

"*You* don't trust me?" he scoffed. "That's bloody rich! After what you've done to me, I should wring your bloody neck! Half the police in England are looking for me because of you . . . And you have the gall to say you don't trust me!"

He pushed her away roughly and stood glowering at her as if resisting the temptation to do her bodily violence. It was not difficult to summon up a sense of outrage. The more he thought about how nasty a piece of work was wrapped up in this doe-eyed bundle of femininity, the easier it was to remind himself that she deserved no mercy from him or anyone else.

"I need time to think. I feel so confused . . ." Her plea was a concession to Chisholm's powers of conviction. She was unsure again. She needed time to make up her mind about him. He gave her the truce she wanted. He wanted a breather himself. He was drained from the bizarre confrontation, with its emotional acrobatics performed on a tightrope of reality.

"Look," he said, his demeanour conciliatory, "why don't you make us both a cup of coffee? We can talk things over in a calm way."

She leapt at the suggestion and invited him to clean himself up while she attended to things in the kitchen.

As he splashed water on his face in a chintz-curtained bathroom, the tension of his masquerade caught up on him. It was as if his whole body wanted to tremble. Yet, his reflection in the mirror was calm enough. He realised that until a few moments ago – when he had actually exposed her lies – he had never quite believed that Anina was a German spy. Now, the last doubts had gone and it brought a dimension of terrifying reality to the charade he had undertaken.

When he returned from the bathroom, she was pouring coffee into two large china mugs. For all her beauty, she had a strained and haggard look. She stirred sugar into her coffee in a preoccupied way. He wondered what was going through her mind. She gave him an indication without looking up from her idle rotation of the spoon in her mug.

"What was it gave you the idea that I was working for Germany?"

He thought about this for a moment.

"It was a calculated guess. It was the only answer that made sense. All the questions I was asked . . . They thought I was a collaborator, you see. Accused me of selling out . . . Your name kept coming up."

"And did you sell out, Hector? Were you a collaborator?"

Chisholm smiled.

"Let's just say that when the Germans had me, I didn't make life too hard for myself. I knew the side my bread was buttered on."

She considered this. After a moment, she asked: "That brooch, Hector – the one you gave me in the Beaumaris . . . Was that a put-up job?"

"Possibly," he replied. "It was innocent enough as far as I was concerned. I must admit I was curious about you . . . They said you were Rick's girlfriend and yet Rick had never mentioned you to me . . . I just didn't know where you fitted in . . . And the penny hadn't dropped then . . . It all seemed genuine enough to me because it was the Yanks who wanted me to look you up and give you the brooch. They were a damned sight more sympathetic to me than my own lot – and I couldn't see any harm in doing what they wanted. That was before . . ."

He let his voice trail away.

"Before what?" she prompted.

"Before I met you . . . Before they found Lomax dead . . . Before they pulled me in and tried to pin his murder on me . . . That was when I started putting two and two together. They *knew* I'd been with you after the concert . . . They knew every damned move I'd made."

"Did you tell them about us . . . Spending the night together?"

"Yes."

He could sense her anxiety as she waited for him to enlarge on the simple affirmative to her question.

"And what did they say?"

"They didn't believe me."

Was it relief that caused her almost imperceptibly to draw in her breath? He went on: "They said I was lying because I was wrong about your room. They said you didn't have a room just along from mine . . . That yours was four floors up. They said the room that we were in belonged to some army colonel called Green. That was when I started to think some very nasty things about you, Anina."

"And yet you came here to me. Why?"

He tried to summon disappointment to the look he gave her.

"Don't you know? Nothing like you ever happened to me before, Anina. Even now I don't want to believe that it was all a game of pretend to you. I think you're probably a bitch, Anina, but you're the loveliest, most desirable bitch that I've ever met. I want you. That's why I came. I want you more than anything else on this whole damned earth."

He felt sick within himself as he tried to put conviction into what he said. The words seemed to pour out without any hesitation but, in his own ears, they sounded hollow and patently false. He wanted to hide his face from her and it was near panic that forced him to conceal his loss of nerve by reaching for her hand across the table and following up with a clumsy lunge that ended with him holding her awkwardly and pressing his lips on to hers.

She pushed him away, struggling to free herself from the unwelcome embrace. He let her go, inwardly cursing himself for ever being persuaded to embark on a pantomime of entrapment for which he had neither taste nor the necessary talent of deceit. It took him a dazed moment to realise that, far from having blown everything, he seemed to have lent authenticity to the part he was playing. His impetuous attempt to cover up his ineptitude as a liar seemed somehow to have given credence to his claim that a lusting desire had overridden all else in motivating his need to turn to her.

Her angry disgust for him was all too real. But it was not his failure to deceive that was the reason for it. It was his presumption that she would fall swooning into his arms and embrace his fantasies with an equal blindness to reality. It was his presumption in believing, even, that she was available. Men did not leap unbidden into her arms: they waited for her command.

Angry as she was, her annoyance was tempered by the sense of power that Chisholm's declaration of dependence had restored to her. If there was one thing that the woman who called herself Anina Calvi understood, it was that weakness in the human male that she had exploited all her life: that drive to possess a woman that blinds him to the bounds of folly. Evidence of that weakness in Chisholm reassured her. It meant that Chisholm's stupidity in seeking her out was not governed by a conscious desire to do her harm but by the same animal instinct that leads a dog unerringly to the kennel of a bitch where once he had been welcomed.

She sought to atone for rejection of his clumsy advances.

"We're both tired," she said. "Why don't we both get some rest? You're safe here. We can decide what we're going to do about things in the morning." Seeing his expression, she added: "There's a spare room. Would you mind, Hector? My mood's all wrong for anything else . . . I'm sorry."

"I thought we might talk a bit more," he said.

"Haven't we done enough talking for one night?"

"I've done most of it. It's your turn now. Should I go on calling you Anina?"

She shrugged.

"Is it important?"

"It is to me."

"The less you know about me, the better. I mean that, Hector."

"I want to know all there is to know about you. And stop calling me Hector. Try Chizz."

"Are you trying to bully me . . . Chizz?"

"I'm trying to come to terms with the fact that I've made love to you but I don't even know your name. It bothers me that all I really know about you is that you're in a line of business that makes a virtue out of mayhem and murder. The bigger the double-cross, the bigger the iron cross . . . Can't you see? I'm trying to get some kind of perspective about the girl I'm crazy for . . . If I'm going to get hanged for you, I need to know things like how in hell you got into such a stinking business in the first place . . ."

"I'm not ashamed of what I do," she interrupted sharply. "I risk my life every minute of the day for what I believe in. And that's more than you can say! You're interested only in your own neck . . . What was it you said? Oh, yes – the side your bread's buttered on. That hardly gives you the right to question my morality."

"Go easy," he protested. "That's rather hitting below the belt."

190

"So what?" she came back waspishly. "That's about the level of your mind."

Chisholm forced a grin.

"I asked for that, didn't I?" He tried a fresh tack. "You know, your English is perfect."

"So is my Spanish, and my German, and my French . . ."

"Where did you go to school? Or is that classified information?"

"Lucerne, Vienna, Paris, Madrid, Dublin . . . My parents travelled a lot."

"But they never got as far as Buenos Aires?"

She had the grace to smile.

"No."

"What happened to the real Anina Calvi?"

"She disappeared."

"That must have been very convenient."

"I shared a flat with her for nearly a year. But I had nothing to do with her . . . disappearance. That was taken care of by others. I simply took her place."

"Why?"

"She had good connections in this country. Not that she had ever been here. The only people here who had met her were people who had been in the Argentine when she was about six years old." She smiled. "Girls change a lot when they grow up. They keep changing the way they do their hair. They dye it. They change their faces with new make-up. It was easy to pass myself off as her. We were alike in the important things . . . height, eye colour . . . We even took the same size of bra. She was heaven-sent for *Schatten Gruppe* . . ."

"*Schatten Gruppe?*"

Her boastful recital had all but carried her away. The last had slipped out. Now, she regretted her talkativeness.

"It's meaningless," she covered up. "A girls' school term . . . The German doesn't usually slip out . . ." Almost defensively, she added: "I *am* a German, you know."

Chisholm elected to appear oblivious of her seeming indiscretion. But he had noted it. He smiled broadly as he mentally prepared the next strike.

"You're quite a girl," he said, with what he hoped was the right note of admiration to put her off guard. "How many of you are working this stolen identity racket for the glory of the Third Reich?"

The directness of the question earned him a penetrating stare.

"I've told you enough," she said testily and, picking up the coffee mugs, carried them over to the sink. He followed her, mentally kicking himself for his stupidity. He should have known better than make a jokey remark about the Third Reich to someone who was probably a fanatical Nazi at heart.

"Look, I'm not wanting you to part with deadly secrets . . ." He was compounding one lie with a bigger one – because that was exactly what he was trying to do. ". . . If we are going to try for Ireland and you have people here who can help, I want to know. We'll need papers, places where we can stay out of sight." He was almost parroting Thorn's instructions to him.

She rinsed a mug under the tap.

"There is someone I can trust," she said thoughtfully. Then she seemed to make a decision. "But I'm not going to risk his cover for you. Or me, for that matter. He's too important. In any case, he won't be back in this country before the thaw . . ." She turned then and the smile she gave came as a surprise. "He and you have a lot in common, if you only knew it."

"Don't tell me he eats peas off his knife, too?" Chisholm said, with calculated flippancy. The joke fell on stony ground.

"Don't mock him," she rebuked. "He's the bravest man I know."

"Have you slept with him?" Chisholm had meant to provoke, but the question managed to sound even more maliciously spiteful than he intended. She glared angrily at him.

"You have a dirty, one-track mind. If you must know, the answer is no. It's never been that way between us." Her expression softened as if there was regret somewhere behind the revelation. It was there, too, in her tone when she added. "He's the one man who could have had me any time, just for the asking . . . His strength alone excited me . . ." She snapped suddenly out of the reverie that seemed to have held her momentarily. Self-consciously, as if Chisholm had caught her thinking aloud, she snapped: "It's really none of your business."

"I'm jealous," he said. "You really think a lot of this bloke?"

"He could break you in two," she retorted with another sudden flaring of anger. "And he might just do that if anything happens to me because of you."

"Thanks for the warning," Chisholm said, with a wry face. She fixed him with a stare that was devoid of warmth. Her pretty lips twisted into a smile that teased. Cruelty glinted in the wide eyes.

"It *is* a warning. Oh, it *is* a warning. Remember it, and remember it well." She laughed, but the sound jarred Chisholm. "We were well named, he and I. He was Quasimodo and I was the gipsy. Beware Quasimodo's revenge, Hector Chisholm. If anything happens to me, you'll have him to reckon with. And he really will break you in small pieces."

Chisholm laughed.

"Quasimodo and Gipsy? Are you having me on?"

She ignored his scorn.

"Just *nommes de guerre*. His choice, not mine. I would have gone for something more classical. Something more Homeric."

"Oh yes, Poseidon and Aphrodite, perhaps?"

She looked at him as if he had said something astonishingly astute for a lower order intelligence.

"Not bad," she said. "Not bad. As a matter of fact, the last time I saw him, I suggested Jason amd Medea would have been appropriate. A little private joke. But he was afraid it might change our luck."

"Oh, I see," said Chisholm, pulling a face. "It's all hokum to me. I'm not really up on the spy business. You'll have to coach me."

"Can't we just call it a night?" she said wearily. "I'm tired and I want to go to bed. To sleep."

"OK, OK." He held up his arms in a token of surrender. "Show me the spare room."

He was not displeased at the progress he had made. She seemed to have accepted him on her own terms rather than his – but she did seem to have accepted him. It was more than he had dared to hope for. He had learned more from her than he had any right to expect and, he realised, he could easily spoil things by pushing her too far. Once or twice he had come perilously close to giving the whole game away.

She showed him into a small but pleasant bedroom with heavy drapes pulled over the mullioned windows he had seen from outside. The wallpaper was bright: a floral mixture with white and pink predominant. The single bed was covered by a quilt that matched the decor.

"It's an old bed but comfortable," she said. "Will you

promise to stay in it?"

"I promise," he said, smiling broadly.

She was about to leave, when he could not resist one final question. She waited for it with a patience that had worn very thin.

"Well?" she said.

"It's about Lomax . . . That night at the Beaumaris . . . Something that's puzzled me."

"What about him?" she asked wearily.

"They said I poisoned him . . . How, I don't know . . . It was because they found a jar of pills in my coat . . . I don't know what they were and I'd no idea they were there . . ."

"What about them?"

He sighed, as if what he had to say was going to be painful.

"I know it must have been you or your Canadian chum who put them there . . ." He saw the frown of annoyance cross her face and held up his hands in a placatory gesture. "OK, we won't go into that. You had your reasons. That's not what's been worrying me. It was Lomax . . . Why did he have to be killed? Why was it necessary?"

"You mean you don't know?" she asked. Her surprise was unhidden. "You're the one who made him suspicious. He made the mistake of running straight to Raoul Gilbert . . ."

"Gilbert?" Chisholm interrupted. "It was Gilbert?"

The question, and his surprise, seemed to puzzle her. Then a truth seemed to dawn on her. She stared at him, her lips slightly parted. Chisholm could not understand why she was looking at him the way she was: as if she had just discovered that he had bubonic plague. He opened his mouth to speak but she cut him short.

"No more, please. Look, I've had enough . . . I'm sorry. I just can't take any more tonight. I'm going to bed."

There was no detaining her this time. With a sharp "goodnight", she was gone. Chisholm shrugged philosophically and, sitting down on the bed, kicked off his shoes. Taking off only his jacket, he switched off the light and groped his way back to the bed. He climbed under the quilt and pulled it about him.

The girl who called herself Anina Calvi went into the adjacent room but not to bed. She slipped out of her housecoat and cotton nightgown and dressed quickly: exchanging her nightwear for slacks and a heavy woollen sweater. Then in stockinged feet, she crossed the room to a bookshelf on a wall facing the big double bed. She ran a finger along the spines of the dozen or so books and selected one. It was a leather-bound edition of *Palgrave's Golden Treasury*, with a brass locking clip securing the covers.

She opened the book and held back the front cover. Inside, the pages had been scooped out to make a snug-fitting resting place for a .25 calibre Astra Firecat automatic. She carefully extracted the tiny Spanish-made gun and checked that it was fully loaded. Then she stretched out on the bed and lay staring at the ceiling, her fingers caressing the cold metal of the gun at her side. She had no thought of sleep.

Thirteen

Shot in the Dark

Chisholm had no intention of falling asleep. He lay under the quilt and allowed himself some quiet amusement at the thought of Thorn and Brockway somewhere outside in the sub-zero weather. By now, he reckoned, they would have bitten their fingernails down to their elbows wondering what had been going on inside the cottage.

They had told Chisholm that they wanted the whole thing wrapped up by morning. There was going to be hell to pay if it wasn't and the wrong people got scent of the night's activities. Thanks mainly to Thorn, the Brighton affair—although officially swept under the carpet—was by no means a dead letter. Under bureaucratic smokescreens of varying ingenuity, put out by both Hibberd and Brockway—and to a lesser extent, Vaughan—Thorn had been allowed to pursue matters in his own unorthodox way. Hibberd, in particular, had been prepared to take on anyone and everyone up to the level of the Joint Chiefs of Staff over his right to assign a man to the unclosed file on the death by stabbing of Lieutenant R. Thomson, US Army.

Without being privy to the almost surreptitious way the three planners of "Thumbscrew" were defying orders from above, Chisholm was aware of a "walking-on-eggs" approach by those most concerned in solving the mysteries of Brighton and St Cyr des Bains. Thorn had kept him involved and informed.

Chisholm knew, for instance, that it had suited Thorn and the others that their interest in Lomax's death had never leaked out. Without reason for doubting otherwise, a coroner had ruled that the Canadian Major's death was accidental: that Lomax had hastened his own death by taking a small quantity

196

of sodium barbitone either in error or in ignorance of the effects the drug would have on him.

There had been one unfortunate and wholly unexpected development. On no stronger a pretext than the discovery of Anina Calvi's photograph among Rick Thomson's personal effects, Thorn had interviewed Colonel E. (Teddy) Green at Combined Operations HQ, where he was a planner and had access to the most sensitive military secrets. From Thorn's point of view, the interview had been totally unproductive. Green had, in the first instance, become extremely flustered over the possibility that his wife might learn of his relationship with the singer. Then, when it dawned on him that Thorn's main concern was the possible transmission of secrets to the Germans via Anina Calvi, Green had become almost ill with shock and refused to answer any questions that would have confirmed his folly or incriminated his paramour.

Half an hour after Thorn had left his office, Green had taken his service revolver and shot himself.

There had been shockwaves: with accusations rumbling through the corridors of power that Green had been needlessly hounded to his death over nothing more heinous than his infatuation for a younger woman. Outrage was expressed that a brilliant officer's patriotism should even have been called into question by implication. The heavy-handed security services and their secret minions were cast as the real villains in the piece, for victimising a man whose only crime was an unwise, but otherwise innocent, affair of the heart.

Hibberd had not escaped censure but, oddly enough, most of the odium had been directed at Brockway, with his known bee in the bonnet about Anina Calvi. The Canadian had blandly denied any part in a vendetta against the singer or her middle-aged boyfriend. Green's death had, however, been taken by Brockway as the strongest indicator to date of Anina's guilt and had hardened his resolve to expose her treachery beyond all shadow of doubt.

Not even Brockway, however, had been prepared to risk the arrest and interrogation of the singer. She had only to remain silent in that event to render such a move counter-productive. They would be no nearer knowing the size and scope of the operation of which she was a part; and failure to disprove her innocence would give their detractors a field day. Brockway's head would roll for a start.

Thorn's idea to use Chisholm to compromise Anina Calvi had appealed instantly to Brockway. It left all their other options open. It was better than hauling her in and trying to break her. Using Chisholm, there was no saying how much she might unwittingly betray if pressurised to do so.

It was Thorn who had discovered the location in Sussex of Anina Calvi's hideaway cottage and learned of her habit of retiring there for days on end. Thorn had then discussed with Chisholm the idea of confronting her in a way that forced her to show her hand. The American's original plan had been to hide himself in the cottage ahead of Chisholm's arrival and be in a position to corroborate the singer's reactions to Chisholm's fugitive role. But that part of the plan had been abandoned as impractical. Concealment in the cottage would have been difficult and the risk of the entire venture being scuppered by Thorn being discovered prematurely was too high.

It had been left to Chisholm, therefore, to do the best he could on his own. He had doubted his ability to carry it off. Thorn had reminded him of Brighton.

"Don't go soft on her now, Chizz," the American had argued. "Just remember the way she tried to sucker you. You know what would have happened if her scheme had worked and you had been charged with murder. She would have sworn blind that you didn't spend the night with her. It would have been her word against yours, with you needing her for an alibi more than she needed you. How she worked the key trick with that Colonel, I don't know – but you can bet your last dollar that she had enough on that guy to make sure that he said just what he was supposed to say. And you would have been cooked! Good grief, Chizz, that poor sap must have known she was creaming secrets out of him, but he was so deep in hock to her that he wouldn't say a word about her even when he got the chance. Instead, he goes and blows his brains out! You're the one who can nail her, Chizz . . . Beat her at her own goddamned game . . . And you've got to nail her good!"

Well, he had nailed her. She had swallowed the fiction that he was wanted for Lomax's murder. And he had forced her to admit her German nationality and the stealing of the real Anina's identity. There was enough information for Thorn and Brockway to take the lid right off the case without running foul of all those people who had been so anxious to protect the person they believed was Anina Calvi. Ironically, Anina Calvi was almost certainly beyond the reach of anyone's protection: dead in some unmarked grave in Spain, most likely.

As he lay in the dark, Chisholm felt a wave of compassion sweep him for that unknown Anina. Poor kid, rotting unmourned while her place had been taken by someone whom she had probably regarded as a friend.

Chisholm looked at his watch. An hour had passed since his reluctant hostess had switched out his light. He eased himself out of the bed and found his shoes and jacket. Crossing to the window, he moved the heavy curtains aside and examined the windows. They were hinged vertically to open outwards. He unlatched the catch on one and pushed. It moved less than an inch and stuck. The timber frame had been damp and swollen, and it had iced up against the sash.

He gave the frame a sharp thump with his fist. The window moved about nine inches and jammed again. Chisholm cursed softly as the noise echoed through the silent house.

She knew what had to be done. Chisholm had to die. He had to be removed as though he had never been. Certainly, any trace that he set foot in the cottage would have to be erased.

But how was the killing to be done?

Ideally, she had to get him out of the cottage and to a place that would serve as both execution ground and graveyard. A possibility was the old gravel quarry behind Knott's Hill. No one ever went near the place – it was remote enough – and the water in the quarry was deep. But what pretext could she use to get him there? Say it was a place where she had money and emergency papers hidden? Maybe. She did not doubt that she had the wit to invent a convincing excuse. The difficult part would be the actual deed.

It would have to be quick, with everything she needed handy: something to weight the body, some rope. Her story would have to be good enough to put him off-guard. Good enough even to get him to do all the hard work – like carrying all that was necessary to make his disappearance permanent. Like Anina Calvi's disappearance had been permanent. She patted the little Firecat, now a comforting weight against her thigh in the flap pocket of her slacks. It would do the job. At close quarters, it was just as deadly as a weapon four times its size. And it would make no more noise than a cork popping.

Damn him! Why had he come here? She felt a surge of

venomous fury for the man in the next room. Things seemed to have been going wrong for her from the moment in Brighton when she had first clapped eyes on him. She had been walking on a razor's edge ever since, with nothing seeming to go right. It had meant one improvisation after another – and now, like the proverbial bad penny, he had turned up here at the cottage, threatening everything.

He had said "they" had been watching her. Just the thought that she had been under surveillance of any kind made her go cold with fear. How much did "they" know or guess? Was she finally compromised, finished?

A sudden sharp noise from the next room made her sit bolt upright on the bed. It was followed by a second sound, even more pronounced. She slid from the bed and moved silently to the door. In the hallway, she hesitated only long enough to palm the baby-sized automatic. She put her ear to the door of the room where she had left Chisholm. There was a clatter of sound that she immediately identified: the crash of a window flying open on its hinges.

She plunged into the room. There was no need to grope for the light. Chisholm was astride the window sill, framed against the starlight glow: his dark figure a silhouette on a screen of filtered grey.

"What are you doing?" she shouted. Her screech was redolent with panic.

The figure in the window froze.

"I'm leaving, sweetheart," came Chisholm's voice. It was cheerful with the resignation of one who has been caught without a prayer and knew it. "Go back to bed, Anina. I'm letting you off the hook. I shouldn't have come here . . . It was a mistake. I'm going."

"No!" she screamed. "No!"

"Sorry, but it's for the best. No more arguments. I'm off. *Auf wiedersehen.*" He started to move and the arm holding the gun came up. She fired.

Chisholm, half-in and half-out of the window, felt the sharp flaming of pain in his chest and then he was falling outwards from the window. He had a sensation of floating gently, as if his body had no more weight than thistledown. But more intense than pain or any other feeling was a kind of disbelief: an overwhelming perception of utter surprise.

* * *

At 2 a.m., Thorn had decided that, with Brockway and the redcap watching the cottage, his own services were not immediately required. There was a long night ahead of them yet. Chisholm had been inside the house now for two hours and that was a good sign. It meant that the girl must have swallowed his story and that the first big hurdle had been cleared. They had to give Chisholm time now to play the cards at his disposal and by persuasion, bluff, or by putting the plain fear of death into her, get the girl to commit herself.

Thorn walked along the lane to the jeep. If Chisholm didn't show himself by six in the morning, they would have to move the vehicles to a less conspicuous spot and be ready for any one of a number of possible developments. If Chisholm came out alone there was no problem. If the girl came out alone or she and Chisholm came out together, the watchers were to tail them at a discreet distance. The same would apply if the girl called the village for a taxi: the transport she most habitually used. Thorn thought that no eventuality had escaped their consideration, even the girl's acceptance of the flee-with-me-to-Ireland proposition that Chisholm had been coached to make. Thorn doubted somehow that it would come to that, but they had to be ready for anything.

At the jeep, Thorn drank a cup of coffee from a Thermos and then sat in the passenger seat dragging pensively on a Chesterfield. The jeep offered no escape from the cold. Better moving about outside than sitting, icing over from the toes up. He stuck the Thermos in the pocket of his coat and headed back towards the cottage. Brockway would be glad of a warming cup, he had no doubt.

He had not reached the bend in the lane when he heard a sharp popping noise followed by a faint cry. It came from the cottage.

The sound had been scarcely loud enough to be a shot – and yet it was the only explanation he could attach to the soft but sudden report. He hurried forward at a run.

Nearer the cottage, both Brockway and the redcap had been alerted by the same sound. They came to the same conclusion as Thorn. It may only have been from a kiddy's popgun – but it had been a shot. Brockway, whispering low and urgently, ordered the redcap to get as close to the cottage as he could and take a look. He cautioned him to move silently.

The redcap was surprisingly light on his feet for a man of his size. He went over the wall silently and, at a low crouch, was quickly across the rime-covered lawn. Heavy service revolver in hand, he began a cautious detour of the cottage, following the edge of cultivated flowerbed against the building. He stayed low, below the level of mullioned windows, his eyes on the frosted panes: alert to any glimpse of movement inside. He caught sight of one window, swung wide open. At the same moment his outstretched hand encountered Chisholm's body entangled grotesquely across a hydrangea bush. It took the redcap several heart-stopping seconds to realise what it was flattening the hydrangea. His exploring fingers, searching across Chisholm's shirt-front for a heartbeat, met a spreading ooze of blood from his chest. He quickly withdrew the hand at a sudden sound above him, from somewhere in the room beyond the open window. He turned soundlessly, easing his weight from one haunch to the other, his raised revolver pointed at the window. With a hand sticky with blood, he unclipped a battery-lamp from his belt and raised it so that he was poised, arms well apart and one leg outstretched for balance: eyes, lamp and gun all trained on the window. He saw the dim outline of head and shoulders appear at the open window.

"Hold it right there!" he warned in a low growl. "You move as much as an eyebrow and you're dead."

He flicked the switch of his lamp. For an instant, caught in the circle of white light, he glimpsed the terrified face of a young woman. He saw her arm rise as if to shield her eyes from the dazzle of the lamp's beam. But if the movement was a reflex born of panic, its intent was not to shy from the light but to extinguish it. Even as the girl's arm came up, her finger was tightening on the Firecat's miniscule trigger. She fired straight at the light, missing it, but hitting the fleshy biceps of the arm in which the lamp was held.

Although the redcap had raised his revolver in threat, the necessity of using it had not crossed his mind. The girl was wanted alive. But now the decision was taken from him. As the Firecat's bullet struck home, a surprise of pain fired a current that leapt from left arm to right across the shoulders of the redcap and caused him to clench his fist in convulsive reaction. The .45 roared in his hand, a thunderclap echo to the Firecat's pop. The face, bathed white in the lamp's beam, disappeared in a fountainburst of blood and tissue as the lamp fell from his hand.

Brockway was first to the scene, with Thorn arriving almost on his heels. Both men had thrown caution to the wind at the loud report of the .45. They found the redcap kneeling, nursing the upper part of his left arm.

His pain was nothing in his anticipation of Brockway's wrath.

"I'm sorry, sir. I think maybe I killed her. She's inside . . . I didn't mean it. The goddamned gun just went off in my hand when I was hit . . ."

Thorn, who had drawn his own .38 Police Positive, slid it back in its holster. He lifted Chisholm clear of the hydrangea bush and bent over him.

"Is he dead, too?" Brockway's question was terse with chagrin.

"I don't think so. But he's in a bad way. Chest wound."

"I'll see to him," Brockway said gruffly. "You check out the girl."

As Brockway knelt at Chisholm's side, Thorn pulled himself up on to the window ledge and eased himself feet first into the bedroom of the cottage. He thumbed the switch of the flashlight.

The girl was sprawled on her back, one arm flung out. Where her left eye had been, there was now only a pulpy red mess. What was left of her head was haloed by a pool of blood.

Thorn switched off the flashlight and leaned out the window. He took a deep breath and welcomed the fresh night air in a gulp through his nostrils.

"She's dead all right," he called to Brockway.

"Damn!" he heard the other man pronounce bitterly to the darkness. Thorn dropped down from the window and joined him. Brockway turned.

"At least, this one's still breathing. But we'll need to get him to hospital fast."

They decided that Thorn should take the truck. It would be quicker than waiting for an ambulance to find the cottage and make a double journey. Thorn was sprinting over the frozen lawn as a shrill blast from Brockway's whistle summoned the second redcap from his post along the road. The Corporal was pounding down the road at the double when Thorn reached the parked vehicles. He rode back to the cottage with Thorn in the truck.

"It's a mess," Thorn warned the Corporal. "One dead, two

wounded. You never saw such a goddamned mess!"

Brockway had done his best to make Chisholm comfortable. Thorn and the Corporal carried him to the truck. The wounded redcap walked alongside. He was shivering from cold and shock. Brockway had managed to get him out of his great-coat and tunic and had wrapped them round Chisholm. At the truck, Thorn took off his coat and draped it round the wounded Canadian's shoulders.

"Thanks," the man murmured. "I'm sorry about the girl." Thorn guessed that Brockway must have given him the rough edge of his tongue.

"It can't be helped now," Thorn said, and helped him into the cab of the truck.

Brockway's bitter disappointment at the turn of events hung over him like a dark cloud. He was to stay at the cottage meantime. It would have to be searched from top to bottom, and a call would have to be made to Vaughan for one of his clean-up squads to remove the girl's body and bypass the legal formalities that a violent death warrants.

"Stay with the skipper," Brockway urged Thorn, referring to Chisholm. "If he found out the least little thing, we got to know what it is. Even if you got to go into the operating theatre with him, you stay with him. He's our only hope."

Thorn stayed with Chisholm. He was never very far away from his side during the next thirty-six hours.

As it happened, the nearest hospital of any size was a US Army hospital less than an hour's drive from the cottage. It was one of several that had sprung up in Southern England during the past year to cater for the steady influx of American troops pouring in from across the Atlantic. The complex of white prefabricated buildings near the village of Beddohampton sprawled across 200 acres of Sussex parkland and was crisscrossed by narrow roads topped with red marl. Chisholm was rushed to the Emergency Unit and within minutes of arrival was stretched on a table under the opaque-screened arc lights of the low-ceilinged theatre.

Gowned like the surgeons and nurses, Thorn watched from a few feet away as the fight for Chisholm's life began. Twice during the next thirty-six hours, Thorn followed the trolley back to the same theatre, where Chisholm underwent further emergency surgery. Then it was back to the oppressively warm side ward to sit by the bedside and wait.

Thorn was not a praying man but he addressed a stream of thought messages to any and every deity tuned in on his vigil. He willed life into the prone, disconcertingly motionless occupant of the bed. Sometimes he spoke to him: whispered encouragement, addressing him with such unlikely endearments as "you stone-faced son-of-a-gun" and "you stiff-necked Limey deck-swabber".

Sometimes Thorn felt angry: at Brockway, at Hibberd, at the world at large – but principally at himself. He knew that if Chisholm did not recover, he would never forgive himself for having placed his life on the line. If anybody should have been lying on that hospital bed fighting for life, then it should have been Cal Thorn. Not this undeserving sea captain.

It ceased to be a matter of concern to Thorn whether Chisholm had gleaned any vital information from the girl who had shot him. He didn't give a goddamn whether or not Brockway ever solved the mystery of Anina Calvi. Thorn only wanted one thing. He wanted Chisholm to live. Nothing else mattered. Nothing.

Thorn's eyes were heavy with sleep, lead-like, when finally Chisholm stirred. The American, struggling against the compulsion to surrender to sleep, had to fight himself to wakefulness. There had been a sound, a movement, from the bed. There, it came again. Just a whimper. He saw Chisholm's eyes flutter open and stare at him vaguely. Then Chisholm spoke.

"I've been dreaming," he said, and smiled weakly. Then the eyes fluttered shut again.

The next time Chisholm stirred, he sustained his wakened state long enough to complain that someone must have sandpapered his throat. He asked for water.

A hovering nurse went to get him an ice-cube to suck. When she came back with it, she was accompanied by a doctor in US captain's uniform. Chisholm looked at the faces. When he saw Thorn, he gave a weak smile of recognition.

"Cal . . . You look worried . . . Something wrong?"

Thorn shook his head, grinning.

"What in hell gave you such an idea? Everything's fine, old friend. Couldn't be better. You're going to be OK."

Chisholm let his head roll to one side. His eyes searched his surroundings. He was in a hospital. What was he doing here? Why did his chest have that dull, tight feeling? He couldn't understand. Then he remembered a flash of light and a feeling of stupefying surprise. Anina Calvi. It started to come back. He closed his eyes. When he opened them again, Thorn was still there. He stared at him.

"I fouled it all up, didn't I? She tried to kill me . . . I can remember . . . I'm sorry, Cal . . . She must have seen through me . . . I'm a lousy actor . . ."

"No. Chizz, you were just great. Just great. Good enough for an Oscar. Look, take it easy, old friend. Don't try to talk if you don't want to. There'll be plenty of time for that . . ."

The doctor in captain's uniform was nodding his head in approval. Thorn was saying the right things. The patient wasn't to be taxed.

"I'll be right here, Chizz," Thorn said. "Anything you want, you just got to say.

Chisholm's eyes closed, opened again, and then sought Thorn's.

"There's one thing you could do for me, Cal," he said gravely.

"You name it, Chizz."

"Could you get a piano in here?"

"A piano!" Thorn's voice rose an octave. Suppressing his surprise, he asked: "What do you want a piano for?"

"To see if I can play a tune on it."

Thorn wrinkled his brow.

"I didn't know you played the piano, Chizz." He looked up at the doctor helplessly, but he was as puzzled as Thorn. He shrugged his shoulders in bewilderment.

Chisholm stayed silent for a moment. He closed his eyes. The corners of his lips started to twitch. His body gave a little convulsive shake. The doctor was quickly at his side. He drew back startled as Chisholm gave a small hiccough of sound, like an involuntary chuckle. Then came another, and another.

Thorn blinked. He and the doctor stared at each other in disbelief. Chisholm was trying not to laugh, and he was failing. He seemed unable to contain the bubbles of laughter. It seemed to cause him pain but he was rocking gently with mirth.

"I really don't want a piano," he managed to say, his eyes bright with a merriment that seemed to bring twinges of hurt as its price. "I was having you on, Cal. It was a joke . . . I was trying to think if there was anything I was worse at than acting. There is . . . It's playing the piano . . . I can't play a damned note!"

Thorn almost choked.

"Why you ... you ... you tricky, two-timing, Limey son-of-a ..." he spluttered. Then he was laughing, too. Helplessly. Even the doctor was grinning in a dazed kind of way.

"Well, I'll be goddamned!" he kept saying over and again. "Well, I'll be goddamned!" It took some moments for the obligations of his office to work back to the surface of his thoughts.

In a kindly way, he damped down the hilarity and reminded Chisholm that he was a very sick man and that, in his case, laughter wasn't really the best medicine. He could aggravate his injury. Chisholm was persuaded to rest some more.

The doctor beckoned to Thorn and drew him to one side.

"He *is* going to be all right, Doctor?" Thorn asked, worried by the doctor's expression.

The doctor smiled.

"Oh, he'll live. I was just going to ask you. Do you think we should hide his clothes?"

Although Brockway, Hibberd and Vaughan all telephoned Thorn at the American hospital with solicitous enquiries about Chisholm's survival chances and expressed genuine relief when they learned that the sea captain was out of danger, all three awaited Thorn's report on his debriefing of Chisholm with an impatience that, to Thorn, seemed indecent. When, finally, the American submitted his report, it was used as the basis of a review of the Anina Calvi case which was speedily circulated to departmental heads in the Intelligence establishment.

The following day, Brockway, Hibberd and Vaughan met for a council of war in Hibberd's office. It was the first time the three had met since the order to abort "Operation Thumb-screw" had been made.

Hibberd tapped the copy of the circulated review, which lay on his desk.

"There are loose ends – a lot of them maybe – but I think, gentlemen, that this document vindicates 'Thumbscrew'. They'll have to re-activate the operation now, even if it's only in a modest way."

"Not a chance," said Vaughan.

His tone was so emphatic that it drew questioning frowns

from the other two.

"You've seen the Brigadier?" Brockway's tone was tentative.

Vaughan nodded.

"He sent for me this morning. I've come straight here from his office." He sighed unhappily. "I'm afraid he was his usual highly objectionable self. He made it quite clear that 'Thumbscrew' is dead and buried and it's going to stay that way."

"I hope the sanctimonious buzzard had the grace to apologise to you for some of the things he said to you last time," Hibberd observed.

Vaughan laughed.

"The Brigadier *never* apologises. He wouldn't know how. As a matter of fact, he succeeded in being only slightly less obnoxious than he was last time. He more or less accused me of aiding and abetting you two to disregard a specific injunction and then covering up for you when you fouled things up."

"But you had nothing to do with the damned thing," protested Hibberd.

"What difference does it make?" Brockway said morosely. "We did foul things up. We should have taken the girl alive."

"So, she's dead! So what?" argued Hibberd. "At least we now know for sure that you were right about her all along. We know, too, that she probably milked enough outa this guy, Green, to blow the whole Dieppe show to the Krauts . . . Hell, all that guy of yours did when he blew her head off was saved us the job of doing it officially!"

Vaughan gave a perplexed little shake of his head.

"Unfortunately that isn't the view that's being taken on high. The Holy Fathers are conceding rather reluctantly that the girl was *probably* an enemy agent and was passing on information from Green and God knows how many others . . . But they are also pointing out that the girl's death was *unfortunate*. That word came up a lot. The lack of detail about what happened to the real Anina Calvi is *unfortunate* . . . Chisholm stopping a bullet was *unfortunate* . . . And having to accept his uncorroborated account of the girl's admissions was *unfortunate* . . . The flimsiness of the evidence about another agent still at large is *unfortunate* . . . Everything about the case is *unfortunate* . . . Oh, except as far as it appears to justify the disobedience of certain American and Canadian intelligence officers. The fact that the girl can no longer speak in her own defence is seen as being exceptionally *fortunate* for the gentlemen concerned."

Hibberd was almost incoherent with outrage.

"They don't think we invented it ... That it's all a goddamned story ... ?"

Vaughan made a face.

"That accusation was never actually made. You know the Brigadier ... He tosses hints in the air like balloons ..." He mimicked the Brigadier's high-pitched manner of speech: "Quite unthinkable, my dear fellow, that any of our side would look on the gal's death as rather provident for them. Quite unthinkable! Depends of course on how much of an embarrassment she was alive, eh what?"

Hibberd was in no way mollified.

"We'll get facts!" he declared, fuming "I'll send Thorn to Spain to find out just what did happen to the Calvi girl. We'll get facts and we'll ram 'em down that whoreson's throat!"

Vaughan glanced at Brockway.

"Gilbert has to be made to talk," he said meaningfully.

"He'll talk!" growled Brockway. "If I have to beat the truth out of him myself, he'll talk! He'll spill everything he knows."

"When will you pull him in?" Vaughan asked.

"All I got to do is say the word and he'll be on ice quicker than you can say knife. I only put it off because I wanted to see you guys first." Brockway looked at Vaughan and Hibberd in turn. "Do I give the word?"

Hibberd arched an eyebrow.

"How about this Sergeant of yours? Weaver, wasn't it? Is he still keeping an eye on Gilbert?"

"He's been closer than a leech ever since your man, Thorn, phoned from the hospital and said Gilbert was the one who was working with the girl."

"I say we pull him in," said Vaughan.

"Me, too," agreed Hibberd.

Brockway nodded.

"It's unanimous then." He looked enquiringly at Hibberd. "Mind if I use your phone, Major? I'd like to make a call to Brighton."

Lieutenant Raoul Gilbert was not in Brighton. Shortly after midday, he had boarded a train for London with half a dozen other officers from the Beaumaris. Sergeant Weaver, with the twenty-four-hour-a-day job of watching Gilbert, had boarded the same train.

The train's arrival in the capital had coincided with the first of a succession of heavy rainstorms rolling over London from the east. By six in the evening, Weaver was at least happy to be out of the rain. But he did not think that the comedian up on the stage was very funny. Half of the comic's jokes were lost on the Canadian because his strident cockney accent went some way to rendering English into a foreign language.

Weaver did not care all that much for burlesque shows in the first place. He would have been much happier in a cinema watching a good western, especially one featuring William Boyd and Gabby Hayes. Weaver was a devoted fan of Hopalong Cassidy. Unfortunately, Gilbert, and his two friends had not sought their amusement at a cinema. They had picked the Windmill Theatre.

The Windmill had some consolation for Weaver. It was better in here in the dry than it had been hanging around outside a succession of pubs while his quarry embarked on what had seemed like a serious attempt at drinking London dry.

Weaver had been surprised when Gilbert and his two companions had entered the Windmill and purchased tickets. He had followed suit and was only a dozen paces behind them when they went into the auditorium.

The three officers had found seats two rows from the front. Weaver seated himself in the empty back row, where he could keep his eye on them: remaining aloof from the steady flow of incomers all pressing to get as near the front as possible. Indeed, Weaver found it rather distasteful that grown men should elbow and push one another in so unseemly a manner to get the prime seats: all in order to drool at the statuesque nudity of the girls on the stage.

So, he viewed the hour-long vaudeville show with its girlie décor and risqué sketches with an air of moral rectitude that was not discernible in the rest of the boisterous audience. He was, therefore, quite unprepared for the general stampede that followed the end of the sixty-minute programme.

As the front rows emptied, latecomers in the rear stalls scrambled across the seats in front in order to secure better positions from which to view the voluptuous torsos and mammary glands that would be exposed to view when the curtain rose for the next house.

Weaver was caught flat-footed and amazed in the undignified mêlée, as the patrons surged over seats and scrambled in the side-aisles to get front seats. He saw Gilbert and his two friends leave by a side exit but was quite powerless himself to get anywhere near them. He had to wait until the throng in the aisle had thinned before fighting his way to the exit they had taken.

When Weaver finally got out of the theatre, he found himself in one of the myriad of lanes off Piccadilly Circus. He scanned the groups of servicemen milling about in the lane like shadowy ghosts. In the dark of the blackout it was impossible to identify anyone. He dashed up an alley after three shapes, only to discover to his consternation that they were navymen. Cursing, he made his way back to Piccadilly Circus, where he ran up and down peering at faces and jostling passers-by with such uncaring frenzy that one aggrieved soldier threatened to rearrange his face in a way that was permanently irremediable.

After twenty minutes, Weaver had to face up to an unpalatable truth: he had lost Gilbert.

The news that Weaver had lost his quarry in London's West End was relayed to Brockway later that night. It did nothing to relieve the choleric mood that had been with him since early afternoon when his order to arrest Gilbert had been temporarily frustrated. The provost commander in Brighton had failed to locate Gilbert and had informed Brockway that he and some other officers from the Beaumaris had gone off to London on forty-eight-hour furloughs.

Brockway decided against alerting Military Police patrols in the capital, knowing that Weaver was on Gilbert's tail and would sooner or later report in: either to let his whereabouts be known to HQ or to request assistance in maintaining the twenty-four-hour surveillance. The last thing Brockway had expected was Weaver to telephone in and report that he had lost his man.

When he did so, Brockway immediately notified the Military Police patrols to be on the lookout for Gilbert. Their only success was that they located the two officers who had accompanied Gilbert to the Windmill. They had no idea where the missing officer was. He had parted company with them outside the Windmill without saying where he was going. They had assumed he had a heavy date, but that was pure speculation.

There was still no sign of Gilbert the next day. Nor did he return to the Beaumaris at the expiry of his furlough. As a matter of course, he was posted absent without leave. Long before this, however, his description had been circulated nationally to all sections of the Civil and Military Police with orders that he was to be arrested on sight.

At the end of a week, he was still missing and not a single sighting of him had been reported. Lieutenant Raoul Gilbert, it seemed, had emerged from the Windmill Theatre into London's blackout and had vanished into thin air.

Fourteen

The Nominated Ship

The questioning seemed to go on forever, long after Chisholm had painstakingly accounted to Thorn every scrap of remembered conversation with the girl who had masqueraded as Anina Calvi. Vaughan came. He was followed by two specialists from the Foreign Office: one an expert on South American affairs, the other an expert on Spain. Brockway came, with a stenographer to record everything that Chisholm could tell him. Hibberd arrived with questions to ask. So did a senior officer of Scotland Yard's Special Branch and a man from MI5.

Then, one day, Thorn appeared with Millie in tow. Vaughan had sought and obtained permission for her to be told the truth about her brother's injury. She had been given, in the strictest confidence, an edited and abridged version of the circumstances leading up to the cottage shooting.

By the end of February, Chisholm was well enough to be taking walks in the hospital grounds. By then, the exhaustive debriefing had ceased and he was vaguely aware that the spy-hunt operation in which he had figured was being regarded in some quarters as the security bungle of the century.

He knew from his interviews with Vaughan and Brockway in particular that both men were being subjected to immense pressures. The strain showed in their faces. They were men burdened by a sense of failure. Confidence had been sapped from them not only as a result of criticism by others but because both men knew that they had not achieved the objectives they had set themselves.

They had ended the spying activities of the woman who had appropriated Anina Calvi's identity and, in some respects, this was a victory – but it was a hollow victory, with no honour for them. Most of the girl's secrets had died with her. They had made no headway in tracking down the mysterious "Quasimodo", to whom she had referred. Nor were they any nearer identifying the *Schatten Gruppe*—or Shadow Squad—whose name she had inadvertently let slip.

Worst of all, not a clue had been found to the whereabouts of Lieutenant Raoul Gilbert, who—the evidence now seemed conclusive—was Lomax's murderer and the traitor of St Cyr des Bains. The fugitive officer had successfully evaded a net spread over the entire British Isles for his capture, and this considerable feat suggested that he must have had an emergency escape route planned for use at a moment's notice.

How Gilbert had been alerted that the net was closing remained a mystery. But, in this respect, the unfortunate Sergeant Weaver was not being held guiltless. It seemed highly possible that Gilbert had become aware of the Sergeant's surveillance and had put his disappearing act into operation with careful calculation. What rankled keenly was that Gilbert's evasion of arrest had become a major blot on the otherwise formidable success record of the anti-espionage forces in Britain.

As each day at Beddohampton marked an improvement in Chisholm's condition, hundreds of unanswered questions haunted him. But, even as they filled his mind in the lonely hours of the night, he forced himself to face the fact that they might have to remain unanswered. Because, as far as he was concerned, the affair was now over. It was finished.

Both Vaughan and Brockway had made this clear to him. His part in the drama had ended with a bullet in the chest. The two spy-hunters were emphatic about that. They both looked on Chisholm as a non-combatant in their kind of war and it shamed them both that he had become a casualty. They had no intention of exposing him in the firing-line again.

On his final visit to the hospital, Vaughan was warm in his thanks for all Chisholm's help and co-operation, especially after the ordeal of his detention.

"Lesser men would never have forgiven us for what you've been through." Vaughan told Chisholm. "You're the only one who has come out of this with your honour and your reputation enhanced." As he shook Chisholm's hand, he said rather wistfully: "In many ways, I envy you, Captain Chisholm. In a month or so, you'll be back on the bridge of a ship and all this will be behind you. You'll be where you belong . . . And me?

Well, I wish I had my own ship again . . . At sea, the air's clean . . ." His voice tailed away almost to inaudibility, his expression soft with a longing that would never be fulfilled. "Yes," he murmured. "I envy you . . ."

A chapter in Chisholm's life seemed to be closing. The enactment of its final scene came on the day that Thorn arrived at Beddohampton to say goodbye. The American had lost some but not all of his ebullience. His chagrin at Chisholm's injury was a personal burden that had not entirely been shed by the sea captain's recovery. Thorn had cast himself as Chisholm's friend and protector and it weighed heavily with him that he had failed in both capacities. No amount of reassurance by Chisholm seemed able to relieve the American of an overwhelming sense of obligation. But there seemed no way open to Thorn to make the amends that he felt were due.

And, now, he was being sent to Spain.

The two men walked along the marled paths of the Beddohampton hospital, saying little. The silences were companionable: mute periods of recognition of the solidity of the friendship they had found.

"I'll be doing what I'm good at in Spain," Thorn said, ending one short period of silence. "I'll be looking for needles in haystacks."

"You don't sound all that enthusiastic."

Thorn smiled.

"I'd sooner stick around in England, looking for that Canadian who did the Houdini act, or trying to get a line on that guy Quasimodo." He shrugged. "This time I gotta do what I'm told. I fly to Gib tomorrow. This time next week, I'll be in Madrid."

"You watch out for yourself there, Cal," Chisholm said, not quite concealing real concern with a jolly-uncle kind of tone. "Franco's mob aren't exactly friendly. And they say the place is hotching with Nazis."

Thorn grinned.

"I'm banking on flushing out a few. Somebody out there must know what happened to the Calvi girl. I intend to dig until I hit paydirt."

"You take care."

Thorn's grin widened.

"I sure hope I can take care of myself better than I took care of you!"

They lapsed into silence again as they walked on. Banks of yellow and purple crocus carpeted the grass: harbingers of spring. War seemed a million miles away. Chisholm sighed.

"The place is not going to be the same without Calvin T. Thorn around."

"That's what your sister, Millie, said."

Chisholm looked at Thorn with a gleam in his eye.

"Have you got designs on my sister, Calvin T. Thorn?"

"You're goddamned right I do," Thorn replied cheerfully. "If you think you've seen the last of me, you're making the mistake of your life. I'll be back!" He glanced sideways at Chisholm. "How would it grab you to have me as a brother-in-law, Chizz?"

Chisholm stared at him.

"Good God . . . You mean you've asked Millie?"

"I ain't asked her nothing," came back Thorn, hastily, his face reddening. "I was just asking you how you liked the idea. That's all."

Chisholm grinned broadly.

"I suppose I could get used to the idea. She could do worse for herself."

For the first time since Chisholm had known him, Thorn seemed all shy and tongue-tied.

"I like her, Chizz. I like her a lot. We've been seeing a bit of each other since you've been in here – but that's as far as it goes. There's been no talk . . . nothing. I just wanted you to know how it was."

"Millie's a big girl now, Cal. She doesn't need my approval in her choice of men friends. So, my opinion doesn't count."

"It does with me," Thorn said. He was as anxious as a schoolboy seeking parental permission to date a cherished daughter. Chisholm eyed the American with a gently teasing smile.

"You know what I should do, Cal? I should try to talk some sense into her . . . Tell her she's crazy to have anything to do with you . . ."

"You'd probably be right," Thorn said miserably.

"Of course, I'd be right," Chisholm went on cheerfully. "But she wouldn't take a blind bit of notice."

Thorn stared at him puzzled.

"You mean you don't mind?"

Chisholm laughed.

"Of course I don't mind! I'm far too fond of both of you. I'd say you were probably made for each other—but that's a conclusion you'll have to work out all for yourselves. I'm staying strictly neutral."

Thorn grinned in a rueful way.

"Millie sure has a mind of her own, don't she?"

"She's a law unto herself," Chisholm said with a smile. "That makes two of you."

When Thorn had gone, the realisation that there would be no more visits from him left Chisholm depressed and anxious to be free of the clockwork boredom of hospital routine. Thorn's visits had been the high point of any day on which they had occurred: not because of the nature of Thorn's job—which dictated most of them—but because of the nature of the man. Chisholm missed him. He counted the days until he could be discharged.

The head offices of the Stockton Steamship Company were in Billiter Street, on the fringe of the few square miles of London known as the City. In the spring of 1943, few buildings in the area had escaped unscathed from the Blitz that had been launched with particular fury on London's East End. From Whitechapel to St Paul's, the bombs had rained down in deadly profusion: devastating properties that had risen from the ashes of another fiery disaster nearly three centuries before.

The Indo-Pacific Marine Insurance building in Billiter Street had survived and was partly habitable. It had suffered some structural damage from blast and fire, but not enough to render most of the offices it housed unfunctionable. From behind the building's buttressed façade, the Stockton Steamship Company continued to conduct its world-wide interests in maritime trading.

Chisholm had joined the Company as a sixteen-year-old apprentice, sailing under the command of its senior master, Captain "Snowy" Grieve. Twelve years later, in 1940, Chisholm had become the line's youngest ever shipmaster. Now, in mid-March 1943, the Stockton headquarters became the regular outward stopping-point in marathon walks he undertook to restore full working capability to a bullet-damaged lung. The American doctors at Beddohampton had told him that the lung would be as good as new if he got himself plenty of exercise and fresh air. "Walk miles," he had been told, and, based again in Millie's Westminster flat, he had taken the edict to heart. His first aim was to get fit, his second to get back to sea. Thus, he concentrated on the first by walking from Westminster to distant Billiter Street every other day; and angled for the second by making a nuisance of himself at the shipping company's head office.

Little of the true reasons for Chisholm's unavailability for service since his escape from France had filtered back to his employers. They had accepted without question a governmental request that he be treated as on indefinite rehabilitation leave. There had been a strong hint that as a result of the time he had spent in enemy-occupied territory, he had come into possession of knowledge that was of value to certain government departments and that the debriefing processes might go on for months. The Company's absolute discretion was sought, with the request that they did not press for fuller details as matters of national security were at stake.

There had been alarm and puzzlement at Billiter Street when the Company had been informed in a letter—marked "Most Secret"—that Captain Chisholm had been of notable service to HM Government in circumstances that could not be revealed until the end of hostilities. He was presently in hospital with a lung complaint from which he was making a good recovery. The writer noted that Captain Chisholm was anxious to return to the Company's service at the earliest possible opportunity and that he would be contacting them in due course. There was, meantime, no other impediment in the way of his return to duty but his health.

The consequence of all this was that, when Chisholm presented himself at Billiter Street—claiming that he was as fit as a fiddle and clamouring for a ship—he was treated like a treasured piece of porcelain that had survived a fall. He was handled with the utmost delicacy while, all the time, he was surreptitiously examined for outward signs of irreparable damage.

In spite of the warmth and genuine relief in the welcome he was given, it soon became clear to Chisholm that the Stockton Company had no intention of rushing him back to sea. They stalled him in the nicest possible way, assuring him that there would be time enough to think of sea duty when he had been pronounced fit by the Company's expensively retained consultant at Greenwich Hospital.

Thus, Chisholm's treks from Westminster to Billiter Street became something of a trial of wills between him and Captain "Snowy" Grieve, now Marine Superintendent and chief executive of the Stockton line. A mentor-disciple relationship between the two men had long since matured to a friendship of firstname informality. Chisholm unashamedly traded on it, determined to wear down Grieve's reluctance to give him a ship. Grieve was equally determined to humour the younger man, while awaiting documentary proof of his fitness.

Grieve did not altogether believe Chisholm's story that he had required "minor surgery" for a "mild chest infection", but all his attempts to get Chisholm to be more forthcoming got nowhere. Indeed, Chisholm became irritatingly vague every time Grieve tried to pump him about his experiences before and after his escape from France.

"How did they treat you on the U-boat?"

"All right. I don't remember much about it."

"Where did they hold you in France?"

"They moved me about. One place was pretty much the same as the next."

On Chisholm's third visit, Grieve was determined to get some straight answers. When Chisholm was as vague as ever, Grieve eyed him fiercely.

"Getting information out of you, Chizz, is like drawing teeth. Your memory wasn't always so bad."

"It was the shots they gave me in hospital, Snowy. Five ccs of amnesia three times a day and four times on Sundays. I'm under orders to forget."

"They gagged you? They made you sign the Secrets Act?"

"In blood. My blood. I needed a transfusion afterwards."

"But we're knee-deep in secrets here, Chizz. You work for us! There are things we're entitled to know."

"Then ask the people who can give you the answers, Snowy. Don't ask me. My lips are sealed."

"I just want to know what the hell happened to you, Chizz. Good God, son, do you know what happened when they told me that there were no survivors from the *Millerby*? That you were gone? I cried, Chizz. I bloody well sat down and cried!"

The older man's admission touched Chisholm deeply. He floundered for a reply. It was as much as he could do to murmur a trite, "I'm sorry". There was more he wanted to say but the words stuck unsaid in his throat, impeded by a lump that seemed to have lodged there.

He was saved further embarrassment by Grieve coming round his desk and putting a fatherly arm round his shoulder.

"I'm a silly old bugger, Chizz. Let's go and have a drink."

He took Chisholm to a club nearby: a watering-hole much frequented by the shipping fraternity and, for whom, it stayed open twenty-four hours a day. Chisholm did not walk back to Westminster that day. Discretion demanded a taxi. Next morning, he felt so unwell that he thought he had suffered a relapse. But a brisk walk along the Embankment as far as Blackfriars Bridge blew the cobwebs from his brain and reassured him that he might survive until nightfall after all. He made a leisurely westward return via the cloistered walks of the Temple and an aproned barman was opening the doors of the Devereux as he emerged through the Judge's Gate. A pint of bitter in the 600-year-old pub gave Chisholm hope that he might live for several more days.

A week later, Chisholm was given the all-clear at Greenwich Hospital.

"If you were an office worker, you could go back to work tomorrow," the consultant physician told Chisholm, "but running a ship at sea is rather different. Give yourself another month before you commit yourself to sea duties. In the meantime, there's no need to come back and see me. You are perfectly sound in wind and limb."

The doctor wrote out a report for the Company while Chisholm waited.

"Shall I send it to Captain Grieve as usual?" he asked.

"I'm on my way to the office now," Chisholm informed him cheerfully. "I'll be happy to give it to Captain Grieve personally."

With the medical report in his hand, Chisholm was knocking on Grieve's office door an hour later. He handed it over to the white-haired Marine Superintendent with a flourish.

Grieve opened the envelope and read the doctor's report. Once or twice as he read, he gave a snort of surprise. When he had finished, he looked across his desk at Chisholm, his eyes wide.

"What in God's name is this about a bullet wound?"

"A bullet wound?" Chisholm had not expected the report to be so detailed. "It was nothing. I thought that would have been censored," he added lamely. "It makes no difference. I'm OK now."

Grieve's eyes were popping.

"For heaven's sake, Chizz! You told me you had a mild chest infection."

Chisholm grinned weakly.

"Lead poisoning?" he suggested tentatively.

Grieve came close to exploding. Chisholm let him rant and rave about being fed lies by the bucketful. At the end of it Chisholm pointed out: "Snowy, there's no point in going on at me. OK, so I got in the way of a bullet and you know – but it's something I just can't talk about. I've given a solemn promise and that's the end of it."

Grieve was far from satisfied.

"All right, Chizz, but you haven't heard the last of this. I won't ask you any more questions but, believe me, there are people I can ask – and I bloody well will!"

In calmer mood, he returned to the subject closer to Chisholm's heart: prospective vacancies for a master mariner. Chisholm was not surprised to hear the Marine Superintendent admit that he had not been exactly truthful himself on that score.

"I wasn't holding off because we don't need you, Chizz," he confessed. "We're desperate for experienced masters. But you're too valuable to risk if you're only half-fit. Hell, other men would have jumped at the chance of taking a decent leave when it was offered them."

"I've been on the beach too damned long," Chisholm complained. "And that medical report says I'm fit."

"Almost," Grieve replied, tapping the report with his finger. "The doc says you may resume full sea duties in a month, OK? So, let's take him at his word. You could do some relieving work for the time being. All the masters in this Company's aren't as averse as you are to a spot of home leave . . . You could give them a chance of it."

Most of the Company's port relief work was carried out by pensioned shipmasters who were too old to go to sea. It was not the kind of work that Chisholm wanted, but he speedily agreed. Better being a port-bound sailor than no sailor at all.

A Stockton-managed ship, the *Empire Fratten*, was due in Birkenhead in four days time. Grieve made arrangements for Chisholm to join as relieving master for the seven days she would spend in the Merseyside port. He would then travel to

Middlesborough to take over the *Fennerby* for ten days. After that, he could more or less have his pick of one of a half dozen new ships due in the UK during April.

"That's a promise, is it?" Chisholm enquired. "You won't keep me on this relieving lark for the duration?"

Grieve smiled at his anxiety.

"Not a chance. I told you we were desperate for experienced masters. I meant it. We'd rather use a Company man than take pot luck from the pool. Next month, we're going to have more ships to manage than we have the officers to man them. You'll get your new command, Chizz – and a brand new ship to go with it. You can take your pick out of the six. I can't offer fairer than that."

Old Snowy Grieve's words filled Chisholm with a rare exhilaration. He had loved the old *Millerby* but only the war had saved her from the scrapyard. The thought of a new ship, hand-picked, was the stuff of dreams.

It made an ironic change from pre-war days when promotion had been slow. "Waiting for dead men's shoes," they had called it. The war had changed all that. Or, rather, it had accelerated the process in a grim way. The men were dying more quickly than their shoes could be filled. They were being killed at the rate of one out of every three.

The reason for the spate of new ships coming available was – as Grieve explained – due to the provision of American capital to sustain Britain's battered merchant fleet. The Stockton line had lost twenty-eight ships through enemy action since 1939. Now, some of these losses were being made good by the outpouring of American dollars to build ships in the yards of Canada and the USA. Hundreds of these ships were now crossing the Atlantic on loan, to be managed and manned by British companies whose fleets had all but disappeared in four years of war.

Grieve told Chisholm about the six new Stockton ships already on the Atlantic on their way to Britain. There was the Baltimore-built Liberty ship, the *Samorna*. Three others were US standard-built "Oceans": the *Ocean Merry*, the *Ocean Streamer*, and the *Ocean Gulfwind*. The remaining two were Canadian-built "Forts": the *Fort Appaloose* and the *Fort Mohican*.

Chisholm's eyes lit up at the last-mentioned.

"Save the *Fort Mohican* for me," he said. On the magic of

name alone, the *Fort Mohican* made the other ships non-starters in his estimation. Ever since boyhood, when he had been enthralled by the works of James Fenimore Cooper, Chisholm had held the name Mohican in a special awe. The word enshrined legends of daring and savage nobility in a way that no other could.

Grieve was amused when Chisholm tried to explain his feeling.

"I know what you mean," he said. "You spent too long reading cowboy and indian stories when you should have been doing your lessons!"

"Perhaps," conceded Chisholm, and would have liked to argue on the subject.

"Don't be in too much of a hurry to put up your shingle on that ship," Grieve warned him good-humouredly. "She has already been earmarked by your Millie's lot."

"Millie's lot?"

"HM Sea Transport," said Grieve, and made it sound ominous.

"Earmarked to do what?" Chisholm asked.

Grieve crossed the room and unlocked a steel-doored safe store. He emerged from it a moment later with a letter file. At his desk again, he selected a single sheet of notepaper.

"I'll quote," he said, as he adjusted horn-rimmed reading glasses over his nose. "Where is it? Ah, yes, here: 'And we have to inform you that the fore-mentioned vessel, while remaining under your management, has been nominated *for hazardous expeditions against the enemy*.'"

If Chisholm's imagination had been fired by the possibility of commanding a ship called the *Fort Mohican*, it would be fair to say that a tremble of eager anticipation gripped him at guessing the nature of activity planned for the ship. *Hazardous expeditions against the enemy*. Surely that meant only one thing. The ship had been earmarked for a role in the Second Front that was the talk of all the newspapers and politicians.

He tried to examine truthfully his own feelings towards the exposure of a ship under his command to the guns of Hitler's Atlantic Wall. And he was surprised at his own eagerness to participate, to be part of the grand assault on Europe. His feelings puzzled him. He hated war. Long before the *Millerby* had gone down he had had his fill of it. Its demands had drained and wearied him. What had happened since the sinking of the *Millerby* should have killed stone dead any desire on his part to seek fresh battlefields. Why then was he now straining at the traces like a starved hawk that had been given the taste of blood?

He knew it was not a death-wish nor any longing for glory. It was not an over-zealous sense of duty nor an intense patriotism. Self-sacrifice did not figure in at all. Nor did his chances of survival – or his disregard of these chances – come anywhere into the reckoning. Almost with a sense of shock, he realised that the fighting heat that raced in his blood rose from some deep-seated anger that demanded expression. It was the same anger that had kept him hanging to his sanity chained to a wall in a windowless cell. It was the same anger that had gripped him in the Beaumaris when he had discovered Lomax's body planted in his room. It was an anger that had been building up since the first day of the war: a war that he had had to fight with, metaphorically, his hands tied behind his back. The Merchant Navyman's war: the sitting target waiting for an unseen enemy to strike. The inability to fight back, the impotence of his role, had wound the clockwork spring of his anger tighter and tighter until it was now at the point where the tension demanded relief. *He wanted to hit back, to lash out with any weapon that came to hand*. It was as simple and basic as that. His war had been *passive*: like a boxer who faces an opponent with instructions not to raise his hands but to keep turning the other cheek to any blow aimed at him. Well, not any more. If an armada of ships and men was going to be launched against the fortress of Europe, Chisholm wanted to be part of it.

It, therefore, became almost an obsession with him as he worked out his relieving stints on the *Empire Fratten* and the *Fennerby*, that he should get the appointment as master of the *Fort Mohican* and sail with her to whatever maelstrom awaited her. The hope of getting that command dominated his thoughts. It became to him the most important thing in his life.

Thus, his expectations were high as a taxi took him and his baggage into Middlesborough from Smith's Dock, where he had handed over the *Fennerby*. By evening, he would be in London and, tomorrow, when he reported at Billiter Street, there would be news of his new ship.

So it was that Snowy Grieve's letter came like a body blow. It was waiting for him in the shipping agent's office at Middlesborough, when he called there to collect his railway warrant for the journey to London.

It was a long and, for Snowy Grieve, a newsy letter. But the relevant passages hit Chisholm between the eyes.

". . . you'll be disappointed to learn that we've decided to keep Freddie Jackman as master of the *Fort Mohican* meantime. He is very happy with her and says that she handled well on the trip over from St John's. We'd like you take over the *Ocean Streamer*, now due in the Clyde on May 1st. She is identical in design to the *Mohican*, except that being Yankee-built she is the welded-hull type . . ."

There was more, but none of it was what Chisholm wanted to hear. Snowy did not even want him to report to Billiter Street for another week, suggesting that he take advantage of this bonus leave because the *Ocean Streamer* was scheduled to be away from home for at least eighteen months.

Neither London, Millie, nor the glorious April weather seemed able to cheer Chisholm. He told himself he was being silly, that he was sulking like a child over a lost toy—but his gloom, at being deprived of the ship he wanted, prevailed. He had set his heart on a prize he had wanted above all others and it had been snatched away from him almost at the moment of possession. Being offered something similar, as a substitute, was no consolation.

The week in London dragged out miserably. When the day came to present himself at Billiter Street, Chisholm was in a scowling bad humour and so seething with resentment that he was ready to reject command of the *Ocean Streamer*, quit the Stockton line and seek a ship by joining the MN Officers Pool. Consequently, he was unprepared for the surprise that waited him when he entered Snowy Grieve's office with a face like thunder.

Sitting in the chair opposite the white-haired Marine Superintendent was Commander Vaughan. Grieve got to his feet.

"I believe you two gentlemen have already met," he said.

Fifteen

New Command

Chisholm shook hands with Vaughan, whose uniform jacket seemed loose and ill-fitting; as if he had lost weight. The Commander looked ill and seemed to have aged in the weeks since Chisholm had last seen him. His eyes were ringed with dark shadows and he had a hollow-cheeked look.

"Commander Vaughan and I have had an interesting chat," said Grieve. "He's in charge of a special security operation that involves two of our ships. But," he glanced at Chisholm, "you know his line of business."

Chisholm was aware of disappointment. He had assumed that *he* was the reason for Vaughan's visit to the office.

"I've changed hats since Captain Chisholm and I last met," Vaughan volunteered for Grieve's benefit.

"Promotion, I hope," said Chisholm.

Vaughan smiled wearily.

"Definitely not that. More of a step sideways. That's the kindest interpretation I can put on it. How about yourself? I believe you're bound for the Clyde and a new ship?"

Chisholm coloured, and stared uncomfortably at Snowy Grieve.

"That's rather a sore point. I was expecting another ship to the one I'm getting."

"Now, Chizz," Grieve said warningly. "Let's not go into that." He smiled at Vaughan. "I think he had rather set his heart on the *Fort Mohican*. He doesn't seem to realise I'm doing him a good turn by letting him have another ship."

Vaughan had looked up sharply. He stared questioningly at Chisholm.

"You wanted the *Fort Mohican*?" He transferred his questioning gaze to Grieve. "Does he know?"

"That she's Sea Transport nominated? Yes," said Grieve, "I told him."

"And you still want her?" Vaughan asked Chisholm.

"Yes," Chisholm said. The look he flashed at Snowy Grieve was defiant. It seemed to pain rather than anger the Marine Superintendent. When Grieve spoke, his tone was patient. He sounded like a man anxious to avoid argument.

"Don't be a bloody fool, Chizz. The *Mohican* isn't for you. You don't have to prove anything . . . You've had a hard war . . . Just because you had some boyhood fancy to play with tomahawks and the name of a red indian tribe still fills your head with crazy notions doesn't mean that I can run a shipping line like I was picking winners for the big race at Aintree. I've got to exercise judgement."

"I see," said Chisholm, with purse-lipped frostiness. "And in your judgement, I wouldn't be suitable for the *Fort Mohican* and the job it has to do . . . Because it's a tough one and the only reason I want the ship is because of some silly schoolboy fancy about a name?"

"Well, isn't it?" Grieve fired back testily.

Chisholm's face darkened.

"No, it damned well isn't!" He waved a hand in a concessionary gesture. "OK, so I said the name appealed to me – but that's not the most important reason. It was what you told me . . . About . . ." He paused involuntarily, not wanting to sound like a glory-hunter. Then he mumbled the phrase that Grieve had quoted to him. ". . . Hazardous expeditions."

Grieve was looking at him, wide-eyed.

"Why, Chizz, why? Haven't you had enough? Do you not know when you've had enough?"

Their stares locked. Grieve's was eloquent with mute appeal. Chisholm's was fierce. Vaughan could have been a million miles away for all that his presence mattered.

"I'll tell you what I've had enough of," Chisholm said, his voice edged with feeling. "I've had enough of slow plodding convoys, sitting waiting for some U-boat commander to get my ship in its sights and blow me out of the water. I've had enough of always being on the receiving end and never hitting back. I want to do something positive in this war. I want to fight back. And if the *Fort Mohican* is going to do some hitting back . . . If she's booked for this Second Front that everybody's shouting about, I want to be on her . . ."

His vehemence seemed to sadden Grieve. The Marine Superintendent did not need to tell Chisholm what he was now able to guess: that the reason he had not been offered the *Fort Mohican* was because Grieve had wanted to shield him from the extreme dangers cloaked behind the words "hazardous expeditions". He did not want to expose Chisholm to more than the day-to-day hazards of the war at sea, which were great enough. He did not want to be the one who ordered him into the cannon's mouth. He had wanted only to protect him.

It was Vaughan who broke the tense silence.

"The *Fort Mohican* has been reserved for special operations, Captain Chisholm, but no one has said a word about Second Front. What gave you that idea?"

"You don't have to be a genius to work it out," said Chisholm impatiently.

Vaughan arched his eyebrows and glanced at Grieve.

"Has anyone said anything to you about Second Front?" he asked.

"No," Grieve answered. "But I must admit I had come to the same conclusion as Hector . . . that that's what you people wanted the *Fort Mohican* for."

"You could both be quite wrong," said Vaughan. "And both of you could be making my job a damned sight more difficult than it is by even speculating on such a possibility. God knows it's difficult enough as it is." He looked from Grieve to Chisholm and back again, his expression severe with reproach. "Captain Grieve, I should appreciate it very much if I could have a further word with you in private . . . If Captain Chisholm will excuse us?"

Chisholm waited for fifteen minutes in an outer office. When Vaughan finally emerged, he indicated to Chisholm that Snowy Grieve wanted to see him.

"I'll wait for you out here," Vaughan said to Chisholm. "When you're finished with Captain Grieve, we'll have our own little chat."

Whatever it was that Vaughan had said to the Marine Superintendent, Chisholm was never to find out. He found the chief executive of the Stockton shipping line in a strangely subdued and chastened mood. No mention was made of what had gone before and there was no discussion. All Grieve had to say was that he had, as a result of his conversation with Vaughan, undergone a change of mind about Chisholm's appointment to the *Fort Mohican*. If Chisholm wanted it, the job was his.

Chisholm and Vaughan left the bomb-scarred Indo-Pacific Marine Insurance building together. Vaughan had a string of other shipping company offices to visit in connection with his new job, but he wanted to talk to Chisholm first. He suggested that they walk and talk. They strolled in Leadenhall Street.

"Thanks for putting in a good word for me with the Old Man," Chisholm said. "How did you do it?"

"A nod and a hint," said Vaughan. "At first he blustered a bit. He's very fond of you, you know. He said it was none of my business who got the *Fort Mohican* job. I said it was my business, and yours . . . And that it was unfinished business."

Chisholm threw him a look.

"And what does that mean?"

"It means that we'll both be working with the Canadian Army again. But that is 'most secret' information, so keep it in under your hat."

Chisholm gave a low whistle.

"I'm intrigued. Is this undercover stuff or what?"

"No repeat performances of Brighton, if that's what you're thinking," Vaughan said with a glimmer of a smile. "No, this is on the up-and-up. And there's an irony in it that I thought would appeal to you. That's why I hinted to Captain Grieve that HM Government would approve if you got the *Fort Mohican* job. You know better than most what a shambles the Dieppe affair was. It gives you a vested interest in helping me to ensure that the 'Husky' operation doesn't suffer the same fate."

"The 'Husky' operation?"

"Yes, that's what they're calling the little exercise ahead of you and the *Fort Mohican* – 'Operation Husky'. Don't ask me for more details now. You'll find out all you need to know soon enough . . . Although, like everyone else involved, you'll be kept guessing about your final destination. You won't get your final orders until you're well at sea."

"Just where do you fit into all this, Commander?"

"I'm in charge of UK security operations for 'Husky'. It will be my job to make sure that Jerry doesn't know where we're going to hit him."

"That's a bit of a change for you, isn't it?" asked Chisholm. Vaughan frowned.

229

"Some might say it's a bit of a comedown. I'm afraid that I didn't exactly cover myself with glory with the business that you and your Canadian friends triggered off. I suppose, if I'm truthful with myself, I should consider myself in disgrace. They've given me my present job as a kind of sop . . . Put me where they think I'll do the least damage."

Chisholm felt strangely embarrassed.

"I'm sorry," he said.

"Don't be sorry for me," Vaughan replied, and summoned up a brave smile. "I'm still in a position to cause confusion to the enemy. And you can help me." He patted Chisholm on the sleeve and there was a twinkle in his eye as he added: "And I can guarantee that this time, no one will put a bullet in you for helping out."

Their strolling had taken them to the entry of Great St Helen's Bishopgate and Vaughan indicated that he would be going out of his way by proceeding further. They moved into the courtyard of the 700-year-old church, away from passers-by.

"Have you heard from Lieutenant Thorn?" Chisholm asked.

Vaughan shook his head. "No, he was in Spain the last I heard."

"Then you won't know if there have been any . . . developments?"

Vaughan smiled at Chisholm's choice of word.

"There have been no 'developments' that I know of. As I told you, I've been stepped sideways – out of harm's way. Brockway and Hibberd will still be beavering away, if I know them, but I'm out of all that now."

Chisholm was disappointed. From the moment he had seen Vaughan in Snowy Grieve's office he had wanted to ask him about Cal Thorn. He had to content himself with the hope that no news was good news.

"I shall be seeing one old acquaintance of yours this week," Vaughan informed him. "Remember Constantine? He's got his third pip now and he's up to his neck in 'Husky'. Shall I tell him to wangle a berth on the *Fort Mohican*?"

"That might be tempting fate," said Chisholm. "But give him my regards. Tell him it was a pity we never had that party in his Mess. He'll know what I mean."

A light southerly breeze was blowing over Brighton from the

Channel, but there was a pleasant warmth in the April sun. The man in the wide-brimmed grey fedora walked with the slow, rolling gait of a seafarer. He wore a black serge suit. The collar of his blue-and-white striped shirt was slightly askew and his tightly knotted blue tie was off the straight, as if both collar and tie were worn as a sop to convention rather than by choice.

He was a big man with a slight stoop to his massive shoulders. His great moon of a face had a benign quality and, indeed, the big man smiled tolerantly as two children on roller skates careered into him as he turned the corner from North Road into Kew Street. He helped one boy to his feet, his kindly grin reassuring the lad.

"Hey, sonny," he said, "you can make yourself a tanner. It's yours if you can tell me how to get to St Nicholas Church."

The boy pointed down the road.

"It's just down there, Mister. You can't miss it. Just turn first right."

The boy neatly caught the sixpence that the stranger tossed in the air.

"Gee, Mister, thanks!" The boy's grin stretched from ear to ear. He called to his friend and they went skating off along the road, the big man's soft chuckling laugh following them.

When he reached the church of St Nicholas, the man in the grey fedora made his way round the side of the 700-year-old building towards the tombs and monuments of the adjacent graveyard. The churchyard was deserted but for one other person. An army officer, with "Canada" flashes at his shoulders, stood at one of the graves. He held a brown-paper-wrapped bunch of daffodils.

The man in the grey fedora approached him.

"Hello, Antoine," he said.

The army officer turned. There was no smile of greeting on his face. He seemed agitated.

"This is bloody madness!" were his first words.

The big man was unruffled. He gently chided the officer that it was no way to greet an old friend on such a beautiful spring day, but his words seemed to have no mollifying effect. The other man was not to be mollified.

"Have you any idea of the trouble I had to get here?" he complained.

"But you're stationed here . . ."

"Not any more, I'm not," snapped the officer. "I've been

running around transit camps in Wales. I had to get a special forty-eight to get down here. The entire division will be on the move next week and I've got the job of shunting them around!"

"Keep cool, Antoine," soothed the man in the grey fedora. "I wouldn't have contacted you like this if it hadn't been an emergency. Let's walk, eh?"

"What do you suggest I do with these goddamned things?" he demanded, holding up the bunch of daffodils. "It wasn't as if they were needed."

"You've changed since we last met, Antoine. I had to be sure it was you. Why don't you leave them . . . ? A small tribute to Martha?"

The officer looked at the daffodils in his hand and then at the stone raised to the memory of Martha Gunn. With a snort of disgust, he tossed the flowers down on the grave.

The man in the fedora had already turned away and the officer fell in step beside him.

"Why have you hauled me down here?" he asked.

"Because I can't reach Esmeralda. I'm worried about her, Antoine. She seems to have disappeared."

"I know," said the man called Antoine, his tone sober. "I think she's dead."

The words were scarcely out of his mouth when he found himself seized by his jacket front and whirled round to face the man in the fedora. Ferocity and anguish contorted the big moon face.

"No!" The single word came out like an animal cry of pain. The big man's fingers were like steel talons digging at the officer's chest. "No!" came the animal sound again.

Eventually, the big man released the other and turned away. Several minutes passed before he made a gesture of apology and signified that he was ready to return to the subject of Esmeralda.

During the next half hour, the two men made several circuits of the churchyard, talking earnestly. They had been talking for some time when the name of Chisholm came up.

"You think he had something to do with Esmeralda's disappearance?" asked the man in the fedora.

"I'm sure of it. He was with her the last time I saw her. The roof should have fallen in on the guy after we'd put Lomax's lights out – but it didn't. It all went wrong. I think the other side tumbled to what we were doing to Chisholm and roped him in to work for them. He's not the innocent fool that Keitler took him for."

The man in the fedora digested this thoughtfully. He stopped in his tracks when his companion said in a faltering voice: "I'm not sure that the British aren't on to me."

The big man's moon face registered a frozen look of horror. His lips moved in a hoarse whisper.

"What makes you say that?"

"This Chisholm . . . and his friends . . . Goddamn it, we dressed the guy up as a ready-made traitor. Instead, he's chummy as hell with one of their top security buffs—a guy called Vaughan. I was interrogated three times by this guy, Vaughan . . . And last week, he turned up again at HQ . . . With a message from Chisholm . . . I near had heart failure . . ."

The man in the fedora looked around the churchyard anxiously.

"Could you have been followed here?"

"No one followed me here. I'm sure! Christ, I'm not an amateur."

The man in the fedora breathed a sigh of relief.

"You probably imagined they were on to you. It gets you like that. I know. I get the jitters myself sometimes . . . You mentioned a message from Chisholm?"

"The message was nothing. It was Vaughan delivering it that gave me the creeps. And what he told me. Chisholm has been given command of one of the invasion ships."

"So?"

"They wouldn't do that if they thought he was two-timing them, would they?"

"The British can be incredibly stupid at times."

"It's too much of a coincidence," the army officer said, his fears far from dissipated. "I don't like it. Not now, when I'm so near the pay-off. It's only a matter of time before I'll be able to give the High Command everything they wanted on a plate: the time and the place of the invasion, and the precise part that will be played in it by an entire new Canadian division. This is the big one. I'm sure of it."

"The Second Front, Antoine? You're sure it's the Second Front this time?"

"It has to be! Christ, the Canadian Division is only going to be a part of this operation. Only a part of it! More than twenty thousand men! I tell you, this is the big one!"

The man in the fedora wanted to hear details. The man called Antoine gave him details: regimental units, their strength in manpower; the military hardware; every component that had been assembled to form a fighting division. He reeled off the names of ships scheduled to load Canadian soldiers and their arms for the military operation, codenamed "Husky". He named more than two dozen ships and the ports of embarkation. The man in the grey fedora memorised all he had been told.

"You have done well, Antoine," he congratulated the officer. "Now, all we have to do is keep our nerve. Together, we will see this through."

"That is not going to be easy without Esmeralda," the officer replied. "We have a communication problem that we didn't have before."

"We'll find a way," promised the man in the fedora. "And we'll make them pay for Esmeralda. You said this man Chisholm was in command of one of the invasion ships. Do you know which ship?"

"The *Fort Mohican*. She's a ten-thousand-ton freighter."

"The one that's embarking at Newport in the Bristol Channel?"

"Yes."

"Can you get yourself on this ship?"

The man called Antoine grimaced.

"It won't be easy, but it's not impossible. Most of our equipment is going on a freighter called the *St Essylt*, and me, too."

"Can't you do a switch?"

"Not without the help of the Navy guy who works these things out to the last pound of weight and square inch of space. But he's a friendly guy. If I can find a good reason for diverting a couple of trucks from one ship to the other, and me with them, I know he'll help."

"You can always say the captain of the *Fort Mohican* is an old comrade and you want to sail with him."

"Thanks but I'll keep Chisholm's name out of it. Then if I do land on his ship, I'll treat it as a great big wonderful surprise. The long arm of coincidence."

"All the best coincidences take very careful planning," said the man in the fedora. He smiled. "Remember that when we meet again, Antoine."

"What do you mean?"

"I mean, Antoine, that next time we meet – and, with luck, that will be quite soon – please don't act surprised. Act as if I am a complete stranger to you. Because I shall do the same. I shall show no sign of recognising you."

The man in the fedora refused to elaborate further. It was not his habit to give notice of his future actions, especially when they were dependent on his ability to overcome a number of intervening obstacles.

The two men parted company. The man in the grey fedora continued to walk in the churchyard of St Nicholas for a further fifteen minutes, enjoying the spring sunshine. Then, he, too, left and walked at a leisurely pace in the direction of the railway station.

Two days after the meeting in the Brighton churchyard, a rendezvous of which he had no knowledge, Vaughan was in his London club. He had stayed there overnight and, after breakfast, found himself with several hours to kill before catching a train to Devizes. He wandered into the reading-room and rummaged through an orderly pile of recent newspapers. He had almost a month's news to catch up with, having been dependent on snatches of heard radio bulletins to keep abreast of recent events.

A tiny item in *The Times* suddenly brought him bolt upright from the depths of his deep leather armchair and then scurrying quickly for the telephone. He dialled and got through immediately to Brockway in Pirbright. What he told the Canadian was enough to bring him hotfoot into London to meet Vaughan.

Vaughan was waiting on the front steps of the club as Brockway dismissed his driver. He ushered Brockway inside with impatient excitement.

The Canadian was scarcely seated before Vaughan was thrusting the week-old copy of *The Times* at him with exhortation to read. The newspaper was folded open at the "Personal" notices and a three-line advertisement had been circled in ink.

The advertisement read:

ANTOINE – Esmeralda does not answer my calls. Essential we meet this week. Bring daffodils for Martha's grave. Wear your Sunday best. – Q.

Brockway read the advertisement several times.

"You think this was inserted by Quasimodo? The Calvi girl's Quasimodo?"

"Well, don't you?" Vaughan's voice was shrill with the impatience that gripped him. "He signs himself 'Q' – and the Calvi girl talked about being the gipsy to her working partner's Quasimodo. The name of the gipsy girl in *The Hunchback of Notre Dame* was Esmeralda!"

Brockway quoted out loud from the advertisement: "Esmeralda does not answer my calls . . ."

"Well, she couldn't, could she?" Vaughan broke in. "She's dead!"

Brockway gave a low whistle.

"Now, you're making sense," he said. "I honestly didn't know what the hell you were driving at on the phone."

"Well, at least you lost no time in getting here. Thank you for that."

Brockway laughed.

"Quicker than trying to find *The Times* down at Pirbright. Now, if it had been the *Toronto Star* . . ." He flicked at the newspaper with a finger. "Hell, this is a week old!"

"But it still gives you something to go on," Vaughan said. "Somebody placed that ad in *The Times*. That means that, with luck, you can get a description of Mr Quasimodo. And the message itself may be able to tell us quite a lot if we can get a good cryptographer on to it right way."

Brockway drummed a hand on the newspaper.

"This could be the break we need. Can I take the paper?"

"I'll tell the librarian it has been appropriated by His Majesty's Armed Forces. Help yourself." Vaughan's face was wreathed in a smile, but it drew no answering smile from Brockway. The Canadian was taking in – as Chisholm had recently done – Vaughan's gaunt appearance: the hollow cheeks, the sunken eyes.

"Are you all right, Commander?" he asked.

"I'm soldiering on," said Vaughan.

"I heard you had been moved."

"We can't stand still." He smiled again. "But I can't get away from the Canadian Army. They're keeping me on my toes."

"If there's anything I can do for you, let me know," said Brockway.

"It might help me get reinstated if you catch Quasimodo," said Vaughan. "And Antoine."

"Yes," mused Brockway, "Antoine. Gilbert, do you think? We'd figured that he was long gone. Do you think he's still holed up somewhere after all this time?"

Vaughan shook his head.

"Until just over a week ago, I might have thought so. But I had a rather strange meeting with another of your Dieppe heroes that has had me thinking ever since . . . He wasn't pleased to see me. He was . . . Well, the only word I can think of is . . . disturbed. Perhaps uneasy describes it better. If I were you, I'd keep an eye on Captain Paul Constantine."

"Constantine?" Brockway's eyes widened. "But we've dredged him and his background clean. He keeps coming up whiter than white."

Vaughan shrugged.

"Maybe it's just my suspicious mind. It was his reaction to me. Something I just couldn't put my finger on." Vaughan was thoughtfully silent for a moment before he added: "His reading habits would interest me. I would certainly like to know if Captain Constantine is in the habit of reading *The Times*."

Vaughan looked at his watch and suddenly stood up.

"Good God, I'll have to fly! Anyway, I've done my little bit . . . I've given you something to think about. I've got to catch a train to Devizes in darkest Wiltshire." He smiled. "I'm giving a lecture on security to five hundred of your Canadian troops."

"Sooner you than me," was Brockway's comment. Vaughan laughed.

"It's not too bad. I'm actually getting quite good at it. I have a very simple and telling text. Only two words, but I find that the Canadians are engraving it on their hearts . . . 'Remember Dieppe'."

When Brockway left Vaughan's club, his first port of call was Scotland Yard. There, he arranged for Special Branch detectives to call at the offices of *The Times* and make enquiries about the person who had placed the advertisement in the "Personal" notices.

His second call was at a Government office in St James's, where he left a copy of the advertisement with a team of experts on crypto-analysis. Then, he returned to Pirbright to await results.

It was evening before he heard from a Special Branch officer.

Brockway's heart sank as he listened to the report. A counter clerk at *The Times* remembered accepting the copy for the small ad but could remember nothing of the person who had placed it; not even if the advertiser had been male or female. A cash payment had been made for three insertions. The name and address of the advertiser had been found to be bogus. Brockway was not going to get a description of the mysterious Q. after all.

It was the next day before the crypto-analysts telephoned Brockway. Their first call was a cautious enquiry to find out if the town of Brighton might have any relevance in the case.

Brockway excitedly confirmed the possibility. Half an hour later, the code expert was on the telephone again. His team were convinced that the message was in plain language, rather than in code, but the information contained in it was lightly disguised.

Antoine, Q., and Esmeralda were clearly pre-arranged cryptonyms for the concealment of identities. And Q. – could this be Quasimodo? – was seeking a meeting with Antoine because Esmeralda was not responding to Q.'s attempts to contact her. The mention of daffodils was possibly a means by which Antoine could identify himself to Q., and the mention of "Sunday best" suggested that a Sunday rendezvous was required. "Best" might suggest the hour. It was a four-letter word, possibly denoting 4 p.m., or perhaps four hours before noon, depending on any pre-arrangement. Alternatively, "b", the second letter of the alphabet might denote 2 p.m. or 2 a.m. There were endless variations.

"Martha's grave" provided what appeared to be a definite location for the meeting, and a search of many guidebooks and other reference works had yielded one interesting discovery. There was in a churchyard in Brighton a "Martha's grave" of some but not outstanding note. Buried in the churchyard of St Nicholas Church was a Martha Gunn, celebrated as "queen" of the dippers: the attendants who looked after sea bathers in the late seventeenth and early eighteenth centuries.

The latter information was sufficient for Brockway to order an immediate watch on the graveyard at St Nicholas in the hope that Antoine and Q. used the place regularly to meet. But that hope faded when the first report from Brighton, after twenty-four hours, was negative. There was a gratuitous footnote to the report. On the grave itself had been found a bunch of daffodils, still partially wrapped in brown paper. The daffodils had withered.

The *Fort Mohican*, with the last of its grain cargo discharged, had been moved from the silo wharf at Avonmouth to a fitting-out berth. Chisholm felt a swell of pride as he stood on the dockside looking up at his ship for the first time. She towered high above him, a veritable giant of a ship compared with the old *Millerby*: ten feet broader in the beam and, with her 441-foot length, nearly a hundred feet longer. Below the deck scuppers, the dark grey of her hull was rust-marked from her Atlantic crossing – but it was staining rather than plate corrosion and Chisholm knew that a wire-brushing and a lick of paint would have her looking smarter than a new pin.

He was unprepared for the sight that met his eyes at deck level. From bow to stern, the ship looked like a building yard that had been struck by a hurricane. The foredeck was a battlefield of strewn shifting boards and unwanted dunnage. Scarcely an inch of deck space could be seen. From the bridge aft, the prospect was little better: stacks of timber everywhere; small mountains of angle-irons, coils of wire and bottle-screws; enough uncut metal piping to keep a plumber in business for a decade; rolls of roofing felt and bolts of canvas; porcelain sinks and metal wash-basins; barrels of rivets; the steel frames and armour of gun-pits under construction; clusters of mobile generators, torpedo-like oxygen bottles, and a confusion of insulated cables running everywhere. Through this chaos moved a small army of carpenters, welders, riggers, electricians and their attendant labourers. The noise of hammering, sawing, rolling winches and bawled communication provided the ant-like activity with an accompaniment of continuous bedlam.

Jackman, the departing master, had to shout to be heard as he took Chisholm on a tour of his new command. He gave no sign of being heartbroken at being relieved of the frenzy and chaos that was the *Fort Mohican*. Indeed, he seemed almost light-headed with incredulity at his good fortune: like a long-term convict who has been unexpectedly handed a free pardon at the beginning of his sentence.

He showed Chisholm the sites on deck where an additional galley and bakery were to be built. The sinks and metal basins on deck were waiting to be housed in a new timber-built ablutions section close by. The juxtaposition of primitive toilet accommodation and catering facility was unfortunate, but deck space was at a premium and every square inch of it would be used in the *Fort Mohican*'s transformation from cargo ship to troop transport.

There was as much activity below decks as there was on the open deck. Squads of workmen were installing cabins and messes in the tween-decks and, in number four hold, rows and rows of lino-topped tables were being installed with hammock rails above them to provide hundreds of men with quarters where they would both eat and sleep. When the work was over, the *Fort Mohican* would be equipped to carry ten times its normal human complement of fifty souls.

Chisholm's first days aboard passed in a daze of consultations. He was besieged from morning until night by relays of contractors, suppliers, port authorities and government officials. In the second week in May, the crew signed on.

Chisholm was not sorry to escape early from the noisy comings and goings of the shipping office for a Sea Transport conference and leave the selection of deck and engine-room personnel to the Chief Officer and Chief Engineer respectively. As a consequence, he missed a small moment of drama.

It occurred when the shipping master discovered that the Donkeyman PO who had been pencilled in for the *Fort Mohican* was not in the shipping office. His name was called several times but, on each occasion, there was no response. After a third call, a man did come forward. He volunteered the information that Davis, the missing donkeyman had returned to his home in the Rhondda Valley because his wife was sick. He no longer wanted the *Fort Mohican* job but he had asked the bearer of this news to take his place and offer his own services.

In the absence of other candidates, the newcomer was given the berth of donkeyman on the *Fort Mohican*.

Robertson, the Chief Engineer, was impressed by his new PO. The man was a Norwegian and Robertson had had a great regard for the competence of Norwegian seafarers ever since he had sailed with them in 1940. A Norwegian ship had plucked him and several other survivors from an open boat in mid-Atlantic.

"Have you sailed in Fort boats before?" Robertson asked the man, whose name was Eric Lander.

"I've just brought one over from the States, sir. The *Fort McGillivary*. We paid off from her three weeks ago, in Cardiff. I was only on her a month, but you get to know your way round an engine-room in that time."

"A month?" queried the engineer.

"Yes, sir." Lander smiled. It gave his moon face a very benign look. "I got the job in New York. I took the place of a guy who fell in the dock and got drowned. They shipped me down from Montreal."

"What were you doing in Montreal?"

"Waiting for the ice on the St Lawrence to break. The ship I was on there was getting a new boiler fitted . . . But she'll be in Montreal another winter yet."

'Why is that?'

"A spark from a welding torch. She was burned out."

"What ship was it?"

"A Dutchman called the *Argo*."

Robertson grinned.

"Don't tell me she was eighteen hundred years old and the Captain's name was Jason."

"No, sir. The Old Man was an Amsterdammer called Van Koch and he was more interested in the golden stuff that comes out of a whisky bottle than he was in any golden fleece."

"I was only joking," said Robertson, with a laugh. "Mind you I did know a ship called the *Argo*. A Baltic trader . . . Finnish. She's probably iced up for the duration, too!" He became suddenly serious, aware that the shipping master was anxious to get the articles signed and that he was holding things up by gossiping. "How soon can you report aboard?" he asked Lander.

"Today, if you want," replied the Norwegian. "I've got all my gear here."

Half an hour later, Lander – a battered suitcase in one hand and a kit-bag across his shoulder – was looking for a taxi to take him to the *Fort Mohican*. He felt pleased with himself. For an outlay of a bottle of whisky and twenty pounds, he had secured Davis' job. Seated finally in a taxi, speeding to Avonmouth docks, he placed his grey fedora hat on the seat beside him and half-heartedly tried to straighten his wayward collar and tie.

Sixteen

The Smokescreen

Almost fifty men were crowded into the saloon and smoke-room of the *Fort Mohican*. Standing on a chair to be seen and heard, Chisholm addressed the crew of his ship.

He gave a short homily of the dangers of careless talk in wartime, belabouring the point that an ill-advised word about a ship's movements could lead to the loss of that ship and the deaths of her crew.

He expressed the hope that no man on his ship would advertise her name by injudicious talk in bus or pub or any public place; nor speculate anywhere about the voyage that lay before them all. It would be a voyage with greater danger, perhaps, than any of them had ever undertaken. The key to its success would be the secrecy exercised by every man on board concerning the ship, her cargo, and her destination.

"Yours are the lives that are at stake," he warned. "Do all of you understand that?"

There was a chorus of affirmative answers. From the serious expressions on the faces of the congregated seamen, it seemed clear that none took the matter lightly. The younger men were awed; vaguely aware that they were committed for a trip that was out of the ordinary. The older hands, all too familiar with the perils of wartime sailing, stood grim-faced and tense. For them, the risks did not have to be spelled out.

Satisfied that his warning had registered, Chisholm directed the attention of the men to three tables in the smoke-room, where the First, Second and Third Officers sat like stall-holders at a charity bazaar, half-hidden by voluminous cardboard crates. He invited the crew to form an orderly queue and file past the three officers, who would issue each man with equipment needed for the voyage. Most of it was for their protection but Chisholm reminded them all that the nature of the gifts they were about to receive should not be broadcast.

One at a time, the men moved past the three tables. From the Third Officer, they each received a blue and orange life-jacket and battery-powered survival light to attach to it. From the Second Officer, each man got a grey steel helmet, heavy seaboot socks and a pair of long woolly drawers. At the end of the line, the Chief Officer dispensed sheepskin waistcoats, balaclava helmets and tiny Norwegian-English phrasebooks. The latter provoked surprise and much comment.

As the file wound slowly past the tables, Chisholm left his officers to it and slipped up the inside stairway to his cabin. Seated in his day-room and drinking coffee from large china mugs were two naval officers. One, a lieutenant called Penrose, was shortly to be joining the *Fort Mohican* as SNOT: the unprepossessing acronym for Senior Naval Officer Transport. He would command the three twenty-five-ton landing-craft the *Fort Mohican* would carry.

The other naval officer was Vaughan.

"How goes the distribution of goodies?" he asked Chisholm.

"Smoothly," Chisholm replied. He eyed Vaughan reproachfully. "I still think it's bloody daft. The Arctic gear and Norwegian handbooks could have waited until we were at sea. Giving them out now is just asking for trouble."

"Don't you trust fifty men to keep a secret?" Vaughan asked.

"It's not a matter of trust. I know human nature. It only needs one of these blokes down there to have one drink too many and get a bit garrulous, and you might as well broadcast your precious secret on the six o'clock news."

Vaughan laughed.

"How about yourself, Captain Chisholm. Can you keep a secret?"

Chisholm stared hard at the other man. This wasn't the Vaughan he knew: the Vaughan who carried the troubles of the world on his shoulders. He seemed to be treating the whole matter of operational security with uncharacteristic frivolity.

"I think I can," Chisholm answered Vaughan frostily. "But, if you don't mind me saying so, keeping secrets seems to be going out of fashion – and common sense with it. Otherwise, you wouldn't have insisted on me handing out the Arctic gear in port. Every stevedore on the ship will have seen the men taking these sheepskin waistcoats and their long johns back to their quarters. Tonight, it'll be the talk of every bar in Newport. By tomorrow, they'll be talking about it in Cardiff and Swansea . . . By next week, the whole bloody world will know we're bound for Norway . . ."

The more Chisholm had railed, the broader had become Vaughan's smile. Chisholm's harangue halted suddenly. His eyes widened as a blinding truth seemed to hit him.

"You devil!" he exclaimed. "You *want* it to leak out that we're going to Norway!"

The look that came to Vaughan's face at the accusation was one of bland innocence.

"That's something that I cannot confirm nor deny," he said with a shrug. Then the smile returned. "But you have a right to know certain things. That's why I asked you if you can keep a secret. I think you should know, for instance, what I've been planning with Lieutenant Penrose for tomorrow."

Chisholm listened, with the air of one who finds education painful, as Vaughan revealed what was laid on for the *Fort Mohican*'s Royal Navy personnel. More than thirty men were involved: landing-craft crews, DEMS gunners, signallers. Next day, they would all be attending a one-day course at the naval barracks.

In the morning, they would be given two lectures – one on tropical diseases and the other on Japanese aircraft indentification. In the afternoon, they would be given typhoid and cholera inoculations and would receive a special issue of tropical KD uniforms and solar topis. Each man would sign, too, for a personal supply of one hundred quinine tablets, one to be taken daily on arrival in equatorial waters.

Two days hence, the naval contingent would embark on the *Fort Mohican*. By then, Vaughan would have moved on to a large army transit camp in the Wye valley, where a large number of Canadian troops were assembling: including 450 who would embark on the *Fort Mohican* when cargo-loading was complete.

"Do not be too surprised," Vaughan told Chisholm, "if the troops who come aboard have the impression that you will be taking them to Greece or Jugoslavia. During their final hours in this country, they will be receiving a series of talks on Balkan politics, Balkan languages, Balkan customs and the finer points of mountain warfare."

After Vaughan had left the ship, Chisholm was soon wishing

that he had not been taken into the Commander's confidence. The knowledge that an elaborate smokescreen was being manufactured to conceal the true destination of "Operation Husky" was something of an embarrassment amid the guarded, almost conspiratorial, conversations of his officers at the *Fort Mohican*'s long dining table. There was not a man on the ship who doubted that he was to take part in a sea-borne assault on occupied Norway – and Chisholm felt like a liar, merely by saying nothing to disabuse them of the idea.

In three weeks, the chaos he had found on the *Fort Mohican* had not disappeared – but it had been given some kind of order. Amidships, the erection on deck of timber houses to contain augmented catering and toilet facilities had been completed in seven days. So, too, had been the work of installing extensive living accommodation in three holds. Simultaneously, 2,000 tons of sand ballast had been loaded and bedded in the hold-bottoms, and timber floors had been built on the levelled sand as a base for the heavy army vehicles soon to be loaded.

The ship had made the short crossing of the Bristol Channel from Avonmouth to Newport for cargo work to begin. It had been an eye-opener to Chisholm to see his new command's astonishing capacity to accommodate the machines and ordnance of war. Lines and lines of army trucks had disappeared from the quay-side to be swallowed up in the great belly of the *Fort Mohican*. Into the forward holds had disappeared a fifty-foot-high dockside mountain of cased petroleum, without very much impression seeming to be made on the hold space. Into No. 2 hold, had gone a seemingly endless procession of 250-lb bombs with RAF markings: sufficient to erase an entire city from the face of the earth.

On the evening after Vaughan's visit, Chisholm quietly surveyed his domain from the level of the lower bridge. The holds were almost full. Two or three more days would see the *Fort Mohican* ready for sea. It would not take long to load the deck cargo, including the landing-craft that would straddle holds two and four.

A lone figure picked his way forward past the new troop galley, footsteps echoing on the board-walk that skirted it. Chisholm recognised the heavy build and distinctive grey hat of the Norwegian donkeyman. It was almost 9 p.m.

"You're late going ashore, Donkeyman," Chisholm called to the man on the deck below. "The pubs will be shut before you get to town."

The big moon face smiled up at Chisholm.

"Oh, I'm not a drinking man, Captain. I do not care about the pubs . . . I leave that to the others. But I like to exercise my legs before I turn in. I go for a walk."

"It's a fine night for it," Chisholm called.

He watched Lander as he reached the quay and walked with his slow, bowling gait past the line of khaki-painted trucks waiting to be shipped on the *Fort Mohican*'s deck.

Lander seldom gave the impression of being in a hurry but, beneath the contented, easy-going exterior he displayed, a rare excitement gripped him. In his pocket was the letter that he had laboured over in the seclusion of his boat-deck cabin for three hours. Its text covered no more than a single sheet of Basildon Bond notepaper, but elaborate care had gone into the wording. Lander had sealed the letter in an addressed envelope and then inserted this in a larger envelope. On the outer envelope, he had stuck a 2½d stamp before penning on a name and an address in London.

Lander's immediate goal on leaving the ship was the General Post Office in Newport. He walked all the way from the docks. It afforded him some amusement that the British postal service would with great efficiency deliver his letter in London within twenty-four-hours. The man to whom it was addressed could be trusted to send it on the next stage of its journey.

Lander dropped the letter into the postbox with a feeling of satisfaction at a job well done. With luck – and enjoying the privacy of a Spanish Embassy diplomatic bag – it would be in Madrid within a week.

With the last of the deck cargo in place and all the dockers gone, the *Fort Mohican* had fallen strangely silent by mid-afternoon. The eerie silence persisted until shortly before midnight, when it ended with a roar of motor-cycle engines. Still astride their machines, the squad of military police methodically barricaded off the access roads to the *Fort Mohican*'s berth by occupying every corner. They were no sooner in position then the first of the covered military trucks began arriving in convoy. They were waved into the hangar-like cargo shed opposite the ship, where they drew up in rows.

At a signal, tail-gates were lowered and canvas flaps thrown aside. Each truck disgorged a quota of helmeted figures

246

carrying battle-packs and weapons. With a minimum of spoken commands – and little sound other than the clank of equipment or the ring of steel-heeled boot on concrete – the Canadian soldiers formed ranks on the quay. Then, without talk of any kind, they trooped in file up the *Fort Mohican*'s gangway. The decks echoed metallically under their boots as they silently went aft and were ushered below.

In under half an hour, more than 450 men had embarked and were out of sight below decks. The trucks that had brought them had gone and the cargo shed was empty. The motor-cycle escorts had roared off in the wake of the trucks with a final chorus of surging throttles.

The troops were still below decks when, at first light, Chisholm gave the order from the *Fort Mohican*'s bridge to single up the moorings. Moments later, the ship was on the move and heading for the choppy waters of the Bristol Channel. She was well clear of the harbour and settled on a south-south-westerly course before the town had begun to stir to the new day.

In Barry Roads, later in the morning, the lone ship joined company with two other freighters and a trawler escort before proceeding into the teeth of a westerly gale – which stiffened as Nash Point was left on the starboard quarter. The unpleasant weather threatened to put into some disarray the time-tabled rota of meal sittings in the *Fort Mohican*'s saloon. Not all the Canadian officers availed themselves of the facilities which they had been invited to share with ship's officers. For the first dinner at sea, Chisholm had asked the Canadian CO and his second-in-command to eat with him and the Chief Engineer at a specially laid table for four in the smoke-room. Little exclusivity was involved in the arrangement. Only a curtain separated the four from the mix of ship and military personnel squeezed round the long saloon dining table.

It was when Chisholm rose from dinner that he came face to face with Captain Paul Constantine. The Canadian was vacating his seat at the saloon table as Chisholm emerged from the smoke-room through the gap in the partially drawn curtain.

They shook hands and exchanged greetings, attracting the attention of those seated around the long table when Constantine introduced the ship's captain not only as an old acquaintance but as a fellow-escaper. Chisholm flushed with embarrassment when Constantine went on to say that he owed

247

his life to Chisholm's magnificent seamanship. All the Canadians wanted to shake his hand and tell him how honoured they were to be aboard his ship.

It was quickly apparent to Chisholm, that Constantine was quite a hero in the eyes of the other officers and seemed to enjoy their adulation. Their esteem owed a lot to the white and blue ribbon of the MC on Constantine's chest and the Dieppe exploits, fast becoming legendary, that had earned it.

Neither Chisholm nor Constantine gave any indication that their encounter was anything other than an extravagant stroke of chance. Chisholm avoided mention of Vaughan and gave no hint that the meeting was not entirely a surprise. Constantine said nothing about having met Vaughan at Divisonal HQ.

"It really is a small world," Chisholm said when, at his invitation, the two men had escaped from the hubbub of the saloon to his day-room. The cliché sounded like a cliché as he handed Constantine a whisky and poured a glass of soda water for himself.

"Not drinking with me?" Constantine enquired.

"Nothing stronger than soda water at sea," replied Chisholm, and waved his glass. "Your good health anyway."

Constantine replied in kind and sipped the whisky. His eyes seemed to smile, but there was no telling from the slight movement of his lipless face whether this was so or not.

"Seen anything of Anina lately?" he asked casually.

"No, not since that night we met in Brighton," Chisholm said. The lie embarrassed him. "How about you, Paul? Have you seen her?"

Constantine shook his head.

"No. She just seemed to fade out of sight altogether. I wondered if you'd heard anything. There were rumours that she'd had an accident . . ."

"What kind of accident?"

"I don't know. It was just talk in the Mess . . . Very vague."

"An accident would have been in the papers," Chisholm suggested.

"Yeah, you'd think so."

They talked briefly about Lomax's death. It had not been mentioned in the papers. The conversation became more and more strained, as if neither man had very much to say to the other. It was a relief to Chisholm when Constantine declined a second drink and said it was time he was getting below.

When the Canadian had gone, Chisholm sat for a time trying to arrive at an explanation for his unease in Constantine's company. He concluded that it arose from his own reluctance to talk about Brighton, Anina, or Lomax. They were part of the past now. And here, on the *Fort Mohican*, he did not want the past to intrude. He did not know if Constantine's presence on board was by accident or design, nor did he care. He knew only that he resented that presence. Constantine was a link in a chain extending back to St Cyr des Bains and beyond. The last link. And, with all that lay ahead, Chisholm would have preferred it not to exist.

Constantine, emerging from the Captain's quarters on to the lower bridge deck, was in no easier frame of mind than Chisholm. Conversation had been like walking in a minefield. Lander had been crazy to think that, because he knew Chisholm, there would be some advantage in being aboard his ship. The opposite was the case. Because he knew Chisholm and Chisholm knew him, he was going to have to be doubly on guard. Constantine was now bitterly regretting the trouble he had taken to ensure that he shipped on the *Fort Mohican* instead of the *St Essylt*. He should have stuck with the *St Essylt* and ignored Lander's orders.

Constantine stood for a moment, gazing down at the crowded midships deck of the *Fort Mohican*. On the port side, was the huddle of new timber housing with smoke belching from the pipe-like chimney atop the second galley. On the starboard side, several large trucks and two jeeps – lashed to angle-irons and bottle-screwed – left little or no deck space for passage fore and aft. He drew no comfort from the congested scene. He felt hemmed in, trapped. It had been a grave mistake to come to this ship. There had been no need for it.

His single consolation was that, before embarking, he had got a letter off to Montreal. Using the Canadian cover address was perhaps a laborious way of getting urgent information back to *Schatten Gruppe* HQ – but it had been proved time and again that attempts at direct radio communication had caused the downfall of more espionage groups than any other means. So *Schatten Gruppe* avoided radio communication except in the most extreme emergencies, as a matter of policy. Constantine knew that they had survived because of it. The SD had made several attempts to infiltrate Britain with radio-carrying agents and all had been conspicuously disastrous.

He knew, too, that use of existing postal systems was not only one of the safest methods of transmission of information but much under-estimated as far as speed of delivery was concerned. He was hopeful that the air letter he had sent to Montreal – ostensibly to a girlfriend – would be delivered within four to seven days. It would be deciphered the day it was received and its main text transmitted in a coded cable from a New York business house to a similar establishment in Madrid within twenty-four hours. Berlin would be in possession of the hard intelligence a few hours after the cable had reached Madrid.

So, it was not outrageous to hope that the intelligence he had despatched in Britain would be undergoing assessment in Berlin inside ten days, having made a 6000-mile round trip. Compared with radio, the method was painfully slow – but it was reasonably sure and afforded the sender a high degree of safety. Even if the letter were to be intercepted by anti-espionage investigators at any stage of its journey, the trail would lead back to a sender who was found not to exist.

Unhappy as he was at being on the *Fort Mohican*, Constantine felt that the main objective of his mission had been achieved with the despatch of his Montreal letter. In it, he had told his German masters that a division of the Canadian Army was embarking in late May or early June for a sea-borne assault of such size that it was undoubtedly the Second Front. He anticipated an Allied involvement of between ten and twelve divisions. First indications had been that the target was North-West France or the Low Countries. This he was now able totally to discount. The attack would come in the Balkans, either Greece or Jugoslavia. He could not be more specific. The Canadians were to be part of a thrust across the Mediterranean, mounted by the Allied armies now massed in North Africa. The attack would take place between the 1st and 7th July.

There was a steady procession of Canadian soldiers moving in and out of the wooden toilet huts on the port side and Constantine looked down at them with a measure of contempt. They were so cocksure that they were going to savage the German Army this time, make the "squareheads" pay bloodily for Dieppe. Poor bloody fools! They were in for the shock of their lives. His only regret was that he would have to share some of their misery with them. It wasn't going to be much fun at the other end. He was going to have his work cut out staying alive. But perhaps he would be able to concentrate on that— surviving. He'd done the bulk of his work when he had got the letter off to Montreal. He had warned the German High Command where to expect the Allies' next big push and he had given them at least three weeks in which to deploy forces to meet it. There was not much more now that he could do. Just keep his head down and see it through.

The *Fort Mohican* was still battling into a fierce wind and blown spray showered over Constantine as he descended to deck level on the weather side. He ducked quickly into the lee of the housing, paying no attention at first to the denim-jacketed figure only a few feet away. Lander was at the open doors of the ship's pantry, where a steward was issuing him with quantities of tea, coffee, sugar and condensed milk. It was when Constantine edged along the passage between hatch coaming and the pantry that he suddenly came face on to Lander. Their eyes met.

Lander's showed no sign of recognition, but he beamed a smile at the Canadian.

"This lot should keep us going, sir," he remarked jovially, holding up his stores. "They don't get rations like this ashore."

Constantine could only stare at the big moon-faced man, not daring to speak. The eyes in the moon face seemed to taunt him. They continued to mock as Lander made an elaborate performance of steering his great bulk round the rooted Canadian and commenting: "That's all right, sir. Don't you move. Just you stand there till you find your sea legs!"

Constantine watched the donkeyman navigate his way aft: stepping nimbly over the wires and bottle-screws that moored a three-ton army truck to the *Fort Mohican*'s deck. Lander did not once look back.

The fierce westerlies that had persisted all the way north through the Irish Sea were showing no sign of abatement when the tiny convoy from Barry Roads steamed into the Firth of Clyde. The *Fort Mohican* rode the short, shallow swell easily but the escort trawler, just ahead, rolled erratically in the choppy beam sea. There was a flurry of winking lights as the ships passed the signal station at Toward Point. The laden troop transport was ordered to part company with her travelling companions once she was beyond the boom defence at Dunoon.

The escort and the two freighters were going on upriver to Glasgow and veered to starboard when the boom was passed. Chisholm sounded two siren blasts–a farewell and signal of intent–as the *Fort Mohican* turned to port. At reduced speed, she threaded her way among a vast armada of ships lying at anchor in the Holy Loch.

When, finally, the *Fort Mohican* was riding at anchor, Chisholm lingered on the bridge. He took in the vista of green hills and assembled shipping with a strange flutter of anticipation in the pit of his stomach. The setting was one of exceptional beauty and tranquillity, but the presence of so many grey ships dressed and ready for war stirred the nerve ends.

If the *Fort Mohican* had seemed titanic in comparison with the trawler that had escorted her from Barry Roads, it was now the *Fort Mohican*'s turn to be dwarfed. A flat-top at anchor, half a mile away, seemed gargantuan compared with the 10,000-ton transport. Beyond the carrier, a cluster of half a dozen troopships–with tiers of decks and funnels large enough to swallow two railway locomotives on end–swung on their cables. A pair of battleships–their great broad beams clad in bulbous armour–wallowed like dosing crocodiles. Sleek cruisers flaunted their trim stacks rakishly, wearing their dazzle-paint like preening dandies at ease.

The sight filled Chisholm with both expectancy and a mounting impatience. He felt like an athlete who was mentally and physically prepared for the main event and had been summoned to the start line. Now, come what may, he was eager for the race to begin.

But he had to curb his impatience. V-Force–as the gathering of naval ships and transports was designated–was not yet fully assembled. Chisholm was to learn that two separate convoys were mustering: a fast and a slow. The slow convoy, including the *Fort Mohican*, would depart several days in advance of the fast, which would contain the big troopers and be screened by the heavy naval ships. The entire force was to be under the command of a former destroyer commander–now promoted to Admiral–who had made headlines all over the world as "Vian of the *Cossack*". Phillip Vian had made history by tracking the German prison ship *Altmark* into a Norwegian fiord and boarding her with a crew of navymen who had screamed into attack with cutlasses, yelling, "The Navy's here!"

The *Fort Mohican* was to spend only five days amid the green mountains of the Holy Loch. To Chisholm, they seemed endless.

The monotony of renewed waiting was relieved briefly by the arrival of more military passengers. A Company of the RAF Regiment came out on a converted ferry-boat and clambered aboard the *Fort Mohican*. Somehow or other, space was found for them in the already crowded tween-decks.

Next day, a pinnace collected Chisholm to take him to the Convoy Conference at Gourock. He returned late in the afternoon, knowing that the waiting was now almost over but more soberly aware than ever of the "hazardous expeditions" that lay ahead. Tucked in his brief-case were the voluminous sealed orders that would remain locked in his safe until the Convoy Commodore gave the order to open them.

In the early light of the following dawn, the anchorage echoed to the rumble of windlasses and the clangour of anchor chains hauled through hawse-pipes. Everywhere, ships were on the move. The vanguard of V-Force was putting to sea.

Seventeen

Convoy

They sailed out through the North Channel and west into the Atlantic. With the coast of Ireland five hundred miles astern, the convoy swung south.

There were four columns of ships, six ships to a column. A single destroyer beat to and fro ahead of the rectangular formation while another patrolled the rear like a snapping collie. Two pairs of destroyers guarded the flanks: sometimes racing ahead and then circling back with a gleaming smile of white water at the bow; sometimes maintaining station sedately abreast the flock.

Almost daily, the normal alarms of the Western Approaches occurred. One of the escort would pick up a contact on her underwater detecting gear and thrash through the ranks of transports with black pennant streaming and great white plumes of exploding depth charges rising in her wake.

The Convoy Commodore drilled his merchantmen with the zeal of a parade-ground martinet; practising them in a variety of manoeuvres. They wheeled from columns of four to columns of two to line ahead. They marched in ranks of six at a synchronised turn to starboard, then resumed their four-columned advance with a ninety-degree alteration to port at a double siren blast from the leader.

They followed intricate zig-zag patterns from the third day out, altering course on the hour, every hour. But, whatever the pattern, the mean course was steadily south. The sky and the sea took on a deeper blue and the sun became warmer on the back as the cloudy ceiling of the northern latitudes was left behind.

The realisation that the *Fort Mohican*'s progress was in-exorably south brought furrows of concern to the brow of one man on the ship. Eric Lander could not at first believe that the early southward sweep was more than a feint. He was sure it was a time-filling ploy before the convoy reversed course and headed north at maximum speed. Like Constantine, he believed that the major object of his assignment had been achieved by giving his masters warning of the much-vaunted Second Front. His letter from Newport should have been in German hands in Madrid even before the *Fort Mohican* had left the Clyde. Already, as a result of it, German divisions from France and the Low Countries might have been deployed to Norway to face a threat that would never materialise.

Lander's mood of self-congratulation at what he imagined would be the intelligence coup of the war changed to deeper and deeper chagrin at every turn of the *Fort Mohican*'s screw. Far from pulling off a feat that would make his name a legend, he had somehow been duped into an act that might cost Germany the war. His despair grew even deeper as a result of a chance conversation with a smugly knowledgeable naval rating who was one of the landing-craft crew.

This pink-faced seaman thought it was an immense joke that most of the merchant ship crewmen had been convinced that the ship was bound for Norway and that most of the Canadian soldiers believed that their destination was the Mediterranean. *He* knew better. Only the Royal Navy personnel had been trusted with the real secret: that the ship was heading for the Far East. *He had a solar topi and a three-month supply of quinine tablets to prove it!*

Lander lost no time in contriving a meeting with Constantine. He did so by spending much time with a hammer and a monkey wrench, apparently dismantling and re-assembling one of the winches near the hatchway of No. 3 hold, where the Canadian officers were quartered. He eventually succeeded in attracting Constantine's attention and engaging him in casual conversation. He suggested that the Canadian officer might like to be shown round the engine-room.

"Why don't you ask the Chief Engineer if it's OK," he suggested. "Tell him the donkeyman's offered to show you around some evening after he has knocked off for the day." No precedent was being set. On the first day out, the Chief Engineer had asked the donkeyman to show three Canadian officers round the engine-room.

That evening, Lander took Constantine on his conducted

tour: showing him the stoke-hold where the firemen worked; how the trimmers worked the bunkers; and then giving him a running commentary on the platforms and gridded catwalks of the engine-room about the workings of the great triple-expansion steam engine.

To complete the tour, Lander suggested descending to the shaft tunnel at the bottom of the ship to view the propeller shaft in whirling motion. Constantine, a little bewildered, followed Lander down the narrow sixty-foot ladder to the bowels of the ship. He found the enclosed space and the noise from the revolving shaft appalling but Lander – speaking through cupped hands close to Constantine's ear – pointed out the virtues. Here, they could be alone and could speak without any chance of being disturbed.

"We've been tricked," he told Constantine gloomily, and went on to relate the circumstances which had led him to warn Berlin of an imminent invasion of Norway. Constantine, who had always found the other man patronising, could not resist a gloat of triumph.

"You're the one who got it wrong," he corrected. "You, not *we*!" he told Lander then that he had used the North American circuit to Madrid to warn Berlin of an Allied invasion of the Balkans during the first week of July.

The likelihood that Constantine's prediction would prove accurate brought no comfort to Lander. He could imagine the confusion created in Berlin by the receipt of two reports from connected sources announcing that landings were imminent in Europe at points as geographically distant from each other as Greece and Northern Norway. The chances were that the High Command would disregard both.

"Do you realise what this means?" he asked a shaken Constantine. "Somehow or other we've got to get a message off this ship. We've got to let our people know the true situation."

The difficulties and risk in attempting anything so desperate dismayed Constantine. It was bad enough that they would have to face the bombs and bullets of their own side without being forced into an action that would almost certainly lead to their exposure and deaths as spies. He made it plain to Lander that what he wanted was impossible. Lander's accusing eyes washed him with contempt.

"Our lives count for nothing!" The donkeyman shouted to be heard above the noise of the whirling propeller shaft. "Have

256

you forgotten the vows you took when you were admitted to *Schatten Gruppe?*"

Constantine turned his head away in shame. He deserved Lander's contempt. His nerve had been failing badly of late. The strain of the last few months had been so great that it had been easy to forget the words he had recited with such earnest passion in the approving presence of Heinrich Himmler and Reinhard Heydrich. He recalled them now: "I, Walther Strasser, willingly surrender my mind, my body and my life to the service and greater glory of my Führer and my Fatherland. I vow to welcome death, and seek no other reward or honour in the service I now embrace with heart and being . . ."

It all seemed so long ago now, so far removed from this oily tunnel and this foreign ship. He straightened himself. Lander had done right to remind him of the code of that elite body to which they both belonged. A tear of pride glistened on the seared flesh at the corner of one eye.

"I apologise," he said. "Thank you for reminding me of my obligations." His voice was scarcely audible against the thunder of the shaft but it rose as he declared firmly: "If I must die, I must die!"

Lander could sense from the other's calm alone that he had reached inside himself and found a new seam of courage. He felt an uplift of emotion. Impulsively, he embraced Constantine in a comradely hug.

"We shall not fail, Walther!" he promised. "We shall not fail!"

If there was anything incongruous in that strangely emotional reaffirmation of purpose between the two men in that tomb-like passage below the ship's waterline, there was none but themselves to judge it so. They were almost as alone and remote from observation in the tunnel as, in the wider scheme of things, they were cut off from friendly aid.

Although Lander – by virtue of military rank and experience – was the senior officer, he found himself deferring to Constantine's ideas on how they should react to the situation confronting them. It was clear to both that, just as the *Fort Mohican*'s crew had been misled into the belief that Norway was the ship's destination, the Canadians might have been falsely lured to believe that the Balkans was the target.

It was essential then that irrefutable knowledge of the precise location of the landing beaches was a prerequisite to any fresh attempt to contact Berlin.

"How can we find out for sure where the landings will be?" Lander lamented bitterly.

"The sealed orders are in the Captain's safe. Maybe I can get hold of them," suggested Constantine.

"No." Lander was emphatic. "I cannot allow you to take so foolish a risk. If you were caught, we would be no further forward."

"The alternative," said Constantine, "is to wait until the orders are opened before we make a move."

"But when will that be?"

"At least four or five days before D-Day. We have to be given time to familiarise ourselves with the terrain and our objectives. They can't keep us in the dark right to the last minute."

Lander considered this.

"Four or five days? Our army moves fast. A lot can be achieved in four or five days. It might just be time enough."

He insisted that Constantine do nothing that might arouse suspicion before the sealed orders were opened.

"Very well," Constantine agreed. "But, after that, we shall have to move quickly. And you must allow me to take the first initiative. If I fail, then it will be up to you."

So it was that Lander deferred to the younger man's wishes. Once there was no more doubt about the convoy's destination, Constantine would act. Lander would remain the hidden reserve, ready to go into action if anything went wrong.

They shook hands solemnly. As their eyes met, Lander wondered why, earlier, he had doubted the resolution of the man who had been born Walther Strasser. There was a gleam in Strasser's eyes that Lander recognised. He had seen its like once before – in an enemy, during the Spanish Civil War – in that moment when he had realised that a fanatical young Communist was never going to break under interrogation. That young man had not only reconciled himself to dying but was exultant that his death would be a personal victory over his Fascist captors. Even in the moment when Lander had raised his revolver and shot him, the young man's eyes had gleamed his scornful disregard for life.

Now Lander glimpsed the same scorn for life in his confederate's eyes. And he was reassured by it. He knew that Strasser was now running on some inner battery of idealistic ervour and that nothing would deter nor deflect him from his chosen course.

At noon on the eighth day out from the Clyde, the convoy altered course to due east. At dusk, the leading escorts were doing their best to shoo from its path the unrepentant stragglers of a Spanish fishing fleet that had been strung out before them across twenty miles of ocean.

The fishing boats were in no hurry to give way to the advancing formation of ships. The fishermen believed they had as much right to operate in international waters as anyone else and they resented having to haul their tackle and concede passage: reversal of peacetime procedure. The Spanish skippers knew, however, that Article 13 of the laws governing the rule of the road at sea was arbitrarily invoked by belligerent maritime powers in time of war. This Article rendered invalid all peacetime procedures and gave right of passage to two or more ships of war or to vessels sailing in convoy.

The neutral Spaniards knew there would be no compensation for tackle severed by unswerving freighters. Nor would there be any redress by law for boats sunk or fishermen drowned through failure on their part to heed repeated warnings to stand clear. So, they moved out of the convoy's path – but with a disdain that constituted a statement on the violation of cherished rights.

The troops on the ships of the convoy reacted with excited interest at the sight of the tiny Spanish boats dotted across the horizon. For them, it was their first visible evidence that the endless wastes of the Atlantic were inhabited by human life outwith their company of ships.

For others, who knew these waters, the sight of the Spanish boats was the source of heavy misgiving. Chisholm, on the bridge of the *Fort Mohican*, was one of many in this category. He watched their tardy concession of seaway with dismay. He knew that if the convoy's presence on the latitude of 36° North was a secret, the secret would not survive the next rising of the sun.

Tom Laird, the Chief Officer, had his glasses trained on the nearest fishing boats. "Trouble," he announced laconically to Chisholm. He had no need to enlarge further.

"With a capital 'T'," agreed Chisholm.

"Only a matter of time," said Laird.

He was not being unduly pessimistic. He spoke from the bitterness of experience. Like Chisholm, he knew that the Germans had agents and informers in every pint-sized Spanish port from the Portuguese border to Algeciras and there would be pesetas in plenty for the first skipper home with news of a British convoy.

"Want me to double the lookouts before morning?" Laird asked Chisholm.

"It's not really worth it, Mr Laird." Chisholm smiled "We're chockablock with lookouts as it is. Last time I did a head count, I reckoned we had twenty pairs of eyes on the job in any one watch. Double that up and we shan't have anybody left to make a cup of tea."

Laird laughed.

"You're right. I haven't got used yet to having so many people swarming over a ship. Changing the watch is like trooping the colour . . . Gunners, bunting-tossers, butchers, bakers and candlestick-makers . . . We've got eyes for every point of the compass . . . Twenty pairs, you say? That ought to be enough."

"No harm in keeping them on their toes. Ask the PO gunner to tour the pits and ginger up his boys. He enjoys it. See our own lads know the score, too. So far, we've had a nice big ocean to hide in – but, tomorrow, we'll be in the Med. Things could get a little hotter – and I'm not talking about the weather."

The darkened ships of the convoy passed through the Straits of Gibraltar shortly before midnight. No bells sounded the changing of the watch. To the north, the lights of Algeciras were strung like a sparkling necklace below the black mountain of rock.

Chisholm, watching the coast of Spain slip by, thought about Cal Thorn. Was he still in Madrid? Had he found any needles in his haystack?

It was nearly one when Chisholm decided to go below. He gave a parting look northwards and murmured softly: "Good luck, Cal, wherever you are."

"Did you say something, sir?"

Chisholm had not heard the Second Officer come out from the wheel-house. He smiled ruefully in the dark.

"I was just thinking out loud, Second Mate. A sure sign of old age . . . I was thinking of our American friends . . ."

"Oh?"

"Yes, Second Mate. Don't you know what day it is?"

"It's Sunday, sir." The younger man felt he had to qualify that. "Has been for just over an hour."

"Yes, Second Mate – and long past my bedtime. It's also the Fourth of July. American Independence Day." Chisholm paused thoughtfully at the top of the bridge ladder, one foot on the step. Almost to himself, he added: "I hope we can get through it without any fireworks."

His wish was not entirely to be fulfilled. There were to be fireworks of a sort before noon. The danger came from the north and was announced by the two flank-riding escorts to port of the convoy with a sudden quick-fire barking of Bofors guns and Pom-pom cannonade.

The morning had started for Chisholm with the distinctive whistle of his bunk-side voice tube wakening him at seven. Laird, on the bridge, could not keep an excited note from his voice.

"We've just taken a signal on the lamp, sir. It's from Commodore to all ships. Sealed orders are to be opened at ten hundred hours today. I thought you'd like to know right away."

Chisholm thanked him and replaced the whistle-cap of the voice tube. He felt a burn of excitement himself. Three hours to go. Then the secret would be out. The target of "Operation Husky" would be known.

When the time came to take the large yellow envelopes from his safe, he found that his hands trembled. He sat down and spent ten minutes alone with the documents before ringing for his steward and asking him to summon Colonel Ruddy, the Canadian CO and Lieutenant Penrose, the Senior Naval Officer.

At the Canadian Colonel's request, a non-denominational service was to be held in the main troop mess-deck at 11 a.m. It was open to every man in the ship who wanted to attend. With the sealed orders embargo lifted, Ruddy now suggested that a special announcement be made at the service to let crew and soldiers know the destination of the *Fort Mohican*. In the absence of a chaplain, Chisholm was prevailed upon to preside. He accepted, without great relish for the task. He had not been much of a church-goer since achieving adulthood.

In spite of his misgivings. he found himself affected by the

261

mood of the men who crowded into the mess-deck of No. 4 hold: packing into every inch of available space and overflowing up the broad companionway that led to the deck. It seemed that every man on the ship unrestricted by watchkeeping duties wanted to be there. A broad mix of religions seemed to offer no deterrent. Among the Canadians were more than a hundred Jews from Montreal. They crowded in alongside Catholics from Quebec and Presbyterians from Ontario. Among the seamen were two Chinese Buddhists, a Salvationist, a Muslim and a hard-drinking fireman who had been heard to boast that he was a lapsed member of the Band of Hope.

The singing was lusty and unrestrained. They sang two verses of the sailor's hymn and a predominance of bass voices invested the haunting melody with a resonant evocation of deep rolling waters. The final lilting plea "for those in peril on the sea" sighed out across the blue ocean like the plaintive call of a great wind.

There were no sermons. "The Soldier's Prayer" – spoken by the Canadian CO – was simple, short and poignant: a gladiatorial affirmation of steadfastness on the eve of battle that transcended the divisions of religion.

They sang part of the 23rd Psalm and ended the service with three verses of "Abide with me". Chisholm then invited Colonel Ruddy to make a special announcement.

"I shall not keep you long in suspense," the Colonel promised, after an excited buzz of anticipation had died down. "I know that in spite of much speculation about our destination, a substantial amount of money has been raised in the form of a sweepstake . . . With a large prize going to the holder of a ticket that correctly names the place where we shall be landing. Those of you who drew lots for sections of coast between Gibraltar and the top of Norway will already have realised that they have lost their stakes . . ."

"Swindle! Fix!" shouted a grinning soldier, who had drawn Denmark. He was hooted at by others who had drawn strips of enemy-occupied real estate between the Pyrenees and Asia Minor.

Colonel Ruddy smiled at the interruption and waited until the banter had subsided.

"About a week from now," he announced, "we hit the beaches of Sicily."

After the shouting and the cheers had died down he read a

message to the Canadian troops from General Bernard Montgomery, welcoming them to that illustrious fighting force, the Eighth Army. Ruddy had finished and was asking the men to disperse in an orderly fashion when, away to the north, the peace of the placid Mediterranean day was shattered by bursts of Bofors and Pom-pom fire.

Almost simultaneously came the short-long, short-long clangour of the *Fort Mohican*'s alarm bells: the warning of air attack.

Chisholm reached the bridge at a run, having to fight his way through the soldiers crowding on deck and blocking the alleyway. He was puzzled that, after the first bursts of gunfire, there had been no more shooting. Yet now, clearly, he could hear the distant drone of aircraft engines.

"One of ours?" Chisholm fired the question at the Third Officer, who was stationed on the extreme wing of the flying bridge scanning the north-west through binoculars.

"No, sir. One of theirs," came the reply. The young officer of the watch pointed with outstretched hand towards the port quarter. A black, pencil-shaped speck was crossing astern of the convoy, a good seven or eight miles away. The aircraft, flying at about 3000 feet, was keeping discreetly out of range of the convoy's guns.

Chisholm borrowed the binoculars and watched as the aircraft banked away and came round on to the reverse of its original course. He noted the twin tails and long slim fuselage. It was a Dornier. Too far from home, he thought, to be the old Do. 17. More likely the new long-range Do. 217. Chisholm handed the binoculars back to the Third Officer.

"I don't think she'll come much closer," he said. "She's just scouting."

It was the expected pattern. First the Spanish fishing boats. The news of an east-bound convoy heading for the Straits would have been flashed to Madrid within hours, and on from there. The reconnaissance plane would have been scrambled in Southern France soon after daylight. Soon, it would be running back to base with precise details of the convoy's composition: how many tankers, how many warships, how many troop-carriers. The convoy's speed would have been noted and its course plotted.

Chisholm reckoned it would taken the Dornier's crew perhaps fifteen minutes to record all the data required for a comprehensive intelligence report. In fact, in just two minutes short of his estimate, the Dornier gave a tilt of its wings and disappeared to the north at speed.

Five minutes later, Chisholm gave the order to stand down from action stations but warned gun crews and lookouts to maintain extra vigilance. He tried to calculate a time-scale to the pattern that was developing.

The reconnaissance aircraft was probably three hours' flying time from base, and some time would be needed for the aircrew's report to be assessed. That meant that an attack by bombers and torpedo-planes was unlikely to be unleashed before nightfall. Therefore, any threat from the air was not likely to materialise until between ten and noon the following morning. Maybe not at all, Chisholm thought hopefully, as a wing of friendly Spitfires from North Africa chose that moment to roar past the convoy. Their appearance was reassuring. It provided Chisholm, however, with a growing conviction that any attack on the convoy would come from below the sea and not above it. It was too much to hope that no U-boats were deployed in the Western Mediterranean. They would learn of the convoy's presence when they surfaced after dark and made radio contact with their base, probably Toulon. Travelling at speed on the surface, they could put themselves more than a hundred miles nearer to the convoy before daybreak.

The thought gave Chisholm a queasy feeling. He remembered all too vividly his last encounter with a U-boat. If there were any about in this area, they would make their presence felt before another day had run its course.

In fact, it was shortly before dawn the following morning that U-593, running on the surface, detected the approach of many ships. Her captain ran his boat to seaward and sat ten miles to the north as the convoy passed. Then he turned east behind the convoy. When the first streaks of day appeared in the east, the U-boat captain dived his ship and – at 100 metres depth – settled on the same course as the convoy, some five miles astern.

A cloudless sky and a sea that was ruffled by the lightest of breezes did little to ease the disquiet that had kept Chisholm awake for most of the night. He had finally given up any attempt to sleep and joined Laird on the morning watch when it was little more than half an hour old. Laird had been glad of the unexpected company and, together, they had watched the dawn come up.

At eight, Chisholm went down with Laird for breakfast and joined in the smalltalk as he ate his bacon and eggs. But, while the others lingered over second cups of coffee, he excused himself and returned to the bridge.

"Just taking the air," he assured the Second Officer, who was taking morning sights of the sun for the run to noon. Chisholm was anxious not to transmit his jumpiness and certainly, by all outward appearances, he presented a picture of unruffled calm: letting the watchkeepers go about their business without interference and quietly scanning sea and sky from the port wing of the flying bridge.

Inwardly, he was the victim of instincts tuned to a fine degree of sensitivity. He was not ruled by fear: more by an acute awareness of the pattern he had seen developing and by the knowledge that there was nothing he could do to arrest it. From experience, he knew that the shock of torpedo attack could come with mind-numbing suddenness and he was bracing himself for it, so that he could react without semblance of panic: coolly and in full control.

No magical insight told him that at that very moment the captain of U-593 was tucked in five miles astern of the convoy, biding his time. Nor that, some two hundred miles to the east, the commander of an Italian submarine was mulling over with his executive officer an overnight signal that a convoy had been sighted between Gibraltar and Algiers.

Far less did Chisholm know that, in addition, to these unseen enemies, another – much closer at hand – was steeling himself for one final, desperate gambit.

Eighteen

First Blood

Cal Thorn sat in the office of the British NIO, Gibraltar. He fidgeted in his chair, unable to keep his hands or feet still: impatience spilling from him. When the door opened, he was out of the chair in a flash and facing the tall Navy officer who entered. Thorn was tense with expectation.

"Well?" He almost shouted the word. "Can it be done?"

"Not a hope in hell," said the NIO flatly.

"But I've got to get on that ship!"

"Sit down, please, Lieutenant," the NIO said. "I'd better acquaint you with the facts of life."

He went on to tell Thorn that it would be easier to land a man on the dark side of the moon than to get Thorn aboard a ship that was sailing in convoy in mid-Mediterranean. It made no difference whatsoever that London had sanctioned *carte blanche* co-operation from whomsoever Thorn demanded it. Even if Thorn's authority had come from God, what he was asking was impossible, repeat, impossible.

"I suppose if you insisted, we could parachute you into the sea in the middle of the convoy," the NIO said sardonically.

"Well, let's do it, goddamn it!" Thorn roared.

The NIO threw up his arms and raised his eyes heavenward as if seeking divine assistance.

"Dear Lord," he murmured. Turning to Thorn, he said in a sad voice: "I was being facetious, Lieutenant. We could parachute you into the sea – but the ships would not stop and pick you up. And that would make the exercise rather pointless. We could find you a less expensive way of committing suicide."

If he thought that was the end of the argument, he was mistaken. Thorn continued to bombard him with ideas on how the problem could be solved. The NIO met them all with a firm shake of the head and one word: "Impossible."

"There must be something I can do," Thorn persisted stubbornly.

"Look," said the NIO wearily, "we can get a signal off to the Convoy Commodore. If, as you insist, there really is an enemy agent on one of those ships, they could have him clapped in irons quicker than wink."

"No!" exploded Thorn. "Even if they shoot the guy, it's not goddamn good enough!" He was pacing like a caged tiger and he turned and faced the NIO with a look of angry despair. "Don't you understand? It's not enough to nail this guy and put him out of action. We've got to find out just what the hell he's been up to! We've got to find out just how much damage he's done . . . Then we've got to nullify it. There's no way it can be done by remote control!"

The NIO shook his head.

"I just don't know what else I can suggest," he said dejectedly. "Unless . . ."

"Unless what?" Thorn prompted.

"Would it do any good if you spoke to the C-in-C? I could arrange for you to see the Admiral this afternoon . . ."

Thorn leapt at the morsel of hope like a dog at a bone. Yes, he would like to see the Admiral if he was the man with the weight. The NIO was relieved. He knew he was risking the Admiral's wrath – but if the Admiral could not make this stubborn American see sense, no one could.

Thorn spent more than an hour with the C-in-C. At the end of it, he was hoarse from arguing his case. Later in the afternoon, he boarded a DC3 that was making a routine flight to Algiers. In Thorn's pocket was a letter from the Admiral to General Dwight D. Eisenhower, enlisting his help.

Walther Strasser, alias Paul Constantine, lay on an upper bunk in one of the tiny four-berth cabins that had been constructed in the tween-decks of the *Fort Mohican*. He lay with his hands behind his head and was staring up at the deck-head rivets above him. He closed his eyes and filled his mind with other pictures. He was twenty-seven years old – and he allowed the days of those years to flicker before him in series of images: tracing with his memory the milestones of a life that he now believed was running its final hours.

This ship was where it was going to end. Beyond tomorrow,

there were no more tomorrows. There was nothing. It would be over. There was no point in considering the dark precipice that was the future, so he turned his mind away from it and let it dwell on all the lonely steps that had led him to its brink.

His childhood had been idyllically happy and bitterly miserable in turn. His first remembered years held vague and fragmentary visions of a cherished time. He could recall the perfumed presence of the woman who had held him at her breast and enveloped him with security and love. There was the cluttered comfort of the Bavarian home, with its music and smell of furniture polish; the gentle smiling faces of his grandparents.

Then had come the terrifying change: the sudden uprooting away from familiar things. There had been the nightmare of a noisy train journey and the endless, more frightening crossing of the Atlantic in a heaving ship that smelled of vomit and urine. The year had been 1920 . . .

The new home in Three Rivers had been strange and shabby and the ten years he had spent in Canada had been years of misery without relief. His mother had hated Canada with its unrelenting winters and alien people – as young Walther had done. At school, he had always been the outsider. Walt Squarehead, they had called him. And worse.

It had almost been a relief when his father, who spent long periods away from home, had been killed in a logging accident. Young Walther and his grieving mother had returned to Germany, thanks to an unexpectedly large sum of compensation paid out by the Sun Life Assurance Company. They paid out more money on Uwe Strasser's death than he had ever seen during his life.

Walther, in his teens, found that he had returned to his spiritual home in the new Germany that was rising out of the old. Adolf Hitler and his brownshirts had seemed like gods. He had espoused the cause of National Socialism at the age of fifteen, joined the SS at eighteen, and been inducted into the SD at twenty-one. Because of his fluent English, he had been an ideal recruit for Himmler at a time when Hitler's henchman was furtively trying to set up an overseas espionage system in direct competition with Canaris' Abwehr. That in turn had led to Walther Strasser's admission to the SD's *Schatten Gruppe*: an elite body within an elite body.

The *Schatten Gruppe* had led to St Cyr des Bains, to England,

and eventually to the *Fort Mohican*. The *Fort Mohican* was where it would end.

Strasser, alias Constantine, looked at his watch. It was almost 5.30. The first dinner sitting in the *Fort Mohican*'s saloon would soon be rising, in time for the next to start at 6 p.m. He had time for a quick wash and tidy-up before catching up with Bob Fenwick, the ship's Second Radio Officer. Strasser had been cultivating his friendship with Fenwick even before the fateful council of war with Lander in the shaft tunnel, and the pair had formed the habit of having a can of beer in Fenwick's cabin before the evening meal. Now, the unsuspecting Fenwick figured prominently in Strasser's plans.

The two junior radio officers shared a cabin on the starboard side. The door was hooked open and a curtain fluttered in the entry as Strasser tapped on the door-frame and announced himself. He found Fenwick drying his face with a towel over the wash-basin. There was no sign of his cabin-mate. Two cans of beer and two glasses sat on the table.

"Pour, will you?" said Fenwick. "I'll be with you as soon as I can find a clean shirt."

Strasser obliged, with an air of apology.

"I feel guilty drinking your beer, Bob."

"Nonsense!" Fenwick grinned broadly as he buttoned his shirt. "You blokes are our guests. We've got to do something to make up for that pit of a hold you've got to sleep in."

"It's not too bad for us. We don't have to stand watches like you guys."

"We get paid for it." laughed Fenwick. "Not very much – but we do get paid for it."

"Don't it get pretty lonely on that midnight-to-four hitch?" Strasser asked amiably, before taking a sip at his beer.

"Yep, the graveyard watch. It can be a bore. But you get used to it."

"Maybe I can sit it out with you one night?" Strasser made the suggestion casually.

"You'd have to be off your head."

"I'm serious. I'd like to. You can show me how things work. Is there any regulation that says you can't have company?"

"Not that I know of. So long as I do my listening stint, nobody's going to say anything."

"That's settled then. I'll look up after midnight. Maybe tonight."

"You really need your head seen to," said Fenwick. "Are all you Canadians crazy?"

"Sure we are." Strasser patted the medal ribbon on his chest. "I got this to prove it. You got to be crazy to get one of them."

It had not been necessary to draw attention to the decoration—an award he had no right to wear—but Strasser had discovered that it was a most useful adjunct to the identity he had assumed. People trusted him readily because of it. They gave him latitude that, with others, would not have been offered. He received no end of respect because of that little ribbon. Fenwick, in particular, was immensely flattered to have a holder of the Military Cross as his special friend. He enjoyed a glory by association—and it was because of this vanity that Strasser had been immodest enough to remind him of the ribbon. He wanted to keep Fenwick compliant.

Taking the reminder almost as a cue, Fenwick indulged his instincts for hero worship throughout dinner. Strasser allowed himself to be lionised, enjoying the part he was playing, But a brief confrontation with Chisholm disturbed him and left him uneasy.

Chisholm, who had scarcely left the bridge all day but had abandoned his vigil to take dinner at six, emerged from behind the smoke-room curtain just as Fenwick had uttered some extravagant sally for Strasser's benefit. Strasser's laughing reply died on his lips as he caught Chisholm's unsmiling start of surprise. It was as if the *Fort Mohican*'s captain had momentarily seen clear through the German's carefully maintained façade.

But Chisholm shuffled with embarrassment.

"Don't let me interrupt your hilarity, gentlemen. I'm just passing through." He nodded to Strasser, who felt a surge of relief. The German realised that Chisholm's embarrassment was occasioned by guilt. The captain had scarcely acknowledged his existence since he had come aboard at Newport. Now he had suffered a qualm of conscience.

Strasser's asumption was only partly correct. Chisholm had indeed felt guilty at avoiding his fellow-escaper from St Cyr des Bains, but that was not the entire reason for the frowning stare that had stopped Strasser in mid-sentence. It was the puzzle of Fenwick's mateyness with the scar-faced hero of Dieppe.

Chisholm had noticed the two men in each other's company before and it had struck him as odd. Fenwick was a rather prim young man—Chisholm hesitated to think of him as pansy-like—but he seemed a most unusual choice of companion for a rugged leatherneck type like Constantine. Unless ... Chisholm put away as unworthy the thought that, as a result of his disfigurement, the Canadian's sexual inclinations had undergone a deviation from the normal.

He was trying to dismiss the matter from his mind and had climbed half way up the bridge ladder when a cataclysmic roar of sound enveloped him. The sudden shock was such that he missed his footing and stumbled on one knee. As he pitched forward, he caught sight in an involuntary backward glance of the massive fire-cloud erupting from the ship closest to the *Fort Mohican* on the port quarter.

Chisholm raced up the remaining steps to the bridge, where Laird had run into the wheel-house and was ringing out the series of "S" signals on the alarm bell to warn of submarine attack.

Footsteps pounded on the deck as men raced to their stations, clutching helmets and fastening on life-jackets as they ran. Soldiers lined the port rail, staring in horror at the stricken vessel as she veered out of line and began to list. Smoke gushed in clouds from her midships section and, already, the ring of axes echoed across the water as men struck at the metal release clasps of the big emergency life rafts. Two rafts plunged in quick succession into the sea and were momentarily hidden by the splashes they created.

Fenwick and Strasser had joined the lines of awe-struck watchers on the *Fort Mohican*'s port side.

Strasser was shaken.

"You'd better get your life-jacket," Fenwick warned him. "We could be next."

"It's down in my quarters."

"Well, get it," Fenwick exhorted him. "It's a thirty-mile swim to the nearest land."

Strasser dashed below, lingering there only long enough to snatch his white WD flotation collar. He had no desire to be caught below decks if a torpedo struck.

"Christ, you were quick," Fenwick commented as he rejoined him, pushing his head through the neck-hole of his preserver.

Fenwick eyed the standard army issue apparatus disdainfully. It was more primitive than the design issued to merchant

271

seamen, being little more than two bags of kapok with a hole for the head.

"Watch yourself with that if we have to jump for it," said the radio officer cheerfully. "They've caused more broken necks than bears thinking about. They were obsolete in the last war."

Strasser looked at him, aghast.

"Are you kidding?"

"I'm giving you a tip," said Fenwick. "If you jump over the side, don't wear it! Keep it in your hand and put it on in the water. That way you'll keep your head on your shoulders."

Strasser shivered. It was one part fear and two parts a sudden quiver of anger. He had resigned himself to death – but not at the hands of the German Navy, and certainly not before he had fulfilled the task on which the whole course of the war might hinge. He found himself quietly hoping that the British destroyers would quickly find the lurking U-boat and either chase it off or sink it. Strasser wanted nothing to jeopardise the final glorious act he had planned for himself. Nothing!

On the bridge, Chisholm and Laird had been as hypnotised by the spectacle of the sinking ship as everyone else.

"It's the big City boat," Laird had identified the ship, his voice thick, as if the loss was personal. In many ways – as to all men of the sea – it was profoundly personal. The U-boat captain had selected his target well. The cargo-passenger liner – listing slightly but sinking on an even keel – was, with a deadweight tonnage of about 14,000 tons, the biggest ship in the convoy.

"Hey, Captain!" a Canadian voice shouted up to the bridge from the foredeck. "Ain't nobody stoppin' to pick up the poor guys in the water?"

Chisholm looked unhappily down at the soldier.

"The Navy will pick them up," he called. He refrained from adding "eventually". The escorts' immediate priorities were hunting the submarine and protecting the rest of their flock. There would be no attempt to rescue survivors from the sinking ship while the convoy was at risk. It was something every seafaring man knew, and accepted.

The big ship was left behind, masts silhouetted against the setting sun, her decks awash. Like a mighty buffalo taken from the moving herd by a hunter's arrow, her death throes would be endured in the loneliness of a trackless waste, without witness. The herd kept moving.

On the *Fort Mohican*, the horror and wonder had peaked and was beginning slightly to subside when, without warning, a second monstrous roar of sound boomed out with ear-splitting ferocity. Stomachs turned to jelly as the thunderous roll, rumbling echo running into rumbling echo, bounced across the ocean like a giant reverberating tumbleweed of sound.

A bubbling black cloud of smoke and billowing orange flame erupted from the foredeck of the ship directly abeam of the *Fort Mohican*. It pillared hundreds of feet in the air and, in a succession of new explosions, a sheet of liquid flame enveloped the ship's bridge housing: darting in furious tongues at every orifice and open space.

The figure of a man, flaming from head to foot, came in a tottering run from the holocaust within the wheel-house. His weaving run took him to the after end of the bridge, where he hit the guard-rail, jack-knifed, and plummeted like a comet through forty feet of space to the deck below. The screams that had accompanied his blind run and final plunge ended abruptly.

Within seconds, what was visible of the ship's bridge beneath the fire-cloud was charred black and liquefying as if the steel superstructure was bleeding molten tar from pores on its surface.

Laird, standing beside Chisholm, uttered an animal cry of sheer horror at what he had seen. Chisholm had bitten so hard into his lip that blood flecked his teeth.

Explosion followed explosion from deep within the tortured ship: convulsions that materialised in fan-shaped eruptions of fireballs, spreading the inferno from stem to stern. The pyrotechnical horror continued until the ship was well astern of the convoy – a sparking orange torch against the darkening sky. Finally, she exploded like a thousand blazing rockets and disappeared. All that remained was a litter of burning debris, hissing and flaming here and there across a wide area of ocean.

Fenwick and Strasser witnessed the fiery end of the ship. It was almost impossible to believe that, a half hour before, she had been sailing proudly on station only a few cables distance from their stance on the *Fort Mohican*'s deck.

Strasser had commented on the almost top-heavy bulk of the ship, with her visible bank of nine landing-craft strung in davits along her starboard side.

"The *St Essylt*," Fenwick had informed him.

Now, having seen the ship's destruction with the loss of countless lives, Strasser's blood seemed to have frozen in his veins. But for Lander, he would have sailed in that ship. It made the gut go icy just to think about it.

Fenwick noticed his companion's involuntary shudder.

"It's getting cool," he said.

Strasser acknowledged that it was. But he was scarcely aware of Fenwick's presence. His mind was still occupied with the twist of chance that had brought him to the *Fort Mohican* instead of the *St Essylt*.

Perhaps it was a good omen for the task ahead of him. It had not been his destiny to die in the *St Essylt*. His destiny was here on this ship. Perhaps Fate had spared him in its fickle way for those few extra hours he needed to perform his final service for Germany and the Führer.

Strasser was surprised at his own calm. He waited on deck, hidden in the shadow of the ladder to the bridge. It was five minutes to midnight. The holstered revolver at his webbing belt gave him a sense of comfort. Although the night was warm, he had put on his battledress tunic. His one big regret was that he could not have worn his true colours. Just for tonight, he would have liked to have worn his black SD uniform, with the scarlet and gold flash that signified membership of the *Schatten Gruppe* elite. He knew that his chances of fulfilling his night's work and getting away with it were remote. There would be no escape. Once he had shown his hand and transmitted his warning from the radio cabin, there would be nowhere to run. He had not finally decided what he should do when the game was up. It was possible that circumstances would decide – but he seemed to be faced with two possibilities.

He could either fight it out to the death or he could surrender with head held high and face the ceremonial of execution.

The latter course tempted him. It meant some prolongation of life: long enough to allow the formality of a trial. It would also permit a period in which to enjoy the triumph he hoped to achieve.

The thought of being held by his enemies – knowing that they could not undo the damage he had inflicted on them – had a strong appeal for him. Instant martyrdom had less appeal. There was no time to savour the victory. And Strasser wanted to savour victory, to enjoy the discomfiture of his enemies openly . . . Not behind a mask but in the full glare of their awe. He wanted them to acknowledge him as the architect of their undoing. They could take away his life but that would be all that they could take from him. They could not take from him the sweet sustaining knowledge that he was the winner and they were the losers.

One minute to midnight. The ship seemed to come briefly to life as the watchkeepers changed over. There was traffic on the bridge ladders and in the alleyways leading fore and aft. Strasser kept checking the time on his watch. Fenwick would now have taken over in the radio cabin. He would give him a few minutes more and then he would move.

He allowed ten more minutes to tick away. The only stirring on deck now was in the vicinity of the troop bakery where the singlet-clad night workers were carrying bags of flour from the dry store to make the hundreds of loaves that would be needed next morning. Strasser straightened his shoulders and, emerging from shadow, stepped resolutely on to the bridge ladder.

He was crossing the pumiced-white wooden deck of the lower bridge when the strident clamour of alarm bells caused him almost to faint with fright. So sudden and unexpected was the piercing assault of sound on his senses that it took him a breathless moment to realise that he had not, like a thief in the night, triggered off some hidden device that had been laid exclusively for his entrapment. He shrank guiltily against the bridge house as the ship came alive with men running to gun stations and soldiers spilling from the holds to find out what was happening.

Strasser was buffeted twice by steel-helmeted crewmen who came pounding up the bridge ladders, heading for the gun-pits on the top bridge. No apologies were offered as he reeled out of the way, cursing.

Anger coursed through him. With so many people awake and milling about the bridge, it would be folly to go near the radio room.

"What the hell's happening, sailor?" he snarled at a latecomer, clutching at the man as he bundled past with helmet and life-jacket in hand.

"Air raid alert," was the perfunctory reply. The man pressed on, interested only in getting to his station.

Strasser made his way down to deck level, fizzing inside with anger and frustration. He had little choice but to postpone his planned takeover of the radio room. He moved aimlessly aft. In the alleyway near the engine-room, a large figure was hunched unconcernedly over the bulwark. It was Lander. He was sipping coffee from a large enamel mug.

"Anywhere a man can enjoy a cigarette in peace?" Strasser asked.

"Sure, soldier. Follow me . . . I'll show you."

Lander led him up a ladder to the boat-deck and into the POs' accommodation. Bosun, carpenter and PO Gunner were all at emergency stations and the small mess-room was empty.

"We can talk here," said Lander, "but make it quick."

Strasser told him of his intended takeover of the radio room. The moon face nodded approval.

"You have a better chance of pulling off a stunt like that than I do. But don't do anything stupid, like getting yourself killed. I'll still be around, remember."

Strasser poured out some of his frustration at being foiled by the alarm bell.

"You can try again tomorrow night," Lander soothed him. "It's still a long way to Sicily."

Lander's confidence made Strasser feel better. In a calmer frame of mind, he left the mess and worked his way forward. He was outside the galley when the roar of aircraft engines made him look skywards. There was nothing to be seen but stars glittering through wispy cloud. There seemed to be a large number of aircraft, flying very high and almost overhead. They were passing right over the convoy from north to south.

In every ship in the convoy, the guns were manned. But none fired. The standing night-time edict was to hold fire unless attacked. The aircraft droned south. Their engines were almost inaudible when the southern horizon began to flash red with leaping and shimmering light. Tiny little sparks began climbing in profusion into the sky and the air trembled with a distant popping that was punctuated by deep resonant thumps. The deeper explosions were accompanied by miniature false sun-rises that streaked the heavens with shivering arcs of pink candescence.

All along the Algerian coast, the Luftwaffe was reminding the inhabitants, both permanent and transitory, that the land the German forces had conceded to the Anglo-Americans was still in the firing line.

At sea, the four columns of darkened ships slipped by like a squadron of phantom cavalry: dim grey shapes in the night with rank upon rank of high masts like lances held erect. The silence was broken only by the muffled rhythm of engine beat and thrusting screw: sounds that were softened by the ghostly shushing hiss of bow knifing away water in swirls of phosphorescent brilliance.

By two in the morning, the last of the raiders had droned away north and the flashing sky to the south was dark and silent. On the ships, the crews stood down from their guns.

The convoy marched on into the night, soon to meet a dawn that came up with a glory that mocked war. As the sun rose higher, it sparkled on a sea as smooth as a painted mirror. Not a fluff of cloud tarnished the great blue bowl of sky. Not a sigh of wind rippled the placid serenity of ocean.

The intrusion of violence, when it came in the afternoon, came as a desecration of Nature. And, again, it came with a totality of surprise so sudden that it paralysed the senses. In spite of the glassy calm of the sea, the telltale shimmer of water that marked the track of speeding torpedo was unobserved. It homed on the leading ship of the third column like an avenging shark, tearing through the ship's steel skin and exploding in her vitals with a thunderous boom.

Chisholm was bent in study over the chart-room table when the blast shook through the wheel-house and chart-room of the *Fort Mohican* like a wind from hell. He rushed to the wheel-house window in time to see a hundred-foot geyser hang for a moment above the ship ahead, obscuring her superstructure.

"Starboard ten," he barked at the helmsman. The Second Officer, who had followed him out of the chart-room, had his finger on the alarm button: sending out series of three-dot rings. There was almost no need. The crash of exploding torpedo had been sufficient to galvanise a rush to action stations. Many of the off-watch men, who had been enjoying the sun, were shirtless.

"Port ten," called out Chisholm. Then, after a moment: "Steady as she goes."

The *Fort Mohican* was quickly overtaking the torpedoed ship, having swung out to avoid collision with her. No ship in that convoy was expendable but, again, the unseen underwater assassin had struck with telling cruelty. If the first victim had been the biggest ship in the convoy, then this latest was undoubtedly the most beautiful. She had a raised forecastle and neat raking stem; her curved accommodation housing was concentrated amidships, with stream-lined flying bridge just forward of the squat, raked funnel. She had grace in every line.

It had possibly been for aesthetic reasons that Rear-Admiral Freddie Hope, the Convoy Commodore, had selected her as his headquarters ship. There was, however, the additional attraction – although she was listed as a fourteen-knot ship – that, flat out, she was capable of eighteen knots.

She would clip through the water at that speed no more. She was mortally wounded. As the *Fort Mohican* came abeam, the Commodore ship's stern was almost underwater and the four-inch gun's crew were stepping off the poop into the sea. The torpedo had struck just abaft the engine-room, blowing a massive hole in the hold where most of her complement of Canadian troops was quartered; and, as a consequence inflating the death toll to awesome proportions.

The sea around the ship was dotted with swimming men. Several life-rafts had been launched, but no boats. Two had been destroyed in the explosion and their shattered shells hung from the starboard davits. There was no time to launch the port-side boats. Her after holds invaded by an enormous rush of water, the ship's sleek bow suddenly rose high out of the sea. It seemed to shudder there for a moment and, then, the doomed vessel dived stern-first to the ocean floor, leaving a cauldron boil of turbulent water to mark where she had disappeared.

It was a sight that Chisholm had witnessed many times: the death of a ship. But it was a sight, he knew, to which he could never become accustomed. He turned away, weighed down by an ineffable sadness.

The convoy forged on eastward. The ranks closed up to conceal the gaps.

There were no more alarms before nightfall, and darkness fell as a welcome cloak. An eerie silence seemed to fall on the ships, as if even the talk in the messes and smoke-rooms had become subdued by events.

In the hour after midnight, Strasser welcomed the silence that had settled on the *Fort Mohican*. It was broken only by the occasional clatter of baking trays from within the galley where the nightly bread-making routine had begun.

Strasser made for the radio cabin by the interior route. He climbed the narrow stairway from the saloon alleyway, tiptoeing past the door to Chisholm's day-room. The next flight of stairs took him to the rear of the chart-room. It was deserted and the double black-out curtains leading out to the wheel-house were closed. He tapped gently on the door to the radio cabin, opened it without waiting for a response, and entered. Fenwick, headphones perched on the back of his head, looked up in surprise.

"I told you I would come," said Strasser.

Fenwick made him welcome and nodded at the spare swivel chair.

"Take a pew. There's absolutely nothing doing tonight. I was listening to the BBC news."

Strasser surveyed the banks of radio equipment occupying two facing walls. He gave a low whistle.

"Gee, you got quite a layout here." He pointed to a tall grey cabinet with a telephone piece cradled at its side. "Is this the RT?"

Fenwick swivelled his chair and nodded.

"Yep, but we hardly ever use it. Range is only about fifty miles. Not much use really, except in an emergency . . . Or coasting."

Strasser transferred his attention to the wall Fenwick had been facing. He noticed the Morse key on the highly polished bench-top.

"This must be the real works here," he said. "Show me how the main transmitter works. Say I wanted to send a short-wave message to Gib. or Port Said, how would I go about it?"

Fenwick loved talking radio to anyone who was even mildly interested. Strasser was very interested—and he was an excellent listener. He listened for fully twenty minutes as Fenwick explained the function of every piece of apparatus in his twelve-feet-by-nine domain. Strasser prompted him by asking him surprisingly shrewd questions.

The radio operator had to break off briefly to fulfil a routine function. It was "All Ships" stuff from Gibraltar. When he turned back to Strasser, he found himself looking up the muzzle of a .38 calibre revolver.

"Make one squeak and I'll shoot you straight between the eyes." Fenwick heard Strasser speak the words but he could not believe that he had heard right.

"Is this a joke, Paul?"

Strasser thrust the muzzle of the revolver brutally into the fleshy fold of skin at Fenwick's throat and forced the operator's chin up until his neck was almost at snapping point. Speaking softly and menacingly, Strasser convinced Fenwick that, if it was a joke, he would not live long enough to laugh at the punchline. He taped the radio officer's mouth with broad adhesive strips, already cut, and then he bound his wrists behind his back with a short piece of cord.

The German worked swiftly. Pushing a badly frightened Fenwick out of the way, he locked the radio room door and wedged the handle with one of the swivel chairs. Then he sat down at the transmitter and donned the earphones. With the revolver in his left hand, he gestured menacingly at Fenwick.

"See that I get this right," he ordered. "I want to transmit on thirty-eight metres."

He checked the set in front of him for both "send" and "receive", flicking the "send" switch to the on position. Then he fiddled with the frequency dials before adjusting the fine tuning and frequency modulation. He worked with the air of a man who knew what he was doing. When he appeared satisfied, he allowed Fenwick to inspect the settings.

"All right?"

The radio operator nodded dumbly. He was pop-eyed with shock at what was happening.

Strasser ignored him then. He began tapping at the key. His speed was only moderate but his sending was good. He repeated a three-letter sequence as a call sign, growing anxious when there was no response. He delicately adjusted the frequency tuner and tried the call sign again. This time there was a speedy crackle of Morse in the headset.

He began his transmission with a six-letter group, which he repeated. Then he transmitted a plain language text. He ended by repeating the six-letter group with which he had started. He listened briefly to an acknowledgement and sat back with a sigh of relief. He was pleased with himself, exhilarated. He had done it. He had doomed "Operation Husky".

Nineteen

Commodore Ship

The whistle-blast from the voice tube, only inches from his head, startled Chisholm into instant wakefulness. He groped for the tube.

"Yes?"

"Second Mate here, sir. Can you come up to the bridge at once?"

"What's up?"

"I don't quite know, sir. The Sparks has locked himself in the radio room and doesn't answer. I think we'll have to break down the door."

"I'll be right up," Chisholm said.

He found Peters, the Second Officer, waiting for him in the chart-room.

"It's not like Bob Fenwick, sir. I gave him a shout to say there was a brew of tea on the go and there was no answer. Usually, he's the one who's yelling for somebody to put the kettle on!"

Chisholm tried the radio room door. Finding it did not yield, he rapped loudly on the panelling.

"Mr Fenwick. Open up, please. This is the Captain."

There was the sound of a chair being moved inside the radio room. Then a voice.

"Just a moment, Captain. Mr Fenwick is tied up right now."

It was not Fenwick's voice but, moments later, when the door opened, it was Fenwick who stood there. His usually neat hair was awry and he was wild-eyed with shock. He stood rubbing his mouth with the back of his hand. The flesh round his lips had a raw-skinned look.

"Are you all right, Mr Fenwick?"

"He's alive and that's something," said a voice from beyond

the partly opened door. Fenwick stood aside, moving the door with him. For the first time, Chisholm saw the second occupant of the radio room.

Strasser, alias Constantine, was sitting in one of the swivel chairs. His heavily scarred face – if the amused eyes were an indicator – was creased in a smile. He was idly toying with a revolver.

Chisholm stared, trying to make sense of the bizarre tableau. Fenwick found his voice.

"The bastard held me up with that gun and tied me up. He's been on the key . . . Transmitting . . ."

Chisholm's mind was racing. Answers to questions he had asked himself a thousand times were avalanching intuitively. But he could not believe that the thoughts pummelling his brain were more than a mad rioting of his imagination. His eyes were riveted on the gun.

"It's all right, Captain. I'm not going to use it," Strasser drawled. "If I'd been going to kill anybody, your young Sparky here would have been the first to go." He grinned grotesquely at Fenwick. "Cheer up, Bob, old chap. You got your reprieve when your pal started hollering for you to get your tea. If he hadn't, I might have just made it out of here without anybody being the wiser – and you would have been deader'n mutton . . ." He grinned again. "I would've had to do it quietly, no gun. Just a quick chop on the neck. That would have been a shame after all the beers you've bought me."

"Let me have that gun, Paul," Chisholm said quietly. He took a step inside the cabin and held out his hand.

Strasser handed him the revolver without demur.

"What are you going to do with me?" he asked.

"We're going to have a chat. And you're going to do most of the talking, Paul. We'll go down to my cabin." Chisholm turned to the Second Mate. "Get somebody to rouse out Colonel Ruddy, Mr Peters. Tell him we've got a problem that can't wait until morning. Tell him one of his officers has been trying to send messages to the Germans . . ."

"Not trying, Captain," Strasser corrected. "I got an acknowledgement. Message received and understood. If you don't believe me, wait until we get to Sicily. We should get a very warm reception."

Colonel Josef Reitlinger did not know what kind of reception to expect when he was summoned to the Operations Room in the *Wolfsschanze* just as he was preparing to step into his bath. He was told only that the Führer wished to see him immediately.

Reitlinger dressed hastily and yet took care to see that his expensively cut SD uniform was sitting neatly. His vanity about his appearance was a byword. He surveyed himself in his mirror and wasted precious seconds brushing a hair away from his shoulder, where a red and gold flash indicated his membership of the elite *Schatten Gruppe*. Reitlinger was, in fact, *Schatten Gruppe*'s permanent headquarters man at OKW in Rastenberg, East Prussia.

Satisfied with his appearance, Reitlinger walked the short distance from his quarters to the Operations Room bunker. He regretted having to postpone his bath. It would have freshened him up and made him more able to cope with the Führer's ways. One never knew from one meeting to the next just what to expect from Germany's leader. Having been up for most of the night, Reitlinger did not feel at his best and he was more than a little apprehensive. He was still smarting from his last interview with Hitler, only four hours previously.

Then, Reitlinger had taken it upon himself to have the Führer wakened in order to acquaint him personally with the dramatic signal from Walther Strasser, which had been picked up in France and relayed immediately to Rastenberg. The SD Colonel had been sure that Hitler would have been as excited as he had been to receive confirmation that an Allied attack on Sicily was imminent.

Instead, Hitler had been furious at having been disturbed with a piece of intelligence about the Mediterranean war. He had been expecting news from the Eastern Front of German gains in the battles around Kursk. When he had discovered that he had been wakened over something that had nothing to do with the Kursk situation – with which he seemed obsessed – he had stormed angrily at Reitlinger and sent him off with a flea in his ear.

Now, Reitlinger fervently hoped, the Führer was regretting his outburst and, in the light of day, was prepared to acknowledge the significance of Strasser's warning. There was every possibility that Strasser had gambled his life in order to despatch a message from the heart of the enemy taskforce approaching Sicily and it would be a bitter injustice to him and to *Schatten Gruppe* if his warning went unheeded.

Hitler was thoughtfully studying a wall map of the Russian front when Reitlinger was admitted to the Operations Room. The SD Colonel waited discreetly until his presence was acknowledged. He did not have long to wait.

"Ah, Reitlinger, it's you! You took your time getting here." Hitler eyed him severely.

"I am sorry, my Führer. I was about to get into the bath . . ."

Hitler waved aside his explanations. He pointed to a sheet of paper on the table beside him.

"Have a look at that, "he commanded. "I shall be interested to know what you make of it."

Reitlinger picked up the paper. It was a signal from Kriegsmarine, Berlin, and gave a summary of joint German Navy and Luftwaffe intelligence reports from Oslo. The signal was marked "Most Urgent" and timed 0950 hours, 7th July.

Reitlinger read that sea and air reconnaissance units had sighted a large enemy taskforce approaching Northern Norway. The report named several ships of the British Home Fleet that had been definitely identified from aerial photographs and also two large American warships, believed to be the *North Dakota* and the *Alabama*.

"An invasion force?" Reitlinger framed the words tentatively as a question.

"You tell me, Reitlinger. Some days ago, you showed me a *Schatten Gruppe* report stating that the Anglo-Americans were about to launch a second front in Norway. Then, some time after that you produced another saying that we could expect a sea attack with twelve or more divisions in Western Greece or Jugoslavia during the first week in July. Early this morning, you wakened me to tell me that Greece would not be attacked but that a landing in Sicily could be expected within the next three days . . ."

"But if two taskforces are at sea . . ." Reitlinger stammered. "That must mean a two-pronged attack . . . One in the north and one in the south . . ."

"Or they could be diversions," said Hitler.

"The British would not send an entire division of Canadians to the Mediterranean as a ruse," Reitlinger insisted stoutly. "We have a man actually on one of their invasion ships. He took a desperate risk this morning to warn us that Sicily is where they are heading."

"And you think we should believe him?"

"Yes, my Führer."

"You said his message was not even in cipher. Which means that the enemy probably read it, too. Perhaps they will change their minds about attacking Sicily . . . Or perhaps it suits them to let us think they will attack Sicily and strike somewhere else. What do you think, Reitlinger?"

"I think we should reinforce southern Sicily with the utmost speed, Führer."

Hitler scowled at him, his small eyes sparkling.

"As we have reinforced Greece with Divisions from France, and Norway with divisions from the Low Countries?"

Reitlinger was not deterred by the scorn in Hitler's voice.

"The Antoine signal told us to treat all previous warnings about Norway and the Balkans as the Second Front locations as incorrect."

"So! The fleet our pilots have been flying against in the northern seas does not exist?"

"It could be a diversion, as you suggested."

"And what about the Abwehr reports from Spain. The same reports, Reitlinger, that your *Schatten Gruppe* checked so carefully and endorsed. You said that the documents found on the body of that British officer washed up by the sea were genuine. And they pinpointed Greece as the objective of this so-called 'Operation Husky' – not Sicily!"

"They seemed genuine, Führer."

"And this signal from Antoine? You think it is genuine?"

"I would stake my life on it."

"You may be doing just that," Hitler said meaningfully. "You may be doing just that."

Reitlinger flushed.

"Does that mean, my Führer, that reinforcements will be rushed to Sicily?"

Hitler turned his head away, tilting his nose in the air in a manner that made it plain to Reitlinger that command decisions were not his concern.

"If action is required, it will be taken," the leader of the German nation said loftily.

Nearly 2000 miles away, the Algerian port of Bougie shimmered under a morning heat haze as HMS *Tavendale* nosed through Avant-Port – the most outlying of three dock areas – and headed for the gap between Jetée Sud and Jetée Est. Clear of the two breakwaters, *Tavendale* wheeled forty-five degrees to port and increased speed.

The notes of a bugle call echoed down from Fort Abd-el-Kader as the destroyer steadied on a course that would take her out of the Gulf of Bougie. This clarion salute from the battlements at the north end of the harbour was in no way connected with *Tavendale*'s departure but, to Cal Thorn on the destroyer's deck, it seemed amusingly appropriate.

At no other time since he had put on the uniform of the US Army had he experienced the feeling quite so utterly that he was a soldier off to battle. Part of the reason was that Thorn, in the past, had never quite accepted that he was a soldier – more a cop who dressed up as a soldier. Today was different. Today, he felt much more soldier than cop.

More than anything, it was the gaiters that made him feel warrior-like; not the lightweight field jacket he wore over his shirt, nor the sandy-finished bucket of a helmet on his head. It was not even the personal armoury strapped about him: the M1 sub-machine-gun, the forty-five pistol that had replaced his Police Positive, and the pouch of spare mags. It was the gaiters! The canvas leggings worn over his OD trousers really made him feel like an itinerant infantryman off in search of a shooting war.

They had kitted him out in Algiers and flown him up the coast to Bougie as soon as GHQ had heard that *Tavendale* was temporarily detaching from escort duty with the convoy to land survivors from the torpedoed Commodore ship. The convoy's disastrous loss had brought a dramatic turnabout in Thorn's fortunes. Stuck in Algiers, he had been resigned to the fact that not even Eisenhower was going to help him reach the *Fort Mohican*. The *Fort Mohican* and the convoy were unreachable. And they would have remained unreachable but for HMS *Tavendale*.

She had berthed at Bougie with three hundred survivors crowding her deck. Among them had been Rear-Admiral Freddie Hope, who had no intention of letting a ducking in the Mediterranean deprive him of his command. He was passionately determined to return to the convoy and see "Operation Husky" through to the end. This intent, and certain circumstances, gave Thorn the time he needed to fly from Algiers and join HMS *Tavendale*. The circumstantial factors were that Commodore Hope had leg and rib injuries which demanded overnight treatment in hospital, and that *Tavendale* was the sole means of his return to the convoy.

Thorn had spent an illuminating half hour with Commodore Hope and his aide before *Tavendale* had sailed from Bougie. The American had thought that the irascible old seadog was going to have a seizure when he had revealed why it was so imperative for him to reach the *Fort Mohican*. Shock, outrage, fury . . . mildly describe how Commodore Hope reacted. Thorn had to listen to a diatribe about "vipers in bosoms", "infamy" and "treacherous jackals" before the Commodore warmed up to the theme of the fate likely to befall traitors found in *his* convoy. The merits of "hanging from the nearest yard-arm" were aired at some length.

Thorn had been glad to escape to the deck of *Tavendale* to watch the departure from Bougie. Cape Carbon was disappearing behind the land haze when he was joined by the Commodore's aide, a beanpole two-ringer called Ingledew.

"That's quite a fire-eater you got back there," Thorn commented. Ingledew grinned.

"Freddie's bark is a lot worse than his bite. His leg's giving him a lot of pain and he's flaming mad at the Jerries for sinking his ship under him. But he's not a bad sort under all the bluster. He sent me out to tell you that he's decided to do you a good turn. You want to get aboard the *Fort Mohican* . . . So, we're all going aboard the *Fort Mohican*. He's making her the new Commodore ship."

"Well, good for him!" Thorn exclaimed.

"Don't get too ecstatic," Ingledew warned. "Freddie can be an interfering old bugger. He probably wants to get his hands on this traitor of yours and personally wring his neck."

On the *Fort Mohican*, as noon approached, the man who had betrayed "Operation Husky" was temporarily forgotten. He was under lock and key in the ship's tiny hospital, with two armed Canadians guarding the door. Chisholm was studying a signal from Senior Naval Officer, Escorts, flashed by lamp. It said: "Reduce speed and rendezvous with HMS *Tavendale* five miles astern convoy. When *Tavendale* joins you, stop engines and make ready for Commodore to board your ship."

Other ships were warned of the manoeuvre by a flurry of flag signals emanating from the Senior Escort and repeated throughout the convoy. Chisholm conned the *Fort Mohican* out of column and instructed the signalman to run up the international code flag "D", warning following ships to keep clear.

The rear ships had passed and *Fort Mohican* was at half speed, a mile behind the tail rank when there was another flurry of flag signals up ahead; also a series of siren blasts and a sudden flaring of signal lamps. The front of the convoy seemed in disarray, with ships manoeuvring in all directions.

The signals yeoman was at Chisholm's elbow, his glasses trained ahead. He was brilliant at his job and seemed to know the Mersigs manual by heart.

"It's the leading ship, column one, sir," he piped out. "She's sighted torpedo tracks, oh-four-five degrees. They're taking evasive action."

Now, a flank escort was flashing the *Fort Mohican*. The yeoman disappeared from the wheel-house at a run and Chisholm heard his hasty ascent of the ladder to the top bridge. Seconds later, came the shutter sounds of the ten-inch signal lamp as he acknowledged the escort's lamp. Chisholm left the wheel-house and waited directly under the signal-lamp platform for the yeoman to relay the text of the message he was receiving. The navyman called out each word as it came: "Rejoin . . . convoy . . . at . . . once . . . Take . . . up . . . station . . . three . . . six."

"Got it," Chisholm acknowledged to the signaller on the monkey-island and, returning to the wheel-house, jangled the engine telegraph to full speed.

"Starboard five," he called to the helmsman. "When she answers, steady on the last ship in the third column."

"Aye aye, sir."

They slowly overhauled the convoy, now reforming its orderly ranks. The torpedoes had passed clean through without hitting a ship. Away to port, one of the escorts had raised a contact and was attacking with a pattern of depth charges. The depth charge attack continued long after *Fort Mohican* was secure again with the flock and the hunting destroyer had been left on the horizon, still engaged in her duel.

A new signal flashed from the Senior Escort to *Fort Mohican*. It said simply: "We shall try again this afternoon."

The Mediterranean was as flat as a mill-pond when *Fort Mohican* dropped behind the convoy for a second time and stopped engines, with *Tavendale* a few cables off on the starboard beam. *Tavendale* lowered a whaler and, through his glasses, Chisholm watched three men clamber down a ladder to join the boat's crew. First down was a naval officer, built like an elongated matchstick. He was followed by an American soldier with what appeared to be full battle kit. Last into the boat was the recognisable figure of Rear-Admiral Freddie Hope. Below his uniform white shorts, his left leg was heavily bandaged.

The crew pulled away from the destroyer with long easy strokes of the oars. The crossing to the merchantman took less than ten minutes. The three passengers were climbing up the jacob's ladder streamed from the *Fort Mohican*'s side, when all hell broke loose.

There was a tragi-comic element of absurdity in what happened – and it is debatable whose was the greater surprise among the parties involved. With only the distant drumming of the convoy's propellers echoing on his hydrophones, the captain of U-593 had no reason to believe that, when he ordered his ship up to periscope depth, he would find anything other than an empty ocean in his immediate vicinity: nothing more than the masts and smoke of the convoy five miles ahead. It must have come as a heart-stopping shock as he revolved his search periscope to find that his U-boat was flanked on one side by a stationary troop transport with trucks and landing-craft on her deck and, on the other by a Royal Navy destroyer.

The black cylinder of periscope, feathering a foaming white trail in the calm sea, was seen simultaneously by the *Fort Mohican*'s starboard-side gunners and those on *Tavendale*'s port side. Without waiting for orders, both sets of gunners opened up a concerted stream of Oerlikon fire at the same moment. There was some imprudence in their enthusiasm: because of the low angle of fire and the proximity of the two motionless ships to each other. It was as if the two ships had opened fire on each other. The sea between them became a maelstrom of arcing tracer shells, which seemed to bounce off the water and leap upward again in paths that took them between deck and rigging.

Chisholm, conscious only that his ship was a sitting duck, was less concerned that the *Fort Mohican*'s shells were leaping over the destroyer's bridge in a deadly spray than that his own was at risk. He ordered full steam ahead.

Tavendale's captain was no less speedy off the mark and, with a mushroom of oily smoke from her funnel, the destroyer surged forward. Willing hands helped three shaking passengers over the *Fort Mohican*'s gunwale as the first depth charges from *Tavendale* exploded so nearby that the merchantman's plated hull trembled with the blast and threatened to shake apart.

A cheer went up from the Canadian soldiers lining the *Fort Mohican*'s deck as part of the U-boat's pressure hull briefly broke the surface of the sea in the wake of *Tavendale*'s attack. It seemed that the submarine had been thrown on her side, but the whale-like flank vanished in a swirl of water and was seen no more. As *Tavendale* wheeled for a second attack, the merchant ship was running from the scene, shaking throughout her frame as the engineers pushed her speed to an unprecedented thirteen knots. She was two miles distant when a pattern of high white plumes and booming explosions announced *Tavendale*'s renewed attack.

Throughout all the action, the boat-crew who had rowed the Commodore's party to the *Fort Mohican*, were left to drift. The boat was a speck on the horizon as the merchant ship overhauled the convoy and sought the safety of its ranks.

Rear-Admiral Freddie Hope arrived somewhat shaken on Chisholm's bridge. He was spluttering angrily at having nearly been deposited in the Mediterranean for the second time in successive days.

"You bloody near drowned me!" he roared at Chisholm without preamble. "What kind of a bloody captain are you?"

Chisholm, whose hand was extended to shake the Commodore's, resisted the impulse to throw the newcomer into the sea. He controlled his anger sufficiently to snarl: "I'm the kind of captain who puts his ship first!"

To his surprise, a broad grin appeared on the Commodore's face.

"Good for you, Captain. I'd have done the same thing myself!" He stuck out a hand. "Freddie Hope's the name. May I have permission to join you on your bridge?"

It was not until Chisholm had arranged for the Commodore to be accommodated in his night cabin that Chisholm was informed that the American army officer who had come aboard with Freddie Hope was anxious to see him. Cal Thorn had been shown into the ship's saloon and offered a reviving brandy after the unexpected rigours of his boat trip. Chisholm could not believe his eyes when Cal rose to greet him.

"Permission to come aboard, sir." Thorn's first words were

accompanied by a passable salute. They fell on each other's necks like long-lost brothers.

The simple act of removing his canvas gaiters made Thorn feel more like his old self. It had been fun playing soldiers and sailing to war in a British destroyer but, now, he was a cop again. He got down to work right away.

With a plea to Chisholm to contain for the time being all his bursting curiosity about his surprise appearance and what had led up to it, he questioned the *Fort Mohican*'s captain with a remorseless care for detail about the Canadian called Paul Constantine. Chisholm was only first on the list. Bob Fenwick, the Second Radio Officer, was grilled with the same thoroughness. Then it was the turn of Colonel Ruddy and several of the Canadian officers, all of whom were still in a state of angry shock at the discovery of Constantine's treachery.

It was early evening before Thorn felt that he was in possession of sufficient facts to face the prisoner in the ship's hospital. He invited Chisholm to be present.

"Well, well, well, if it isn't Antoine," Thorn greeted Strasser amiably. The German, who had maintained an air of mocking arrogance towards his captors since his surrender in the radio room and told them nothing, was visibly shaken.

"Who are you?" he asked Thorn.

Thorn smiled.

"You don't know me, Antoine, and you don't need to know. The important thing is that I know you. I've made it my business to know you from the day you arrived in London with Captain Chisholm here. You would be surprised at how well I know you."

"Surprise me," Strasser challenged.

Thorn shrugged unconcernedly.

"What would you like me to tell you? How we twigged you belonged to *Schatten Gruppe*? Would that be surprise enough?"

Strasser was sitting perched on the edge of the single bed looking up at Thorn. If Thorn saw the sudden clench of the German's fists, he gave no indication of having noticed. He planked himself down on one of the two chairs in the room and drew it up so that he could face Strasser from close quarters. Chisholm took the other chair but sat down near the door, content to be a spectator to the confrontation.

Thorn smiled teasingly at Strasser.

"Do *you* want to tell me about you?" he asked. "Or would you prefer me to do the talking?"

"I don't intend to tell you anything about anybody," Strasser replied tightly.

"Have it your own way." Thorn's eyes still teased. "You know you're a pretty lousy operator? You've bungled just about everything you've done."

"Is that so?"

"Yeah, that's a fact. Bumping off Lomax, for instance. A clever enough idea maybe, to slip him a couple of sodium pills. But dumping the body in Captain Chisholm's room wasn't too bright. That was clumsy . . . Real amateurish. Maybe we should have hauled you in there and then."

Strasser sat as tense as an overwound clock. He said nothing.

"Aren't you curious about that?" Thorn went on. "Don't you want to know why we kept you on a string?"

"You're bluffing me," Strasser said.

"Sure we are," Thorn agreed. "We've been bluffing you since you got off the boat from France. We like to give guys like you plenty of rope—and you've had enough to hang yourself a dozen times. We could have taken you any time."

"But you left it too late," snapped Strasser.

Thorn laughed.

"Oh, you mean by letting you send out that message last night? No, Antoine, you blew that one, too. We'd have been disappointed if you hadn't tried something like that." Thorn spread his hands and made a frowning little grimace. "Mind you, we didn't think you would be crazy enough to bust into the radio room and blow your cover the way you did. You must have been real desperate."

There was no arrogance about Strasser now. There was anxiety in the way he hunched himself, scarcely daring to move a muscle. Thorn eyed him with a smile that was intended to appear one of sympathy.

"You can still save your skin, Antoine. You can play ball with us . . . Tell us everything we want to know . . ." Thorn could see the other man tense himself to reject the offer. He forestalled him by saying quickly: "Like the girl told us everything, Antoine. Didn't you think it strange the way she just disappeared from sight? She did the sensible thing. Antoine. She told us all about you. And about your friend 'Q'."

Strasser sagged as if he had been punched in the stomach.

Thorn kept after him with a comment delivered casually, but with the calculated *schadenfreude* of a tossed grenade.

"Hey, that was a real crazy place to meet with your buddy 'Q', wasn't it? A graveyard in Brighton, for heaven's sake!"

Still Strasser said nothing. He could only stare at Thorn, beads of sweat trickling from his temples down the patchy yellow scars and pinched furrows of his disfigured face.

"That face of yours," Thorn said. "They didn't do that to you on purpose, did they? So that nobody who knew the real Constantine would know the difference? The trouble was that some people did notice the difference, didn't they? You covered your slip-ups well when you met some of Constantine's old pals at Brighton . . . Pretended your memory wasn't so hot . . . But Lomax remembered those slips, Antoine. He was going to check you out, wasn't he? That's why he had to be bumped off before he could spill the beans to Captain Chisholm. The mistake he made was running to Gilbert with his suspicions. Gilbert thought he was crazy and he told you . . ."

"Stop!" shouted Strasser.

The smile never left Thorn's face.

"Are you going to play ball, Antoine? I'm giving you a plank to walk over . . . It's the only way you can save your lousy neck . . . You can co-operate. Otherwise, I might just throw you to the Canadians in that hold out there. They don't like traitors, Antoine . . . And they're pretty riled up about you. They'd like to feed you to the fishes. The guards on that door aren't there to keep you in here, Antoine. They're there to keep the others from busting in and taking you apart a piece at a time . . ."

"Stop!" Strasser screamed. "Stop!"

Thorn looked at him expectantly.

"Are you ready to talk?"

The bright, pin-head eyes in the scarred face stared wildly at Thorn.

"I am not a traitor! I am a German officer! My name is Walther Strasser. That is all I am going to tell you. You had better kill me and be done with it. But you had better do it quickly . . . You will all die at Sicily."

Thorn met Strasser's defiant outburst with a broad grin.

"But we are not going to Sicily, Herr Strasser. Hasn't that sunk into your thick skull yet? All those orders you heard about are phoney. They were announced just for your benefit – to see what you would do. You goofed, Herr Strasser. You blew your cover to tell Berlin that we were going to hit Sicily – and we're not going there at all. We're going to Greece!''

Thorn pushed back his chair and stood up. He had the air of a man whose good humour had abruptly evaporated. He turned to Chisholm, who had watched the performance in stunned silence.

"We're wasting our time with this guy, Captain," he said curtly. "For all I care, they can string him up right now."

Chisholm stood up, his expression dazed and questioning. Thorn nodded towards the door.

"Let's go," he said.

Chisholm followed Thorn out to the deck. He watched the American lock the door and pocket the key.

"Nobody goes in there without my say-so," Thorn cautioned the guards.

He said nothing more until he and Chisholm were in Chisholm's day-room. Then, he let out a gasp of air as if he had been holding his breath for several minutes.

"Jesus! he exclaimed. "I could use a drink."

Chisholm looked at him in amazement. He was remembering his own first encounter with Thorn in a hotel room in Brighton and how the American had seemed to have a clairvoyant knowledge of the secrets he had tried to hide. Thorn had seen through his attempt at subterfuge and had had him admitting the truth in the winking of an eye. Now, he had witnessed the American do a similar demolition job on Strasser.

"Were you bluffing down there?" Chisholm asked.

"I just wanted that guy to sweat," Thorn said. "Now, I'll let him stew for a bit." He beamed. "A little bit of inspired guesswork and a few downright lies can work wonders. I think I've got him softened up. How about that drink?"

Chisholm got him a drink from his cabinet. He did not take one himself. Thorn poured the neat whisky down his throat in a single gulp.

"Now we got work to do," he said. "Tonight, we've got to put out a radio message."

"Break radio silence?" Chisholm frowned. "I don't know what the Commodore will say about that."

"I don't give a goddamn what the Commodore says about it," said Thorn. "We go on the air some time after midnight! Where is the old buzzard anyway?"

"The old buzzard's right here," said a voice from the doorway of Chisholm's night cabin. Commodore Freddie Hope, clad in Chisholm's bath-robe and with a towel round his neck, stood glaring at Thorn from the doorway. Thorn grinned at him.

"Well, talk of the devil," he said.

Twenty

Confession

There were five men crowded into the Radio cabin. Fenwick, the Second Radio Officer, was seated at the main transmitter with Thorn in the chair beside him. Chisholm, the Commodore and his aide, Ingledew, were perched against the bench-top behind the two seated men. It was half an hour after midnight.

For what to Fenwick seemed to be the twentieth time, Thorn went over with him the procedure that Strasser had followed only twenty-four hours previously.

"Now you're sure you've got the frequency right?"

"I'm sure," Fenwick said wearily. "The settings are precisely as he left them."

"And he didn't use a standard callsign?"

Fenwick shook his head.

"No. It was a three-letter series – Q-S-V. I read it off the key."

"The key has a double click. You're sure you couldn't have got it wrong?"

"I know what he sent."

"Good," Thorn encouraged. "Now, the message itself . . . You said he started and finished by sending the same six-letter group. This is important. It was probably a code which identified the call as an emergency, or authentic, or both. You said the group was G-O-E-T-H-E?"

"Yes, like the poet and philosopher, Goethe. That's what helped me remember it."

"And it's probably why they picked the name in the first place. German as liver sausage and easily remembered. Now . . . The message itself was in German. Plain language?"

"I'm ninety-nine per cent certain," said Fenwick. "I had a year in the Civilian Shore Wireless Service before I came to sea and most of it was spent taking German traffic."

Thorn turned to Ingledew.

"Have you got our message?"

Ingledew handed him a signal sheet on which a message had been written in block capitals.

"This is the genuine article?" Thorn asked the lanky lieutenant. "No obvious English-isms . . . ? Or what you called them – anglicisms?"

"It's the genuine article," Ingledew confirmed. He had taught German at one of England's top public schools before the war and, because of that, Thorn had recruited him to translate the text of a message he had dictated.

"We're all set then," Thorn said.

Fenwick switched on the transmitter.

"I'll let it warm up before I start," he said.

"Do you think you can do a reasonable copy of Strasser's fist?" Thorn asked.

"He was slow. I'll keep it slow, too. That's all I can promise. If his fist is known at the other end, they'll know right away that it isn't him sending. But I don't think he was a regular at the job. I'm banking on the hope that they wouldn't know his fist from my Uncle Charlie's. Keep you fingers crossed."

The onlookers scarcely dared to breathe when, finally, Fenwick began tapping out the Q-S-V callsign. There was an acknowledgement almost immediately. Deliberately, Fenwick repeated the G-O-E-T-H-E sequence and then started sending the German text that Ingledew had prepared. There was a "message received" burst from the unknown station in France.

When it was over, everyone in the radio cabin wanted to talk at once. The owner of the most piercing voice secured and held the floor.

"I hope you know what you are doing, young man," the Commodore barked, addressing Thorn. "My Lords of the Admiralty may yet have me keelhauled for letting you talk me into this."

"It's a calculated risk we've taken, sir," Thorn replied. "I reckon the Germans have known about this convoy ever since it came through the Straits of Gibraltar. Events have proved it. Breaking radio silence a second time ain't going to make a difference one way or the other. They know exactly where we are – and if they're going to hit us again, they'll hit us, sir. Regardless."

The Commodore fixed Thorn with his hawklike eyes.

"If the worst does come to the worst, Lieutenant, and we finish in the water, there's one word of advice I should like to give you. Do not climb on the same life raft as me!"

With that, the Commodore departed with the avowed intention of getting a couple of hours sleep. He had had none in the previous forty-eight hours, and Freddie Hope was no longer a young man. He left before Thorn had the chance to tell him that he wanted the *Fort Mohican* to break radio silence again the following night.

Thorn had only one nagging worry. He had appended the word "Antoine" to the out-going signal in German, without knowing for certain that Strasser had used the name in his first "Goethe" call. It was a gamble. The Germans might know at a glance that the second message was false.

If they did not, Thorn wondered how they would react to the news that the convoy's progress towards Sicily was a feint and that, during the night of 9th July, its course would be altered for landings to be made between Cape Carbonara and Villaputzu on the island of Sardinia on the night of 10th/11th July.

Strasser was haggard from lack of sleep. Where had the American come from? He seemed to know about *Schatten Gruppe*, about Lomax, about *everything*. Was it possible that they had known who and what he was from the day he had landed from France?

Had the girl really betrayed *Schatten Gruppe*? Was that why the American knew so much? And what about Lander? The American *knew* he had met Lander in Brighton – so, he must know all about Lander, too. Was he being held in another part of the ship?

The questions ate at Strasser's brain like a cancer. And no answers came to him. The longer the night went on, the more depressed he became. Not even the thought, that German forces might already be massing in Sicily to repel the invasion, cheered him. He regretted now not shooting his way out of the radio cabin and going down fighting. Had it been latent cowardice in him that had made him choose to surrender and put off the inevitable end?

The thought made him weep in his loneliness.

Towards dawn, he made a decision.

He stripped the single sheet from his bed. Knotting one end

to the tubular bed-head, he began to wind the sheet into a rope. When it was tightly wound, he looped the unknotted end over a deckhead water-pipe . . .

The crash of the falling chair alerted the guards outside the hospital cabin. Minutes passed before Thorn was located. He arrived still buttoning on his shirt. When he opened the door, the scene inside told it all: Strasser on the floor with the sheet roped round his neck; the chair that had been kicked over.

Strasser lay on the deck sobbing. Thorn looked down at him with shaking head.

"You've bungled it again, Walther," he said sadly. "You can't even make a good job out of killing yourself."

He walked across and picked up the end of sheet that Strasser had anchored to the bed-head with a knot that had slipped the moment it had taken his weight. Strasser's attempt at suicide had done him no more damage than a couple of bruised knees.

Thorn disentangled the sheet from the German's neck and turned him over on to his back. Strasser did not want to look at him. He rolled over, hunching himself in a ball; crying softly to himself. Thorn snorted in disgust and left him where he was. He instructed the guards to throw the German on the bed and suggested that, in future, one of them should remain in the room with Strasser at all times. Strasser was not to be given a second chance to take his own life.

Thorn then returned to the couch in the smoke-room, where he had bedded down for the night. There was still time for an hour's sleep before breakfast.

Chisholm had little time after breakfast to concern himself with the prisoner in the ship's hospital. He was experiencing for the first time a senior Naval presence on his bridge – in the shape of Commodore Freddie Hope – and the frenzied activity that went hand-in-hand with the *Fort Mohican*'s new role as nerve-centre of the convoy. The ships were off Cape Serrat and approaching the narrow Galita Channel in a two-column formation.

Fort Mohican led the port column, with the tail ships of the convoy several miles distant astern. All the merchantmen equipped to do so had streamed their paravanes. For, not only was the mile-wide channel notorious for the unseen underwater rocks around it, it was flanked by known mine-fields and the channel itself was constantly mined from the air by the Luftwaffe.

As the ships passed through, the Galita lived up to its reputation. Gunners on the *Fort Mohican* accounted for one of three floating mines, exploded by rifle fire. There was also a crisis when one ship hooked a mine with her paravane sweep and towed it for some miles before it was cut adrift and exploded.

Even without these diversions, the bridge of the *Fort Mohican* was a mad-house of activity as Freddie Hope bombarded his retinue of ships with one flag hoist after another. The stream of signals varied from course and speed orders to stern rebukes to offending ships for failing to maintain station or for making too much smoke.

It was afternoon before Chisholm had his first real chance of the day to talk to Thorn. The American had not been idle. In the company of Colonel Ruddy and another Canadian officer, who had acted as stenographer, he had spent the morning interrogating Strasser.

"He's a broken man," Thorn told Chisholm.

They were in Chisholm's day-room, and Thorn laid a thick bundle of penned notes on the table between them. There must have been forty pages of foolscap covered by the Canadian officer's looping scrawl.

"The confessions of Walther Strasser," Thorn said.

"You got all that out of him?" Chisholm was incredulous.

"There's more to come. For some reason, he suddenly clammed up on me and went into a kind of stupefied silence . . . He just sat there like he was in a trance. But that's not bad for a morning's work. I warned him I would be back for more."

"You must be pleased," Chisholm said.

Thorn drew a hand wearily over his eyes.

"Pleased? No, that's not how I would have put it. All I've done is get some answers – and that's nothing to crow about. To get them, I had to make a bargain with a murderer . . . And I get no kicks from doing a deal with a cold-blooded killer."

"You did a deal with Constantine? With Strasser, I mean?"

"I showed him the signal we sent off last night. I wanted to see how he reacted. If there was anything in it that was going to make the Germans suspicious that it wasn't genuinely from their boy, Strasser was going to think that we had goofed and he had won the ball game. It was the one chance he had . . ."

"How did he react?"

"Like I had kicked him in the gut. He broke up. On top of

300

trying to kill himself and making a hash of that, I reckon it was all too much for him. He just cracked. He's been running scared for a long time now, Chizz, and today it all caught up with him. What he had for a spine yesterday is all jelly today."

"And the deal you made?"

"No death sentence. On condition that he co-operated and spilled everything. I said I would guarantee it. He gets to live to a ripe old age – but he's got to give us the goods and help us to string the other side along."

"And he agreed? Just like that?"

"Yep."

"But . . . After that message . . . Surely the Jerries won't trust him now. Aren't you overrating his value to our side?"

"He's of no use to our side," Thorn said flatly. "Not now. Not as a double agent. What I wanted out of him, Chizz – and what I got – is the complete goods on *Schatten Gruppe*."

Chisholm frowned, his eyes on Thorn as if something troubled him.

"You knew about him, Cal, didn't you? You knew about him even before you arrived on the ship? You weren't surprised when I told you we had him under lock and key. How long have you known he was working for the Germans?"

Thorn smiled.

"I wasn't holding out, if that's what you're hinting at, Chizz. I've known about him for about a week. Less than that. There was a long story of a cable waiting for me from Hibberd when I got to Gib from Madrid. They had begun to suspect Constantine, or Strasser as we know him now, even before you left England. It's a long story, and complicated."

"I'd like to hear it, Cal."

Thorn told Chisholm then, as simply as he could and skipping, as not essential to Chisholm, some of the details of how counter-espionage forces in both Europe and North America had become involved.

He told how, at Vaughan's suggestion, Brockway had kept a close eye on the officer they knew as Paul Constantine. But the only questionable act they had been able to attribute to him had been his switch of ships from the *St Essylt* to the *Fort Mohican*. This was not construed as necessarily sinister. Vaughan had himself told Constantine that Chisholm was down for command of the *Fort Mohican* and and – because the pair were acquainted – it was just possible that he had engineered the switch to be reunited with a friend.

Thorn, meantime, had been busy in Madrid and had traced a connection between the girl who had impersonated Anina Calvi and a wine exporter who had frequent German visitors. The American had been intrigued to discover that the volume of business communications passing between the Madrid wine firm and a New York company did not seem to be justified by actual trade. He had asked Hibberd to have the New York company investigated. The consequent discovery that the New York business house was headed by a former leading light in the American Nazi Bund had led to an intensification of American undercover activities centred on New York and Madrid.

In Madrid, Thorn had successfully inserted a trusted Spanish agent into the wine exporter's office as a typist. This young woman had attempted to monitor all incoming communications and pass the details to Thorn. Most proved innocuous but the girl noticed that whenever certain coded cables arrived, her boss made a telephone call and a German visitor would call on him within the hour. The girl was told to obtain copies of the next batch of cables and managed to get hold of four.

Thorn had the cables passed to an Embassy cryptographer. When the cryptographer broke the codes, Thorn had his breakthrough. Three of the cables gave details of shipping movements in and around the port of New York. One gave details of the movement of a Canadian army division from England to the Mediterranean and its involvement in a twelve-division attack on Western Greece or Jugoslavia scheduled for the first week in July. The source was named as "Antoine".

Thorn had informed Hibberd in London at once, whereupon he was ordered to place the Madrid operation in the hands of the "residents" and proceed immediately to Gibraltar to await further orders.

These orders had named Constantine as the likely origin of the "Operation Husky" information being passed to the Germans and instructed Thorn to use a special *carte blanche* authority, endorsed by the Combined Chiefs of Staff, to intercept the convoy in the Gibraltar approaches and get himself aboard the *Fort Mohican*. Once on board, he was to ascertain the extent of the enemy agent's activities and intentions and to take such measures as he deemed fit to curtail and counteract them.

Unfortunately for Thorn, he had been delayed getting to Gibraltar and the convoy had already passed through the Straits when he got there. He told Chisholm how, but for the tragic irony of events, he never would have made it to the *Fort Mohican*. If *Tavendale* had not gone into Bougie with survivors, he would probably still have been kicking his heels in Algiers.

"Well you made it, and you've got your man," Chisholm said. "What was it that made Vaughan and the others in England so sure he *was* your man?"

Thorn cocked an eyebrow.

"Didn't I tell you?" he asked, and then answered his own question. "No, I didn't. It was because they found Gilbert."

"Gilbert!"

"The Canadian who did the disappearing act while you were in hospital. Some kids found his body under rubble on a London bomb-site. He'd been dead close on five months."

"How did he die?"

"Strasser told me this morning. He did it . . . With a knife . . . He cut his throat."

Chisholm's face showed his revulsion.

"No wonder you didn't much like doing a deal with him!"

"Gilbert wasn't Strasser's only victim, Chizz. He rubbed out Lomax, too. He's just a hood. Chizz. The nasty thing about the way he did for Gilbert was the way he conned Gilbert. Gilbert thought he was his best buddy. He trusted Strasser completely. That's what cost him his life, and Lomax's. Do you remember meeting Lomax in Brighton, Chizz? You said that you convinced him you weren't a sex fiend and you'd never stooged for the Nazis . . . and Lomax's suspicions were aroused?"

Chisholm remembered only too well. He recalled how the Canadian had reacted, too.

"Lomax took off like an avenging fury. He said he had some checking up to do . . ."

"It was Constantine he was going to check up on," interrupted Thorn. "Twice apparently, Constantine had treated guys who knew him well like he'd never set eyes on them in his life. Both guys spoke to Lomax about it. They were hurt more than puzzled. They thought Constantine maybe backed away from them because of his face, that it had changed him. Anyway, Lomax remembered the incidents when you spoke to him. He realised he'd been wrong about you and that maybe one of his own crowd wasn't quite who he pretended to be. The guy had to be Constantine, the hero of Dieppe, and a chronic amnesia case when his old buddies showed up."

Chisholm's face wrinkled in thought as he dredged his memory, remembering the shock events of Brighton and their aftermath. They had suspected Gilbert of being in cahoots with Anina. She had said that Lomax had gone running to *Gilbert* after he and Chisholm had put the record straight.

"Let me get this straight, Cal," Chisholm said. "When Lomax suddenly got suspicious of Constantine, why did he rush off and tell Gilbert?"

"He wanted Gilbert to get hold of Constantine's dental records from *before* Dieppe and do an ID check."

"What did Gilbert do?"

"He thought Lomax was crazy. Constantine was his buddy. Gilbert humoured Lomax at the time and then ran straight to Constantine to tell him that the Major had flipped his lid."

"And Constantine doctored Lomax's Ovaltine?"

"His milk of magnesia to be precise. Lomax had a fetish about taking the stuff regularly. Strasser . . . Constantine . . . must have ground down about half a pound of barbiturate to lace his bottle – because Lomax took only a couple of spoonfuls. Not that he needed much to kill him."

"Was there anything in the autopsy report about milk of magnesia?"

"Yeah, it mentioned traces of the stuff. And a bottle was found in Lomax's quarters. It was analysed, along with a lot of other stuff, and it was clean. It wasn't of course the bottle Lomax had supped from. You-know-who made sure the loaded bottle was never found."

Chisholm frowned.

"Not many people have the medical knowledge to pull a thing like that, Cal. Would you have known that a brain-damage victim could be bumped off with sleeping pills? How the hell did Constantine know? When you think of it, he was bloody quick off the mark."

"He was well briefed, Chizz. Not just about Lomax and how easily he could be wasted – but about you, too. About all of you who were in that goddamned booby-hatch in France."

"Hold on a bit, Cal," Chisholm protested mildly. "The Ritz Hotel it wasn't – but booby-hatch is putting it a bit strong."

"Not the way Strasser tells it."

"What do you mean?"

"I mean," said Thorn, weighing his words carefully, "that every guy who was in that compound at St Cyr des Bains was a potential nutcase. And, forgive me saying it, that includes you. Hell, Chizz, you know better than anyone that they had you labelled for crazy. You were a candidate when they wheeled you off that submarine, although they didn't take any real interest in you until you escaped from that first nut-house and landed in the Gestapo funny farm. That was where they started to take your brain apart like you were a laboratory specimen . . . And that's just what you were to them: a research specimen that they kept in a bottle with a number on it."

Chisholm could only stare at Thorn in disbelief, while part of his mind was remembering fragments of an indelible horror and piecing them together so that a picture of a monstrous truth began to form. Thorn continued relentlessly, turning over more jigsaw pieces to the light until the pattern could not be denied. He progressed to the establishment of St Cyr des Bains.

"St Cyr was where you graduated to, Chizz. As an expendable but possibly useful commodity. You can maybe even count yourself lucky that they did send you there. You were one of their failures. They couldn't break you, but they didn't throw you out with the trash because they thought they could use you. You had the makings of a patsy, Chizz. Somebody they could use to draw attention away from their guy, Strasser. You maybe thought it was your idea that you could steal a boat and get away to England – but it wasn't your idea, Chizz. It was their idea. They had to make it easy, but not so easy that it roused too many suspicions. And when you got to England, Chizz, if there were any suspicions, you were the one who was going to smell of stinking fish. You were the one who was going to reek of treachery and selling out your country."

Chisholm could recall only too vividly how close the treachery label had come to sticking.

"What I can't fathom, Cal, is why they picked on me. Why me?"

"Because your measurements were right, Chizz. And because you were there. It was maybe as simple as that. You just happened to be in the wrong place at the wrong time."

Chisholm listened in a stunned awe as Thorn went on to tell him of the secrets of St Cyr des Bains, as he had prised them out of Walther Strasser.

The centre was run by the Nazi Security Service as an experimental station, being controlled by a hitherto unknown operational group specialising in different aspects of psychological warfare. Keitler headed the research team investigating victims of psychological disturbance and their possible use against the Reich's enemies.

He was particularly interested in subverting for the Nazi cause enemy casualties whose injuries or war shock had made vulnerable to mind manipulation: the end result being that they exchanged their former loyalties for new ones in tune with Nazi aims. He believed that a soldier who had suffered maiming or disfigurement – and was acutely disturbed psychologically as a result – could be persuaded to blame all his misfortune not on the enemy who had inflicted his injuries, but on the political system or government in whose service he had lost a limb or an eye or his reason.

Paul Constantine had been a typical casualty in this category: badly wounded at Dieppe and suffering the trauma of losing a leg. Unfortunately for Keitler, the real Constantine had shown no inclination to change sides during a spell under SD observation in the security wing of a military hospital near Dieppe. Indeed, the reverse had been the case. Although he was the only survivor from an entire Company, Constantine's spirit was unbroken and he had remained openly defiant of his captors.

It was not quite a coincidence that Walther Strasser had landed in the same hospital as Constantine. At the time of Dieppe, Strasser had been in Germany doing undercover work for the SD in a prison camp for British RAF officers. In the guise of a shot-down RCAF flier, he had been inserted as an informer to worm intelligence secrets from the prisoners.

With the large influx of Canadian prisoners after Dieppe, Strasser had been summoned to France to do similar intelligence work. The aircraft ferrying him to France had, however, crash-landed and Strasser had been taken to hospital suffering from severe burns.

It was as the result of a chance meeting at the hospital between Strasser's commander in *Schatten Gruppe* and Colonel Keitler that the idea had been born to substitute Strasser for Constantine and return him to England with the specific aim of uncovering Allied plans for a Second Front in Europe.

Strasser, still recovering from his burns, was installed in a room with Constantine, with orders to extract every detail of the Canadian's past life and to study his personality. The unsuspecting Constantine showed no inhibitions in sharing his closest secrets with the disfigured Strasser, whom he believed to be a fellow-survivor from the Dieppe massacre.

When the time came, both men left the hospital for "convalescence" at St Cyr des Bains. Only one of them had actually arrived there: Strasser. And he was admitted as Lieutenant Paul Constantine.

"And that was just about where I came in," said Chisholm, interrupting Thorn's flow. "Strasser probably didn't stop at passing himself off as Constantine, I bet he kept Keitler informed about everything that went on inside the wire."

"He did that all right," Thorn agreed. "But don't think Keitler stopped at having an insider to tell tales. He had that whole compound of yours wired for sound anyway – microphones all over the place. You and the other guys were his guinea-pigs and there wasn't a thing went on in that place that he didn't know about. He knew all along that the nurse . . . What was her name . . . ?"

"Nicole. Nicole Baril."

"Yeah. He knew she was in the Resistance. Knew all along. Because they'd penetrated the Resistance Group before she got the job at the hospital. Keitler had his own insider on the girl's father's boat. They had the whole Resistance operation stitched up long before you got to the hospital. They needed it for the escape. Keitler knew all about the escape plan long before it happened. And he let it happen – because it was the one way they could get Strasser to England. You, Lomax, Gilbert, the others . . . You were all puppets, Chizz. Keitler pulled the strings and you guys did what you were supposed to do."

Thorn's words flooded the dark recesses of Chisholm's mind with bright light. Haunting puzzles ceased to be half-remembered mysteries as the underlying reasons for them suddenly became all too starkly clear.

"In some ways, you were a gift from the gods to Keitler," Thorn was saying. "The French had no idea that Keitler was wise to them and they'd been digging in their heels about letting loose a bunch of Canadians in the Channel in one of their boats. And the British Navy were being awkward, too. They wouldn't send a boat to pick up escapers. Keitler needed a genuine, twenty-four-carat sailor to persuade the French to go ahead with an escape that would get Strasser out. You were not only available, Chizz, you were tailor-made for the job. All softened up in a Gestapo prison, with reports to Keitler on his desk about your violence under drugs and your bloody-minded obduracy when you weren't doped up to the eyeballs."

Chisholm was remembering again the windowless cell and the chains. He said to Thorn: "There was a doctor I looked on as my one and only guardian angel, Cal. I know now . . . I worked it out some time ago . . . that he couldn't have been. The Germans called him The Schoolmaster . . ."

"He was no angel, Chizz. He was part of the treatment."

"Strasser knew him?"

"Strasser was one of his pupils at the *Schatten Gruppe* spy school. Strasser called him Der Schulleiter. He's an expert, or used to be, on criminal psychology. Strasser knew all about you being softened up by him for Keitler. I told you he was well briefed on all you guys who got out with him."

"What do you mean, 'softened up for Keitler'?"

"A lot of police forces use the kind of interrogation technique they treated you to. It's classic. Without chaining the prisoner up or working him over with a rubber hose, that is. The rough and the smooth, they call it. First, you rough the prisoner up, then you kill him with kindness and sweet understanding. The prisoner hates the first interrogator but he thinks the second is on his side and trusts him. Nobody is ever going to blame you, Chizz, for thinking this Schoolmaster guy was an angel from heaven. That's just what he must have seemed."

"I must have been blind," said Chisholm. "And stupid! I should have listened to Rick Thomson, Cal. He was the only one who really tumbled to what they were doing to us. He said Keitler was evil."

"Evil's an understatement, Chizz. That guy was really trying to bend your minds. He had you all charted for your likes, your dislikes, your phobias, your strengths, your weaknesses . . . To turn you against each other . . . To turn you against all you ever believed in . . . He was trying to make healthy minds sick and sick minds sicker . . ."

"And the bastard's probably still doing it!" Chisholm said, with a shiver of revulsion.

Thorn nodded unhappily.

"I'm afraid he is. The only consolation I have, Chizz, is that it didn't work with you. He didn't make a Nazi out of you—or Lomax, or Gilbert, or the others who got out with you."

"And Rick Thomson, You're forgetting Rick Thomson. Keitler failed with him, too. Whatever else they did, it's what they did to Rick that I'll never be able to forgive, Cal. He was just a kid . . . A poor helpless kid with only one foot."

Thorn was strangely silent. The fact that he was silent and the look on his face drew a questioning stare from Chisholm. Thorn spoke at last.

"There's something you should know about Rick Thomson," he said softly. He took a deep breath and then added quickly: "Strasser killed Rick Thomson, Chizz."

The American watched Chisholm's face. He saw pain register as Chisholm was reminded of his discovery of Rick's body. The emotion was transient. It gave way to bitter anger.

"Chizz, you won't do anything silly? Strasser's our prisoner." Thorn's tone was almost apologetic.

"No, no . . ." Chisholm shook his head with a weary sadness. "Although I'd like to wring that bastard's neck!" He clenched his fists. "The galling thing is . . . that . . . That the stinking sewer rat's on my ship!"

"And I made a deal with him, Chizz. His life for all the dirt I can squeeze out of him. It sticks in my craw, too. I'm sorry."

Chisholm got up out of his seat and went to stare through the circle of open port. But he was blind to the framed vista of davit-strung lifeboat and sea beyond. His expression was bleak and, when he spoke without facing Thorn, so was his tone.

"Revenge is supposed to be a useless, sterile way of settling wrongs, Cal . . . Maybe it is . . . But God knows I'm tempted to go and lay hands on that bastard down there. I would enjoy lashing him to a couple of fire-bars and watching his face as I pushed him over the side . . ."

"But you're not going to do it, Chizz."

Chisholm turned and faced Thorn.

"No, Cal, I'm not going to do it. But I'll tell you this. You keep Walther Strasser well out of my sight. If I clap eyes on him again, my good intentions might not just be able to stand the strain!"

To Thorn's surprise, Chisholm crossed to the cabinet next his desk and extracted a bottle and two glasses.

"I hate to break a golden rule," he said over his shoulder, "but, for once, I find myself in need of a strong drink. Will you join me?"

Thorn accepted a glass of whisky and raised it.

"I won't propose a toast to crime and punishment. But maybe you'll settle for confusion to our enemies?"

"I'll drink to that, "Chisholm said. "Damnation to them all!" He drained the glass and put it down on the table. He regarded Thorn quizzically.

"You were telling me that Strasser killed Rick. Did he actually admit it?"

"With much anguish and a flood of crocodile tears. He was particularly anxious that you shouldn't find out. He's scared of you, Chizz. Scared of what you might do."

"I've told you I won't lay a finger on him if he's kept out of my sight. Did he say why he killed Rick?"

Thorn nodded.

"He said it was an accident. That it was quite unplanned. What he said would have made more sense to you than it did to me. I've only got a hazy idea of the layout of the compound where you were locked up . . . He said something about you going out of the block after getting hold of a pair of scissors from some nurse – a French girl that Keitler had fixed to take the place of the one called Nicole . . ."

"She was working for Keitler, too?" Chisholm's interruption was shrill with astonishment.

"The whole escape was rigged, Chizz. I told you that."

Chisholm subsided into his chair and let Thorn continue.

"Anyway, Chizz, when you had gone out, Strasser went along to your end of the hut to try to talk Rick Thomson out of escaping. Why, I don't know – but it's not all that important, because Rick never got the chance. Strasser found him dismantling one of the roof microphones Keitler had installed to listen to your conversations . . . And he realised that the escape would be cancelled for certain if you or any of the Canadians tumbled to the fact that the whole goddamned block was wired out like Radio City . . ."

"So Strasser stabbed Rick with the scissors?"

"He said there was a struggle."

"I can imagine!" Chisholm said bitterly. "It must have been hard getting the better of a man who couldn't stand up without crutches."

Their discussion was interrupted by a sharp knocking at the day-room door. With a frown of annoyance at the interruption,

Chisholm got up and opened the door. Outside, astride the weather-step between the alleyway and the lower bridge deck and with his back propping open the sprung mosquito door, was Lander, the donkeyman.

Twenty-One

D-Day Minus One

The moon face beamed at Chisholm.

"Chief Engineer sent me to have a look at your shower, Captain. Seems the Commodore complained to him that he got scalded. Said the regulator wasn't working right."

"Oh? I didn't know. You'd better come in and have a look at it." Chisholm stood aside and held the door open to allow Lander through, hefting his tool-box.

Lander nodded amiably at Thorn as Chisholm led the way through the day-room into the night cabin. Chisholm pointed.

"The bathroom's in there." Lander followed his pointing hand.

"Big fellow," Thorn observed when Chisholm rejoined him.

"Norwegian," said Chisholm. "Got shoulders on him like the hunchback of Notre Dame."

"Quasimodo?" Thorn said with a smile. And they both laughed. From the bathroom came the metallic sound of a hammer applied to a locked monkey-wrench. "Sounds like he's knocking your bathroom to pieces," Thorn said, but Chisholm had already dismissed the donkeyman from his thoughts.

"Did you get anything out of Strasser about Anina's pal Quasimodo, Cal?"

Thorn shook his head.

"I'd just got round to Quasimodo when Strasser went into his trance. He just kept staring at me like I'd grown a spare head. But he'll talk, don't you worry. If he doesn't all deals are off and he'll be guest of honour at a neck-tie party!"

Thorn picked up the pile of notes from the table in front of them and idly straightened them on the table-top.

"The important thing is, Chizz, that volume one of the Strasser story is quite a document. He talked a lot about *Schatten*

Gruppe and how they operate. We know where to start looking for the likes of Quasimodo now. He'll be on the records somewhere, that's for sure. One way or another, we'll find him."

"What exactly is *Schatten Gruppe*, Cal?"

"You dug up our very first lead on them, Chizz. From Anina Calvi, remember? Strasser has given us more. According to him, the group is Himmler's brainchild – part of the *Sicherheitsdienst*, the SS Security Service, or SD for short. Its function covers espionage, sabotage, psychological warfare and undercover work in POW camps like Strasser was doing. The name means shadow group."

"And both Anina and Strasser were part of it?"

"Yeah – and both hand-picked for their backgrounds and fluency in English. *Schatten Gruppe* seems to specialise in acquiring the identities of foreign nationals who have good track records with the Allies, known sympathies. Or, as in Strasser's case, the cover of a serving officer who had shown conspicuous bravery in the field."

"So, Quasimodo could be anything from a pilot in the RAF to a general in the Polish Army?" ·

"Or a New York banker, or a Swiss opera singer. We don't know. All we know is that they got over from Europe and through our screening system in the past year or so. That means we've got them on the books. And, by hell, we'll find them!"

Thorn stood up and handed the Strasser interrogation notes to Chisholm.

"Have a look at these when you get the chance, Chizz. You know the St Cyr set-up better than anyone. You may have some observations to make. Things that may mean nothing to the likes of me could make sense to you."

"Can I save them for later?"

"Sure, but keep 'em out of sight. They're for your eyes only."

Chisholm took a key ring from his pocket and unlocked the top drawer of his desk.

"I'll put them in here beside my trusty thirty-eight," he said, and put the notes in the drawer on top of the Webley revolver that lay inside. He locked the drawer again and returned the keys to his pocket.

Everyone who could find an excuse for being there, off-watch or on, was on the bridge of the *Fort Mohican*. All three deck officers were there. With them was the quaintly designated SNOT and his CPO. The Commodore was there, with Ingledew at his shoulder. Chisholm and Thorn were there. The top bridge and upper gun-pits seemed to be crowded with more than the normal complement of gunners and signallers. The two officer apprentices were perched on the rail of the binnacle box with as good a view as any. And the spectacle they beheld was one to imprint itself on the memory.

From his vantage-point on the port wing of the bridge, Chisholm watched it unfold. It did so like a page in a history book – and the feeling that stirred in the master of the *Fort Mohican* was that he and his ship were indeed at the centre of a unique moment in history. After four weary years of war and the discouragement of battle after battle lost, this surely was the turning-point: the great return to Europe.

Wherever Chisholm turned his eyes, he could see ships. From horizon to horizon, the sea was massed with ships. Ships of every shape and every size and every calling. To north and south and east and west, the masts pointed like the trees of a great forest: their ranks extending over the horizon and beyond sight below the curved rim of the earth's face.

There were large, stately troopships; wide-beamed battleships; iron-clad cruisers; scurrying destroyers; ponderous, tank-like landing-ships. Columns of workmanlike freighters rose abreast of lumbering gun-ships and flat-bottomed rocket-ships. Ocean-going tugs kept company with regal Cape liners, sleek, three-funnel ferryboats and squat corvettes.

This was the hour of rendezvous.

From Alexandria, from Durban, from Bizerta, from Tripoli and from ports between – they were arriving. From the desert heat of Benghazi and Tobruk they came. From Sousse and from Derna. From the cold distant waters of the Clyde.

The meeting place was the stretch of Mediterranean Sea that separates the islands of Malta and Sicily. Within a rectangle of ocean, thirty miles long by twenty-five miles across, more than three thousand ships gathered. They formed the mightiest sea armada ever assembled in war or peace. Packed into the warships and the troopships were more than 160,000 men, comprising sixteen fighting divisions: some four divisions more than would be needed a year later to make the assault on Hitler's Atlantic Wall.

Thorn, standing at Chisholm's side, was awed at the sight of such a majestic array of power.

"Doesn't it make you a kind of glad what side you're on?" he said to Chisholm in a hushed tone.

"I've waited four long years for this," Chisholm said softly. "All of a sudden it doesn't seem to matter too much if we find the Jerries sitting on the beaches waiting for us. They're never going to stop this lot. Not in a million years."

They were joined from the wheel-house by Commodore Freddie Hope. The Commodore was anxious about the weather. Storm-clouds were scudding from the north-east, carried by a wind that seemed to be increasing in force by the minute. The waves in the rising sea were whipped white at their caps.

"I don't like the look of that sky," the Commodore said. "We could be in for a night of it."

"We'll cope, sir," Chisholm promised optimistically. "The sea has to get up a bit yet to get as bad as the Firth of Clyde."

The Commodore smiled.

"Always look on the bright side, eh? By God, Captain, you're right. We never died of winter yet. What I need is a tot. We all do. Nothing like a spot of grog to cheer the troops. A large spot!" He canted his head to one side and bawled: "Signalman!"

The signals yeoman was on the top bridge. He seemed to dispense with the need to touch the upright ladder with his feet in his hurried descent and arrived with a crash at the Commodore's feet as if he had dropped out of the sky.

"Yes, sir?"

"Make a signal from Commodore to all ships, yeoman," the Commodore barked. "We sailed with Hope. We arrive with Hope. God be with you tomorrow. Hope be with you always." He nudged Chisholm with his elbow. "Do you get the pun, Captain? The Nelson touch, eh?" The signalman was about to dash off but a roar from the Commodore stopped him in his tracks. "I hadn't finished," he bawled. "End the signal: 'Splice the mainbrace!' "

"Aye aye, sir," replied the yeoman, with a marked note of enthusiasm in his voice.

The Commodore turned again to Chisholm.

"I'm afraid we'll have to use your rum," he said. "Do you think your ship's bond might rise to six hundred large tots?"

"I'm sure we can find enough to go round," Chisholm replied with a smile. "And since this is on the Navy, shall we send the bill to the Admiralty?"

The Commodore frowned fiercely.

"Certainly not! This is on me. Put it down on my ward-room drinks account." Then he smiled impishly. "But be sure you catch me before I leave the ship and get me to sign you a chit."

From early evening – when the convoys merged – the huge armada sailed towards Western Greece, passing beyond the south-eastern tip of Sicily.

Second Radio Officer Fenwick, in the normal run of things, would have turned in at about 7.30 in the evening to be fresh for watch at midnight – but, tonight, he had been asked by Chisholm to relieve the Third RO for a brief spell at 8.30. So he did not go to his bunk as usual. The Third RO was mystified by this unusual change in procedure but left the radio-room to Fenwick without enlightenment on why his watch was being interrupted.

Chisholm, Thorn and Ingledew joined Fenwick in the radio room as soon as the puzzled junior operator had left the bridge.

"Here's your message for tonight," Thorn told Fenwick, and handed him the second "Goethe" signal that Ingledew had prepared in German text. A few moments later, Fenwick was tapping on the key, having had an immediate response to his Q-S-V callsign.

The wind had risen. By nine, it was battering at the canvas flap-covers of the flag lockers and threatening to tear them off. The Third Officer left the wheel-house to give the duty signalman a hand to secure them. The *Fort Mohican* was pitching and rolling more heavily than at any time since she had been in the Atlantic latitudes of Biscay.

Watching the spray break over the plunging forecastle-head from the shelter of the wheel-house, Chisholm heard the shrill note of the Third Officer's whistle from the after end of the bridge. He was summoning the standby man of the deck watch, and Chisholm wondered why. He went to investigate.

Twenty-one-year-old Evan Morgan had left the signalman to attend to the wind-whipped locker covers and was peering down at the deck from the after rail of the bridge.

"Something up, Mr Morgan?"

The Third Officer turned at Chisholm's voice from behind him.

"There's a deck cargo truck loose on the starboard side of number three hatch, sir. I can't see which one it is but I can hear it moving about."

Chisholm peered over into the darkness. He, too, could hear a metallic grinding followed by a crashing sound that kept time with the motion of the ship. One of the army trucks down there *was* sliding against the hatch coaming and causing the noise but, like Morgan, Chisholm could not identify the offending vehicle.

"You wanted me, sir?"

The stand-by AB from the watch had reached the lower bridge and had called up to the Third Officer.

"There's something loose alongside number three, Willis. Find out what it is and let me know."

"Aye aye, sir."

"I'll go down with him and have a look-see, Mr Morgan," Chisholm offered. "You look after the shop up here – and the Commodore."

"Aye aye, sir. Thank you."

Below, Chisholm found that a fifteen-hundredweight truck had worked loose from its wire lashings and was slamming into a three tonner with every starboard roll of the ship. When the ship rolled to port, the truck was crashing against the coaming of the bunker hatch.

"Get the Bosun and the Chippy," Chisholm ordered the standby man. "And we'll need some gear – a block and tackle, spikes, crow-bars and some chain stoppers."

The seaman reappeared some minutes later, followed by the Bosun and Lander, the donkeyman.

"Chippy's getting the gear from his shop," the Bosun said. The newcomers surveyed the problem. A four-by-three timber chock that had anchored the front wheels of the truck fore and aft had worked its way over the two deck angle-irons keeping it in place. This had reduced the tension on the thwartships lashings and was allowing the front of the truck to slew from side to side.

"For a start, we'll need to get that timber back in place and the front wheels back over it," Chisholm pointed out.

"How do we lift the front end of the truck?" asked the Bosun. "We can't rig a tackle from a sky hook."

"We lift it by hand," said Lander.

The Bosun threw the donkeyman a look that was less than grateful.

"Thanks very much for the advice!" he growled. "There's no bloody room to move, never mind lift the damned thing! If that's the brightest idea you can come up with, you great Skow-wegian, I've got a better one. Why don't you go back and finish your supper?"

The big donkeyman laughed. "There's nothing to it! You go back and finish your supper, Bosun. I could do it myself."

"He's right, Bosun," Chisholm said. "If it can be done."

"We'll give it a try then," the Bosun said, in a tone that was far from optimistic. "Give me a hand, young Willis."

He moved towards the truck – which still slithered away from the coaming with every starboard roll – and Willis and the standby man edged cautiously after him. Their movements were restricted by the lashings on a jeep immediately forward of the wayward truck. Chisholm crawled closer, with the intention of propelling the timber chock into place if the wheels could be lifted clear of it. Lander watched, grinning. The carpenter, loaded with gear, arrived at that moment and he, too, watched with interest.

The Bosun and the seaman cautiously got hands on the bumper of the moving truck but were defeated by the rolling of the ship. They were unable to keep their feet rooted and moved with the ship, ready to leap clear if the truck's weight proved too much for them. It did prove too much for them. They managed to raise the front wheels two inches above the deck but, when the ship lurched to port, they let go and leapt clear. Chisholm, manoeuvring the timber chock had to look lively to scramble clear himself.

Lander pushed the Bosun out the the way impatiently and – placing his feet firmly on the deck where there was space to plant them – took hold of the truck's bumper. With a great intake of breath, he lifted.

The front wheels of the truck came nine inches clear of the deck and Lander held the weight even when the ship rolled to starboard.

"Now!" he roared, and Chisholm and the Bosun rolled the timber chock, working it into place hard against the angle-irons. Lander, pushing with the weight of his body, dropped the front of the truck neatly against the chock.

They worked quickly then, shackling the truck temporarily in position with chains and winding the stoppers tight with spikes and securing them so that they did not run back. Once the truck was rendered immobile by the temporary restraints, new wire lashings were reeved and secured with bottle-screws.

Chisholm thanked the men, singling out Lander for special appreciation. Had he not witnessed the donkeyman's feat of strength, he would not have believed it possible. He returned to his cabin to wash up and change his clothing, still awed by the Norwegian's strongman act.

The clock in the day-room was at ten when, refreshed, Chisholm whistled up to the bridge to check that all was well. Morgan confirmed that it was and that the Commodore hoped to look down in about half an hour or so, as previously arranged, to share a supper of coffee and sandwiches. It was going to be a long night for Commodore and Captain and, after midnight, neither could expect any rest.

Chisholm fished his keyring from his pocket. He had at least thirty minutes to himself and he had still not read the notes on Strasser's interrogation. There was no time like the present.

Key in hand, he went to open the desk drawer where he had put Thorn's notes. As he inserted the key, he noticed a slight scarring and splintering of the varnish-work on the drawer's lip above the lock, where it had closed with the desk. The drawer pulled open without any need to turn the key. There were marks on the desk and drawer as if it had been forced. Yet, the lock was down.

Chisholm turned the key in the open drawer and the metal locking tongue shot up. He found he could depress it easily again with the ball of his hand. It was a mystery. He knew he had left the drawer locked. Obviously, whoever had prised it open had depressed the locking tongue as he had done and closed the drawer again to conceal the mischief.

The notes on Strasser still lay in the drawer, but untidily – as if they had been read and hurriedly replaced. Chisholm took the notes out. As he straightened the papers, his glance went to the open drawer. There was no sign of the Webley. He pulled the drawer open as far as it would go.

Not only had the Webley disappeared, so, too, had two cardboard containers in which there had been four dozen bullets.

* * *

Thorn inspected the damaged drawer.

"Who's had access to your cabin since this afternoon?" He glanced round at Chisholm, his eyebrows tilted in a querying frown.

"Just about everybody, Cal. I've been on the bridge most of the time myself . . . But Colonel Ruddy had an officers' conference in here this evening. The Commodore and his sidekick ate down here tonight. The Chief Steward and half the catering staff have been in and out all day. Laird was in for the logbook . . . The Second Mate was in for the Sicily pilot book . . . The donkeyman was working next door . . . The Chief Engineer was here with the bunkers report . . ."

"Who would steal a thirty-eight? And why? Who would have known it was there?" Thorn was frowning into space, thinking aloud.

"A souvenir-hunter?" Chisholm asked, without conviction.

"If anybody wanted a gun, there are enough on this ship easier got at than yours. Why go to the trouble of busting into your desk?"

"Maybe it wasn't the gun they were after. They saw it there and just took it."

Thorn looked sharply at Chisholm.

"What do you mean?"

"I mean those papers of yours."

"The papers weren't touched."

"They were touched all right. I've just straightened them out. They just weren't taken."

Thorn stared at Chisholm, puzzled.

"What are you driving at, Chizz?"

"I don't know," he said, causing the American to give a snort of exasperation. Chisholm ignored it. He was mentally piecing together a jigsaw of thoughts, sensing rather than seeing an end-picture to the jumble. The Norwegian donkeyman, Lander, loomed largely in the confused images but, for the moment, the only thing to connect the man with the theft of the gun was known opportunity. Lander had had the best opportunity. When he had been working in the bathroom next door, the day-room had been empty except for the period that Thorn and Chisholm himself had been there.

There was something else – but the thought was so outrageous that Chisholm hesitated even to whisper it in Thorn's presence.

"Don't go away," he said suddenly to Thorn, and moved purposefully towards the door.

"Where are you going?"

"To have a word with the Chief Engineer. That's where I'll be if anyone comes looking for me. OK? I shan't be five minutes."

The Chief Engineer was stretched out on his bunk with his clothes on. He was reading an eighteen-month-old copy of *Popular Gardening* in the dim glow of his bunk-light. He looked up in surprise at Chisholm's sudden manifestation in the middle of his cabin after the most perfunctory knock to announce his arrival.

Chisholm dispensed with the need for preamble.

"That Norwegian donkeyman of ours, Jock . . . What do you know about him? Where did we get him?"

Chief Engineer Jock Robertson managed to suppress his surprise at having his privacy invaded by the ship's captain at ten at night. He answered Chisholm's questions from the edge of his bunk with the good nature of one who had long since ceased to be amazed by the eccentricities of deck officers in general and master mariners in particular.

In answer to Chisholm's unexpected cross-examination, he told all he knew about Eric Lander: that Lander's last ship had been another "Fort", the *Fort McGillivary*, which he had joined in New York as a replacement. He had been a replacement on the *Fort Mohican*, too, having got the job of a man called Davis who had failed to show up at the shipping office to sign the articles.

There was more – and the more Chisholm heard, the more his heart raced with an absurd excitement. Cautioning Robertson not to repeat their conversation to anyone, he hurried forward to his quarters to share his discoveries with Thorn.

Cal Thorn was in Chisholm's day-room, eating his way through a heaped plate of chicken sandwiches. The captain's steward – having arrived with a towel-wrapped tray for Chisholm and the Commodore – had insisted that the American should have his own late repast.

Thorn was on his fourth sandwich when Chisholm burst in, wind-swept and rain-spattered from the short journey along the deck. Thorn greeted him with a broad grin.

"Hey, you look like your tail's on fire about something."

"I know who Quasimodo is, Cal. He's on this ship!"

The flat declaration took Thorn by surprise. He shot out of his chair.

"Say that again, Chizz."

"I know who Quasimodo is. And don't say I'm crazy."

"Nobody's saying you're crazy. Just tell me what the hell you're on about. Who is Quasimodo:"

"He's the one who took my Webley."

"Tell me who he is, for Christ's sake!"

"No, Cal. I want you to put the pieces together like I did – and then tell me it makes sense."

"What pieces, Chizz?" Thorn bristled with impatience.

Chisholm ignored the other man's agitation, refusing to be ruffled.

"First, this *Schatten Gruppe*, Cal – the way they operate. Explain what you meant when you said they acquired the identities of foreign nationals with good track records. Explain that."

"I meant just what I said. Jesus, Chizz, don't play games with me!"

"I'm not playing games. Explain what you meant."

Thorn threw his hands in the air with the despair of an afflicted Job. When he spoke it was with the forced calm of an adult humouring a particularly trying child.

"*Schatten Gruppe* are very clever and very nasty people, Chizz. They get their agents cover identities by killing people like Anina Calvi and substituting a ringer. And what I meant by foreign nationals was non-German nationals. The Calvi girl, for instance, was Argentinian . . . A girl from a family that was outspokenly pro-British . . . *Schatten Gruppe* probably stalked her for months before they bumped her off and put their own girl in her place . . ."

"What other kind of people would they use?" Chisholm broke in.

"Well, Constantine's the only one we know about for sure. But they'd go for people like him, too – escaped prisoners. Guys whose credentials are good – or appear to be good. Like, say, a Dutch resistance fighter who turns up in England on a shot-up boat and says he wants to join the Free Dutch Navy . . . He'd be screened, of course, but if his story held up, he'd be home and dry. He'd be accepted . . ."

"How about a Norwegian seaman?"

"Same would apply," said Thorn. "If his story held up, he'd be in. Hell, Chizz, something like ten thousand escapers and refugees are getting out of Nazi Europe every year—Czechs, Poles, Danes, Norwegians, French, our own guys from POW camps . . . God knows how many Nazis slip through with them."

"We've got a Norwegian seaman on this ship, Cal."

Thorn flashed a look at Chisholm.

"The big fella? The one who was knocking your bathroom to hell this afternoon?"

"He's our Quasimodo, Cal. I'm sure of it."

Thorn did not seem impressed.

"Yeah? What makes you so sure?"

"You just drew a picture of a *Schatten Gruppe* agent, Cal. Lander, the donkeyman on this ship, fits it."

"Tell me more."

"Jock Robertson, the Chief Engineer, noticed he was different, a cut above the kind of man you get in his job. He says Lander knows more about ships' engines than any donkeyman he's ever met. Jock says Lander could do *his* job. He's wasted as a donkeyman."

Thorn took Chisholm's drift immediately.

"Are you trying to tell me that, if this guy Lander is a Kraut posing as a Norwegian, he's probably a qualified engineer? That he took a lower-ranked job because it maybe fits the cover he's using?"

"Yes."

"You've got to have more to go on that that. Maybe the Norwegians educate their donkeymen better than you guys."

"There is more. There's something fishy about him being on this ship at all. He turned up at the shipping office the day we were signing on and talked his way into the job when the man who should have got it didn't show up."

"Could be coincidence. And, in any case, if he's Quasimodo, why should he go to the trouble of getting on this ship?"

"I don't known. Maybe to team up with Strasser."

Thorn made a face.

"I suppose it's possible. What else is there?"

"The things that Anina told me about Quasimodo. Do you remember what she said?"

"Some of it," said Thorn. "Not much of it made sense, as I recall."

"She said Quasimodo was out of the country in February."

"So?"

"Lander was in Canada in February."

"He's a seaman. He travels. So what?"

"Anina said he wouldn't be back until the thaw. The *thaw*. Lander's ship was iced up in Montreal."

Thorn did a quick mental calculation.

"Strasser met Quasimodo in Brighton in April. It's April before the St Lawrence opens for ships most years. He couldn't have been in two places at once, Chizz."

"Lander left his ship in Montreal before the ice melted, Cal. His ship had a nasty accident. She was gutted by fire."

Thorn gave a soft whistle of appreciation.

"Sabotage?"

"Who knows? But if there was a *Schatten Gruppe* agent in the crew . . ." Chisholm let his inference hang in the air, before adding: "The ship's name, Cal, was the *Argo*."

Thorn frowned.

"That's supposed to mean something?"

"Anina said she thought a more appropriate cover name for Quasimodo would be Jason. In Greek legend, Cal, the name of Jason's ship was the *Argo*."

The sharp change of Thorn's expression told Chisholm that this time he had penetrated the barrier of doubts that the American had been raising. He was beginning to see a seam of logic in the suspicions that Chisholm was unveiling one at a time. There was still one more.

"Cal, do you remember everything that Anina told me? There was one thing you quizzed me about a lot when I was in hospital . . . A possible clue to Quasimodo's physical appearance. You wanted to build a description of him, remember?"

Thorn thought about this.

"I'm remembering," he said. "We were pretty sure he was a big guy, and maybe ugly. The girl talked about him like she was the beauty and he was the beast . . . Like maybe he really was hunchbacked or something."

"There was more, Cal."

"Yeah. She said she admired his strength . . . That's right. Something about him being the bravest strongest guy she knew. Yeah, he was big enough to break you in pieces."

Chisholm was smiling as if he had just won the pot at poker.

"The *strongest* guy she knew," he repeated. "Well, I have news for you. Lander is the strongest guy I've ever seen, Cal. It wasn't the stolen gun that made me think he was Quasimodo . . . That may have been in the back of my mind, the link – but it was remembering Anina's words. His strength. His sheer bloody strength! I wouldn't have believed it if I hadn't seen it with my own eyes! Tonight, Cal! Not an hour ago! I saw Lander lift an army truck off the deck by its front bumper!"

Thorn stared at Chisholm. There was no doubt in his mind that Chisholm had a strong *prima facie* case against Lander. But this was no time for congratulations. What were the implications, even if there was one chance in a thousand that Chisholm was right? Somebody had read Strasser's incomplete confessions and had perhaps stolen a gun to distract attention from that fact. If it had been Quasimodo, had he found the confessions while looking for something else? And if so, what? Had he just taken the chance to rifle the captain's desk in the hope that he would find something useful? Perhaps he had been afraid – with some justification – that Strasser was on the point of betraying him . . .

"Strasser!" Thorn exclaimed, ignoring Chisholm's clear expectancy of a quite different reaction. "Strasser!" he repeated. There was no point in speculating further on whether Chisholm was right or wrong or whether Lander was or was not Quasimodo. Strasser would tell them. *Strasser knew!*

Reitlinger was sweating. And the oppressive heat of the OKW bunker in Rastenberg was not entirely responsible. Reitlinger had seen others castigated in front of the Headquarters Staff before, but with nothing like the fury that Adolf Hitler had laced into him.

What Reitlinger resented more than anything else was the obvious enjoyment the assorted generals were getting from his humiliation. He knew they were jealous of *Schatten Gruppe* and that they considered it a ratbag organisation compared with the Abwehr, but that only made his misery more acute. The Führer himself had always had a soft spot for *Schatten Gruppe*, with its party allegiance disputed by none. He had criticised *Schatten Gruppe* before, of course, but tonight Hitler had gone beyond the bounds of criticism.

He had damned the whole service as a bunch of blockheaded

incompetents who could not be trusted to tie their own bootlaces without making a hash of it. And there was, in his eyes, no greater nor more incompetent blockhead than Reitlinger himself.

The last signal from "Antoine" had started Hitler off on his tirade. Yet another change in the direction of "Operation Husky"! It was not to be Norway, or Greece, or Sicily, or Sardinia, or Jugoslavia. No, if the signal was to be believed, the attack was now to come on the heel of Italy and the Gulf of Taranto.

"Your agents are useless!" Hitler screamed at Reitlinger, glaring at him. "We would be better employing palm-readers and crystal-gazers to forecast the movements of the enemy. You have been duped, Reitlinger! The Anglo-Americans are the ones who are sending you these signals. They are doing so to distract us from the real objective – Greece!"

"Yes, my Führer." Reitlinger could do no more than agree. He longed only to be gone from this room and away from the eyes of those smirking generals. He suddenly detected a slight mellowing in the Führer's tone.

"You may be thankful, Reitlinger, that we chose to ignore your precious signals – all of them! Think yourself lucky that, some weeks ago, we had the foresight to strengthen our forces in Greece substantially."

Thorn left Chisholm and the Commodore to enjoy their supper. Emerging from a tangle of double black curtains and a mosquito-door that was sprung like a bear-trap, he stumbled out into the darkness of the lower bridge. The deterioration in the weather shocked him. The wind howled round the grey housing, whipping at his legs. It provided only a foretaste of its ferocity, as he discovered when he rounded the end of the bridge-house and the full force of rain and buffeting squall hit him. He was wet through before he reached the main deck.

At the foot of the ladder, he was surprised to see no sign of the guard who should have been watching the hospital door. The deck was deserted. He felt a surge of anger. Wet and unpleasant as it was, there was no excuse for the guard not being at his post.

Thorn looked around. He checked the saloon alleyway, but there was no guard sheltering there. Nor was there any sign of life among the trucks on the deck, where more meagre protection from the weather was available. The entire midships section of the ship was quite deserted. The weather, it seemed, had not only driven the guard below, but everyone else.

Thorn tried the hospital door. It was unlocked. Too late, Thorn regretted not having kept the key. He had left it in the custody of the outside guard when he had decreed that the guard should be split: one outside and one inside with Strasser.

When Thorn opened the door, it dragged torn blackout curtain out with it. The interior was in pitch darkness. He did not dare switch on the light and break the strick blackout regulations, so he kicked the heavy curtain material away from the storm step and went inside, pulling the door closed after him. He groped for the light switch.

The room flooded with light.

He drew back involuntarily at the sight which met his eyes. The Canadian guard who had been left with Strasser was sprawled on his back, his head at an odd angle from his body. His neck was broken. The man's rifle was propped in a corner. The bed where Strasser had lain was empty.

It was not until he turned that Thorn saw Strasser. He was supended by the belt-loop in the waist band of his trousers from a hook in the bulkhead just inside the door. He hung there, legs and arms drooping, his doubled body swaying like a pendulum with the motion of the ship. His head and hair were covered in blood. His killer must have beaten him brutally before despatching him in the same manner as the guard. Strasser's neck was broken.

Twenty-Two

D-Day

The storm showed no sign of abating. Chisholm paced the bridge like a soul in torment. It required a considerable effort of concentration to keep his mind on the part his ship was playing as leader and marker in the intricate manoeuvring of the ships of the convoy. In broad daylight, the task would have been hazardous enough. In dark and stormy conditions, the chances of collision and chaos were increased a hundredfold. Nor was Chisholm's responsibility made less onerous by the fact that the convoy's Commodore was directing operations from *his* bridge. If anything, the Commodore's presence on the *Fort Mohican* increased the strain on her master in a variety of ways. He had to defer to the Commodore's overall command while retaining ultimate responsibility for his own vessel.

No matter that Chisholm knew that his place was on the bridge and that his first priority was to get the *Fort Mohican* to Sicily, he could not shut himself off from the anxiety that was undermining his ability to think straight. *Where the hell was Lander?* It had been two hours now since Thorn had raised the alarm, but a posse of thirty men had failed to find him.

Chisholm blamed himself for their failure. Thorn had pointed out that the donkeyman probably still believed his cover was secure and he had wanted to surprise Lander in his cabin, with one volunteer acting as his back-up. Chisholm had vetoed that. He had seen what Lander had done to Strasser and the guard in the hospital. And he could guess what had happened to the second guard, who was still missing: neck broken and heaved over the side most likely.

Chisholm had wanted no chances taken with Lander. He had insisted on calling out an entire rifle flight of the RAF Regiment to cordon off the PO's quarters and assist Thorn.

The commotion they had made must have been what had alerted Lander, of course. He must have seen or heard the RAF soldiers and guessed they were coming for him. Thorn and his warriors had burst into Lander's cabin, only to find it empty. They were certain now that he had not been in it for some time before they had gone charging in, but had watched them prepare to do so from the roof of the PO's quarters, where he had been breaking into an ammunition locker. There, they had found evidence that he had left the scene in a hurry: some of his tools and a cardboard box in which he had been stacking Oerlikon incendiary shells. Chisholm had shuddered to think what Lander might have intended with the incendiary shells. The *Fort Mohican* was a floating arsenal. She would not burn like the *Argo*. A spark in the right place and she would go up like Krakatoa!

Over an hour had passed since Chisholm had delegated Laird to help Thorn and his troops carry out a systematic search of the ship. Now, with every minute that passed without news that Lander had been found, Chisholm became more edgy.

He was not the only one on the bridge whose nerves were raw. Commodore Freddie Hope was like a cat on hot bricks: leaping about the wheel-house one minute and out on the extreme wing of the flying bridge the next, as the ships executed course alterations, hopefully, in concert. It was, however, the weather that preoccupied the Commodore. It posed a major threat to the success of the landings – greater even than the shells and the bombs of the enemy. Freddie Hope agonised to Chisholm over the possibility that landing-craft loaded with sea-sick troops would never make it to the beach. He had visions of the craft being swamped and overturned in heavy seas, with thousands of men drowned before they could even fire a shot. As the storm reached its full fury just after midnight, the spectre of unmitigated disaster rode the screaming wind like an apocalyptic horseman.

Midnight was the critical hour for the slow ships of V-Force. It was then that the drilling manoeuvres, rehearsed so assiduously in the wide Atlantic, were undertaken as the final examination.

The mighty armada of many convoys was now well to the east of Sicily. At midnight, the great assembly of ships split and turned to approach the island in two tight-ranked rectangular formations in the shape of a wide-angled Vee. One leg sailed towards the strip of coast that runs from Cape Passero north towards Syracuse. The other approached the beaches that run west from Cape Passero to Gela.

The *Fort Mohican*'s destination was the bay made by the curve of shore on the west side of Cape Passero, between the American assault around Gela and the main thrust of Eighth Army forces on the east side of the Cape. A blue lamp winked out from the *Fort Mohican*, signalling speed, course to be steered, and the hour and minute that the order was to be executed. When the minute arrived, Commodore Freddie Hope nodded to Chisholm.

"Now, Captain," he said.

Chisholm ordered the helm to port and sounded two blasts on the siren. Astern and abeam of *Fort Mohican*, the other ships were turning in unison. They steadied on the new course, adjusting station from the new column leaders. Four columns sailing east had become six columns sailing north.

At 0100, the second formation change was executed. It was followed by another and another until the convoy was strung out in two columns. Now, with *Fort Mohican* leading the starboard column, the port column reduced speed and tagged on behind; so that all twenty-one ships steamed in line ahead with the escorts spread out along the flanks.

Ahead of the *Fort Mohican*, a solitary minesweeper criss-crossed in front of the line of transports for passage through the minefields that flanked the south-eastern approaches to Sicily. It was now 0230 and the beaches of Cape Passero were less than thirty miles away. Up ahead, the fast ships of V-Force should have been dropping the assault troops. The first attack was timed for 0200, so that the big ships could be up and away before the slower transports pushed through to their anchorages a quarter-mile offshore at 0600.

Chisholm scanned the horizon ahead through his night glasses. It was dark and silent, Either the first assault was going uneventfully and with total surprise or the big ships were behind schedule because of the gale.

"Damnit, Captain, I do believe the wind's dropping!"

Chisholm turned to find Freddie Hope at his shoulder.

"At least the squalls have stopped," Chisholm said. "Visibility's good." Since they had altered course away from the direction of the weather, its bite had become much less noticeable. Similarly, the sea – now running on the quarter – was deceptive. It seemed to have dropped but its sudden benignity could be due to the fact that they were running with it rather than into it.

"Perhaps it will work in our favour," the Commodore said. "The weather I mean. The Jerries and the Eyeties will have taken one look at it last night and all gone to bed."

"I hope you're right," Chisholm replied. They were interrupted at that moment by Laird. What he had to report was not encouraging. Lander had still not been found. One of the trimmers had seen or imagined he had seen somebody in the bunkers and it had been there that Laird had concentrated his search. He was covered in coal dust, and despondent.

"I'm convinced he must have got into one of the forward holds," he told Chisholm. "The rest of the ship is crawling with men . . . There's no way he couldn't have been spotted if he'd tried to hide anywhere between here and the steering flat. He must have gone forward. Is it right he has a gun?"

"My thirty-eight was stolen from my desk," Chisholm said. "We think he has it."

"I was going to have another look in holds one and two, sir – but that mightn't be such a bright idea if he's got a gun. We should maybe leave it until daylight, when we can get some hatch covers off."

"In case there's shooting?"

"A spark from a squaddie's boot could blow our fore-end to the far side of Malta, sir. We don't want bullets flying around down there. The officer in charge of the RAF boys is being bloody awkward, too. He got his hands dirty in the stoke-hold and he's more of a hindrance than a help."

"Maybe I'd better have a word with him."

"It would help if somebody straightened him out. He's down in the engine-room with your American friend."

Chisholm turned to the Commodore.

"If it's OK with you, sir, I'd like to go below for ten minutes. We may be in as much danger from this maniac as we are from all the Jerries in Sicily – and I want him nabbed. I'll leave Mr Laird in charge here."

"You go and catch that blighter, Captain," Freddie Hope urged cheerfully. "Nothing's going to happen up here for a couple of hours. At least, I sincerely hope not. We've got a straight run in. I would suggest though that we go to action

331

stations at oh-four-hundred."

Chisholm phoned down to the engine-room and they located the RAF Regiment officer for him. The man, whose name was Bullock and whose nickname was unrepeatable in polite company, wanted to argue with Chisholm over the telephone. Chisholm cut him short and arranged to meet him at the top of the engine-room, where he would be waiting for him in two minutes.

Bullock, a rather portly, bumptious individual, was waiting for him on the gridded crosswalk that linked the two doors giving entry to the engine-room.

"We're wasting our bloody time looking for this fellow," he greeted Chisholm. "What we should do is sit on the deck and wait for him to come out of his hideyhole. He'll surface sooner or later, you mark my words. He'll stick his nose out like a rat looking for water. This ship's bloody filthy . . . Look at the mess I'm in from coal."

"I'm sorry you've been inconvenienced," Chisholm said through bared teeth. "I would not have asked for your help if the safety of the ship had not been at stake. The man we are looking for is quite capable of blowing us all out of the water and I would have thought that it was in your interest as well as mine that we caught him as soon as possible. He is bound to be desperate – and every minute that he's at large, the more time we're giving him to cause God knows what kind of damage."

Bullock's lip curled.

"Come off it, Captain. What could one man possibly do?"

Chisholm held his anger in check.

"I'm sure one man is not enough to frighten you, sir," he said icily. "But, by God, what this one could do frightens me. I have a vivid imagination, you see. I can imagine what will happen when several thousand tons of octane and high explosives are suddenly ignited. There will be a big bang. A bang that would make further discussion irrelevant."

"One man could do this?"

"With an oily rag and a lighted match. In fact, he wouldn't need the oily rag."

In the glow of light from the engine-room below, Bullock's face twitched, as if he might suddenly be seasick.

"I didn't know that," he said. "I thought we were looking for some seaman who'd caught a touch of the sun and gone off his rocker."

"You were told that he was armed and dangerous . . . And I am telling you now just how dangerous." Chisholm tried to inject patience into his voice. "The important thing is that we locate him. We've got to know where he is. We've got to keep looking."

"And if we find him?"

"Better if there is no shooting. We don't want to do by accident the very thing we're trying to stop him from doing. We've got to cut off his escape routes . . . Corner him. Then, we may be able to persuade him to give himself up."

Chisholm tried to explain to Bullock how the ship was compartmented and where to post men while others searched, section by section. He got the impression that he would have been employed more profitably talking in Urdu to a brick wall. Bullock was not the brightest of intelligences he had ever encountered and his glib assurances that he comprehended fully did not inspire confidence. Chisholm realised that the man he should have been talking to was Cal Thorn. The American would know how to organise things. He asked Bullock if he knew where Thorn was.

"Oh, the Yank? He was in the engine-room about ten minutes ago but one of your chaps wanted him to go and have a look at a ventilator or something. On the boat-deck, I think he said."

Chisholm tried the port boat-deck first. Thorn was not there. Nor, as he well knew, were there any ventilators. Had Bullock got it wrong? Or had Thorn been directed to the engine-room vents or those with access from the boat decks?

Chisholm skirted the engine-room skylight, which was closed for blackout purposes. At the after end was one of the two ladders leading to the roof of the POs' accommodation, where Lander had broken into the ammunition locker. It was where, too, they reckoned Lander must have been skulking when they had gone looking for him in his cabin. Chisholm climbed up to inspect the housing top, with its clutter of ammunition lockers and the fresh-water tank that fed the stewards' and engineers' toilets.

There was nothing unusual to be seen. It was when Chisholm descended the ladder on the starboard side that he noticed the big open barrel of ventilator shaft and realised that something was out of place. The absence of a cowl from the top of the ventilator shaft was not unusual—some had still to be shipped after being closed for the winter crossing of the North Atlantic – but what was unusual was that the shaft was uncovered. The heavy round board and canvas weather-proofing sleeve that normally sealed off the open neck of the shaft were missing. This surely was what Cal Thorn had been summoned from the engine-room to investigate.

Chisholm found the circular timber trap and its heavy sleeve lying against the engine-room skylight. He left them where they were and peered down the dark well of ventilator shaft. Although the shaft did not lead directly to the engine space, it amplified the heavy beat of the engines: the sound echoing through an open doorway twelve feet from the top. The doorway through which the sound was funnelling opened on to the top crosswalk of the engine-room. Chisholm was, in fact, standing directly over the great watertight bulkhead that sealed the engine space off from the after end of the ship. The ventilator shaft itself ran down to the bottom of the ship, abaft the watertight bulkhead, taking air when the ventilating cowl was in place to the propeller-shaft tunnel.

It occurred to Chisholm – as it had probably occurred to the person who had brought it to Thorn's attention – that this must have been Lander's escape route when he had eluded Thorn's posse. At considerable risk, the donkeyman must have wedged himself with arms and legs within the cylindrical neck of the shaft and worked his way down to the doorway below. Then, he had either entered the engine-room or he had continued via the ladder to the shaft tunnel opening, sixty feet below.

On an impulse, Chisholm decided to check the shaft tunnel. He was not tempted to take Lander's probable route and returned to deck level and the engine-room by orthodox ways. Entering the ventilator shaft from the cross-walk doorway, he began the descent of the vertical runged ladder. With his first few careful steps, the thought struck him that he was volun-tarily exposing himself to a claustrophobic's nightmare. With each step the horror of enclosure became more pronounced. He paused and looked up. A great distance away, overhead, was a faint glimmer of light from the open doorway. Below – a long way yet, it seemed – was a tiny square of meagre light. He felt like an ant trapped in a giant capillary tube from which all light had been excluded except for pinhead glows at the extremes. The awareness of being totally immured was overwhelming. He only had to sway slightly and his shoulders and back rubbed the steel walls of the narrow shaft, reinforcing his rising dread.

Chisholm fought the welling panic. Your fear is entirely in your mind, he told himself. Control it. Make your mind serve you as your hands and muscles serve you. Make your mind *obey*. Free it! Free it to obey, as your body and limbs are free to obey. Your legs and your arms are not *chained*. You can climb up or you can climb down. Your mind is *free*. You are the master of yourself—as you are master of this ship.

He began to climb down, exhilarated at his own courage: at his own victory. He was totally in control. There was, nevertheless, a measure of relief to feel his feet on solid decking. He peered along the shaft tunnel. Having defeated the perilous vertical hazard of the ladder shaft, the slightly greater horizontal space of the tunnel before him had no terror.

He walked slowly aft. The metal catwalk was slippery with oil and water and the whirling thrust-shaft screamed at his ear-drums as it drove three tons of propeller weight through the sea to complete one revolution every second.

Chisholm walked the full length of the shaft tunnel to the stern, where a ladder led up to the emergency steering flat. It was an eerie place, this tunnel, with its scanty lighting and monstrous revolving steel cylinder that spat out oil and water in all directions from the surface of its drum-like girth. It was no place for a claustrophobic, here nearly thirty feet below the level of the sea. A sea that swished and surged against the plates of the hull to provide a strangely menacing accompaniment to the deafening noise of whirling shaft and thrashing propeller.

As he had walked along the catwalk, his footsteps ringing metallic against the dripping walls of the narrow cavern enclosing him, Chisholm's eyes had searched for a single sign to tell him that Lander might have passed the same way. He had seen none but, in spite of this, something nagged uneasily at his mind. There had been nothing out of place, except . . . Except what? Something had registered vaguely.

Bilge boards! That was it. Two bilge boards had been lifted. Nothing sinister about that. The greasers went down in the tunnel bilges all the time to make sure that the suction boxes were clear and the pumps were not labouring in vain. The boards might have been left off through carelessness, or simply as a reminder that there was a troublesome rose below.

Chisholm retraced his steps along the catwalk. And there they were: two bilge boards stacked above the partially opened bay. Steadying himself on a stanchion supporting the catwalk rail, he lowered himself to peer into the bilge.

A hand suddenly reached out of the shadowed depths of the bilge and seized the front of his jacket. He felt himself yanked head-first into the bilge, turning head over heels in the process. The backs of his legs struck the boards above the bilge with bruising force as he was pulled down through the narrow rectangular opening into the bilge bay. There was a foot of water, thick with oil and scum, slushing in the bottom of the bilge. Chisholm splashed into it, scarcely aware of its chill and slime as his assailant beat at him with his free hand. The other retained its claw-like hold on Chisholm's clothing.

He had no opportunity to defend himself. He was thrown down brutally and there was a brief stunning pain as his head struck against a steel half-diamond strapping the frame of the bilge. He went out like a light.

Lander, still holding Chisholm by the jacket front, threw the limp body down like a rag doll and climbed out of the bilge bay. Then he put the bilge boards back, marrying them and stamping them down into place. His eye went to a neat pile of carpenter's wedges, stacked in a recess for emergency use. A malicious smile crossed Lander's face. He took two of the wedges and inserted them in cracks between the bilge boards. Then he stamped them down with his booted heel until the bilge top was wedged solid.

Lander laughed out loud. If the Captain ever woke up, he was going to have an interesting time trying to get out of the bilge.

Cal Thorn had come to the conclusion that Chisholm must be playing hide-and-seek with him. Thorn had gone to the bridge to tell him that he had found out how Lander had accomplished his vanishing act, but Chisholm was not on the bridge. He had gone down to the engine-room to see Bullock. Thorn had made the journey down to the engine-room via the fiddley and the stoke-hold, only to find that he had once again missed the ship's captain. Then, Thorn had learned from the plummy-voiced RAF Regiment officer who was assisting the search for Lander, that Chisholm had gone back to the bridge. Thorn made yet another fruitless journey to the bridge.

Now, he was getting worried. Where the hell was Chisholm? Nobody seemed to know. Ranging around the midships section, Thorn found himself buttonholed by the officer who, five minutes earlier, had directed him to the bridge. Bullock was beginning to panic and wanted Thorn's help. Did Thorn know where the entry to No. 1 hold was? The Captain had wanted men posted at all the hold and hatch entries but, according to Bullock, had not been to clear with his directions.

Thorn advised him to ask one of the ship's crew and Bullock would have dashed off if Thorn had not detained him and queried him again about Chisholm's movements. The only crumb of information forthcoming was that Bullock had told the Captain about "the ventilator on the boat-deck". Had Thorn tried there?

Thorn made for the boat-deck. No sign of Chisholm on the starboard side. He climbed the short ladder behind the engine-room skylight to cross to the port side. In passing, he peered down the ventilator space that he suspected Lander of having used earlier to keep out of sight. Staring down the well, he marvelled at Lander's nerve in venturing into such a death trap. Thorn – by consulting one of the ship's engineers – had already established that there were several escape routes Lander might have taken after climbing down the ventilator hole: to the engine-room, or to either the stewards' or engineers' quarters, or to the deck via both, or straight down to the shaft tunnel. All of these places had been searched at least once without a trace of Lander being found.

A sound from deep in the ventilator shaft made Thorn draw back warily from the open shaft-top. He crouched, listening, before peering cautiously down again. Someone was climbing up the ladder. He could see movement far below as the faint light at the bottom of the shaft was intermittently obscured. It occurred to Thorn that the open ventilator, with its top off, remained an escape route that Lander might use a second time. He retrieved the circular trap that fitted over the opening and manoeuvred it into place. The heavy board was about three feet in diameter and fitted snugly over the rim like a lid on a jar.

The sleeve-like canvas cover completed the sealing process. Thorn speedily secured the rope ties. Then he hurried down to the deck and entered the engine-room from the steward's alleyway. He moved silently along the crosswalk to the opened watertight door that gave access to the ventilator shaft above and the ladder to the shaft tunnel below. He drew his revolver.

The man climbing the ladder was now almost at the top,

level with the doorway. His movements were very slow, deliberate, as if caution and stealth were a calculated necessity.

Thorn waited. He would allow the man to emerge through the door on to the crosswalk. It might not, after all, be Lander and Thorn had no wish to scare an innocent seaman into a sixty-foot fall.

The man was now on top of the ladder. Why did he not come out? Thorn strained to hear his movements, but it was impossible against the thunderous piston-beat of the engine big ends, rising and falling relentlessly in the great cavern below the crosswalk.

The man did not emerge through the watertight door-space. Thorn heard scraping sounds, from *above* the level of the door. The unseen man was climbing above the top of the ladder into the ventilator tube. It had to be Lander!

Thorn unclipped a heavy rubber-sheathed flashlight from his belt and, holding it in his left hand, gun in right, he leaned out through the door space. He flashed the light upward into the ventilator shaft.

Lander was hunched in the shaft like a great spider: shoulders against one side and knees against the other. He craned round as the light caught him.

"Come down slowly," Thorn ordered, "hands where I can see them. Any tricks and you get a bullet right up your fat ass."

Lander ignored him. He started working his way higher up the ventilator. Thorn heard his cry of rage as he encountered the timber trap at the top and his quick curse as he failed to move it.

"There's no way out," Thorn called. "Come down like I said. Nice and slow."

Lander's answer was to launch an arm-blow at the wooden vent-top. There was a splintering sound but the canvas sleeve encasing the top held firm. Lander now tried to turn his body. Supporting himself against the sheer sides by pressure of his forearms and his haunches, he tried to thrust himself upward through the obstruction with a heave of his great shoulders and arched back. The cover began to give but, with the effort, Lander could not sustain the pressure of his arms and thighs. He slipped.

Thorn pulled his head and shoulders clear of the doorway as Lander started to fall. The big man braked his downward momentum briefly by spreading himself against the cylinder wall but, inch by inch, he slipped; his clothes sliding on the smooth metal surface. Suddenly, he plunged.

There was a momentary snagging as his arm hooked on the top of the ladder where it protruded in his path but bone snapped with a loud crack as his weight propelled him downwards. Thorn heard the hurtling body thud against ladder and wall at irregular intervals as Lander tumbled through sixty feet to end in a broken, bloody sprawl far below.

Chisholm came to in darkness. He was half immersed in stinking water that lapped around his body. His head throbbed with pain but he found he could move his aching arms and legs. He tried to turn on to his hands and knees but the tomb in which he was encased kept moving, throwing him from side to side.

Somewhere above him was a fearful noise, like a giant drill boring into solid rock beyond his darkness. Its intensity was unbearable, as if rivets were being driven into his skull.

The noise suddenly held a meaning for him. It was the propeller shaft. He remembered then what had happened. The open bilge space . . . Lander! Lander had been hiding in the bilge space, with the covers off for air: unseen but seeing, like a scorpion in a crevice.

Chisholm tried to stand up. He did so gingerly. His stooped head and arched shoulders encountered the bilge boards enclosing him. He tried to push them upwards. They would not move. Panic began to well in him. An old familiar panic. All his life enclosed spaces had filled him with fear. Now the very worst had happened. He was trapped in a space where it was impossible even to stand upright. He was entombed alive. The ultimate fear had realised.

He fought the panic. Chisholm repeated aloud to himself the thought that had come to his aid on the ladder. That he was the master of his ship and that he must be the master of himself.

To master a ship he had to know the ship. He realised he knew no ship like he now knew himself. There was no hideous depth within himself unexplored – no deep that he had not reached in the loneliness of a prison cell, with fetters about his arms and legs. He had scraped the bottom of his private hell, not once but many times. With the realisation came the knowledge that he was unafraid.

Here, in the stygian dark, he could even smile at the strange irony that he should think of himself and his ship in terms of known depths. Here he was trapped in the deepest remoteness of his ship and instead of concentrating on the practical problem, he was clouding the issue by concerning himself with the intangible dimensions of emotional stress. The problem was not one of the mind with an abstract answer. He had to think in practical terms, without emotion getting in the way.

When Chisholm found he could do so, it was knowledge of his ship, much more than self-knowledge, that inspired him to seek a way out. Although the bilge boards over his head resisted all his attempts to move them, he reasoned that other bilge bays in the shaft tunnel might not have covers so tightly jammed in place. He, therefore, had to get out of the bay in which he was trapped.

His knowledge of their construction told Chisholm that the steel plating that separated one bilge bay from the next was broken at every frame with lightening holes to permit the passage of water from one to the other. The unknown quantity was whether the lightening holes were big enough to allow the passage of a human body.

He groped his way along the watery bottom to the nearest dividing plate. Some ships, he knew, had oval-shaped lightening holes only twelve inches in height. Others had circle-shaped holes. His groping fingers revealed to him that in the *Fort Mohican* the apertures were circular. He was not reassured by the size of the lightening hole that he found. He doubted if the space he found was much more than eighteen inches in diameter.

His first attempt to wriggle through almost ended in disaster. He stuck at the shoulders and almost drowned as he swallowed mouthfuls of the stinking water sloshing around his face. Almost weeping with effort, he disentangled himself and began to strip off all his clothes. When he was naked, he groped forward again: extending both arms before him and projecting his body through the narrow opening in the steel plate so that he was elongated like a high diver at his moment of entry into a pool. It worked. He was through into the next bay.

The test now was to see if the bilge boards in this bay could be moved from underneath. Chisholm stood up, slowly, and found that the board immediately above him rose against the pressure of his bent neck and shoulders. He brought hands and arms into play and pushed the bilge board clattering away. He blinked at the sudden admission of the shaft tunnel's meagre light. He pushed a second board out of the way and clambered free. Groggily, he made his way along the catwalk towards the ladder.

Thorn, inspecting Lander's broken body, turned to see what looked like a spectre approach from the far end of the tunnel. It took him a moment to recognise the naked man as Chisholm. His body was covered in oily slime and blood was smeared on his face and shoulders.

"Jesus Christ!" he exclaimed with awe.

"No, Cal," Chisholm said. "It's just me."

The dawn was coming in on tiptoe from the east: pale streaks of grey turning to white, to soft gold. Cape Passero was a dark inch-high corrugation against the horizon. A distant thunder rumbled from the shore above the bay. Gunfire.

Dotted lines of red curved lazily above the skyline. Tracer shells.

Commodore Freddie Hope lowered his night glasses with the calm detachment of an ornithologist who has seen and noted a familiar species of bird from the shelter of his hide. His tone, when he spoke to Chisholm at his side, was dispassionate.

"It would appear that our assault forces have engaged the enemy, Captain."

Chisholm smiled at the other man's neutral tone and felt a glow of admiration for the Commodore. The old fellow was one of the most excitable of men he had ever met but, right now, his emotions were all battened down out of sight. Self-discipline, Navy style. Chisholm was ready to bet that a sixteen-inch shell passing through the rigging in the next instant would not have caused the old buzzard – as Thorn had tagged him – to bat an aristocratic eyebrow.

The mine-sweeper still maintained its constant crossing and re-crossing of the *Fort Mohican*'s path. Astern, the long tail of ships behind the *Fort Mohican* was stretched out in an eight-mile line.

"We look a fine couple of cripples," Freddie Hope said to Chisholm, eyeing him in the improving light. Chisholm's head was swathed in a bandage. The Commodore's left leg was bound – as if the limb were mummified – from thigh to ankle. It looked odd the way the wrapping emerged from the wide leg of his tropical white shorts.

"I feel fine," Chisholm said and, for no reason he could have explained, added "I feel like a free man!"

The remark seemed to surprise the Commodore. It also seemed to please him mightily.

"Yes!" he agreed with enthusiasm. "Yes, Captain! You are a free man! That's what we all are! But how appropriate that you should declare it now with . . . With such joy . . ." He beamed at Chisholm, and then his eyes softened wistfully. "I suppose, when you come to think about it, that's why we're here."

The yeoman of signals approached the pair, and hovered respectfully.

"Excuse me, sir . . . Captain. Do you want the big ensign up at sunrise? Lieutenant Ingledew wants the Commodore's flag hoisted."

Commodore and Captain turned simultaneously to face the signalman. Both eyed the great mountain of bunting he clutched in his arms.

"Yes, signalman," It was Chisholm who answered. "Please hoist them both—the Commodore's pennant to the truck of the signal-mast and our ensign to the mainmast gaff." He turned to Freddie Hope. "Have you seen it, sir—our battle ensign? It's the biggest damned flag I've ever seen."

The Commodore smiled proudly.

"I insisted on all the ships in *my* convoy getting the things," he said. "When my ships are in sight of the enemy, I want to see them properly dressed." He nodded curtly to the yeoman. "See to it!"

As the yeoman moved off, the Commodore called him back.

"And put a signal down the line, yeoman. Commodore to all ships. Hoist battle ensigns."

"Aye aye, sir."

As the golden edge of the sun tipped the horizon, the colours fluttered out bravely from the ships of the line: great blood-coloured red ensigns, the size of hatch tarpaulins.

From the bridge of the *Fort Mohican*, the land ahead began to take on a discernible identity. Before the ship lay a blue bay fringed with golden sand. Above the beach, the land undulated green towards hills scattered with vineyards. Smoke and the noise of battle drifted from the pleasant land.

Chisholm conned his ship ever closer to the golden beach: half a mile, a quarter of a mile.

"Stand by the port anchor," he bellowed to Laird on the

forecastle-head. To the Third Mate in the wheel-house, he called: "Full astern engines."

"Aye aye, sir," came Laird's voice from the forecastle. "Full astern, sir," came Morgan's voice from the wheel-house.

"Let go the port anchor, Mr Laird."

"Aye aye, sir."

There was a rumble of chain in the hawse-pipe and the splash as the anchor hit the water.

"Stop engines, Third Mate."

"Stop engines, sir," Morgan echoed. The telegraph jangled.

The *Fort Mohican* rode safely at anchor. All around came the rumble of chains and the splashing contact of anchors breaking the waters of the bay. Chisholm went into the wheel-house to ring "finished with engines". When that was acknowledged, he rang the telegraph back to "Stand by engines". Steam would be maintained twenty-four hours a day.

He found Thorn looking at Sicily from the lower bridge.

"Well, Cal, we're here," Chisholm said.

Thorn nodded in the direction of the shore.

"It gives me a funny feeling, Chizz. That there is Hitler's Europe – and this is where we start taking it away from him. Right here."

"Sure, Cal." Chisholm grinned. "We'll start right after breakfast. It's going to be a long hard day."

They went down to breakfast together.

BESTSELLING BOOKS FROM TOR

MORE BESTSELLERS FROM TOR